WASHINGTON IRVING was born in
New York City on April 3, 1783.
Though trained for the law, he turned to writing.
The Rabelaisian humor of *A History of New York
from the Beginning of the World to the End of the
Dutch Dynasty* (1809), written under the name of
Diedrich Knickerbocker, won him wide popularity.
In 1815 Irving journeyed to England to manage a
branch of the family business. This ended in failure,
and he was compelled to write to support himself.
International fame came with the publication of
The Sketch Book of Geoffrey Crayon, Gent. (1819-
1820). In 1826 Irving went to Spain on a diplomatic
assignment. His three-year stay there inspired the
writing of *The History of the Life and Voyages of
Christopher Columbus* (1828), and *The Alhambra*
(1832). In 1829 he was assigned to London as
Secretary of the United States Legation, and after
extensive traveling, served as Minister to Spain from
1842 to 1846. In 1846 Irving returned to his home
in Tarrytown, New York, where he worked and
studied until his death on November 28, 1859.

THE SKETCH BOOK

OF GEOFFREY CRAYON, GENT.

---

by Washington Irving

I have no wife nor children, good or bad, to provide for. A mere spectator of other men's fortunes and adventures, and how they play their parts, which, methinks, are diversely presented unto me, as from a common theatre or scene.

—BURTON

With an Afterword by PERRY MILLER
Revised and Updated Bibliography

A SIGNET CLASSIC

SIGNET CLASSIC
Published by the Penguin Group
Penguin Books USA Inc., 375 Hudson Street,
New York, New York 10014, U.S.A.
Penguin Books Ltd, 27 Wrights Lane,
London W8 5TZ, England
Penguin Books Australia Ltd, Ringwood,
Victoria, Australia
Penguin Books Canada Ltd, 10 Alcorn Avenue,
Toronto, Ontario, Canada M4V 3B2
Penguin Books (N.Z.) Ltd, 182–190 Wairau Road,
Auckland 10, New Zealand

Penguin Books Ltd, Registered Offices:
Harmondsworth, Middlesex, England

Published by Signet Classic, an imprint of Dutton Signet,
a division of Penguin Books USA Inc.

24   23   22   21   20   19

 REGISTERED TRADEMARK—MARCA REGISTRADA

Printed in the United States of America

CONTENTS

PREFACE TO THE REVISED EDITION

The following papers, with two exceptions, were written in England, and formed but part of an intended series, for which I had made notes and memorandums. Before I could mature a plan, however, circumstances compelled me to send them piecemeal to the United States, where they were published from time to time in portions or numbers. It was not my intention to publish them in England, being conscious that much of their contents would be interesting only to American readers, and in truth, being deterred by the severity with which American productions had been treated by the British press.

By the time the contents of the first volume had appeared in this occasional manner, they began to find their way across the Atlantic, and to be inserted, with many kind encomiums, in the *London Literary Gazette*. It was said also that a London bookseller intended to publish them in a collective form. I determined, therefore, to bring them forward myself, that they might at least have the benefit of my superintendence and revision. I accordingly took the printed numbers which I had received from the United States to Mr. John Murray, the eminent publisher, from whom I had already received friendly attentions, and left them with him for examination, informing him that should he be inclined to bring them before the public, I had materials enough on hand for a second volume. Several days having elapsed without any communication from Mr. Murray, I addressed a note to him, in which I construed his silence into a tacit rejection of my work, and begged that the numbers I had left with him might be returned to me. The following was his reply:

MY DEAR SIR,

I entreat you to believe that I feel truly obliged by your kind intentions toward me, and that I entertain the most unfeigned respect for your most tasteful talents. My house is completely filled with work people at this time, and I have only an office to transact business in; and yesterday I was wholly occupied, or I should have done myself the pleasure of seeing you.

If it would not suit me to engage in the publication of your present work it is only because I do not see that scope in the nature of it which would enable me to make those satisfactory accounts between us, without which I really feel no satisfaction in engaging—but I will do all I can to promote their circulation, and shall be most ready to attend to any future plan of yours.

> With much regard, I remain, dear sir,
> Your faithful servant,
> JOHN MURRAY

This was disheartening, and might have deterred me from any further prosecution of the matter had the question of republication in Great Britain rested entirely with me; but I apprehended the appearance of a spurious edition. I now thought of Mr. Archibald Constable as publisher, having been treated by him with much hospitality during a visit to Edinburgh; but first I determined to submit my work to Sir Walter (then Mr.) Scott, being encouraged to do so by the cordial reception I had experienced from him at Abbotsford a few years previously, and by the favorable opinion he had expressed to others of my earlier writings. I accordingly sent him the printed numbers of *The Sketch Book* in a parcel by coach, and at the same time wrote to him, hinting that since I had had the pleasure of partaking of his hospitality, a reverse had taken place in my affairs which made the successful exercise of my pen all-important to me; I begged him, therefore, to look over the literary articles I had forwarded to him, and, if he thought they would bear European republication, to ascertain whether Mr. Constable would be inclined to be the publisher.

The parcel containing my work went by coach to Scott's address in Edinburgh; the letter went by mail to his residence in the country. By the very first post I received a reply, before he had seen my work.

"I was down at Kelso," said he, "when your letter reached Abbotsford. I am now on my way to town, and will converse with Constable, and do all in my power to forward your views—I assure you nothing will give me more pleasure."

The hint, however, about a reverse of fortune had struck the quick apprehension of Scott, and, with that practical and efficient good will which belonged to his nature, he had already devised a way of aiding me.

A weekly periodical, he went on to inform me, was about to be set up in Edinburgh, supported by the most respectable talents and amply furnished with all the necessary information. The appointment of the editor, for which ample funds were provided, would be five hundred pounds sterling a year, with the reasonable prospect of further advantages. This situation, being apparently at his disposal, he frankly offered to me. The work, however, he intimated, was to have somewhat of a political bearing, and he expressed an apprehension that the tone it was desired to adopt might not suit me. "Yet I risk the question," added he, "because I know no man so well qualified for this important task, and perhaps because it will necessarily bring you to Edinburgh. If my proposal does not suit, you need only keep the matter secret, and there is no harm done. 'And for my love I pray you wrong me not.' If, on the contrary, you think it could be made to suit you, let me know as soon as possible, addressing Castle Street, Edinburgh."

In a postscript, written from Edinburgh, he adds, "I am just come here, and have glanced over *The Sketch Book*. It is positively beautiful, and increases my desire to *crimp* you, if it be possible. Some difficulties there always are in managing such a matter, especially at the outset; but we will obviate them as much as we possibly can."

The following is from an imperfect draft of my reply, which underwent some modifications in the copy sent:

"I cannot express how much I am gratified by your letter. I had begun to feel as if I had taken an unwarrantable liberty; but, somehow or other, there is a genial sunshine about you that warms every creeping thing into heart and confidence. Your literary proposal both surprises and flatters me, as it evinces a much higher opinion of my talents than I have myself."

I then went on to explain that I found myself peculiarly unfitted for the situation offered to me, not merely by my political opinions, but by the very constitution and habits of my mind. "My whole course of life," I observed, "has been desultory, and I am unfitted for any periodically recurring task, or any stipulated labor of body or mind. I have no command of my talents, such as they are, and have to watch the varyings of my mind as I would those of a weathercock. Practice and training may bring me more into rule; but at present I am as useless for regular service as one of my own country Indians or a Don Cossack.

"I must, therefore, keep on pretty much as I have begun; writing when I can, not when I would. I shall occasionally shift my residence and write whatever is suggested by objects before me, or whatever rises in my imagination; and hope to write better and more copiously by and by.

"I am playing the egotist, but I know no better way of answering your proposal than by showing what a very good-for-nothing kind of being I am. Should Mr. Constable feel inclined to make a bargain for the wares I have on hand, he will encourage me to further enterprise; and it will be something like trading with a gypsy for the fruits of his prowlings, who may at one time have nothing but a wooden bowl to offer, and at another time a silver tankard."

In reply, Scott expressed regret, but not surprise, at my declining what might have proved a troublesome duty. He then recurred to the original subject of our correspondence; entered into a detail of the various terms upon which arrangements were made between authors and booksellers, that I might take my choice; expressing the most encouraging confidence of the success of my work, and of previous works which I had produced in America. "I did no more," added he, "than open the trenches with Constable, but I am sure if you will take the trouble to write to him, you will find him disposed to treat your overtures with every degree of attention. Or, if you think it of consequence in the first place to see me,

I shall be in London in the course of a month, and whatever my experience can command is most heartily at your command. But I can add little to what I have said above, except my earnest recommendation to Constable to enter into the negotiation." *

Before the receipt of this most obliging letter, however, I had determined to look to no leading bookseller for a launch, but to throw my work before the public at my own risk, and let it sink or swim according to its merits. I wrote to that effect to Scott, and soon received a reply:

"I observe with pleasure that you are going to come forth in Britain. It is certainly not the very best way to publish on one's own account; for the booksellers set their face against the circulation of such works as do not pay an amazing toll to themselves. But they have lost the art of altogether damming up the road in such cases between the author and the public, which they were once able to do as effectually as Diabolus in John Bunyan's Holy War closed up the windows of my Lord Understanding's mansion. I am sure of one thing, that you have only to be known to the British public to be admired by them, and I would not say so unless I really was of that opinion.

"If you ever see a witty but rather local publication called *Blackwood's Edinburgh Magazine,* you will find some notice of your works in the last number: the author is a friend of mine, to whom I have introduced you in your literary capacity. His name is Lockhart, a young man of very considerable talent, and who will soon be

---

* I cannot avoid subjoining in a note a succeeding paragraph of Scott's letter, which, though it does not relate to the main subject of our correspondence, was too characteristic to be omitted. Some time previously I had sent Miss Sophia Scott small duodecimo American editions of her father's poems published in Edinburgh in quarto volumes; showing the "nigromancy" of the American press, by which a quart of wine is conjured into a pint bottle. Scott observes: "In my hurry, I have not thanked you in Sophia's name for the kind attention which furnished her with the American volumes. I am not quite sure I can add my own, since you have made her acquainted with much more of papa's folly than she would ever otherwise have learned, for I had taken special care they should never see any of those things during their earlier years. I think I told you that Walter is sweeping the firmament with a feather like a maypole, and indenting the pavement with a sword like a scythe—in other words, he has become a whiskered hussar in the 18th dragoons."

intimately connected with my family. My faithful friend Knickerbocker is to be next examined and illustrated. Constable was extremely willing to enter into consideration of a treaty for your works, but I foresee will be still more so when

> Your name is up, and may go
> From Toledo to Madrid.

—— And that will soon be the case. I trust to be in London about the middle of the month, and promise myself great pleasure in once again shaking you by the hand."

The first volume of *The Sketch Book* was put to press in London as I had resolved, at my own risk, by a bookseller unknown to fame, and without any of the usual arts by which a work is trumpeted into notice. Still some attention had been called to it by the extracts which had previously appeared in the *Literary Gazette,* and by the kind word spoken by the editor of that periodical, and it was getting into fair circulation when my worthy bookseller failed before the first month was over, and the sale was interrupted.

At this juncture Scott arrived in London. I called to him for help, as I was sticking in the mire, and, more propitious than Hercules, he put his own shoulder to the wheel. Through his favorable representations, Murray was quickly induced to undertake the future publication of the work which he had previously declined. A further edition of the first volume was struck off and the second volume was put to press, and from that time Murray became my publisher, conducting himself in all his dealings with that fair, open, and liberal spirit which had obtained for him the well-merited appellation of the Prince of Booksellers.

Thus, under the kind and cordial auspices of Sir Walter Scott, I began my literary career in Europe; and I feel that I am but discharging, in a trifling degree, my debt of gratitude to the memory of that golden-hearted man in acknowledging my obligations to him. But who of his literary contemporaries ever applied to him for aid or counsel that did not experience the most prompt, generous, and effectual assistance!

W.I.

THE SKETCH BOOK

THE AUTHOR'S ACCOUNT OF HIMSELF

> "I am of this mind with Homer, that as the snaile that crept out of her shel was turned eftsoons into a toad, and thereby was forced to make a stoole to sit on; so the traveller that stragleth from his owne country is in a short time transformed into so monstrous a shape, that he is faine to alter his mansion with his manners, and to live where he can, not where he would."
>
> LYLY'S EUPHUES

I was always fond of visiting new scenes, and observing strange characters and manners. Even when a mere child I began my travels, and made many tours of discovery into foreign parts and unknown regions of my native city, to the frequent alarm of my parents and the emolument of the town crier. As I grew into boyhood, I extended the range of my observations. My holiday afternoons were spent in rambles about the surrounding country. I made myself familiar with all its places famous in history or fable. I knew every spot where a murder or robbery had been committed, or a ghost seen. I visited the neighboring villages, and added greatly to my stock of knowledge by noting their habits and customs and conversing with their sages and great men. I even journeyed one long summer's day to the summit of the most distant hill, whence I stretched my eye over many a mile of terra incognita, and was astonished to find how vast a globe I inhabited.

This rambling propensity strengthened with my years. Books of voyages and travels became my passion, and in devouring their contents, I neglected the regular exercises of the school. How wistfully would I wander about the pier heads in fine weather and watch the parting ships, bound to distant climes—with what longing eyes would I

13

gaze after their lessening sails and waft myself in imagination to the ends of the earth!

Further reading and thinking, though they brought this vague inclination into more reasonable bounds, only served to make it more decided. I visited various parts of my own country, and had I been merely a lover of fine scenery I should have felt little desire to seek elsewhere its gratification, for on no country have the charms of nature been more prodigally lavished. Her mighty lakes, like oceans of liquid silver; her mountains, with their bright aerial tints; her valleys, teeming with wild fertility; her tremendous cataracts, thundering in their solitudes; her boundless plains, waving with spontaneous verdure; her broad, deep rivers, rolling in solemn silence to the ocean; her trackless forests, where vegetation puts forth all its magnificence; her skies, kindling with the magic of summer clouds and glorious sunshine—no, never need an American look beyond his own country for the sublime and beautiful of natural scenery.

But Europe held forth the charms of storied and poetical association. There were to be seen the masterpieces of art, the refinements of highly cultivated society, the quaint peculiarities of ancient and local custom. My native country was full of youthful promise: Europe was rich in the accumulated treasures of age. Her very ruins told the history of times gone by, and every moldering stone was a chronicle. I longed to wander over the scenes of renowned achievement—to tread, as it were, in the footsteps of antiquity, to loiter about the ruined castle, to meditate on the falling tower, to escape, in short, from the commonplace realities of the present and lose myself among the shadowy grandeurs of the past.

I had, besides all this, an earnest desire to see the great men of the earth. We have, it is true, our great men in America: not a city but has an ample share of them. I have mingled among them in my time, and been almost withered by the shade into which they cast me, for there is nothing so baleful to a small man as the shade of a great one, particularly the great man of a city. But I was anxious to see the great men of Europe, for I had read in the works of various philosophers that all animals degenerated in America, and man among the number. A great man of Europe, thought I, must therefore be as superior to a great man of America as a peak of the Alps to a highland of the Hudson; and in this idea I was confirmed by observing the comparative importance and swelling magnitude of many English travelers among us, who, I was assured, were very little people in their own country. I will visit this land of wonders, thought I, and see the gigantic race from which I am degenerated.

It has been either my good or evil lot to have my roving passion gratified. I have wandered through different countries, and witnessed many of the shifting scenes of life. I cannot say that I have studied them with the eye of a philosopher, but rather with the sauntering gaze with which humble lovers of the picturesque stroll from the window of one print shop to another, caught sometimes by the delineations of beauty, sometimes by the distortions of caricature, and sometimes by the loveliness of landscape. As it is the fashion for modern tourists to travel pencil in hand and bring home their portfolios filled with sketches, I am disposed to get up a few for the entertainment of my friends. When, however, I look over the hints and memorandums I have taken down for the purpose, my heart almost fails me at finding how my idle humor has led me aside from the great objects studied by every regular traveler who would make a book. I fear I shall give equal disappointment with an unlucky landscape painter, who had traveled on the continent, but, following the bent of his vagrant inclination, had sketched in nooks and corners and byplaces. His sketch book was accordingly crowded with cottages and landscapes and obscure ruins, but he had neglected to paint St. Peter's, or the Coliseum; the cascade of Terni, or the bay of Naples; and had not a single glacier or volcano in his whole collection.

THE VOYAGE

Ships, ships, I will descrie you
    Amidst the main,
I will come and try you,
What you are protecting,
    And projecting,
      What's your end and aim.
One goes abroad for merchandise and trading,
Another stays to keep his country from invading,
A third is coming home with rich and wealthy lading.
    Halloo! my fancie, whither wilt thou go?

                        OLD POEM

To an American visiting Europe, the long voyage he has to make is an excellent preparative. The temporary absence of worldly scenes and employments produces a state of mind peculiarly fitted to receive new and vivid impressions. The vast space of waters that separates the hemispheres is like a blank page in existence. There is no gradual transition, by which, as in Europe, the features and population of one country blend almost imperceptibly with those of another. From the moment you lose sight of the land you have left, all is vacancy until you step on the opposite shore and are launched at once into the bustle and novelties of another world.

In traveling by land, there is a continuity of scene and a connected succession of persons and incidents that carry on the story of life and lessen the effect of absence and separation. We drag, it is true, "a lengthening chain" at each remove of our pilgrimage; but the chain is unbroken: we can trace it back link by link, and we feel that the last still grapples us to home. But a wide sea voyage severs us at once. It makes us conscious of being cast loose from the secure anchorage of settled life, and sent adrift upon a doubtful world. It interposes a gulf, not merely imaginary but real, between us and our homes—a gulf subject to tempest and fear and uncertainty, rendering distance palpable and return precarious.

Such, at least, was the case with myself. As I saw the

last blue line of my native land fade away like a cloud in the horizon, it seemed as if I had closed one volume of the world and its concerns, and had time for meditation before I opened another. That land, too, now vanishing from my view, which contained all most dear to me in life; what vicissitudes might occur in it, what changes might take place in me before I should visit it again! Who can tell, when he sets forth to wander, whither he may be driven by the uncertain currents of existence, or when he may return, or whether it may ever be his lot to revisit the scenes of his childhood?

I said that at sea all is vacancy; I should correct the expression. To one given to daydreaming and fond of losing himself in reveries, a sea voyage is full of subjects for meditation; but then they are the wonders of the deep and of the air, and rather tend to abstract the mind from worldly themes. I delighted to loll over the quarter railing, or climb to the maintop, of a calm day, and muse for hours together on the tranquil bosom of a summer's sea; to gaze upon the piles of golden clouds just peering above the horizon, fancy them some fairy realms, and people them with a creation of my own; to watch the gentle undulating billows, rolling their silver volumes, as if to die away on those happy shores.

There was a delicious sensation of mingled security and awe with which I looked down from my giddy height on the monsters of the deep at their uncouth gambols. Shoals of porpoises tumbling about the bow of the ship, the grampus slowly heaving his huge form above the surface, or the ravenous shark, darting, like a specter, through the blue waters. My imagination would conjure up all that I had heard or read of the watery world beneath me, of the finny herds that roam its fathomless valleys, of the shapeless monsters that lurk among the very foundations of the earth, and of those wild phantasms that swell the tales of fishermen and sailors.

Sometimes a distant sail, gliding along the edge of the ocean, would be another theme of idle speculation. How interesting this fragment of a world, hastening to rejoin the great mass of existence! What a glorious monument of human invention, which has in a manner triumphed over wind and wave; has brought the ends of the world into communion; has established an interchange of blessings, pouring into the sterile regions of the north all the luxuries of the south; has diffused the light of knowledge and the charities of cultivated life; and has thus bound together those scattered portions of the human race, between which nature seemed to have thrown an insurmountable barrier.

We one day descried some shapeless object drifting at a distance. At sea, everything that breaks the monotony of the surrounding expanse attracts attention. It proved to be the mast of a ship that must have been completely wrecked, for there were the remains of handkerchiefs by which some of the crew had fastened themselves to this spar to prevent their being washed off by the waves. There was no trace by which the name of the ship could be ascertained. The wreck had evidently drifted about for many months; clusters of shellfish had fastened about it, and long seaweeds flaunted at its sides. But where, thought I, is the crew? Their struggle has long been over—they have gone down amidst the roar of the tempest—their bones lie whitening among the caverns of the deep. Silence, oblivion, like the waves, have closed over them, and no one can tell the story of their end. What sighs have been wafted after that ship! What prayers offered up at the deserted fireside of home! How often has the mistress, the wife, the mother, pored over the daily news, to catch some casual intelligence of this rover of the deep! How has expectation darkened into anxiety—anxiety into dread—and dread into despair! Alas! Not one memento may ever return for love to cherish. All that may ever be known is that she sailed from her port, "and was never heard of more!"

The sight of this wreck, as usual, gave rise to many dismal anecdotes. This was particularly the case in the evening, when the weather, which had hitherto been fair, began to look wild and threatening, and gave indications of one of those sudden storms which will sometimes break in upon the serenity of a summer voyage. As we sat around the dull light of a lamp in the cabin that made the gloom more ghastly, everyone had his tale of shipwreck and disaster. I was particularly struck with a short one related by the captain.

"As I was once sailing," said he, "in a fine, stout ship across the banks of Newfoundland, one of those heavy fogs which prevail in those parts rendered it impossible for us to see far ahead even in the daytime; but at night the weather was so thick that we could not distinguish any object at twice the length of the ship. I kept lights at the masthead, and a constant watch forward to look out for fishing smacks, which are accustomed to lie at anchor on the banks. The wind was blowing a smacking breeze, and we were going at a great rate through the water. Suddenly the watch gave the alarm of 'a sail ahead!' It was scarcely uttered before we were upon her. She was a small schooner, at anchor, with her broadside toward us. The crew were all asleep, and had neglected to hoist a light. We struck her just amidships. The force, the size, the weight of our vessel bore her down below the waves; we passed over her and were hurried on our course. As the crashing wreck was sinking beneath us, I had a glimpse of two or three half-naked wretches rushing from her cabin; they just started from their beds to be swallowed shrieking by the waves. I heard their drowning cry mingling with the wind. The blast that bore it to our ears swept us out of all farther hearing. I shall never forget that cry! It was some time before we could put the ship about, she was under such headway. We returned, as nearly as we could guess, to the place where the smack had anchored. We cruised about for several hours in the dense fog. We fired signal guns and listened if we might hear the halloo of any survivors, but all was silent—we never saw or heard anything of them more."

I confess these stories, for a time, put an end to all my fine fancies. The storm increased with the night. The sea was lashed into tremendous confusion. There was a fearful, sullen sound of rushing waves and broken surges. Deep called unto deep. At times the black column of clouds overhead seemed rent asunder by flashes of lightning, which quivered along the foaming billows and made the succeeding darkness doubly terrible. The thunders bellowed over the wild waste of waters, and were echoed and prolonged by the mountain waves. As I saw the ship staggering and plunging among these roaring caverns, it seemed miraculous that she regained her balance or preserved her buoyancy. Her yards would dip into the water: her bow was almost buried beneath the waves. Sometimes an impending surge appeared ready to overwhelm her, and nothing but a dexterous movement of the helm preserved her from the shock.

When I retired to my cabin, the awful scene still followed me. The whistling of the wind through the rigging sounded like funereal wailings. The creaking of the masts, the straining and groaning of bulkheads as the ship labored in the weltering sea were frightful. As I heard the waves rushing along the sides of the ship and roaring in my very ear, it seemed as if Death were raging around this floating prison, seeking for his prey: the mere starting of a nail, the yawning of a seam, might give him entrance.

A fine day, however, with a tranquil sea and favoring breeze, soon put all these dismal reflections to flight. It is impossible to resist the gladdening influence of fine weather and fair wind at sea. When the ship is decked out in all her canvas, every sail swelled, and careering gaily over the curling waves, how lofty, how gallant she appears—how she seems to lord it over the deep!

I might fill a volume with the reveries of a sea voyage, for with me it is almost a continual reverie—but it is time to get to shore.

It was a fine sunny morning when the thrilling cry of "land!" was given from the masthead. None but those who have experienced it can form an idea of the delicious throng of sensations which rush into an American's bosom when he first comes in sight of Europe. There is a volume of associations with the very name. It is the land of promise, teeming with everything of which his childhood has heard or on which his studious years have pondered.

From that time until the moment of arrival, it was all feverish excitement. The ships of war that prowled like guardian giants along the coast; the headlands of Ireland, stretching out into the channel; the Welsh mountains, towering into the clouds; all were objects of intense interest. As we sailed up the Mersey, I reconnoitered the shores with a telescope. My eye dwelt with delight on neat cottages, with their trim shrubberies and green grass plots. I saw the moldering ruin of an abbey overrun with ivy, and the taper spire of a village church rising from the brow of a neighboring hill—all were characteristic of England.

The tide and wind were so favorable that the ship was enabled to come at once to the pier. It was thronged with people; some, idle lookers-on, others, eager expectants of friends or relatives. I could distinguish the merchant to whom the ship was consigned. I knew him by his calculating brow and restless air. His hands were thrust into his pockets; he was whistling thoughtfully, and walking to and fro, a small space having been accorded him by the crowd, in deference to his temporary importance. There were repeated cheerings and salutations interchanged between the shore and the ship as friends happened to recognize each other. I particularly noticed one young woman of humble dress but interesting demeanor. She was leaning forward from among the crowd; her eye hurried over the ship as it neared the shore to catch some wished-for countenance. She seemed disappointed and agitated, when I heard a faint voice call her name. It was from a poor sailor who had been ill all the voyage and had excited the sympathy of everyone on board. When the weather was fine, his messmates had spread a mattress for him on deck in the shade, but of late his illness had so increased that he had taken to his hammock, and only breathed a wish that he might see his wife before he died. He had been helped on deck as we came up the river, and was now leaning against the shrouds, with a countenance so wasted, so pale, so ghastly that it was no wonder even the eye of affection did not recognize him. But at the sound of his voice, her eye darted on his features; it read, at once, a whole volume of sorrow; she clasped her hands, uttered a faint shriek, and stood wringing them in silent agony.

All now was hurry and bustle. The meetings of acquaintances—the greetings of friends—the consultations of men of business. I alone was solitary and idle. I had no friend to meet, no cheering to receive. I stepped upon the land of my forefathers—but felt that I was a stranger in the land.

ROSCOE

————In the service of mankind to be
A guardian god below; still to employ
The mind's brave ardor in heroic aims,
Such as may raise us o'er the grovelling herd,
And make us shine forever—that is life.

THOMSON

One of the first places to which a stranger is taken in Liverpool is the Atheneum. It is established on a liberal and judicious plan; it contains a good library and spacious reading room, and is the great literary resort of the place. Go there at what hour you may, you are sure to find it filled with grave-looking personages, deeply absorbed in the study of newspapers.

As I was once visiting this haunt of the learned, my attention was attracted to a person just entering the room. He was advanced in life, tall, and of a form that might once have been commanding, but it was a little bowed by time—perhaps by care. He had a noble Roman style of countenance, a head that would have pleased a painter; and though some slight furrows on his brow showed that wasting thought had been busy there, yet his eye still beamed with the fire of a poetic soul. There was something in his whole appearance that indicated a being of a different order from the bustling race around him.

I inquired his name, and was informed that it was Roscoe. I drew back with an involuntary feeling of veneration. This, then, was an author of celebrity; this was one of those men whose voices have gone forth to the ends of the earth, with whose minds I have communed even in the solitudes of America. Accustomed, as we are in our country, to know European writers only by their

22

works, we cannot conceive of them, as of other men, engrossed by trivial or sordid pursuits and jostling with the crowd of common minds in the dusty paths of life. They pass before our imaginations like superior beings, radiant with the emanations of their genius and surrounded by a halo of literary glory.

To find, therefore, the elegant historian of the Medici mingling among the busy sons of traffic at first shocked my poetical ideas; but it is from the very circumstances and situation in which he has been placed that Mr. Roscoe derives his highest claims to admiration. It is interesting to notice how some minds seem almost to create themselves, springing up under every disadvantage and working their solitary but irresistible way through a thousand obstacles. Nature seems to delight in disappointing the assiduities of art with which she would rear legitimate dullness to maturity, and to glory in the vigor and luxuriance of her chance productions. She scatters the seeds of genius to the winds, and though some may perish among the stony places of the world and some be choked by the thorns and brambles of early adversity, yet others will now and then strike root even in the clefts of the rock, struggle bravely up into sunshine, and spread over their sterile birthplace all the beauties of vegetation.

Such has been the case with Mr. Roscoe. Born in a place apparently ungenial to the growth of literary talent, in the very market place of trade; without fortune, family connections, or patronage; self-prompted, self-sustained, and almost self-taught, he has conquered every obstacle, achieved his way to eminence, and, having become one of the ornaments of the nation, has turned the whole force of his talents and influence to advance and embellish his native town.

Indeed, it is this last trait in his character which has given him the greatest interest in my eyes, and induced me particularly to point him out to my countrymen. Eminent as are his literary merits, he is but one among the many distinguished authors of this intellectual nation. They, however, in general, live but for their own fame or their own pleasures. Their private history presents no lesson to the world, or, perhaps, a humiliating one of human frailty and inconsistency. At best, they are prone to steal away from the bustle and commonplace of busy existence, to indulge in the selfishness of lettered ease, and to revel in scenes of mental but exclusive enjoyment.

Mr. Roscoe, on the contrary, has claimed none of the accorded privileges of talent. He has shut himself up in no garden of thought, nor elysium of fancy, but has gone forth into the highways and thoroughfares of life; he has planted bowers by the wayside for the refreshment of the pilgrim and the sojourner, and has opened pure fountains where the laboring man may turn aside from the dust and heat of the day and drink of the living streams of knowledge. There is a "daily beauty in his life," on which mankind may meditate and grow better. It exhibits no lofty and almost useless, because inimitable, example of excellence, but presents a picture of active yet simple and imitable virtues, which are within every man's reach, but which, unfortunately, are not exercised by many, or this world would be a paradise.

But his private life is peculiarly worthy of the attention of the citizens of our young and busy country, where literature and the elegant arts must grow up side by side with the coarser plants of daily necessity, and must depend for their culture, not on the exclusive devotion of time and wealth, nor the quickening rays of titled patronage, but on hours and seasons snatched from the pursuit of worldly interests by intelligent and public-spirited individuals.

He has shown how much may be done for a place in hours of leisure by one master spirit, and how completely it can give its own impress to surrounding objects. Like his own Lorenzo de' Medici, on whom he seems to have fixed his eye as on a pure model of antiquity, he has interwoven the history of his life with the history of his native town, and has made the foundations of its fame the monuments of his virtues. Wherever you go in Liverpool, you perceive traces of his footsteps in all that is elegant and liberal. He found the tide of wealth flowing merely in the channels of traffic; he has diverted from it invigorating rills to refresh the garden of literature. By his own example and constant exertions he has effected that union of commerce and the intellectual pursuits, so eloquently recommended in one of his latest writings,* and has practically proved how beautifully they may be brought to harmonize and to benefit each other. The noble institutions for literary and scientific purposes, which reflect such credit on Liverpool and are giving such an impulse to the public mind, have mostly been originated and have all been effectively promoted by Mr. Roscoe; and when we consider the rapidly increasing opulence and magnitude of that town, which promises to vie in commercial importance with the metropolis, it will be perceived that in awakening an ambition of mental improvement among its inhabitants he has effected a great benefit to the cause of British literature.

In America, we know Mr. Roscoe only as the author; in Liverpool he is spoken of as the banker, and I was told of his having been unfortunate in business. I could not pity him, as I heard some rich men do. I considered him far above the reach of pity. Those who live only for the world, and in the world, may be cast down by the frowns of adversity, but a man like Roscoe is not to be overcome by the reverses of fortune. They do but drive him in upon the resources of his own mind, to the superior society of his own thoughts, which the best of men are apt sometimes to neglect, and to roam abroad in search of less worthy associates. He is independent of the world around him. He lives with antiquity and posterity; with antiquity, in the sweet communion of studious retirement; and with posterity, in the generous aspirings after future renown. The solitude of such a mind is its state of highest enjoyment. It is then visited by those elevated meditations which are the proper aliment of noble souls, and are, like manna, sent from heaven, in the wilderness of this world.

While my feelings were yet alive on the subject, it was my fortune to light on further traces of Mr. Roscoe. I was riding out with a gentleman to view the environs of Liverpool, when he turned off, through a gate, into some ornamented grounds. After riding a short distance, we came to a spacious mansion of freestone, built in the Grecian style. It was not in the purest taste, yet it had an air of elegance, and the situation was delightful. A fine

*Address on the opening of the Liverpool Institution.

lawn sloped away from it, studded with clumps of trees, so disposed as to break a soft, fertile country into a variety of landscapes. The Mersey was seen winding a broad, quiet sheet of water through an expanse of green meadowland, while the Welsh mountains, blended with clouds and melting into distance, bordered the horizon.

This was Roscoe's favorite residence during the days of his prosperity. It had been the seat of elegant hospitality and literary retirement. The house was now silent and deserted. I saw the windows of the study, which looked out upon the soft scenery I have mentioned. The windows were closed—the library was gone. Two or three ill-favored beings were loitering about the place, whom my fancy pictured into retainers of the law. It was like visiting some classic fountain that had once welled its pure waters in a sacred shade, but finding it dry and dusty, with the lizard and the toad brooding over the shattered marbles.

I inquired after the fate of Mr. Roscoe's library, which had consisted of scarce and foreign books, from many of which he had drawn the materials for his Italian histories. It had passed under the hammer of the auctioneer, and was dispersed about the country. The good people of the vicinity thronged like wreckers to get some part of the noble vessel that had been driven on shore. Did such a scene admit of ludicrous associations, we might imagine something whimsical in this strange irruption in the regions of learning. Pygmies rummaging the armory of a giant and contending for the possession of weapons which they could not wield. We might picture to ourselves some knot of speculators, debating with calculating brow over the quaint binding and illuminated margin of an obsolete author; of the air of intense but baffled sagacity with which some successful purchaser attempted to dive into the black-letter bargain he had secured.

It is a beautiful incident in the story of Mr. Roscoe's misfortunes, and one which cannot fail to interest the studious mind, that the parting with his books seems to have touched upon his tenderest feelings, and to have been the only circumstance that could provoke the notice of his muse. The scholar only knows how dear these silent yet eloquent companions of pure thoughts and innocent hours become in the seasons of adversity. When all that is worldly turns to dross around us, these only retain their steady value. When friends grow cold and the converse of intimates languishes into vapid civility and commonplace, these only continue the unaltered countenance of happier days and cheer us with that true friendship which never deceived hope, nor deserted sorrow.

I do not wish to censure; but, surely, if the people of Liverpool had been properly sensible of what was due to Mr. Roscoe and themselves, his library would never have been sold. Good worldly reasons may, doubtless, be given for the circumstance, which it would be difficult to combat with others that might seem merely fanciful; but it certainly appears to me such an opportunity as seldom occurs, of cheering a noble mind struggling under misfortunes, by one of the most delicate but most expressive tokens of public sympathy. It is difficult, however, to estimate a man of genius properly who is daily before our eyes. He becomes mingled and confounded with other men. His great qualities lose their novelty, we become too familiar with the common materials which form the basis even of the loftiest character. Some of Mr. Roscoe's townsmen may regard him merely as a man of business; others as a politician; all find him engaged like themselves in ordinary occupations, and surpassed, perhaps, by themselves on some points of worldly wisdom. Even that amiable and unostentatious simplicity of character which gives the nameless grace to real excellence may cause him to be undervalued by some coarse minds, who do not know that true worth is always void of glare and pretension. But the man of letters who speaks of Liverpool speaks of it as the residence of Roscoe. The intelligent traveler who visits it inquires where Roscoe is to be seen. He is the literary landmark of the place, indicating its existence to the distant scholar. He is, like Pompey's column at Alexandria, towering alone in classic dignity.

The following sonnet, addressed by Mr. Roscoe to his books on parting with them, is alluded to in the preceding article. If anything can add effect to the pure feeling and elevated thought here displayed, it is the conviction that the whole is no effusion of fancy, but a faithful transcript from the writer's heart.

TO MY BOOKS

As one who, destined from his friends to part,
    Regrets his loss, but hopes again erewhile
    To share their converse and enjoy their smile,
And tempers as he may affliction's dart;

Thus, loved associates, chiefs of elder art,
    Teachers of wisdom, who could once beguile
    My tedious hours, and lighten every toil,
I now resign you; nor with fainting heart;

For pass a few short years, or days, or hours,
    And happier seasons may their dawn unfold,
    And all your sacred fellowship restore:
When, freed from earth, unlimited its powers,
    Mind shall with mind direct communion hold,
    And kindred spirits meet to part no more.

THE WIFE

The treasures of the deep are not so precious
As are the conceal'd comforts of a man
Locked up in woman's love. I scent the air
Of blessings, when I come but near the house.
What a delicious breath marriage sends forth . . .
The violet bed's not sweeter.

MIDDLETON

I have often had occasion to remark the fortitude with
which women sustain the most overwhelming reverses
of fortune. Those disasters which break down the spirit
of a man and prostrate him in the dust seem to call forth
all the energies of the softer sex, and give such intrepidity
and elevation to their character that at times it approaches to sublimity. Nothing can be more touching
than to behold a soft and tender female, who had been
all weakness and dependence and alive to every trivial
roughness while treading the prosperous paths of life,
suddenly rising in mental force to be the comforter and
support of her husband under misfortune, and abiding
with unshrinking firmness the bitterest blasts of adversity.

As the vine, which has long twined its graceful foliage
about the oak and been lifted by it into sunshine, will,
when the hardy plant is rifted by the thunderbolt, cling
around it with its caressing tendrils and bind up its shattered boughs, so is it beautifully ordered by Providence,
that woman, who is the mere dependent and ornament of
man in his happier hours, should be his stay and solace
when smitten with sudden calamity, winding herself into
the rugged recesses of his nature, tenderly supporting
the drooping head, and binding up the broken heart.

I was once congratulating a friend, who had around
him a blooming family, knit together in the strongest af-

fection. "I can wish you no better lot," said he, with enthusiasm, "than to have a wife and children. If you are prosperous, there they are to share your prosperity; if otherwise, there they are to comfort you." And, indeed, I have observed that a married man falling into misfortune is more apt to retrieve his situation in the world than a single one, partly because he is more stimulated to exertion by the necessities of the helpless and beloved beings who depend upon him for subsistence, but chiefly because his spirits are soothed and relieved by domestic endearments, and his self-respect kept alive by finding that, though all abroad is darkness and humiliation, yet there is still a little world of love at home, of which he is the monarch. Whereas a single man is apt to run to waste and self-neglect, to fancy himself lonely and abandoned, and his heart to fall to ruin like some deserted mansion for want of an inhabitant.

These observations call to mind a little domestic story, of which I was once a witness. My intimate friend, Leslie, had married a beautiful and accomplished girl who had been brought up in the midst of fashionable life. She had, it is true, no fortune, but that of my friend was ample; and he delighted in the anticipation of indulging her in every elegant pursuit and administering to those delicate tastes and fancies that spread a kind of witchery about the sex. "Her life," said he, "shall be like a fairy tale."

The very difference in their characters produced a harmonious combination: he was of a romantic and somewhat serious cast; she was all life and gladness. I have often noticed the mute rapture with which he would gaze upon her in company, of which her sprightly powers made her the delight; and how, in the midst of applause, her eye would still turn to him, as if there alone she sought favor and acceptance. When leaning on his arm, her slender form contrasted finely with his tall, manly person. The fond confiding air with which she looked up to him seemed to call forth a flush of triumphant pride and cherishing tenderness, as if he doted on his lovely burden for its very helplessness. Never did a couple set forward on the flowery path of early and well-suited marriage with a fairer prospect of felicity.

It was the misfortune of my friend, however, to have embarked his property in large speculations; and he had not been married many months when, by a succession of sudden disasters, it was swept from him, and he found himself reduced almost to penury. For a time he kept his situation to himself, and went about with a haggard countenance and a breaking heart. His life was but a protracted agony; and what rendered it more insupportable was the necessity of keeping up a smile in the presence of his wife, for he could not bring himself to overwhelm her with the news. She saw, however, with the quick eyes of affection that all was not well with him. She marked his altered looks and stifled sighs, and was not to be deceived by his sickly and vapid attempts at cheerfulness. She tasked all her sprightly powers and tender blandishments to win him back to happiness, but she only drove the arrow deeper into his soul. The more he saw cause to love her, the more torturing was the thought that he was soon to make her wretched. A little while, thought he, and the smile will vanish from that cheek— the song will die away from those lips—the luster of those eyes will be quenched with sorrow; and the happy heart, which now beats lightly in that bosom, will be weighed down like mine, by the cares and miseries of the world.

At length he came to me one day and related his whole situation in a tone of the deepest despair. When I heard him through, I inquired, "Does your wife know all this?" At the question he burst into an agony of tears. "For God's sake!" cried he, "if you have any pity on me, don't mention my wife; it is the thought of her that drives me almost to madness!"

"And why not?" said I. "She must know it sooner or later; you cannot keep it long from her, and the intelligence may break upon her in a more startling manner than if imparted by yourself, for the accents of those we love soften the hardest tidings. Besides, you are depriving yourself of the comforts of her sympathy; and not merely that, but also endangering the only bond that can keep hearts together—an unreserved community of thought and feeling. She will soon perceive that something is secretly preying upon your mind; and true love will not brook reserve; it feels undervalued and out-raged when even the sorrows of those it loves are concealed from it."

"Oh, but, my friend! To think what a blow I am to give to all her future prospects—how I am to strike her very soul to the earth by telling her that her husband is a beggar! That she is to forego all the elegancies of life—all the pleasures of society—to shrink with me into indigence and obscurity! To tell her that I have dragged her down from the sphere in which she might have continued to move in constant brightness—the light of every eye—the admiration of every heart! How can she bear poverty? She has been brought up in all the refinements of opulence. How can she bear neglect? She has been the idol of society. Oh! It will break her heart—it will break her heart!"

I saw his grief was eloquent, and I let it have its flow, for sorrow relieves itself by words. When his paroxysm had subsided and he had relapsed into moody silence, I resumed the subject gently, and urged him to break his situation at once to his wife. He shook his head mournfully but positively.

"But how are you to keep it from her? It is necessary she should know it, that you may take the steps proper to the alteration of your circumstances. You must change your style of living—nay," observing a pang to pass across his countenance, "don't let that afflict you. I am sure you have never placed your happiness in outward show—you have yet friends, warm friends, who will not think the worse of you for being less splendidly lodged; and surely it does not require a palace to be happy with Mary——"

"I could be happy with her," cried he, convulsively, "in a hovel! I could go down with her into poverty and the dust! I could—I could— God bless her! God bless her!" cried he, bursting into a transport of grief and tenderness.

"And believe me, my friend," said I, stepping up and grasping him warmly by the hand, "believe me, she can be the same with you. Aye, more: it will be a source of pride and triumph to her—it will call forth all the latent energies and fervent sympathies of her nature, for she will rejoice to prove that she loves you for yourself. There is in every true woman's heart a spark of heavenly fire, which lies dormant in the broad daylight of prosperity, but which kindles up, and beams and blazes in the dark hour of adversity. No man knows what the wife of his bosom is—no man knows what a ministering angel she is—until he has gone with her through the fiery trials of this world."

There was something in the earnestness of my manner and the figurative style of my language that caught the excited imagination of Leslie. I knew the auditor I had to deal with; and following up the impression I had made, I finished by persuading him to go home and unburden his sad heart to his wife.

I must confess, notwithstanding all I had said, I felt some little solicitude for the result. Who can calculate on the fortitude of one whose life has been a round of pleasures? Her gay spirits might revolt at the dark downward path of low humility suddenly pointed out before her, and might cling to the sunny regions in which they had hitherto reveled. Besides, ruin in fashionable life is accompanied by so many galling mortifications, to which in other ranks it is a stranger. In short, I could not meet Leslie the next morning without trepidation. He had made the disclosure.

"And how did she bear it?"

"Like an angel! It seemed rather to be a relief to her mind, for she threw her arms around my neck and asked if this was all that had lately made me unhappy. But, poor girl," added he, "she cannot realize the change we must undergo. She has no idea of poverty but in the abstract; she has only read of it in poetry, where it is allied to love. She feels as yet no privation; she suffers no loss of accustomed conveniences nor elegancies. When we come practically to experience its sordid cares, its paltry wants, its petty humiliations—then will be the real trial."

"But," said I, "now that you have got over the severest task, that of breaking it to her, the sooner you let the world into the secret the better. The disclosure may be mortifying, but then it is a single misery, and soon over; whereas you otherwise suffer it, in anticipation, every

hour in the day. It is not poverty so much as pretense
that harasses a ruined man—the struggle between a
proud mind and an empty purse—the keeping up a hollow show that must soon come to an end. Have the
courage to appear poor and you disarm poverty of its
sharpest sting." On this point I found Leslie perfectly
prepared. He had no false pride himself, and as to his
wife, she was only anxious to conform to their altered
fortunes.

Some days afterward he called upon me in the evening. He had disposed of his dwelling house and taken a
small cottage in the country, a few miles from town.
He had been busied all day in sending out furniture.
The new establishment required few articles, and those
of the simplest kind. All the splendid furniture of his
late residence had been sold, excepting his wife's harp.
That, he said, was too closely associated with the idea of
herself; it belonged to the little story of their loves, for
some of the sweetest moments of their courtship were
those when he had leaned over that instrument and listened to the melting tones of her voice. I could not but
smile at this instance of romantic gallantry in a doting
husband.

He was now going out to the cottage, where his wife
had been all day superintending its arrangement. My
feelings had become strongly interested in the progress
of this family story, and, as it was a fine evening, I offered to accompany him.

He was wearied with the fatigues of the day, and as he
walked out fell into a fit of gloomy musing.

"Poor Mary!" at length broke, with a heavy sigh, from
his lips.

"And what of her?" asked I. "Has anything happened
to her?"

"What," said he, darting an impatient glance. "Is it
nothing to be reduced to this paltry situation—to be
caged in a miserable cottage—to be obliged to toil almost in the menial concerns of her wretched habitation?"

"Has she then repined at the change?"

"Repined! She has been nothing but sweetness and
good humor. Indeed, she seems in better spirits than I

have ever known her; she has been to me all love, and tenderness, and comfort!"

"Admirable girl!" exclaimed I. "You call yourself poor, my friend; you never were so rich—you never knew the boundless treasures of excellence you possess in that woman."

"Oh! But, my friend, if this first meeting at the cottage were over, I think I could then be comfortable. But this is her first day of real experience; she has been introduced into a humble dwelling, she has been employed all day in arranging its miserable equipments, she has for the first time known the fatigues of domestic employment, she has for the first time looked around her on a home destitute of everything elegant—almost of everything convenient—and may now be sitting down, exhausted and spiritless, brooding over a prospect of future poverty."

There was a degree of probability in this picture that I could not gainsay, so we walked on in silence.

After turning from the main road up a narrow lane so thickly shaded with forest trees as to give it a complete air of seclusion, we came in sight of the cottage. It was humble enough in its appearance for the most pastoral poet, and yet it had a pleasing rural look. A wild vine had overrun one end with a profusion of foliage; a few trees threw their branches gracefully over it, and I observed several pots of flowers tastefully disposed about the door and on the grass plot in front. A small wicket gate opened upon a footpath that wound through some shrubbery to the door. Just as we approached, we heard the sound of music—Leslie grasped my arm; we paused and listened. It was Mary's voice singing, in a style of the most touching simplicity, a little air of which her husband was peculiarly fond.

I felt Leslie's hand tremble on my arm. He stepped forward to hear more distinctly. His step made a noise on the gravel walk. A bright, beautiful face glanced out at the window and vanished, a light footstep was heard, and Mary came tripping forth to meet us; she was in a pretty rural dress of white, a few wild flowers were twisted in her fine hair, a fresh bloom was on her cheek, her whole countenance beamed with smiles—I had never seen her look so lovely.

"My dear George," cried she, "I am so glad you are come! I have been watching and watching for you, and running down the lane, and looking out for you. I've set out a table under a beautiful tree behind the cottage, and I've been gathering some of the most delicious strawberries, for I know you are fond of them—and we have such excellent cream—and everything is so sweet and still here. . . . Oh!" said she, putting her arm within his and looking up brightly in his face. "Oh, we shall be so happy!"

Poor Leslie was overcome. He caught her to his bosom, he folded his arms around her, he kissed her again and again—he could not speak, but the tears gushed into his eyes; and he has often assured me that, though the world has since gone prosperously with him, and his life has, indeed, been a happy one, yet never has he experienced a moment of more exquisite felicity.

RIP VAN WINKLE

A POSTHUMOUS WRITING OF DIEDRICH KNICKERBOCKER

By Woden, God of Saxons,
From whence comes Wensday, that is Wodensday,
Truth is a thing that ever I will keep
Unto thylke day in which I creep into
My sepulchre——

CARTWRIGHT

[The following Tale was found among the papers of the late Diedrich Knickerbocker, an old gentleman of New York, who was very curious in the Dutch history of the province and the manners of the descendants from its primitive settlers. His historical researches, however, did not lie so much among books as among men, for the former are lamentably scanty on his favorite topics, whereas he found the old burghers, and still more their wives, rich in that legendary lore so invaluable to true history. Whenever, therefore, he happened upon a genuine Dutch family, snugly shut up in its low-roofed farmhouse, under a spreading sycamore, he looked upon it as a little clasped volume of black letter and studied it with the zeal of a bookworm.

The result of all these researches was a history of the province during the reign of the Dutch governors, which he published some years since. There have been various opinions as to the literary character of his work, and, to tell the truth, it is not a whit better than it should be. Its chief merit is its scrupulous accuracy, which indeed was a little questioned on its first appearance, but has since been completely established, and it is now admitted into all historical collections as a book of unquestionable authority.

The old gentleman died shortly after the publication of his work, and now that he is dead and gone, it cannot do much harm to his memory to say that his time might have been much better employed in weightier labors. He, however, was apt to ride his hobby his own way; and though it did now and then kick up the dust a little in the eyes of his neighbors and grieve the spirit of some friends, for whom he felt the truest deference and affection, yet his errors and follies are remembered "more in sorrow than in anger," and it begins to be suspected that he never intended to injure or offend. But however his memory may be appreciated by critics, it is still held dear by many folks, whose good opinion is well worth having; particularly by certain biscuit bakers, who have gone so far as to imprint his likeness on their new-year cakes, and have thus given him a chance for immortality, almost equal to being stamped on a Waterloo Medal, or a Queen Anne's Farthing.]

———————

Whoever has made a voyage up the Hudson must remember the Kaatskill Mountains. They are a dismembered branch of the great Appalachian family, and are seen away to the west of the river, swelling up to a noble height and lording it over the surrounding country. Every change of season, every change of weather, indeed, every hour of the day produces some change in the magical hues and shapes of these mountains, and they are regarded by all the good wives, far and near, as perfect barometers. When the weather is fair and settled, they are clothed in blue and purple, and print their bold outlines on the clear evening sky; but, sometimes, when the rest of the landscape is cloudless, they will gather a hood of gray vapors about their summits, which, in the last rays of the setting sun, will glow and light up like a crown of glory.

At the foot of these fairy mountains, the voyager may have descried the light smoke curling up from a village, whose shingle roofs gleam among the trees, just where the blue tints of the upland melt away into the fresh green of the nearer landscape. It is a little village of great antiquity, having been founded by some of the Dutch colonists in the early times of the province, just about the beginning of the government of the good Peter Stuyvesant (may he rest in peace!), and there were some of the houses of the original settlers standing within a few years, built of small yellow bricks brought from Holland, having latticed windows and gable fronts, surmounted with weathercocks.

In that same village, and in one of these very houses (which, to tell the precise truth, was sadly time-worn and weather-beaten), there lived many years since, while the country was yet a province of Great Britain, a simple, good-natured fellow of the name of Rip Van Winkle. He was a descendant of the Van Winkles who figured so gallantly in the chivalrous days of Peter Stuyvesant, and accompanied him to the siege of Fort Christina. He inherited, however, but little of the martial character of his ancestors. I have observed that he was a simple, good-natured man; he was, moreover, a kind neighbor, and an obedient, henpecked husband. Indeed, to the latter circumstance might be owing that meekness of spirit which gained him such universal popularity, for those men are most apt to be obsequious and conciliating abroad who are under the discipline of shrews at home. Their tempers, doubtless, are rendered pliant and malleable in the fiery furnace of domestic tribulation, and a curtain lecture is worth all the sermons in the world for teaching the virtues of patience and long-suffering. A termagant wife may, therefore, in some respects, be considered a tolerable blessing; and if so, Rip Van Winkle was thrice blessed.

Certain it is that he was a great favorite among all the good wives of the village, who, as usual with the amiable sex, took his part in all family squabbles and never failed, whenever they talked those matters over in their evening gossipings, to lay all the blame on Dame Van Winkle. The children of the village, too, would shout with joy whenever he approached. He assisted at their sports, made their playthings, taught them to fly kites and shoot marbles, and told them long stories of ghosts, witches, and Indians. Whenever he went dodging about the village, he was surrounded by a troop of them, hanging on his skirts, clambering on his back, and playing a thousand tricks on him with impunity; and not a dog would bark at him throughout the neighborhood.

The great error in Rip's composition was an insuperable aversion to all kinds of profitable labor. It could not be from the want of assiduity or perseverance, for he would sit on a wet rock, with a rod as long and heavy as a Tartar's lance, and fish all day without a murmur, even though he should not be encouraged by a single nibble. He would carry a fowling piece on his shoulder for hours together, trudging through woods and swamps and up hill and down dale to shoot a few squirrels or wild pigeons. He would never refuse to assist a neighbor even in the roughest toil, and was a foremost man at all country frolics for husking Indian corn or building stone fences; the women of the village, too, used to employ him to run their errands and to do such little odd jobs as their less obliging husbands would not do for them. In a word, Rip was ready to attend to anybody's business but his own; but as to doing family duty and keeping his farm in order, he found it impossible.

In fact, he declared it was of no use to work on his farm; it was the most pestilent little piece of ground in the whole country; everything about it went wrong, and would go wrong, in spite of him. His fences were continually falling to pieces; his cow would either go astray or get among the cabbages; weeds were sure to grow quicker in his fields than anywhere else; the rain always made a point of setting in just as he had some outdoor work to do; so that though his patrimonial estate had dwindled away under his management, acre by acre, until there was little more left than a mere patch of Indian corn and potatoes, yet it was the worst-conditioned farm in the neighborhood.

His children, too, were as ragged and wild as if they belonged to nobody. His son Rip, an urchin begotten in his own likeness, promised to inherit the habits, with the old clothes, of his father. He was generally seen trooping like a colt at his mother's heels, equipped in a pair of his father's cast-off galligaskins, which he had much ado to hold up with one hand as a fine lady does her train in bad weather.

Rip Van Winkle, however, was one of those happy mortals of foolish, well-oiled dispositions who take the world easy, eat white bread or brown, whichever can be got with least thought or trouble, and would rather starve on a penny than work for a pound. If left to himself, he would have whistled life away in perfect contentment; but his wife kept continually dinning in his ears about his idleness, his carelessness, and the ruin he was bringing on his family. Morning, noon, and night, her tongue was incessantly going, and everything he said or did was sure to produce a torrent of household eloquence. Rip had but one way of replying to all lectures of the kind, and that, by frequent use, had grown into a habit. He shrugged his shoulders, shook his head, cast up his eyes, but said nothing. This, however, always provoked a fresh volley from his wife, so that he was fain to draw off his forces and take to the outside of the house—the only side which, in truth, belongs to a henpecked husband.

Rip's sole domestic adherent was his dog, Wolf, who was as much henpecked as his master, for Dame Van Winkle regarded them as companions in idleness, and even looked upon Wolf with an evil eye as the cause of his master's going so often astray. True it is, in all points of spirit befitting an honorable dog, he was as courageous an animal as ever scoured the woods—but what courage can withstand the ever-during and all-besetting terrors of a woman's tongue? The moment Wolf entered the house his crest fell, his tail drooped to the ground, or curled between his legs, he sneaked about with a gallows air, casting many a sidelong glance at Dame Van Winkle, and at the least flourish of a broomstick or ladle he would fly to the door with yelping precipitation.

Times grew worse and worse with Rip Van Winkle as years of matrimony rolled on; a tart temper never mellows with age, and a sharp tongue is the only edged tool that grows keener with constant use. For a long while he used to console himself, when driven from home, by frequenting a kind of perpetual club of the sages, philosophers, and other idle personages of the village, which held its sessions on a bench before a small inn, designated by a rubicund portrait of His Majesty George the Third. Here they used to sit in the shade through a long, lazy summer's day, talking listlessly over village gossip or telling endless sleepy stories about nothing. But it would have been worth any statesman's money to have heard the profound discussions that sometimes took place when by chance an old newspaper fell into their hands from some passing traveler. How solemnly they would listen to the contents, as drawled out by Derrick Van Bummel, the schoolmaster, a dapper, learned little man who was not to be daunted by the most gigantic word in the dictionary; and how sagely they would deliberate upon public events some months after they had taken place.

The opinions of this junto were completely controlled
by Nicholas Vedder, a patriarch of the village and landlord of the inn, at the door of which he took his seat
from morning till night, just moving sufficiently to avoid
the sun and keep in the shade of a large tree, so that the
neighbors could tell the hour by his movements as accu-
rately as by a sundial. It is true he was rarely heard
to speak, but smoked his pipe incessantly. His adherents, however (for every great man has his adherents),
perfectly understood him, and knew how to gather his
opinions. When anything that was read or related displeased him, he was observed to smoke his pipe vehemently and to send forth short, frequent, and angry puffs;
but when pleased, he would inhale the smoke slowly and
tranquilly and emit it in light and placid clouds, and sometimes, taking the pipe from his mouth and letting the fragrant vapor curl about his nose, would gravely nod his
head in token of perfect approbation.

From even this stronghold the unlucky Rip was at
length routed by his termagant wife, who would suddenly
break in upon the tranquillity of the assemblage and call
the members all to naught; nor was that august personage,
Nicholas Vedder himself, sacred from the daring tongue
of this terrible virago, who charged him outright with
encouraging her husband in habits of idleness.

Poor Rip was at last reduced almost to despair, and his
only alternative, to escape from the labor of the farm
and clamor of his wife, was to take gun in hand and
stroll away into the woods. Here he would sometimes
seat himself at the foot of a tree and share the contents
of his wallet with Wolf, with whom he sympathized as a
fellow sufferer in persecution. "Poor Wolf," he would say,
"thy mistress leads thee a dog's life of it; but never mind,
my lad, whilst I live thou shalt never want a friend to
stand by thee!" Wolf would wag his tail, look wistfully
in his master's face, and if dogs can feel pity, I verily believe he reciprocated the sentiment with all his heart.

In a long ramble of the kind of a fine autumnal
day, Rip had unconsciously scrambled to one of the highest parts of the Kaatskill Mountains. He was after his
favorite sport of squirrel shooting, and the still solitudes had echoed and re-echoed with the reports of his

gun. Panting and fatigued, he threw himself, late in the afternoon, on a green knoll, covered with mountain herbage, that crowned the brow of a precipice. From an opening between the trees he could overlook all the lower country for many a mile of rich woodland. He saw at a distance the lordly Hudson, far, far below him, moving on its silent but majestic course, with the reflection of a purple cloud or the sail of a lagging bark here and there sleeping on its glassy bosom, and at last losing itself in the blue highlands.

On the other side he looked down into a deep mountain glen, wild, lonely, and shagged, the bottom filled with fragments from the impending cliffs, and scarcely lighted by the reflected rays of the setting sun. For some time Rip lay musing on this scene. Evening was gradually advancing; the mountains began to throw their long blue shadows over the valleys. He saw that it would be dark long before he could reach the village, and he heaved a heavy sigh when he thought of encountering the terrors of Dame Van Winkle.

As he was about to descend, he heard a voice from a distance, hallooing, "Rip Van Winkle! Rip Van Winkle!" He looked around, but could see nothing but a crow winging its solitary flight across the mountain. He thought his fancy must have deceived him, and turned again to descend, when he heard the same cry ring through the still evening air, "Rip Van Winkle! Rip Van Winkle!" At the same time Wolf bristled up his back and, giving a low growl, skulked to his master's side, looking fearfully down into the glen. Rip now felt a vague apprehension stealing over him; he looked anxiously in the same direction and perceived a strange figure slowly toiling up the rocks, and bending under the weight of something he carried on his back. He was surprised to see any human being in this lonely and unfrequented place, but supposing it to be some one of the neighborhood in need of his assistance, he hastened down to yield it.

On nearer approach he was still more surprised at the singularity of the stranger's appearance. He was a short, square-built old fellow, with thick, bushy hair and a grizzled beard. His dress was of the antique Dutch fashion—a cloth jerkin strapped around the waist and several pairs

of breeches, the outer one of ample volume, decorated
with rows of buttons down the sides and bunches at the
knees. He bore on his shoulder a stout keg that seemed full
of liquor, and made signs for Rip to approach and assist
him with the load. Though rather shy and distrustful of
this new acquaintance, Rip complied with his usual alacrity, and mutually relieving one another, they clambered
up a narrow gully, apparently the dry bed of a mountain
torrent. As they ascended, Rip every now and then heard
long rolling peals, like distant thunder, that seemed to
issue out of a deep ravine, or rather cleft, between lofty
rocks, toward which their rugged path conducted. He
paused for an instant, but supposing it to be the muttering
of one of those transient thunder showers which often
take place in mountain heights, he proceeded. Passing
through the ravine, they came to a hollow, like a small
amphitheater, surrounded by perpendicular precipices,
over the brinks of which impending trees shot their
branches, so that you only caught glimpses of the azure
sky and the bright evening cloud. During the whole
time, Rip and his companion had labored on in silence,
for though the former marveled greatly what could be
the object of carrying a keg of liquor up this wild mountain, yet there was something strange and incomprehensible about the unknown that inspired awe and checked
familiarity.

On entering the amphitheater, new objects of wonder
were to be seen. On a level spot in the center was a company of odd-looking personages playing at ninepins.
They were dressed in a quaint, outlandish fashion; some
wore short doublets, others jerkins, with long knives in
their belts, and most of them had enormous breeches, of
similar style with that of the guide's. Their visages, too,
were peculiar; one had a large beard, broad face, and
small piggish eyes, the face of another seemed to consist
entirely of nose and was surmounted by a white sugar-
loaf hat set off with a little red cock's tail. They all had
beards, of various shapes and colors. There was one
who seemed to be the commander. He was a stout old
gentleman, with a weather-beaten countenance; he wore a
laced doublet, broad belt and hanger, high-crowned hat
and feather, red stockings, and high-heeled shoes, with

roses in them. The whole group reminded Rip of the figures in an old Flemish painting, in the parlor of Dominie Van Shaick, the village parson, and which had been brought over from Holland at the time of the settlement.

What seemed particularly odd to Rip was that though these folks were evidently amusing themselves, yet they maintained the gravest faces, the most mysterious silence, and were, withal, the most melancholy party of pleasure he had ever witnessed. Nothing interrupted the stillness of the scene but the noise of the balls, which, whenever they were rolled, echoed along the mountains like rumbling peals of thunder.

As Rip and his companion approached them, they suddenly desisted from their play and stared at him with such fixed, statuelike gaze and such strange, uncouth, lackluster countenances that his heart turned within him and his knees smote together. His companion now emptied the contents of the keg into large flagons and made signs to him to wait upon the company. He obeyed with fear and trembling; they quaffed the liquor in profound silence and then returned to their game.

By degrees Rip's awe and apprehension subsided. He even ventured, when no eye was fixed upon him, to taste the beverage, which he found had much of the flavor of excellent Hollands. He was naturally a thirsty soul and was soon tempted to repeat the draft. One taste provoked another; and he reiterated his visits to the flagon so often that at length his senses were overpowered, his eyes swam in his head, his head gradually declined, and he fell into a deep sleep.

On waking, he found himself on the green knoll whence he had first seen the old man of the glen. He rubbed his eyes—it was a bright, sunny morning. The birds were hopping and twittering among the bushes, and the eagle was wheeling aloft and breasting the pure mountain breeze. "Surely," thought Rip, "I have not slept here all night." He recalled the occurrences before he fell asleep. The strange man with a keg of liquor—the mountain ravine—the wild retreat among the rocks—the woebegone party at ninepins—the flagon—"Oh! That flagon! That wicked flagon!" thought Rip. "What excuse shall I make to Dame Van Winkle?"

He looked around for his gun, but in place of the clean, well-oiled fowling piece he found an old firelock lying by him, the barrel encrusted with rust, the lock falling off, and the stock worm-eaten. He now suspected that the grave roysters of the mountain had put a trick upon him, and, having dosed him with liquor, had robbed him of his gun. Wolf, too, had disappeared, but he might have strayed away after a squirrel or partridge. He whistled after him and shouted his name, but all in vain; the echoes repeated his whistle and shout, but no dog was to be seen.

He determined to revisit the scene of the last evening's gambol, and if he met with any of the party, to demand his dog and gun. As he rose to walk, he found himself stiff in the joints and wanting in his usual activity. "These mountain beds do not agree with me," thought Rip, "and if this frolic should lay me up with a fit of the rheumatism, I shall have a blessed time with Dame Van Winkle." With some difficulty he got down into the glen; he found the gully up which he and his companion had ascended the preceding evening, but to his astonishment a mountain stream was now foaming down it, leaping from rock to rock and filling the glen with babbling murmurs. He, however, made shift to scramble up its sides, working his toilsome way through thickets of birch, sassafras, and witch hazel, and sometimes tripped up or entangled by the wild grapevines that twisted their coils or tendrils from tree to tree and spread a kind of network in his path.

At length he reached to where the ravine had opened through the cliffs to the amphitheater, but no traces of such opening remained. The rocks presented a high, impenetrable wall over which the torrent came tumbling in a sheet of feathery foam and fell into a broad, deep basin, black from the shadows of the surrounding forest. Here, then, poor Rip was brought to a stand. He again called and whistled after his dog; he was only answered by the cawing of a flock of idle crows, sporting high in air about a dry tree that overhung a sunny precipice, and who, secure in their elevation, seemed to look down and scoff at the poor man's perplexities. What was to be done? The morning was passing away, and Rip felt famished for want of his breakfast. He grieved to give up his dog and gun; he dreaded to meet his wife, but it would not do to starve among the mountains. He shook his head, shouldered the rusty firelock, and, with a heart full of trouble and anxiety, turned his steps homeward.

As he approached the village he met a number of people, but none whom he knew, which somewhat surprised him, for he had thought himself acquainted with every one in the country around. Their dress, too, was of a different fashion from that to which he was accustomed. They all stared at him with equal marks of surprise, and whenever they cast their eyes upon him invariably stroked their chins. The constant recurrence of this gesture induced Rip, involuntarily, to do the same, when, to his astonishment, he found his beard had grown a foot long!

He had now entered the skirts of the village. A troop of strange children ran at his heels, hooting after him and pointing at his gray beard. The dogs, too, not one of which he recognized for an old acquaintance, barked at him as he passed. The very village was altered; it was larger and more populous. There were rows of houses which he had never seen before, and those which had been his familiar haunts had disappeared. Strange names were over the doors—strange faces at the windows—everything was strange. His mind now misgave him; he began to doubt whether both he and the world around him were not bewitched. Surely this was his native village, which he had left but the day before. There stood the Kaatskill Mountains—there ran the silver Hudson at a distance—there was every hill and dale precisely as it had always been. Rip was sorely perplexed. "That flagon last night," thought he, "has addled my poor head sadly!"

It was with some difficulty that he found the way to his own house, which he approached with silent awe, expecting every moment to hear the shrill voice of Dame Van Winkle. He found the house gone to decay—the roof fallen in, the windows shattered, and the doors off the hinges. A half-starved dog that looked like Wolf was skulking about it. Rip called him by name, but the cur snarled, showed his teeth, and passed on. This was an unkind cut indeed. "My very dog," sighed poor Rip, "has forgotten me!"

He entered the house, which, to tell the truth, Dame

Van Winkle had always kept in neat order. It was empty, forlorn, and apparently abandoned. This desolateness overcame all his connubial fears—he called loudly for his wife and children; the lonely chambers rang for a moment with his voice, and then all again was silence.

He now hurried forth and hastened to his old resort, the village inn—but it too was gone. A large, rickety, wooden building stood in its place, with great gaping windows, some of them broken and mended with old hats and petticoats, and over the door was painted, "the Union Hotel, by Jonathan Doolittle." Instead of the great tree that used to shelter the quiet little Dutch inn of yore, there now was reared a tall, naked pole, with something on the top that looked like a red nightcap, and from it was fluttering a flag, on which was a singular assemblage of stars and stripes—all this was strange and incomprehensible. He recognized on the sign, however, the ruby face of King George, under which he had smoked so many a peaceful pipe; but even this was singularly metamorphosed. The red coat was changed for one of blue and buff, a sword was held in the hand instead of a scepter, the head was decorated with a cocked hat, and underneath was painted in large characters, GENERAL WASHINGTON.

There was, as usual, a crowd of folk about the door, but none that Rip recollected. The very character of the people seemed changed. There was a busy, bustling, disputatious tone about it, instead of the accustomed phlegm and drowsy tranquillity. He looked in vain for the sage Nicholas Vedder, with his broad face, double chin, and fair long pipe, uttering clouds of tobacco smoke instead of idle speeches; or Van Bummel, the schoolmaster, doling forth the contents of an ancient newspaper. In place of these, a lean, bilious-looking fellow, with his pockets full of handbills, was haranguing vehemently about rights of citizens—elections—members of congress—liberty—Bunker's Hill—heroes of seventy-six—and other words, which were a perfect Babylonish jargon to the bewildered Van Winkle.

The appearance of Rip, with his long, grizzled beard, his rusty fowling piece, his uncouth dress, and an army of women and children at his heels, soon attracted the attention of the tavern politicians. They crowded around him, eying him from head to foot with great curiosity. The orator bustled up to him and, drawing him partly aside, inquired "on which side he voted?" Rip stared in vacant stupidity. Another short but busy little fellow pulled him by the arm, and, rising on tiptoe, inquired in his ear, "whether he was Federal or Democrat?" Rip was equally at a loss to comprehend the question; when a knowing, self-important old gentleman in a sharp cocked hat made his way through the crowd, putting them to the right and left with his elbows as he passed, and, planting himself before Van Winkle, with one arm akimbo, the other resting on his cane, his keen eyes and sharp hat penetrating, as it were, into his very soul, demanded in an austere tone, "what brought him to the election with a gun on his shoulder, and a mob at his heels, and whether he meant to breed a riot in the village?" "Alas! Gentlemen," cried Rip, somewhat dismayed, "I am a poor, quiet man, a native of the place, and a loyal subject of the king, God bless him!"

Here a general shout burst from the bystanders. "A tory! A tory! A spy! A refugee! Hustle him! Away with him!" It was with great difficulty that the self-important man in the cocked hat restored order; and, having assumed a tenfold austerity of brow, demanded again of the unknown culprit what he came there for and whom he was seeking. The poor man humbly assured him that he meant no harm, but merely came there in search of some of his neighbors, who used to keep about the tavern.

"Well—who are they? Name them."

Rip bethought himself a moment, and inquired, "Where's Nicholas Vedder?"

There was a silence for a little while, when an old man replied, in a thin, piping voice, "Nicholas Vedder! Why, he is dead and gone these eighteen years! There was a wooden tombstone in the churchyard that used to tell all about him, but that's rotten and gone too."

"Where's Brom Dutcher?"

"Oh, he went off to the army in the beginning of the war; some say he was killed at the storming of Stony Point—others say he was drowned in a squall at the foot of Antony's Nose. I don't know—he never came back again."

"Where's Van Bummel, the schoolmaster?"

"He went off to the wars, too, was a great militia general, and is now in congress."

Rip's heart died away at hearing of these sad changes in his home and friends, and finding himself thus alone in the world. Every answer puzzled him, too, by treating of such enormous lapses of time and of matters which he could not understand: war—congress—Stony Point. He had no courage to ask after any more friends, but cried out in despair, "Does nobody here know Rip Van Winkle?"

"Oh, Rip Van Winkle!" exclaimed two or three. "Oh, to be sure! That's Rip Van Winkle yonder, leaning against the tree."

Rip looked, and beheld a precise counterpart of himself as he went up the mountain: apparently as lazy, and certainly as ragged. The poor fellow was now completely confounded. He doubted his own identify, and whether he was himself or another man. In the midst of his bewilderment, the man in the cocked hat demanded who he was, and what was his name?

"God knows," exclaimed he, at his wit's end. "I'm not myself—I'm somebody else—that's me yonder—no—that's somebody else got into my shoes—I was myself last night, but I fell asleep on the mountain, and they've changed my gun, and everything's changed, and I'm changed, and I can't tell what's my name, or who I am!"

The bystanders began now to look at each other, nod, wink significantly, and tap their fingers against their foreheads. There was a whisper also about securing the gun and keeping the old fellow from doing mischief, at the very suggestion of which the self-important man in the cocked hat retired with some precipitation. At this critical moment a fresh, comely woman pressed through the throng to get a peep at the gray-bearded man. She had a chubby child in her arms, which, frightened at his looks, began to cry. "Hush, Rip," cried she, "hush, you little fool; the old man won't hurt you." The name of the child, the air of the mother, the tone of her voice, all awakened a train of recollections in his mind. "What is your name, my good woman?" asked he.

"Judith Gardenier."

"And your father's name?"

"Ah, poor man, Rip Van Winkle was his name, but it's twenty years since he went away from home with his gun, and never has been heard of since—his dog came home without him; but whether he shot himself, or was carried away by the Indians, nobody can tell. I was then but a little girl."

Rip had but one question more to ask; but he put it with a faltering voice:

"Where's your mother?"

"Oh, she too had died but a short time since; she broke a blood vessel in a fit of passion at a New England peddler."

There was a drop of comfort, at least, in this intelligence. The honest man could contain himself no longer. He caught his daughter and her child in his arms. "I am your father!" cried he. "Young Rip Van Winkle once— old Rip Van Winkle now! Does nobody know poor Rip Van Winkle?"

All stood amazed, until an old woman, tottering out from among the crowd, put her hand to her brow and, peering under it in his face for a moment, exclaimed, "Sure enough! It is Rip Van Winkle—it is himself! Welcome home again, old neighbor. Why, where have you been these twenty long years?"

Rip's story was soon told, for the whole twenty years had been to him but as one night. The neighbors stared when they heard it; some were seen to wink at each other and put their tongues in their cheeks, and the self-important man in the cocked hat, who, when the alarm was over, had returned to the field, screwed down the corners of his mouth and shook his head—upon which there was a general shaking of the head throughout the assemblage.

It was determined, however, to take the opinion of old Peter Vanderdonk, who was seen slowly advancing up the road. He was a descendant of the historian of that name, who wrote one of the earliest accounts of the province. Peter was the most ancient inhabitant of the village, and well versed in all the wonderful events and traditions of the neighborhood. He recollected Rip at once and corroborated his story in the most satisfactory manner. He assured the company that it was a fact, handed down from his ancestor the historian, that the Kaatskill Mountains had always been haunted by strange beings. That it was affirmed that the great Hendrick Hudson, the first discoverer of the river and country, kept a kind of vigil there every twenty years, with his crew of the *Half Moon,* being permitted in this way to revisit the scenes of his enterprise and keep a guardian eye upon the river and the great city called by his name. That his father had once seen them in their old Dutch dresses playing at ninepins in a hollow of the mountain, and that he himself had heard, one summer afternoon, the sound of their balls, like distant peals of thunder.

To make a long story short, the company broke up and returned to the more important concerns of the election. Rip's daughter took him home to live with her; she had a snug, well-furnished house, and a stout, cheery farmer for a husband, whom Rip recollected for one of the urchins that used to climb upon his back. As to Rip's son and heir, who was the ditto of himself, seen leaning against the tree, he was employed to work on the farm, but evinced a hereditary disposition to attend to anything else but his business.

Rip now resumed his old walks and habits; he soon found many of his former cronies, though all rather the worse for the wear and tear of time, and preferred making friends among the rising generation, with whom he soon grew into great favor.

Having nothing to do at home, and being arrived at that happy age when a man can be idle with impunity, he took his place once more on the bench at the inn door and was reverenced as one of the patriarchs of the village, and a chronicle of the old times "before the war." It was some time before he could get into the regular track of gossip, or could be made to comprehend the strange events that had taken place during his torpor. How that there had been a revolutionary war—that the country had thrown off the yoke of old England—and that, instead of being a subject of his Majesty George the Third, he was now a free citizen of the United States. Rip, in fact, was no politician—the changes of states and empires made but little impression on him; but there was one species of despotism under which he had long groaned, and that was—petticoat government. Happily that was at an end; he had got his neck out of the yoke of matrimony and could go in and out whenever he pleased, without dreading the tyranny of Dame Van Winkle. Whenever her name was mentioned, however, he shook his head, shrugged his shoulders, and cast up his eyes, which might pass either for an expression of resignation to his fate or joy at his deliverance.

He used to tell his story to every stranger that arrived at Mr. Doolittle's hotel. He was observed, at first, to vary on some points every time he told it, which was, doubtless, owing to his having so recently awaked. It at last settled down precisely to the tale I have related, and not a man, woman, or child in the neighborhood but knew it by heart. Some always pretended to doubt the reality of it, and insisted that Rip had been out of his head, and that this was one point on which he always remained flighty. The old Dutch inhabitants, however, almost universally gave it full credit. Even to this day they never hear a thunderstorm of a summer afternoon about the Kaatskill but they say Hendrick Hudson and his crew are at their game of ninepins; and it is a common wish of all henpecked husbands in the neighborhood, when life hangs heavy on their hands, that they might have a quieting draft out of Rip Van Winkle's flagon.

NOTE

The foregoing Tale, one would suspect, had been suggested to Mr. Knickerbocker by a little German superstition about the Emperor Frederick *der Rothbart* and the Kypphaüser mountain. The subjoined note, however, which he had appended to the tale, shows that it is an absolute fact, narrated with his usual fidelity:

"The story of Rip Van Winkle may seem incredible to many, but nevertheless I give it my full belief, for I know the vicinity of our old Dutch settlements to have been very subject to marvelous events and appearances. Indeed, I have heard many stranger stories than this, in the villages along the Hudson, all of which were too well authenticated to admit of a doubt. I have even talked with Rip Van Winkle myself, who, when last I saw him, was a very venerable old man and so perfectly rational and consistent on every other point that I think no conscientious person could refuse to take this into the bargain; nay, I have seen a certificate on the subject taken before a country justice and signed with a cross, in the justice's own handwriting. The story, therefore, is beyond the possibility of doubt.

D. K."

POSTSCRIPT

The following are traveling notes from a memorandum book of Mr. Knickerbocker:

The Kaatsberg, or Catskill Mountains, have always been a region full of fable. The Indians considered them the abode of spirits, who influenced the weather, spreading sunshine or clouds over the landscape, and sending good or bad hunting seasons. They were ruled by an old squaw spirit, said to be their mother. She dwelt on the highest peak of the Catskills and had charge of the doors of day and night, to open and shut them at the proper hour. She hung up the new moons in the skies and cut up the old ones into stars. In times of drought, if properly propitiated, she would spin light summer clouds out of cobwebs and morning dew and send them off from the crest of the mountain, flake after flake, like flakes of carded cotton, to float in the air; until, dissolved by the heat of the sun, they would fall in gentle showers, causing the grass to spring, the fruits to ripen, and the corn to grow an inch an hour. If displeased, however, she would brew up clouds black as ink, sitting in the midst of them like a bottle-bellied spider in the midst of its web; and when these clouds broke, woe betide the valleys!

In old times, say the Indian traditions, there was a kind of Manitou or Spirit, who kept about the wildest recesses of the Catskill Mountains, and took a mischievous pleasure in wreaking all kinds of evils and vexations upon the red men. Sometimes he would assume the form of a bear, a panther, or a deer, lead the bewildered hunter a weary chase through tangled forests and among ragged rocks, and then spring off with a loud ho! ho! leaving him aghast on the brink of a beetling precipice or raging torrent.

The favorite abode of this Manitou is still shown. It is a great rock or cliff on the loneliest part of the mountains, and, from the flowering vines which clamber about it and the wild flowers which abound in its neighborhood, is known by the name of the Garden Rock. Near the foot of it is a small lake, the haunt of the solitary bittern, with water snakes basking in the sun on the leaves of the pond lilies which lie on the surface. This place was held in great awe by the Indians, insomuch that the boldest hunter would not pursue his game within its precincts. Once upon a time, however, a hunter who had lost his way penetrated to the Garden Rock, where he beheld a number of gourds placed in the crotches of trees. One of these he seized and made off with, but in the hurry of his retreat he let it fall among the rocks, when a great stream gushed forth, which washed him away and swept him down precipices, where he was dashed to pieces, and the stream made its way to the Hudson and continues to flow to the present day; being the identical stream known by the name of the Kaaters-kill.

ENGLISH WRITERS ON AMERICA

"Methinks I see in my mind a noble and puissant nation, rousing herself like a strong man after sleep, and shaking her invincible locks: methinks I see her as an eagle, mewing her mighty youth, and kindling her undazzled eyes at the full midday beam."

MILTON ON THE LIBERTY OF THE PRESS

It is with feelings of deep regret that I observe the literary animosity daily growing up between England and America. Great curiosity has been awakened of late with respect to the United States, and the London press has teemed with volumes of travels through the Republic; but they seem intended to diffuse error rather than knowledge, and so successful have they been, that, notwithstanding the constant intercourse between the nations, there is no people concerning whom the great mass of the British public have less pure information or entertain more numerous prejudices.

English travelers are the best and the worst in the world. Where no motives of pride or interest intervene, none can equal them for profound and philosophical views of society or faithful and graphical descriptions of external objects; but when either the interest or reputation of their own country comes in collision with that of another, they go to the opposite extreme, and forget their usual probity and candor in the indulgence of splenetic remark and an illiberal spirit of ridicule.

Hence, their travels are more honest and accurate the more remote the country described. I would place implicit confidence in an Englishman's descriptions of the regions beyond the cataracts of the Nile, of unknown islands in the Yellow Sea, of the interior of India, or of any

other tract which other travelers might be apt to picture
out with the illusions of their fancies; but I would cautiously receive his account of his immediate neighbors,
and of those nations with which he is in habits of most
frequent intercourse. However I might be disposed to trust
his probity, I dare not trust his prejudices.

It has also been the peculiar lot of our country to be
visited by the worst kind of English travelers. While men
of philosophical spirit and cultivated minds have been
sent from England to ransack the poles, to penetrate the
deserts, and to study the manners and customs of barbarous nations, with which she can have no permanent intercourse of profit or pleasure, it has been left to the
broken-down tradesman, the scheming adventurer, the
wandering mechanic, the Manchester and Birmingham
agent to be her oracles respecting America. From such
sources she is content to receive her information respecting a country in a singular state of moral and physical
development, a country in which one of the greatest political experiments in the history of the world is now performing, and which presents the most profound and
momentous studies to the statesman and the philosopher.

That such men should give prejudicial accounts of
America is not a matter of surprise. The themes it offers
for contemplation are too vast and elevated for their
capacities. The national character is yet in a state of fer-
mentation; it may have its frothiness and sediment, but its
ingredients are sound and wholesome; it has already given
proofs of powerful and generous qualities, and the whole
promises to settle down into something substantially excellent. But the causes which are operating to strengthen
and ennoble it, and its daily indications of admirable
properties, are all lost upon these purblind observers,
who are only affected by the little asperities incident to its
present situation. They are capable of judging only of the
surface of things, of those matters which come in contact with their private interests and personal gratifications.
They miss some of the snug conveniences and petty comforts which belong to an old, highly finished, and over-
populous state of society, where the ranks of useful labor
are crowded and many earn a painful and servile subsistence by studying the very caprices of appetite and

self-indulgence. These minor comforts, however, are all-important in the estimation of narrow minds, which either do not perceive or will not acknowledge that they are more than counterbalanced among us by great and generally diffused blessings.

They may, perhaps, have been disappointed in some unreasonable expectation of sudden gain. They may have pictured America to themselves an El Dorado, where gold and silver abounded and the natives were lacking in sagacity, and where they were to become strangely and suddenly rich in some unforeseen but easy manner. The same weakness of mind that indulges absurd expectations produces petulance in disappointment. Such persons become embittered against the country on finding that there, as everywhere else, a man must sow before he can reap, must win wealth by industry and talent, and must contend with the common difficulties of nature and the shrewdness of an intelligent and enterprising people.

Perhaps, through mistaken or ill-directed hospitality, or from the prompt disposition to cheer and countenance the stranger prevalent among my countrymen, they may have been treated with unwonted respect in America; and having been accustomed all their lives to consider themselves below the surface of good society, and brought up in a servile feeling of inferiority, they become arrogant on the common boon of civility. They attribute to the lowliness of others their own elevation, and underrate a society where there are no artificial distinctions, and where, by any chance, such individuals as themselves can rise to consequence.

One would suppose, however, that information coming from such sources, on a subject where the truth is so desirable, would be received with caution by the censors of the press; that the motives of these men, their veracity, their opportunities of inquiry and observation, and their capacities for judging correctly, would be rigorously scrutinized before their evidence was admitted, in such sweeping extent, against a kindred nation. The very reverse, however, is the case, and it furnishes a striking instance of human inconsistency. Nothing can surpass the vigilance with which English critics will examine the credibility of the traveler who publishes an account of some distant and comparatively unimportant country. How warily will they compare the measurements of a pyramid, or the descriptions of a ruin, and how sternly will they censure any inaccuracy in these contributions of merely curious knowledge, while they will receive, with eagerness and unhesitating faith, the gross misrepresentations of coarse and obscure writers, concerning a country with which their own is placed in the most important and delicate relations. Nay, they will even make these apocryphal volumes textbooks, on which to enlarge with a zeal and an ability worthy of a more generous cause.

I shall not, however, dwell on this irksome and hackneyed topic; nor should I have adverted to it but for the undue interest apparently taken in it by my countrymen and certain injurious effects which I apprehend it might produce upon the national feeling. We attach too much consequence to these attacks. They cannot do us any essential injury. The tissues of misrepresentations attempted to be woven around us are like cobwebs woven around the limbs of an infant giant. Our country continually outgrows them. One falsehood after another falls off of itself. We have but to live on, and every day we live a whole volume of refutation.

All the writers of England united, if we could for a moment suppose their great minds stooping to so unworthy a combination, could not conceal our rapidly growing importance and matchless prosperity. They could not conceal that these are owing, not merely to physical and local, but also to moral causes—to the political liberty, the general diffusion of knowledge, the prevalence of sound moral and religious principles, which give force and sustained energy to the character of a people, and which, in fact, have been the acknowledged and wonderful supporters of their own national power and glory.

But why are we so exquisitely alive to the aspersions of England? Why do we suffer ourselves to be so affected by the contumely she has endeavored to cast upon us? It is not in the opinion of England alone that honor lives and reputation has its being. The world at large is the arbiter of a nation's fame; with its thousand eyes it witnesses a nation's deeds, and from their collective testimony is national glory or national disgrace established.

For ourselves, therefore, it is comparatively of but little importance whether England does us justice or not; it is, perhaps, of far more importance to herself. She is instilling anger and resentment into the bosom of a youthful nation, to grow with its growth and strengthen with its strength. If in America, as some of her writers are laboring to convince her, she is hereafter to find an invidious rival and a gigantic foe, she may thank those very writers for having provoked rivalship and irritated hostility. Everyone knows the all-pervading influence of literature at the present day, and how much the opinions and passions of mankind are under its control. The mere contests of the sword are temporary; their wounds are but in the flesh, and it is the pride of the generous to forgive and forget them. But the slanders of the pen pierce to the heart; they rankle longest in the noblest spirits; they dwell ever present in the mind and render it morbidly sensitive to the most trifling collision. It is but seldom that any one overt act produces hostilities between two nations; there exists, most commonly, a previous jealousy and ill will, a predisposition to take offense. Trace these to their cause, and how often will they be found to originate in the mischievous effusions of mercenary writers, who, secure in their closets, and for ignominious bread, concoct and circulate the venom that is to inflame the generous and the brave.

I am not laying too much stress upon this point, for it applies most emphatically to our particular case. Over no nation does the press hold a more absolute control than over the people of America, for the universal education of the poorest classes makes every individual a reader. There is nothing published in England on the subject of our country that does not circulate through every part of it. There is not a calumny dropped from English pen, nor an unworthy sarcasm uttered by an English statesman, that does not go to blight good will and add to the mass of latent resentment. Possessing, then, as England does, the fountainhead whence the literature of the language flows, how completely is it in her power, and how truly is it her duty, to make it the medium of amiable and magnanimous feeling—a stream where the two nations might meet together and drink in peace and kindness. Should she, however, persist in turning it to waters of bitterness, the time may come when she may repent her folly. The present friendship of America may be of but little moment to her, but the future destinies of that country do not admit of a doubt; over those of England there lower some shadows of uncertainty. Should, then, a day of gloom arrive, should these reverses overtake her from which the proudest empires have not been exempt, she may look back with regret at her infatuation, in repulsing from her side a nation she might have grappled to her bosom, and thus destroying her only chance for real friendship beyond the boundaries of her own dominions.

There is a general impression in England that the people of the United States are inimical to the parent country. It is one of the errors which have been diligently propagated by designing writers. There is, doubtless, considerable political hostility and a general soreness at the illiberality of the English press; but, generally speaking, the prepossessions of the people are strongly in favor of England. Indeed, at one time, they amounted, in many parts of the Union, to an absurd degree of bigotry. The bare name of Englishman was a passport to the confidence and hospitality of every family, and too often gave a transient currency to the worthless and the ungrateful. Throughout the country there was something of enthusiasm connected with the idea of England. We looked to it with a hallowed feeling of tenderness and veneration, as the land of our forefathers—the august repository of the monuments and antiquities of our race—the birthplace and mausoleum of the sages and heroes of our paternal history. After our own country, there was none in whose glory we more delighted—none whose good opinion we were more anxious to possess—none toward which our hearts yearned with such throbbings of warm consanguinity. Even during the late war, whenever there was the least opportunity for kind feelings to spring forth, it was the delight of the generous spirits of our country to show that, in the midst of hostilities, they still kept alive the sparks of future friendship.

Is all this to be at an end? Is this golden band of kindred sympathies, so rare between nations, to be broken forever? Perhaps it is for the best; it may dispel an illusion which might have kept us in mental vassalage, which might have interfered occasionally with our true interests, and prevented the growth of proper national pride. But it is hard to give up the kindred tie! And there are feelings dearer than interest—closer to the heart than pride—that will still make us cast back a look of regret, as we wander farther and farther from the paternal roof and lament the waywardness of the parent that would repel the affections of the child.

Shortsighted and injudicious, however, as the conduct of England may be in this system of aspersion, recrimination on our part would be equally ill-judged. I speak not of a prompt and spirited vindication of our country, nor the keenest castigation of her slanderers; but I allude to a disposition to retaliate in kind, to retort sarcasm and inspire prejudice, which seems to be spreading widely among our writers. Let us guard particularly against such a temper, for it would double the evil instead of redressing the wrong. Nothing is so easy and inviting as the retort of abuse and sarcasm; but it is a paltry and an unprofitable contest. It is the alternative of a morbid mind, fretted into petulance, rather than warmed into indignation. If England is willing to permit the mean jealousies of trade or the rancorous animosities of politics to deprave the integrity of her press and poison the fountain of public opinion, let us beware of her example. She may deem it her interest to diffuse error and engender antipathy for the purpose of checking emigration; we have no purpose of the kind to serve. Neither have we any spirit of national jealousy to gratify, for as yet, in all our rivalships with England, we are the rising and the gaining party. There can be no end to answer, therefore, but the gratification of resentment—a mere spirit of retaliation; and even that is impotent. Our retorts are never republished in England; they fall short, therefore, of their aim. But they foster a querulous and peevish temper among our writers; they sour the sweet flow of our early literature and sow thorns and brambles among its blossoms. What is still worse, they circulate through our own country, and, as far as they have effect, excite virulent national prejudices. This last is the evil most especially to be deprecated. Governed, as we are, entirely by public opinion, the utmost care should be taken to preserve the purity of the public mind. Knowledge is power, and truth is knowledge; whoever, therefore, knowingly propagates a prejudice willfully saps the foundation of his country's strength.

The members of a republic, above all other men, should be candid and dispassionate. They are, individually, portions of the sovereign mind and sovereign will, and should be enabled to come to all questions of national concern with calm and unbiased judgments. From the peculiar nature of our relations with England, we must have more frequent questions of a difficult and delicate character with her than with any other nation, questions that affect the most acute and excitable feelings; and as, in the adjusting of these, our national measures must ultimately be determined by popular sentiment, we cannot be too anxiously attentive to purify it from all latent passion or prepossession.

Opening, too, as we do, an asylum for strangers from every portion of the earth, we should receive all with impartiality. It should be our pride to exhibit an example of one nation, at least, destitute of national antipathies, and exercising not merely the overt acts of hospitality but those more rare and noble courtesies which spring from liberality of opinion.

What have we to do with national prejudices? They are the inveterate diseases of old countries, contracted in rude and ignorant ages, when nations knew but little of each other, and looked beyond their own boundaries with distrust and hostility. We, on the contrary, have sprung into national existence in an enlightened and philosophic age, when the different parts of the habitable world and the various branches of the human family have been indefatigably studied and made known to each other; and we forego the advantages of our birth if we do not shake off the national prejudices as we would the local superstitions of the old world.

But above all let us not be influenced by any angry feelings so far as to shut our eyes to the perception of what is really excellent and amiable in the English character. We are a young people, necessarily an imitative one, and must take our examples and models, in a great degree, from the existing nations of Europe. There is no country more worthy of our study than England. The spirit of her constitution is most analogous to ours. The manners of her people—their intellectual activity—their freedom of opinion—their habits of thinking on those subjects which concern the dearest interests and most sacred charities of private life, are all congenial to the American character, and, in fact, are all intrinsically excellent; for it is in the moral feeling of the people that the deep foundations of British prosperity are laid, and however the superstructure may be time-worn or overrun by abuses, there must be something solid in the basis, admirable in the materials, and stable in the structure of an edifice that so long has towered unshaken amidst the tempests of the world.

Let it be the pride of our writers, therefore, discarding all feelings of irritation, and disdaining to retaliate the illiberality of British authors, to speak of the English nation without prejudice, and with determined candor. While they rebuke the indiscriminating bigotry with which some of our countrymen admire and imitate everything English merely because it is English, let them frankly point out what is really worthy of approbation. We may thus place England before us as a perpetual volume of reference, wherein are recorded sound deductions from ages of experience; and while we avoid the errors and absurdities which may have crept into the page, we may draw thence golden maxims of practical wisdom wherewith to strengthen and to embellish our national character.

RURAL LIFE IN ENGLAND

Oh! friendly to the best pursuits of man,
Friendly to thought, to virtue, and to peace,
Domestic life in rural pleasures past!

COWPER

The stranger who would form a correct opinion of the English character must not confine his observations to the metropolis. He must go forth into the country; he must sojourn in villages and hamlets; he must visit castles, villas, farmhouses, cottages; he must wander through parks and gardens; along hedges and green lanes; he must loiter about country churches; attend wakes and fairs and other rural festivals; and cope with the people in all their conditions, and all their habits and humors.

In some countries the large cities absorb the wealth and fashion of the nation; they are the only fixed abodes of elegant and intelligent society, and the country is inhabited almost entirely by boorish peasantry. In England, on the contrary, the metropolis is a mere gathering place, or general rendezvous, of the polite classes, where they devote a small portion of the year to a hurry of gaiety and dissipation, and, having indulged this kind of carnival, return again to the apparently more congenial habits of rural life. The various orders of society are therefore diffused over the whole surface of the kingdom, and the most retired neighborhoods afford specimens of the different ranks.

The English, in fact, are strongly gifted with the rural feeling. They possess a quick sensibility to the beauties of nature and a keen relish for the pleasures and employments of the country. This passion seems inherent in them. Even the inhabitants of cities, born and brought up among brick walls and bustling streets, enter with facility into rural habits and evince a tact for rural occupation. The merchant has his snug retreat in the vicinity of the metropolis, where he often displays as much pride and zeal in the cultivation of his flower garden and the maturing of his fruits as he does in the conduct of his business and the success of a commercial enterprise. Even those less fortunate individuals who are doomed to pass their lives in the midst of din and traffic contrive to have something that shall remind them of the green aspect of nature. In the most dark and dingy quarters of the city, the drawing-room window resembles frequently a bank of flowers; every spot capable of vegetation has its grass plot and flower bed; and every square its mimic park, laid out with picturesque taste and gleaming with refreshing verdure.

Those who see the Englishman only in town are apt to form an unfavorable opinion of his social character. He is either absorbed in business or distracted by the thousand engagements that dissipate time, thought, and feeling in this huge metropolis. He has, therefore, too commonly a look of hurry and abstraction. Wherever he happens to be, he is on the point of going somewhere else; at the moment he is talking on one subject, his mind is wandering to another; and while paying a friendly visit, he is calculating how he shall economize time so as to pay the other visits allotted in the morning. An immense metropolis, like London, is calculated to make men selfish and uninteresting. In their casual and transient meetings, they can but deal briefly in commonplaces. They present but the cold superficies of character—its rich and genial qualities have no time to be warmed into a flow.

It is in the country that the Englishman gives scope to his natural feelings. He breaks loose gladly from the cold formalities and negative civilities of town, throws off his habits of shy reserve, and becomes joyous and freehearted. He manages to collect around him all the conveniences and elegancies of polite life, and to banish its restraints. His country seat abounds with every requisite, either for studious retirement, tasteful gratification, or rural exercise. Books, paintings, music, horses, dogs, and sporting implements of all kinds are at hand. He puts no constraint either upon his guests or himself, but in the true spirit of hospitality provides the means of enjoyment, and leaves everyone to partake according to his inclination.

The taste of the English in the cultivation of land and in what is called landscape gardening is unrivaled. They have studied Nature intently, and discover an exquisite sense of her beautiful forms and harmonious combinations. Those charms, which in other countries she lavishes in wild solitudes, are here assembled around the haunts of domestic life. They seem to have caught her coy and furtive graces and spread them, like witchery, about their rural abodes.

Nothing can be more imposing than the magnificence of English park scenery. Vast lawns that extend like sheets of vivid green, with here and there clumps of gigantic trees, heaping up rich piles of foliage; the solemn pomp of groves and woodland glades, with the deer trooping in silent herds across them, the hare, bounding away to the covert, or the pheasant, suddenly bursting upon the wing; the brook, taught to wind in natural meanderings or expand into a glassy lake; the sequestered pool, reflecting the quivering trees, with the yellow leaf sleeping on its bosom, and the trout roaming fearlessly about its limpid waters, while some rustic temple or sylvan statue, grown green and dank with age, gives an air of classic sanctity to the seclusion.

These are but a few of the features of park scenery; but what most delights me is the creative talent with which the English decorate the unostentatious abodes of middle life. The rudest habitation, the most unpromising and scanty portion of land, in the hands of an Englishman of taste becomes a little paradise. With a nicely discriminating eye, he seizes at once upon its capabilities and pictures in his mind the future landscape. The sterile spot grows into loveliness under his hand; and yet the operations of art which produce the effect are scarcely to be perceived. The cherishing and training of some trees, the cautious pruning of others, the nice distribution of flowers and plants of tender and graceful foliage, the introduction of a green slope of velvet turf, the partial opening to a peep of blue distance or silver gleam of water, all these are managed with a delicate tact, a pervading yet quiet assiduity, like the magic touchings with which a painter finishes up a favorite picture.

The residence of people of fortune and refinement in the country has diffused a degree of taste and elegance in rural economy that descends to the lowest class. The very laborer, with his thatched cottage and narrow slip of ground, attends to their embellishment. The trim hedge, the grass plot before the door, the little flower bed bordered with snug box, the woodbine trained up against the wall and hanging its blossoms about the lattice, the pot of flowers in the window, the holly, providently planted about the house to cheat winter of its dreariness and to throw in a semblance of green summer to cheer the fireside, all these bespeak the influence of taste, flowing down from high sources and pervading the lowest levels of the public mind. If ever Love, as poets sing, delights to visit a cottage, it must be the cottage of an English peasant.

The fondness for rural life among the higher classes of the English has had a great and salutary effect upon the national character. I do not know a finer race of men than the English gentlemen. Instead of the softness and effeminacy which characterize the men of rank in most countries, they exhibit a union of elegance and strength, a robustness of frame and freshness of complexion which I am inclined to attribute to their living so much in the open air and pursuing so eagerly the invigorating recreations of the country. These hardy exercises produce also a healthful tone of mind and spirits, and a manliness and simplicity of manners, which even the follies and dissipations of the town cannot easily pervert and can never entirely destroy. In the country, too, the different orders of society seem to approach more freely, to be more disposed to blend and operate favorably upon each other. The distinctions between them do not appear to be so marked and impassable as in the cities. The manner in which property has been distributed into small estates and farms has established a regular gradation from the nobleman, through the classes of gentry, small landed proprietors, and substantial farmers, down to the laboring peasantry; and while it has thus banded the extremes of society together, has infused into each intermediate rank a spirit of independence. This, it must be confessed, is not so universally the case at present as it was formerly, the larger estates having, in late years of distress, absorbed the smaller, and, in some parts of the country, almost annihilated the sturdy race of small farmers. These, however, I believe, are but casual breaks in the general system I have mentioned.

In rural occupation there is nothing mean and debasing. It leads a man forth among scenes of natural grandeur and beauty; it leaves him to the workings of his own mind, operated upon by the purest and most elevating of external influences. Such a man may be simple and rough, but he cannot be vulgar. The man of refinement, therefore, finds nothing revolting in an intercourse with the lower orders in rural life, as he does when he casually mingles with the lower orders of cities. He lays aside his distance and reserve and is glad to waive the distinctions of rank and to enter into the honest, heartfelt enjoyments of common life. Indeed, the very amusements of the country bring men more and more together; and the sound of hound and horn blends all feelings into harmony. I believe this is one great reason why the nobility and gentry are more popular among the inferior orders in England than they are in any other country, and why the latter have endured so many excessive pressures and extremities without repining more generally at the unequal distribution of fortune and privilege.

To this mingling of cultivated and rustic society may also be attributed the rural feeling that runs through British literature; the frequent use of illustrations from rural life; those incomparable descriptions of nature that abound in the British poets, that have continued down from "the Flower and the Leaf" of Chaucer and have brought into our closets all the freshness and fragrance of the dewy landscape. The pastoral writers of other countries appear as if they had paid Nature an occasional visit, and become acquainted with her general charms; but the British poets have lived and reveled with her

—they have wooed her in her most secret haunts—they have watched her minutest caprices. A spray could not tremble in the breeze, a leaf could not rustle to the ground, a diamond drop could not patter in the stream, a fragrance could not exhale from the humble violet, nor a daisy unfold its crimson tints to the morning, but it has been noticed by these impassioned and delicate observers, and wrought up into some beautiful morality.

The effect of this devotion of elegant minds to rural occupations has been wonderful on the face of the country. A great part of the island is rather level, and would be monotonous were it not for the charms of culture; but it is studded and gemmed, as it were, with castles and palaces, and embroidered with parks and gardens. It does not abound in grand and sublime prospects, but rather in little home scenes of rural repose and sheltered quiet. Every antique farmhouse and moss-grown cottage is a picture; and as the roads are continually winding, and the view is shut in by groves and hedges, the eye is delighted by a continual succession of small landscapes of captivating loveliness.

The great charm, however, of English scenery is the moral feeling that seems to pervade it. It is associated in the mind with ideas of order, of quiet, of sober, well-established principles, of hoary usage and reverent custom. Everything seems to be the growth of ages of regular and peaceful existence. The old church of remote architecture, with its low, massive portal, its gothic tower, its windows rich with tracery and painted glass in scrupulous preservation, its stately monuments of warriors and worthies of the olden time, ancestors of the present lords of the soil, its tombstones, recording successive generations of sturdy yeomanry whose progeny still plow the same fields and kneel at the same altar; the parsonage, a quaint, irregular pile, partly antiquated, but repaired and altered in the tastes of various ages and occupants; the stile and footpath leading from the churchyard, across pleasant fields, and along shady hedgerows, according to an immemorial right of way; the neighboring village, with its venerable cottages, its public green sheltered by trees, under which the forefathers of the present race have sported; the antique family mansion, standing apart in some little rural domain, but looking down with a protecting air on the surrounding scene: all these common features of English landscape evince a calm and settled security, a hereditary transmission of home-bred virtues and local attachments that speak deeply and touchingly for the moral character of the nation.

It is a pleasing sight of a Sunday morning, when the bell is sending its sober melody across the quiet fields, to behold the peasantry in their best finery, with ruddy faces and modest cheerfulness, thronging tranquilly along the green lanes to church; but it is still more pleasing to see them in the evenings, gathering about their cottage doors and appearing to exult in the humble comforts and embellishments which their own hands have spread around them.

It is this sweet home feeling, this settled repose of affection in the domestic scene, that is, after all, the parent of the steadiest virtues and purest enjoyments; and I cannot close these desultory remarks better than by quoting the words of a modern English poet, who has depicted it with remarkable felicity:

> Through each gradation, from the castled hall,
> The city dome, the villa crown'd with shade,
> But chief from modest mansions numberless,
> In town or hamlet, shelt'ring middle life,
> Down to the cottaged vale, and straw-roof'd shed;
> This western isle hath long been famed for scenes
> Where bliss domestic finds a dwelling-place;
> Domestic bliss, that, like a harmless dove,
> (Honor and sweet endearment keeping guard,)
> Can center in a little quiet nest
> All that desire would fly for through the earth;
> That can, the world eluding, be itself
> A world enjoy'd; that wants no witnesses
> But its own sharers, and approving heaven;
> That, like a flower deep hid in rocky cleft,
> Smiles, though 'tis looking only at the sky.*

*From a poem on the death of the Princess Charlotte, by the Reverend Rann Kennedy, A.M.

THE BROKEN HEART

> I never heard
> Of any true affection, but 'twas nipt
> With care, that, like the caterpillar, eats
> The leaves of the spring's sweetest book, the rose.
>   MIDDLETON

It is a common practice with those who have outlived the susceptibility of early feeling, or have been brought up in the gay heartlessness of dissipated life, to laugh at all love stories and to treat the tales of romantic passion as mere fictions of novelists and poets. My observations on human nature have induced me to think otherwise. They have convinced me that, however the surface of the character may be chilled and frozen by the cares of the world, or cultivated into mere smiles by the arts of society, still there are dormant fires lurking in the depths of the coldest bosom, which, when once enkindled, become impetuous and are sometimes desolating in their effects. Indeed, I am a true believer in the blind deity and go to the full extent of his doctrines. Shall I confess it? I believe in broken hearts and the possibility of dying of disappointed love. I do not, however, consider it a malady often fatal to my own sex; but I firmly believe that it withers down many a lovely woman into an early grave.

Man is the creature of interest and ambition. His nature leads him forth into the struggle and bustle of the world. Love is but the embellishment of his early life, or a song piped in the intervals of the acts. He seeks for fame, for fortune, for space in the world's thought, and dominion over his fellow men. But a woman's whole life is a history of the affections. The heart is her world: it is there her ambition strives for empire; it is there her avarice seeks for hidden treasures. She sends forth her sympathies on adventure; she embarks her whole soul in the traffic of affection; and if shipwrecked, her case is hopeless—for it is a bankruptcy of the heart.

To a man, the disappointment of love may occasion some bitter pangs; it wounds some feelings of tenderness; it blasts some prospects of felicity. But he is an active being—he may dissipate his thoughts in the whirl of varied occupation, or may plunge into the tide of pleasure; or, if the scene of disappointment be too full of painful associations, he can shift his abode at will, and, taking as it were the wings of the morning, can "fly to the uttermost parts of the earth, and be at rest."

But woman's is comparatively a fixed, a secluded, and a meditative life. She is more the companion of her own thoughts and feelings; and if they are turned to ministers of sorrow, where shall she look for consolation? Her lot is to be wooed and won; and if unhappy in her love, her heart is like some fortress that has been captured, and sacked, and abandoned, and left desolate.

How many bright eyes grow dim—how many soft cheeks grow pale—how many lovely forms fade away into the tomb, and none can tell the cause that blighted their loveliness! As the dove will clasp its wings to its side and cover and conceal the arrow that is preying on its vitals, so is it the nature of woman to hide from the world the pangs of wounded affection. The love of a delicate female is always shy and silent. Even when fortunate, she scarcely breathes it to herself; but when otherwise, she buries it in the recesses of her bosom, and there lets it cower and brood among the ruins of her peace. With her the desire of the heart has failed. The great charm of existence is at an end. She neglects all the cheerful exercises which gladden the spirits, quicken the pulses, and send the tide of life in healthful currents through the veins. Her rest is broken—the sweet refreshment of sleep is poisoned by melancholy dreams—"dry sorrow drinks her blood," until her enfeebled frame sinks under the slightest external injury. Look for her, after a little while, and you find friendship weeping over her untimely grave and wondering that one who but lately glowed with all the radiance of health and beauty should so speedily be brought down to "darkness and the worm." You will be told of some wintry chill, some casual indisposition, that laid her low—but no one knows of the mental malady which previously sapped her strength and made her so easy a prey to the spoiler.

She is like some tender tree, the pride and beauty of the grove, graceful in its form, bright in its foliage, but with the worm preying at its heart. We find it suddenly withering when it should be most fresh and luxuriant. We see it drooping its branches to the earth and shedding leaf by leaf until, wasted and perished away, it falls even in the stillness of the forest; and as we muse over the beautiful ruin, we strive in vain to recollect the blast or thunderbolt that could have smitten it with decay.

I have seen many instances of women running to waste and self-neglect, and disappearing gradually from the earth almost as if they had been exhaled to heaven; and have repeatedly fancied that I could trace their death through the various declensions of consumption, cold, debility, languor, melancholy, until I reached the first symptom of disappointed love. But an instance of the kind was lately told to me; the circumstances are well known in the country where they happened, and I shall but give them in the manner in which they were related.

Everyone must recollect the tragical story of young E——, the Irish patriot; it was too touching to be soon forgotten. During the troubles in Ireland, he was tried, condemned, and executed on a charge of treason. His fate made a deep impression on public sympathy. He was so young, so intelligent, so generous, so brave, so everything that we are apt to like in a young man. His conduct under trial, too, was so lofty and intrepid. The noble indignation with which he repelled the charge of treason against his country, the eloquent vindication of his name, and his pathetic appeal to posterity, in the hopeless hour of condemnation, all these entered deeply into every generous bosom, and even his enemies lamented the stern policy that dictated his execution.

But there was one heart whose anguish it would be impossible to describe. In happier days and fairer fortunes, he had won the affections of a beautiful and interesting girl, the daughter of a late, celebrated Irish barrister. She loved him with the disinterested fervor of a woman's first and early love. When every worldly maxim arrayed itself against him, when blasted in fortune and disgrace and danger darkened around his name, she loved him the more ardently for his very sufferings. If, then, his fate could awaken the sympathy even of his foes, what must have been the agony of her whose whole soul was occupied by his image! Let those tell who have had the portals of the tomb suddenly closed between them and the being they most loved on earth, who have sat at its threshold, as one shut out in a cold and lonely world, whence all that was most lovely and loving had departed.

But then the horrors of such a grave! So frightful, so dishonored! There was nothing for memory to dwell on that could soothe the pang of separation—none of those tender though melancholy circumstances which endear the parting scene, nothing to melt sorrow into those blessed tears, sent like the dews of heaven to revive the heart in the parting hour of anguish.

To render her widowed situation more desolate, she had incurred her father's displeasure by her unfortunate attachment, and was an exile from the paternal roof. But could the sympathy and kind offices of friends have reached a spirit so shocked and driven in by horror, she would have experienced no want of consolation, for the Irish are a people of quick and generous sensibilities. The most delicate and cherishing attentions were paid her by families of wealth and distinction. She was led into society, and they tried by all kinds of occupation and amusement to dissipate her grief and wean her from the tragic story of her love. But it was all in vain. There are some strokes of calamity which scathe and scorch the soul—which penetrate to the vital seat of happiness —and blast it, never again to put forth bud or blossom. She never objected to frequent the haunts of pleasure, but was as much alone there as in the depths of solitude, walking about in a sad reverie, apparently unconscious of the world around her. She carried with her an inward woe that mocked at all the blandishments of friendship and "heeded not the song of the charmer, charm he never so wisely."

The person who told me her story had seen her at a masquerade. There can be no exhibition of far-gone wretchedness more striking and painful than to meet it in such a scene. To find it wandering like a specter, lonely and joyless, where all around is gay—to see it dressed out in the trappings of mirth and looking so wan and woebegone, as if it had tried in vain to cheat the poor heart into a momentary forgetfulness of sorrow. After strolling through the splendid rooms and giddy crowd with an air of utter abstraction, she sat herself down on the steps of an orchestra, and, looking about for some time with a vacant air that showed her insensibility to the garish scene, she began, with the capriciousness of a sickly heart, to warble a little plaintive air. She had an exquisite voice, but on this occasion it was so simple, so touching, it breathed forth such a soul of wretchedness that she drew a crowd mute and silent around her, and melted everyone into tears.

The story of one so true and tender could not but excite great interest in a country remarkable for enthusiasm. It completely won the heart of a brave officer, who paid his addresses to her, and thought that one so true to the dead could not but prove affectionate to the living. She declined his attentions, for her thoughts were irrevocably engrossed by the memory of her former lover. He, however, persisted in his suit. He solicited not her tenderness, but her esteem. He was assisted by her conviction of his worth, and her sense of her own destitute and dependent situation, for she was existing on the kindness of friends. In a word, he at length succeeded in gaining her hand, though with the solemn assurance that her heart was unalterably another's.

He took her with him to Sicily, hoping that a change of scene might wear out the remembrance of early woes. She was an amiable and exemplary wife and made an effort to be a happy one, but nothing could cure the silent and devouring melancholy that had entered into her very soul. She wasted away in a slow but hopeless decline, and at length sunk into the grave, the victim of a broken heart.

It was on her that Moore, the distinguished Irish poet, composed the following lines:

She is far from the land where her young hero sleeps,
  And lovers around her are sighing;
But coldly she turns from their gaze, and weeps,
  For her heart in his grave is lying.

She sings the wild songs of her dear native plains,
  Every note which he loved awaking—
Ah! little they think, who delight in her strains,
  How the heart of the minstrel is breaking!

He had lived for his love—for his country he died,
  They were all that to life had entwined him—
Nor soon shall the tears of his country be dried,
  Nor long will his love stay behind him!

Oh! make her a grave where the sunbeams rest,
  When they promise a glorious morrow;
They'll shine o'er her sleep, like a smile from the west,
  From her own loved island of sorrow!

THE ART OF BOOKMAKING

"If that severe doom of Synesius be true—'It is a greater
offence to steal dead men's labor, than their clothes,' what
shall become of most writers?"

BURTON'S ANATOMY OF MELANCHOLY

I have often wondered at the extreme fecundity of the
press, and how it comes to pass that so many heads on
which nature seemed to have inflicted the curse of barren-
ness should teem with voluminous productions. As a man
travels on, however, in the journey of life, his objects
of wonder daily diminish and he is continually finding
out some very simple cause for some great matter of
marvel. Thus have I chanced, in my peregrinations about
this great metropolis, to blunder upon a scene which un-
folded to me some of the mysteries of the bookmaking
craft, and at once put an end to my astonishment.

I was one summer's day loitering through the great
saloons of the British Museum with that listlessness with
which one is apt to saunter about a museum in warm
weather, sometimes lolling over the glass cases of min-
erals, sometimes studying the hieroglyphics on an Egyptian mummy, and sometimes trying, with nearly equal
success, to comprehend the allegorical paintings on the
lofty ceilings. While I was gazing about in this idle way,
my attention was attracted to a distant door, at the end
of a suite of apartments. It was closed, but every now and
then it would open and some strange-favored being,
generally clothed in black, would steal forth and
glide through the rooms, without noticing any of the surrounding objects. There was an air of mystery about

this that piqued my languid curiosity, and I determined to attempt the passage of that strait and to explore the unknown regions beyond. The door yielded to my hand with that facility with which the portals of enchanted castles yield to the adventurous knight-errant. I found myself in a spacious chamber, surrounded with great cases of venerable books. Above the cases, and just under the cornice, were arranged a great number of black-looking portraits of ancient authors. About the room were placed long tables, with stands for reading and writing, at which sat many pale, studious personages, poring intently over dusty volumes, rummaging among moldy manuscripts, and taking copious notes of their contents. A hushed stillness reigned through this mysterious apartment, excepting that you might hear the racing of pens over sheets of paper, or occasionally, the deep sigh of one of these sages as he shifted his position to turn over the page of an old folio, doubtless arising from that hollowness and flatulency incident to learned research.

Now and then one of these personages would write something on a small slip of paper and ring a bell, whereupon a familiar would appear, take the paper in profound silence, glide out of the room, and return shortly loaded with ponderous tomes, upon which the other would fall tooth and nail with famished voracity. I had no longer a doubt that I had happened upon a body of Magi, deeply engaged in the study of occult sciences. The scene reminded me of an old Arabian tale, of a philosopher shut up in an enchanted library, in the bosom of a mountain, which opened only once a year, where he made the spirits of the place bring him books of all kinds of dark knowledge, so that at the end of the year, when the magic portal once more swung open on its hinges, he issued forth so versed in forbidden lore as to be able to soar above the heads of the multitude and to control the powers of nature.

My curiosity being now fully aroused, I whispered to one of the familiars, as he was about to leave the room, and begged an interpretation of the strange scene before me. A few words were sufficient for the purpose. I found that these mysterious personages, whom I had mistaken for Magi, were principally authors, and in the very act of manufacturing books. I was, in fact, in the reading room of the great British Library—an immense collection of volumes of all ages and languages, many of which are now forgotten, and most of which are seldom read; one of these sequestered pools of obsolete literature to which modern authors repair and draw buckets full of classic lore, or "pure English, undefiled," wherewith to swell their own scanty rills of thought.

Being now in possession of the secret, I sat down in a corner and watched the process of this book manufactory. I noticed one lean, bilious-looking wight, who sought none but the most worm-eaten volumes, printed in black letter. He was evidently constructing some work of profound erudition that would be purchased by every man who wished to be thought learned, placed upon a conspicuous shelf of his library, or laid open upon his table, but never read. I observed him, now and then, draw a large fragment of biscuit out of his pocket and gnaw; whether it was his dinner, or whether he was endeavoring to keep off that exhaustion of the stomach produced by much pondering over dry works, I leave to harder students than myself to determine.

There was one dapper little gentleman in bright-colored clothes, with a chirping, gossiping expression of countenance, who had all the appearance of an author on good terms with his bookseller. After considering him attentively, I recognized in him a diligent getter-up of miscellaneous works which bustled off well with the trade. I was curious to see how he manufactured his wares. He made more stir and show of business than any of the others, dipping into various books, fluttering over the leaves of manuscripts, taking a morsel out of one, a morsel out of another, "line upon line, precept upon precept, here a little and there a little." The contents of his book seemed to be as heterogeneous as those of the witches' caldron in *Macbeth*. It was here a finger and there a thumb, toe of frog and blind-worm's sting, with his own gossip poured in like "baboon's blood," to make the medley "slab and good."

After all, thought I, may not this pilfering disposition be implanted in authors for wise purposes; may it not be the way in which Providence has taken care that the seeds of knowledge and wisdom shall be preserved from age to age, in spite of the inevitable decay of the works in which they were first produced? We see that nature has wisely, though whimsically, provided for the conveyance of seeds from clime to clime, in the maws of certain birds, so that animals, which, in themselves, are little better than carrion, and apparently the lawless plunderers of the orchard and the cornfield, are, in fact, Nature's carriers to disperse and perpetuate her blessings. In like manner, the beauties and fine thoughts of ancient and obsolete authors are caught up by these flights of predatory writers and cast forth again to flourish and bear fruit in a remote and distant tract of time. Many of their works, also, undergo a kind of metempsychosis and spring up under new forms. What was formerly a ponderous history revives in the shape of a romance, an old legend changes into a modern play, and a sober philosophical treatise furnishes the body for a whole series of bouncing and sparkling essays. Thus it is in the clearing of our American woodlands; where we burn down a forest of stately pines, a progeny of dwarf oaks start up in their place, and we never see the prostrate trunk of a tree moldering into soil, but it gives birth to a whole tribe of fungi.

Let us not, then, lament over the decay and oblivion into which ancient writers descend; they do but submit to the great law of nature, which declares that all sublunary shapes of matter shall be limited in their duration, but which decrees, also, that their elements shall never perish. Generation after generation, both in animal and vegetable life, passes away, but the vital principle is transmitted to posterity and the species continue to flourish. Thus, also, do authors beget authors, and having produced a numerous progeny, in a good old age they sleep with their fathers, that is to say, with the authors who preceded them—and from whom they had stolen.

While I was indulging in these rambling fancies, I had leaned my head against a pile of reverend folios. Whether it was owing to the soporific emanations from these works, or to the profound quiet of the room, or to the lassitude arising from much wandering, or to an unlucky

habit of napping at improper times and places with which
I am grievously afflicted, so it was that I fell into a doze.
Still, however, my imagination continued busy, and indeed the same scene remained before my mind's eye,
only a little changed in some of the details. I dreamed
that the chamber was still decorated with the portraits of
ancient authors, but that the number was increased.
The long tables had disappeared, and in place of the
sage Magi I beheld a ragged, threadbare throng, such
as may be seen plying about the great repository of
cast-off clothes, Monmouth Street. Whenever they seized
upon a book, by one of those incongruities common to
dreams, methought it turned into a garment of foreign or
antique fashion, with which they proceeded to equip
themselves. I noticed, however, that no one pretended to
clothe himself from any particular suit, but took a sleeve
from one, a cape from another, a skirt from a third, thus
decking himself out piecemeal, while some of his original
rags would peep out from among his borrowed finery.

There was a portly, rosy, well-fed parson, whom I observed ogling several moldy polemical writers through
an eyeglass. He soon contrived to slip on the voluminous mantle of one of the old fathers, and, having pur-
loined the gray beard of another, endeavored to look
exceedingly wise; but the smirking commonplace of his
countenance set at naught all the trappings of wisdom.
One sickly looking gentleman was busied embroidering a
very flimsy garment with gold thread drawn out of several
old court dresses of the reign of Queen Elizabeth. Another had trimmed himself magnificently from an illuminated manuscript, had stuck a nosegay in his bosom,
culled from "The Paradise of Daintie Devices," and having put Sir Philip Sidney's hat on one side of his head,
strutted off with an exquisite air of vulgar elegance. A
third, who was but of puny dimensions, had bolstered
himself out bravely with the spoils from several obscure
tracts of philosophy so that he had a very imposing
front; but he was lamentably tattered in rear, and I perceived that he had patched his small clothes with scraps
of parchment from a Latin author.

There were some well-dressed gentlemen, it is true,
who only helped themselves to a gem or so, which spar-

kled among their own ornaments without eclipsing them.
Some, too, seemed to contemplate the costumes of the
old writers, merely to imbibe their principles of taste,
and to catch their air and spirit; but I grieve to say
that too many were apt to array themselves from top to
toe in the patchwork manner I have mentioned. I shall not
omit to speak of one genius, in drab breeches and gaiters
and an Arcadian hat, who had a violent propensity to
the pastoral, but whose rural wanderings had been confined to the classic haunts of Primrose Hill and the solitudes of the Regent's Park. He had decked himself in
wreaths and ribbons from all the old pastoral poets, and,
hanging his head on one side, went about with a fantas-
tical lackadaisical air, "babbling about green fields." But
the personage that most struck my attention was a
pragmatical old gentleman, in clerical robes, with a
remarkably large and square but bald head. He entered
the room wheezing and puffing, elbowed his way through
the throng with a look of sturdy self-confidence, and
having laid hands upon a thick Greek quarto, clapped it
upon his head and swept majestically away in a formidable frizzled wig.

In the height of this literary masquerade, a cry suddenly resounded from every side of "Thieves! thieves!"
I looked, and lo! the portraits about the wall became
animated! The old authors thrust out, first a head, then
a shoulder from the canvas, looked down curiously for
an instant upon the motley throng, and then descended
with fury in their eyes to claim their rifled property. The
scene of scampering and hubbub that ensued baffles all
description. The unhappy culprits endeavored in vain to
escape with their plunder. On one side might be seen half
a dozen old monks, stripping a modern professor; on another, there was sad devastation carried into the ranks
of modern dramatic writers. Beaumont and Fletcher, side
by side, raged around the field like Castor and Pollux,
and sturdy Ben Jonson enacted more wonders than
when a volunteer with the army in Flanders. As to the
dapper little compiler of farragos, mentioned some time
since, he had arrayed himself in as many patches and
colors as Harlequin, and there was as fierce a contention
of claimants about him as about the dead body of

Patroclus. I was grieved to see many men to whom I had been accustomed to look up with awe and reverence fain to steal off with scarce a rag to cover their nakedness. Just then my eye was caught by the pragmatical old gentleman in the Greek grizzled wig, who was scrambling away in sore affright with half a score of authors in full cry after him! They were close upon his haunches. In a twinkling off went his wig; at every turn some strip of raiment was peeled away, until in a few moments, from his domineering pomp, he shrunk into a little, pursy "chopped bald shot" and made his exit with only a few tags and rags fluttering at his back.

There was something so ludicrous in the catastrophe of this learned Theban that I burst into an immoderate fit of laughter, which broke the whole illusion. The tumult and the scuffle were at an end. The chamber resumed its usual appearance. The old authors shrunk back into their picture frames and hung in shadowy solemnity along the walls. In short, I found myself wide awake in my corner, with the whole assemblage of bookworms gazing at me with astonishment. Nothing of the dream had been real, but my burst of laughter, a sound never before heard in that grave sanctuary, and so abhorrent to the ears of wisdom as to electrify the fraternity.

The librarian now stepped up to me and demanded whether I had a card of admission. At first I did not comprehend him, but I soon found that the library was a kind of literary "preserve," subject to game laws, and that no one must presume to hunt there without special license and permission. In a word, I stood convicted of being an arrant poacher, and was glad to make a precipitate retreat, lest I should have a whole pack of authors let loose upon me.

A ROYAL POET

Though your body be confined,
    And soft love a prisoner bound,
Yet the beauty of your mind
    Neither check nor chain hath found.
    Look out nobly, then, and dare
    Even the fetters that you wear.
                                FLETCHER

On a soft, sunny morning in the genial month of May, I made an excursion to Windsor Castle. It is a place full of storied and poetical associations. The very external aspect of the proud old pile is enough to inspire high thought. It rears its irregular walls and massive towers, like a mural crown, around the brow of a lofty ridge, waves its royal banner in the clouds, and looks down, with a lordly air, upon the surrounding world.

On this morning the weather was of that voluptuous vernal kind which calls forth all the latent romance of a man's temperament, filling his mind with music and disposing him to quote poetry and dream of beauty. In wandering through the magnificent saloons and long echoing galleries of the castle, I passed with indifference by whole rows of portraits of warriors and statesmen, but lingered in the chamber where hang the likenesses of the beauties which graced the gay court of Charles the Second; and as I gazed upon them, depicted with amorous, half-disheveled tresses and the sleepy eye of love, I blessed the pencil of Sir Peter Lely, which had thus enabled me to bask in the reflected rays of beauty. In traversing also the "large green courts," with sunshine beaming on the gray walls, and glancing along the velvet turf, my mind was engrossed with the image of the tender, the gallant, but hapless Surrey, and his account of his loiterings about them in his stripling days, when enamored of the Lady Geraldine—

"With eyes cast up unto the maiden's tower,
With easie sighs, such as men draw in love."

In this mood of mere poetical susceptibility, I visited the ancient Keep of the Castle, where James the First of Scotland, the pride and theme of Scottish poets and historians, was for many years of his youth detained a prisoner of state. It is a large, gray tower that has stood the brunt of ages, and is still in good preservation. It stands on a mound, which elevates it above the other parts of the castle, and a great flight of steps leads to the interior. In the armory, a Gothic hall furnished with weapons of various kinds and ages, I was shown a coat of armor, hanging against the wall, which had once belonged to James. Hence I was conducted up a staircase to a suite of apartments of faded magnificence, hung with storied tapestry, which formed his prison, and the scene of that passionate and fanciful amour, which has woven into the web of his story the magical hues of poetry and fiction.

The whole history of this amiable but unfortunate prince is highly romantic. At the tender age of eleven he was sent from home by his father, Robert III, and destined for the French court, to be reared under the eye of the French monarch, secure from the treachery and danger that surrounded the royal house of Scotland. It was his mishap, in the course of his voyage, to fall into the hands of the English, and he was detained prisoner by Henry IV, notwithstanding that a truce existed between the two countries.

The intelligence of his capture, coming in the train of many sorrows and disasters, proved fatal to his unhappy father. "The news," we are told, "was brought to him while at supper, and did so overwhelm him with grief, that he was almost ready to give up the ghost into the hands of the servant that attended him. But being carried to his bed-chamber, he abstained from all food, and in three days died of hunger and grief at Rothesay." *

James was detained in captivity above eighteen years; but though deprived of personal liberty, he was treated with the respect due to his rank. Care was taken to in-

*Buchanan.

struct him in all the branches of useful knowledge cultivated at that period and to give him those mental and personal accomplishments deemed proper for a prince. Perhaps, in this respect, his imprisonment was an advantage, as it enabled him to apply himself the more exclusively to his improvement and quietly to imbibe that rich fund of knowledge and to cherish those elegant tastes which have given such a luster to his memory. The picture drawn of him in early life by the Scottish historians is highly captivating, and seems rather the description of a hero of romance than of a character in real history. He was well learned, we are told, "to fight with the sword, to joust, to tournay, to wrestle, to sing and dance; he was an expert mediciner, right crafty in playing both of lute and harp, and sundry other instruments of music, and was expert in grammar, oratory, and poetry." *

With this combination of manly and delicate accomplishments fitting him to shine both in active and elegant life and calculated to give him an intense relish for joyous existence, it must have been a severe trial, in an age of bustle and chivalry, to pass the springtime of his years in monotonous captivity. It was the good fortune of James, however, to be gifted with a powerful poetic fancy and to be visited in his prison by the choicest inspirations of the muse. Some minds corrode and grow inactive under the loss of personal liberty; others grow morbid and irritable; but it is the nature of the poet to become tender and imaginative in the loneliness of confinement. He banquets upon the honey of his own thoughts, and, like the captive bird, pours forth his soul in melody.

> Have you not seen the nightingale,
>   A pilgrim coop'd into a cage,
> How doth she chant her wonted tale,
>   In that her lonely hermitage!
> Even there her charming melody doth prove
> That all her boughs are trees, her cage a grove.†

Indeed, it is the divine attribute of the imagination that it is irrepressible, unconfinable; that when the real

*Ballenden's Translation of Hector Boyce.
†Roger L'Estrange.

world is shut out it can create a world for itself, and with a necromantic power can conjure up glorious shapes and forms and brilliant visions to make solitude populous and irradiate the gloom of the dungeon. Such was the world of pomp and pageant that lived around Tasso in his dismal cell at Ferrara, when he conceived the splendid scenes of his Jerusalem; and we may consider the "King's Quair," composed by James during his captivity at Windsor, as another of those beautiful breakings forth of the soul from the restraint and gloom of the prison house.

The subject of the poem is his love for the Lady Jane Beaufort, daughter of the Earl of Somerset and a princess of the blood royal of England, of whom he became enamored in the course of his captivity. What gives it a peculiar value is that it may be considered a transcript of the royal bard's true feelings and the story of his real loves and fortunes. It is not often that sovereigns write poetry, or that poets deal in fact. It is gratifying to the pride of a common man to find a monarch thus suing, as it were, for admission into his closet, and seeking to win his favor by administering to his pleasures. It is a proof of the honest equality of intellectual competition, which strips off all the trappings of factitious dignity, brings the candidate down to a level with his fellow men, and obliges him to depend on his own native powers for distinction. It is curious, too, to get at the history of a monarch's heart and to find the simple affections of human nature throbbing under the ermine. But James had learned to be a poet before he was a king; he was schooled in adversity and reared in the company of his own thoughts. Monarchs have seldom time to parley with their hearts or to meditate their minds into poetry, and had James been brought up amidst the adulation and gaiety of a court we should never, in all probability, have had such a poem as the Quair.

I have been particularly interested by those parts of the poem which breathe his immediate thoughts concerning his situation, or which are connected with the apartment in the tower. They have thus a personal and local charm, and are given with such circumstantial truth, as to make the reader present with the captive in his prison and the companion of his meditations.

Such is the account which he gives of his weariness of spirit and of the incident which first suggested the idea of writing the poem. It was the still midwatch of a clear, moonlight night; the stars, he says, were twinkling as fire in the high vault of heaven, and "Cynthia rinsing her golden locks in Aquarius." He lay in bed, wakeful and restless, and took a book to beguile the tedious hours. The book he chose was Boetius' *Consolations of Philosophy,* a work popular among the writers of that day, and which had been translated by his great prototype Chaucer. From the high eulogium in which he indulges, it is evident this was one of his favorite volumes while in prison; and indeed it is an admirable textbook for meditation under adversity. It is the legacy of a noble and enduring spirit, purified by sorrow and suffering, bequeathing to its successors in calamity the maxims of sweet morality and the trains of eloquent but simple reasoning by which it was enabled to bear up against the various ills of life. It is a talisman, which the unfortunate may treasure up in his bosom, or, like the good King James, lay upon his nightly pillow.

After closing the volume, he turns its contents over in his mind and gradually falls into a fit of musing on the fickleness of fortune, the vicissitudes of his own life, and the evils that had overtaken him even in his tender youth. Suddenly he hears the bell ringing to matins; but its sound, chiming in with his melancholy fancies, seems to him like a voice exhorting him to write his story. In the spirit of poetic errantry, he determines to comply with this intimation; he therefore takes pen in hand, makes with it a sign of the cross to implore a benediction, and sallies forth into the fairyland of poetry. There is something extremely fanciful in all this, and it is interesting as furnishing a striking and beautiful instance of the simple manner in which whole trains of poetical thought are sometimes awakened and literary enterprises suggested to the mind.

In the course of his poem, he more than once bewails the peculiar hardness of his fate; thus doomed to lonely and inactive life, and shut up from the freedom and pleasure of the world, in which the meanest animal indulges unrestrained. There is a sweetness, however, in his very complaints; they are the lamentations of an amiable and social spirit at being denied the indulgence of its kind and generous propensities. There is nothing in them harsh nor exaggerated; they flow with a natural and touching pathos and are perhaps rendered more touching by their simple brevity. They contrast finely with those elaborate and iterated repinings which we sometimes meet with in poetry; the effusions of morbid minds sickening under miseries of their own creating and venting their bitterness upon an unoffending world. James speaks of his privations with acute sensibility, but having mentioned them, passes on, as if his manly mind disdained to brood over unavoidable calamities. When such a spirit breaks forth into complaint, however brief, we are aware how great must be the suffering that extorts the murmur. We sympathize with James, a romantic, active, and accomplished prince, cut off in the lustihood of youth from all the enterprise, the noble uses, and vigorous delights of life, as we do with Milton, alive to all the beauties of nature and glories of art, when he breathes forth brief but deep-toned lamentations over his perpetual blindness.

Had not James evinced a deficiency of poetic artifice, we might almost have suspected that these lowerings of gloomy reflection were meant as preparative to the brightest scene of his story, and to contrast with that refulgence of light and loveliness, that exhilarating accompaniment of bird and song, and foliage and flower, and all the revel of the year with which he ushers in the lady of his heart. It is this scene, in particular, which throws all the magic of romance about the old Castle Keep. He had risen, he says, at daybreak, according to custom, to escape from the dreary meditations of a sleepless pillow. "Bewailing in his chamber thus alone," despairing of all joy and remedy, "fortired of thought and wobegone," he had wandered to the window, to indulge the captive's miserable solace of gazing wistfully upon the world from which he is excluded. The window looked forth upon a small garden which lay at the foot of the tower. It was a quiet, sheltered spot, adorned with arbors and green alleys, and protected from the passing gaze by trees and hawthorn hedges.

> Now was there made, fast by the tower's wall,
>   A garden faire, and in the corners set
> An arbour green with wandis long and small
>   Railed about, and so with leaves beset
> Was all the place and hawthorn hedges knet,
>   That lyf* was none, walkyng there forbye
>   That might within scarce any wight espye.
>
> So thick the branches and the leves grene,
>   Beshaded all the alleys that there were,
> And midst of every arbour might be sene
>   The sharpe, grene, swete juniper,
> Growing so fair, with branches here and there,
>   That as it seemed to a lyf without,
>   The boughs did spread the arbour all about.
>
> And on the small grene twistis† set
>   The lytel swete nightingales, and sung
> So loud and clear, the hymnis consecrate
>   Of lovis use, now soft, now loud among,
> That all of the garden and the wallis rung
> Right of their song——

It was the month of May, when everything was in bloom; and he interprets the song of the nightingale into the language of his enamored feeling:

> Worship, all ye that lovers be, this May,
>   For of your bliss the kalends are begun,
> And sing with us, away, winter, away,
>   Come, summer, come, the sweet season and sun.

As he gazes on the scene and listens to the notes of the birds, he gradually relapses into one of those tender and undefinable reveries which fill the youthful bosom in this delicious season. He wonders what this love may be, of which he has so often read and which thus seems breathed forth in the quickening breath of May, and melt-

---

*Lyf, Person. †Twistis, small boughs or twigs.
  Note.—The language of the quotations is generally modernized.

ing all nature into ecstasy and song. If it really be so
great a felicity, and if it be a boon thus generally dis-
pensed to the most insignificant beings, why is he alone
cut off from its enjoyments?

> Oft would I think, O Lord, what may this be,
>   That love is of such noble myght and kynde?
> Loving his folke, and such prosperitee
>   Is it of him, as we in books do find:
>   May be oure hertes setten* and unbynd:
> Hath he upon our hertes such maistrye?
> Or is all this but feynit fantasye?
>
> For giff he be of so grete excellence,
>   That he of every wight hath care and charge,
> What have I gilt† to him, or done offense,
>   That I am thral'd, and birdis go at large?

In the midst of his musing, as he casts his eye downward, he beholds "the fairest and the freshest young
floure" that ever he had seen. It is the lovely Lady Jane,
walking in the garden to enjoy the beauty of that
"fresh May morrowe." Breaking thus suddenly upon his
sight, in the moment of loneliness and excited susceptibility, she at once captivates the fancy of the romantic
prince and becomes the object of his wandering wishes,
the sovereign of his ideal world.

There is, in this charming scene, an evident resemblance to the early part of Chaucer's "Knight's Tale,"
where Palamon and Arcite fall in love with Emilia, whom
they see walking in the garden of their prison. Perhaps
the similarity of the actual fact to the incident which he
had read in Chaucer may have induced James to dwell
on it in his poem. His description of the Lady Jane is
given in the picturesque and minute manner of his master, and being doubtless taken from the life, is a perfect
portrait of a beauty of that day. He dwells, with the
fondness of a lover, on every article of her apparel, from
the net of pearl, splendent with emeralds and sapphires
that confined her golden hair, even to the "goodly chaine
of small orfeverye" ‡ about her neck, whereby there hung

Setten, incline.   †*Gilt*, what injury have I done, etc.
‡Wrought gold.

a ruby in shape of a heart, that seemed, he says, like a spark of fire burning upon her white bosom. Her dress of white tissue was looped up to enable her to walk with more freedom. She was accompanied by two female attendants, and about her sported a little hound decorated with bells, probably the small Italian hound of exquisite symmetry which was a parlor favorite and pet among the fashionable dames of ancient times. James closes his description by a burst of general eulogium:

> In her was youth, beauty, with humble port,
>   Bounty, richesse, and womanly feature;
> God better knows than my pen can report,
>   Wisdom, largesse,* estate,† and cunning‡ sure,
> In every point so guided her measure,
>   In word, in deed, in shape, in countenance,
>   That nature might no more her child advance.

The departure of the Lady Jane from the garden puts an end to this transient riot of the heart. With her departs the amorous illusion that had shed a temporary charm over the scene of his captivity, and he relapses into loneliness, now rendered tenfold more intolerable by this passing beam of unattainable beauty. Through the long and weary day he repines at his unhappy lot, and when evening approaches and Phoebus, as he beautifully expresses it, had "bade farewell to every leaf and flower," he still lingers at the window, and, laying his head upon the cold stone, gives vent to a mingled flow of love and sorrow, until, gradually lulled by the mute melancholy of the twilight hour, he lapses, "half sleeping, half swoon," into a vision, which occupies the remainder of the poem and in which is allegorically shadowed out the history of his passion.

When he wakes from his trance, he rises from his stony pillow, and, pacing his apartment, full of dreary reflections, questions his spirit, whither it has been wandering; whether, indeed, all that has passed before his dreaming fancy has been conjured up by preceding circumstances, or whether it is a vision, intended to comfort and assure him in his despondency. If the latter, he prays

Largesse, bounty.   †*Estate,* dignity.   ‡*Cunning,* discretion.

that some token may be sent to confirm the promise of
happier days, given him in his slumbers. Suddenly, a
turtle dove of the purest whiteness comes flying in at the
window and alights upon his hand, bearing in her bill a
branch of red gilliflower, on the leaves of which is written,
in letters of gold, the following sentence:

> Awake! awake! I bring, lover, I bring
>   The newis glad that blissful is, and sure
> Of thy comfort; now laugh, and play, and sing,
>   For in the heaven decretit is thy cure.

He receives the branch with mingled hope and dread,
reads it with rapture; and this, he says, was the first
token of his succeeding happiness. Whether this is a mere
poetic fiction, or whether the Lady Jane did actually send
him a token of her favor in this romantic way, remains
to be determined according to the faith or fancy of
the reader. He concludes his poem by intimating that the
promise conveyed in the vision and by the flower is fulfilled by his being restored to liberty and made happy in
the possession of the sovereign of his heart.

Such is the poetical account given by James of his love
adventures in Windsor Castle. How much of it is
absolute fact, and how much the embellishment of fancy,
it is fruitless to conjecture; let us not, however, reject
every romantic incident as incompatible with real life,
but let us sometimes take a poet at his word. I have
noticed merely those parts of the poem immediately connected with the tower, and have passed over a large part
written in the allegorical vein so much cultivated at that
day. The language, of course, is quaint and antiquated,
so that the beauty of many of its golden phrases will
scarcely be perceived at the present day; but it is impossible not to be charmed with the genuine sentiment,
the delightful artlessness and urbanity which prevail
throughout it. The descriptions of nature too, with which
it is embellished, are given with a truth, a discrimination, and a freshness worthy of the most cultivated periods of the art.

As an amatory poem, it is edifying in these days of
coarser thinking to notice the nature, refinement, and
exquisite delicacy which pervade it, banishing every gross

thought or immodest expression and presenting female loveliness clothed in all its chivalrous attributes of almost supernatural purity and grace.

James flourished nearly about the time of Chaucer and Gower and was evidently an admirer and studier of their writings. Indeed, in one of his stanzas he acknowledges them as his masters, and in some parts of his poem we find traces of similarity to their productions, more especially to those of Chaucer. There are always, however, general features of resemblance in the works of contemporary authors which are not so much borrowed from each other as from the times. Writers, like bees, toll their sweets in the wide world; they incorporate with their own conceptions the anecdotes and thoughts current in society, and thus each generation has some features in common, characteristic of the age in which it lived.

James belongs to one of the most brilliant eras of our literary history and establishes the claims of his country to a participation in its primitive honors. While a small cluster of English writers are constantly cited as the fathers of our verse, the name of their great Scottish compeer is apt to be passed over in silence; but he is evidently worthy of being enrolled in that little constellation of remote but never-failing luminaries who shine in the highest firmament of literature, and who, like morning stars, sang together at the bright dawning of British poesy.

Such of my readers as may not be familiar with Scottish history (though the manner in which it has of late been woven with captivating fiction has made it a universal study) may be curious to learn something of the subsequent history of James and the fortunes of his love. His passion for the Lady Jane, as it was the solace of his captivity, so it facilitated his release, it being imagined by the court that a connection with the blood royal of England would attach him to its own interests. He was ultimately restored to his liberty and crown, having previously espoused the Lady Jane, who accompanied him to Scotland and made him a most tender and devoted wife.

He found his kingdom in great confusion, the feudal chieftains having taken advantage of the troubles and irregularities of a long interregnum to strengthen themselves in their possessions and place themselves above the power of the laws. James sought to found the basis of his power in the affections of his people. He attached the lower orders to him by the reformation of abuses, the temperate and equable administration of justice, the encouragement of the arts of peace, and the promotion of everything that could diffuse comfort, competency, and innocent enjoyment through the humblest ranks of society. He mingled occasionally among the common people in disguise, visited their firesides, entered into their cares, their pursuits, and their amusements, informed himself of the mechanical arts and how they could best be patronized and improved, and was thus an all-pervading spirit, watching with a benevolent eye over the meanest of his subjects. Having in this generous manner made himself strong in the hearts of the common people, he turned himself to curb the power of the factious nobility, to strip them of those dangerous immunities which they had usurped, to punish such as had been guilty of flagrant offenses, and to bring the whole into proper obedience to the crown. For some time they bore this with outward submission, but with secret impatience and brooding resentment. A conspiracy was at length formed against his life, at the head of which was his own uncle, Robert Stewart, Earl of Athol, who, being too old himself for the perpetration of the deed of blood, instigated his grandson Sir Robert Stewart, together with Sir Robert Graham and others of less note, to commit the deed. They broke into his bedchamber at the Dominican Convent near Perth, where he was residing, and barbarously murdered him by oft-repeated wounds. His faithful queen, rushing to throw her tender body between him and the sword, was twice wounded in the ineffectual attempt to shield him from the assassin; and it was not until she had been forcibly torn from his person that the murder was accomplished.

It was the recollection of this romantic tale of former times and of the golden little poem which had its birthplace in this Tower that made me visit the old pile with more than common interest. The suit of armor hanging up in the hall, richly gilt and embellished, as if to figure in the tournay, brought the image of the gallant and ro-

mantic prince vividly before my imagination. I paced
the deserted chambers where he had composed his poem;
I leaned upon the window and endeavored to persuade
myself it was the very one where he had been visited
by his vision; I looked out upon the spot where he had
first seen the Lady Jane. It was the same genial and joyous
month; the birds were again vying with each other in
strains of liquid melody; everything was bursting into
vegetation and budding forth the tender promise of the
year. Time, which delights to obliterate the sterner memorials of human pride, seems to have passed lightly over
this little scene of poetry and love and to have withheld
his desolating hand. Several centuries have gone by, yet
the garden still flourishes at the foot of the Tower. It
occupies what was once the moat of the Keep; and
though some parts have been separated by dividing walls,
yet others have still their arbors and shaded walks, as
in the days of James, and the whole is sheltered, blooming,
and retired. There is a charm about a spot that has been
printed by the footsteps of departed beauty and consecrated by the inspirations of the poet which is heightened, rather than impaired, by the lapse of ages. It is,
indeed, the gift of poetry to hallow every place in
which it moves, to breathe around nature an odor more
exquisite than the perfume of the rose, and to shed over it
a tint more magical than the blush of morning.

Others may dwell on the illustrious deeds of James as
a warrior and legislator, but I have delighted to view him
merely as the companion of his fellow men, the benefactor of the human heart, stooping from his high estate to
sow the sweet flowers of poetry and song in the paths of
common life. He was the first to cultivate the vigorous
and hardy plant of Scottish genius, which has since become so prolific of the most wholesome and highly fla-
vored fruit. He carried with him into the sterner regions
of the north all the fertilizing arts of southern refinement.
He did everything in his power to win his countrymen to
the gay, the elegant, and gentle arts, which soften and
refine the character of a people and wreathe a grace
around the loftiness of a proud and warlike spirit. He
wrote many poems, which, unfortunately for the fullness
of his fame, are now lost to the world; one, which is still

preserved, called "Christ's Kirk of the Green," shows how diligently he had made himself acquainted with the rustic sports and pastimes which constitute such a source of kind and social feeling among the Scottish peasantry, and with what simple and happy humor he could enter into their enjoyments. He contributed greatly to improve the national music, and traces of his tender sentiment and elegant taste are said to exist in those witching airs still piped among the wild mountains and lonely glens of Scotland. He has thus connected his image with whatever is most gracious and endearing in the national character; he has embalmed his memory in song and floated his name to after ages in the rich streams of Scottish melody. The recollection of these things was kindling at my heart as I paced the silent scene of his imprisonment. I have visited Vaucluse with as much enthusiasm as a pilgrim would visit the shrine at Loretto, but I have never felt more poetical devotion than when contemplating the old Tower and the little garden at Windsor and musing over the romantic loves of the Lady Jane and the Royal Poet of Scotland.

THE COUNTRY CHURCH

A gentleman!
What, o' the woolpack? or the sugar-chest?
Or lists of velvet? which is't, pound, or yard,
You vend your gentry by?

BEGGAR'S BUSH

There are few places more favorable to the study of
character than an English country church. I was once
passing a few weeks at the seat of a friend, who resided
in the vicinity of one, the appearance of which particularly struck my fancy. It was one of those rich morsels
of quaint antiquity which give such a peculiar charm to
English landscape. It stood in the midst of a country
filled with ancient families and contained, within its cold
and silent aisles, the congregated dust of many noble
generations. The interior walls were encrusted with monuments of every age and style. The light streamed through
windows dimmed with armorial bearings, richly emblazoned in stained glass. In various parts of the church
were tombs of knights and high-born dames, of gorgeous
workmanship, with their effigies in colored marble. On
every side the eye was struck with some instance of
aspiring mortality, some haughty memorial which human pride had erected over its kindred dust, in this
temple of the most humble of all religions.

The congregation was composed of the neighboring
people of rank, who sat in pews, sumptuously lined and
cushioned, furnished with richly gilded prayerbooks and
decorated with their arms upon the pew doors; of the
villagers and peasantry, who filled the back seats and a
small gallery beside the organ; and of the poor of the
parish, who were ranged on benches in the aisles.

99

The service was performed by a snuffling, well-fed vicar, who had a snug dwelling near the church. He was a privileged guest at all the tables of the neighborhood, and had been the keenest fox hunter in the country, until age and good living had disabled him from doing anything more than ride to see the hounds throw off and make one at the hunting dinner.

Under the ministry of such a pastor, I found it impossible to get into the train of thought suitable to the time and place; so, having, like many other feeble Christians, compromised with my conscience by laying the sin of my own delinquency at another person's threshold, I occupied myself by making observations on my neighbors.

I was as yet a stranger in England and curious to notice the manners of its fashionable classes. I found, as usual, that there was the least pretension where there was the most acknowledged title to respect. I was particularly struck, for instance, with the family of a nobleman of high rank, consisting of several sons and daughters. Nothing could be more simple and unassuming than their appearance. They generally came to church in the plainest equipage, and often on foot. The young ladies would stop and converse in the kindest manner with the peasantry, caress the children, and listen to the stories of the humble cottagers. Their countenances were open and beautifully fair, with an expression of high refinement but, at the same time, a frank cheerfulness and an engaging affability. Their brothers were tall and elegantly formed. They were dressed fashionably but simply, with strict neatness and propriety but without any mannerism or foppishness. Their whole demeanor was easy and natural, with that lofty grace and noble frankness which bespeak freeborn souls that have never been checked in their growth by feelings of inferiority. There is a healthful hardiness about real dignity that never dreads contact and communion with others, however humble. It is only spurious pride that is morbid and sensitive and shrinks from every touch. I was pleased to see the manner in which they would converse with the peasantry about those rural concerns and field sports in which the gentlemen of this country so much delight. In these conversations there was neither haughtiness on the one part nor servility on the other, and you were only reminded of the difference of rank by the habitual respect of the peasant.

In contrast to these was the family of a wealthy citizen who had amassed a vast fortune, and, having purchased the estate and mansion of a ruined nobleman in the neighborhood, was endeavoring to assume all the style and dignity of an hereditary lord of the soil. The family always came to church *en prince*. They were rolled majestically along in a carriage emblazoned with arms. The crest glittered in silver radiance from every part of the harness where a crest could possibly be placed. A fat coachman, in a three-cornered hat, richly laced, and a flaxen wig curling close around his rosy face, was seated on the box, with a sleek Danish dog beside him. Two footmen, in gorgeous liveries, with huge bouquets and gold-headed canes, lolled behind. The carriage rose and sunk on its long springs with peculiar stateliness of motion. The very horses champed their bits, arched their necks, and glanced their eyes more proudly than common horses, either because they had caught a little of the family feeling or were reined up more tightly than ordinary.

I could not but admire the style with which this splendid pageant was brought up to the gate of the churchyard. There was a vast effect produced at the turning of an angle of the wall; a great smacking of the whip, straining and scrambling of horses, glistening of harness, and flashing of wheels through gravel. This was the moment of triumph and vainglory to the coachman. The horses were urged and checked until they were fretted into a foam. They threw out their feet in a prancing trot, dashing about pebbles at every step. The crowd of villagers sauntering quietly to church opened precipitately to the right and left, gaping in vacant admiration. On reaching the gate, the horses were pulled up with a suddenness that produced an immediate stop and almost threw them on their haunches.

There was an extraordinary hurry of the footman to alight, pull down the steps, and prepare everything for the descent on earth of this august family. The old citizen first emerged his round, red face from out the door, looking about him with the pompous air of a man accustomed to rule on 'Change and shake the Stock Market with a nod. His consort, a fine, fleshy, comfortable dame, followed him. There seemed, I must confess, but little pride in her composition. She was the picture of broad, honest, vulgar enjoyment. The world went well with her, and she liked the world. She had fine clothes, a fine house, a fine carriage, fine children, everything was fine about her; it was nothing but driving about and visiting and feasting. Life was to her a perpetual revel; it was one long Lord Mayor's day.

Two daughters succeeded to this goodly couple. They certainly were handsome, but had a supercilious air that chilled admiration and disposed the spectator to be critical. They were ultrafashionable in dress; and, though no one could deny the richness of their decorations, yet their appropriateness might be questioned amidst the simplicity of a country church. They descended loftily from the carriage and moved up the line of peasantry with a step that seemed dainty of the soil it trod on. They cast an excursive glance around that passed coldly over the burly faces of the peasantry, until they met the eyes of the nobleman's family, when their countenances immediately brightened into smiles and they made the most profound and elegant courtesies, which were returned in a manner that showed they were but slight acquaintances.

I must not forget the two sons of this aspiring citizen, who came to church in a dashing curricle, with outriders. They were arrayed in the extremity of the mode, with all that pedantry of dress which marks the man of questionable pretensions to style. They kept entirely by themselves, eying everyone askance that came near them, as if measuring his claims to respectability; yet they were without conversation, except the exchange of an occasional cant phrase. They even moved artificially, for their bodies, in compliance with the caprice of the day, had been disciplined into the absence of all ease and freedom. Art had done everything to accomplish them as men of fashion, but nature had denied them the nameless grace. They were vulgarly shaped, like men formed for the common purposes of life, and had that air of supercilious assumption which is never seen in the true gentleman.

I have been rather minute in drawing the pictures of these two families, because I considered them specimens of what is often to be met with in this country—the unpretending great and the arrogant little. I have no respect for titled rank, unless it be accompanied with true nobility of soul, but I have remarked in all countries where artificial distinctions exist that the very highest classes are always the most courteous and unassuming. Those who are well assured of their own standing are least apt to trespass on that of others, whereas nothing is so offensive as the aspirings of vulgarity which thinks to elevate itself by humiliating its neighbor.

As I have brought these families into contrast, I must notice their behavior in church. That of the nobleman's family was quiet, serious, and attentive. Not that they appeared to have any fervor of devotion, but rather a respect for sacred things and sacred places, inseparable from good breeding. The others, on the contrary, were in a perpetual flutter and whisper; they betrayed a continual consciousness of finery and a sorry ambition of being the wonders of a rural congregation.

The old gentleman was the only one really attentive to the service. He took the whole burden of family devotion upon himself, standing bolt upright and uttering the responses with a loud voice that might be heard all over the church. It was evident that he was one of those thorough church and king men who connect the idea of devotion and loyalty, who consider the Deity, somehow or other, of the government party, and religion "a very excellent sort of thing that ought to be countenanced and kept up."

When he joined so loudly in the service, it seemed more by way of example to the lower orders, to show them that, though so great and wealthy, he was not above being religious; as I have seen a turtle-fed alderman swallow publicly a basin of charity soup, smacking his lips at every mouthful and pronouncing it "excellent food for the poor."

When the service was at an end, I was curious to

witness the several exits of my groups. The young noblemen and their sisters, as the day was fine, preferred strolling home across the fields, chatting with the country people as they went. The others departed as they came, in grand parade. Again were the equipages wheeled up to the gate. There was again the smacking of whips, the clattering of hoofs, and the glittering of harness. The horses started off almost at a bound; the villagers again hurried to right and left; the wheels threw up a cloud of dust; and the aspiring family was rapt out of sight in a whirlwind.

THE WIDOW AND HER SON

Pittie olde age, within whose silver haires
Honour and reverence evermore have rain'd.
MARLOWE'S TAMBURLAINE

Those who are in the habit of remarking such matters must have noticed the passive quiet of an English landscape on Sunday. The clacking of the mill, the regularly recurring stroke of the flail, the din of the blacksmith's hammer, the whistling of the plowman, the rattling of the cart, and all other sounds of rural labor are suspended. The very farm dogs bark less frequently, being less disturbed by passing travelers. At such times I have almost fancied the winds sunk into quiet, and that the sunny landscape, with its fresh green tints melting into blue haze, enjoyed the hallowed calm.

Sweet day, so pure, so calm, so bright,
The bridal of the earth and sky.

Well was it ordained that the day of devotion should be a day of rest. The holy repose which reigns over the face of nature has its moral influence; every restless passion is charmed down, and we feel the natural religion of the soul gently springing up within us. For my part, there are feelings that visit me in a country church, amid the beautiful serenity of nature, which I experience nowhere else; and if not a more religious, I think I am a better man on Sunday than on any other day of the seven.

During my recent residence in the country, I used frequently to attend at the old village church. Its shadowy aisles, its moldering monuments, its dark oaken paneling, all reverend with the gloom of departed years, seemed to fit it for the haunt of solemn meditation; but being in a wealthy, aristocratic neighborhood, the glitter of fashion penetrated even into the sanctuary, and I felt myself continually thrown back upon the world by the frigidity and pomp of the poor worms around me. The only being in the whole congregation who appeared thoroughly to feel the humble and prostrate piety of a true Christian was a poor, decrepit old woman bending under the weight of years and infirmities. She bore the traces of something better than abject poverty. The lingerings of decent pride were visible in her appearance. Her dress, though humble in the extreme, was scrupulously clean. Some trivial respect, too, had been awarded her, for she did not take her seat among the village poor, but sat alone on the steps of the altar. She seemed to have survived all love, all friendship, all society, and to have nothing left her but the hopes of heaven. When I saw her feebly rising and bending her aged form in prayer, habitually conning her prayerbook, which her palsied hand and failing eyes would not permit her to read but which she evidently knew by heart, I felt persuaded that the faltering voice of that poor woman arose to heaven far before the responses of the clerk, the swell of the organ, or the chanting of the choir.

I am fond of loitering about country churches, and this was so delightfully situated that it frequently attracted me. It stood on a knoll, around which a small stream made a beautiful bend and then wound its way through a long reach of soft meadowy scenery. The church was surrounded by yew trees which seemed almost coeval with itself. Its tall Gothic spire shot up lightly from among them, with rooks and crows generally wheeling about it. I was seated there one still, sunny morning, watching two laborers who were digging a grave. They had chosen one of the most remote and neglected corners of the churchyard, where, from the number of nameless graves around, it would appear that the indigent and friendless were huddled into the earth. I was told that the new-made grave was for the only son of a poor widow. While I was meditating on the distinctions of worldly rank, which extend thus down into the very dust, the toll of the bell announced the approach of the funeral. They were the obsequies of poverty, with which pride had nothing to do. A coffin of the plainest materials, without pall or other covering, was borne by some of the villagers. The sexton walked before with an air of cold indifference. There were no mock mourners in the trappings of affected woe, but there was one real mourner who feebly tottered after the corpse. It was the aged mother of the deceased—the poor old woman whom I had seen seated on the steps of the altar. She was supported by a humble friend who was endeavoring to comfort her. A few of the neighboring poor had joined the train, and some children of the village were running hand in hand, now shouting with unthinking mirth and now pausing to gaze, with childish curiosity, on the grief of the mourner.

As the funeral train approached the grave, the parson issued from the church porch, arrayed in the surplice, with prayerbook in hand, and attended by the clerk. The service, however, was a mere act of charity. The deceased had been destitute and the survivor was penniless. It was shuffled through, therefore, in form, but coldly and unfeelingly. The well-fed priest moved but a few steps from the church door; his voice could scarcely be heard at the grave, and never did I hear the funeral service, that sublime and touching ceremony, turned into such a frigid mummery of words.

I approached the grave. The coffin was placed on the ground. On it were inscribed the name and age of the deceased—"George Somers, aged 26 years." The poor mother had been assisted to kneel down at the head of it. Her withered hands were clasped, as if in prayer, but I could perceive by a feeble rocking of the body and a convulsive motion of her lips that she was gazing on the last relics of her son with the yearnings of a mother's heart.

Preparations were made to deposit the coffin in the earth. There was that bustling stir which breaks so harshly on the feelings of grief and affection; direc-

tions given in the cold tones of business, the striking of
spades into sand and gravel, which, at the grave of
those we love, is, of all sounds, the most withering. The
bustle around seemed to waken the mother from a
wretched reverie. She raised her glazed eyes and looked
about with a faint wildness. As the men approached
with cords to lower the coffin into the grave, she wrung
her hands and broke into an agony of grief. The poor
woman who attended her took her by the arm, endeavoring to raise her from the earth and to whisper something
like consolation—"Nay, now—nay, now—don't take it
so sorely to heart." She could only shake her head and
wring her hands, as one not to be comforted.

As they lowered the body into the earth, the creaking of the cords seemed to agonize her; but when, on
some accidental obstruction, there was a justling of the
coffin, all the tenderness of the mother burst forth, as if
any harm could come to him who was far beyond the
reach of worldly suffering.

I could see no more—my heart swelled into my throat
—my eyes filled with tears—I felt as if I were acting a
barbarous part in standing by and gazing idly on this
scene of maternal anguish. I wandered to another part
of the churchyard, where I remained until the funeral
train had dispersed.

When I saw the mother slowly and painfully quit-
ting the grave, leaving behind her the remains of all
that was dear to her on earth and returning to silence
and destitution, my heart ached for her. What, thought
I, are the distresses of the rich! They have friends to
soothe—pleasures to beguile—a world to divert and dissipate their griefs. What are the sorrows of the young!
Their growing minds soon close above the wound—their
elastic spirits soon rise beneath the pressure—their green
and ductile affections soon twine around new objects.
But the sorrows of the poor, who have no outward appli-
ances to soothe; the sorrows of the aged, with whom
life at best is but a wintry day, and who can look for
no aftergrowth of joy; the sorrows of a widow, aged,
solitary, destitute, mourning over an only son, the last
solace of her years: these are indeed sorrows which
make us feel the impotency of consolation.

It was some time before I left the churchyard. On my way homeward I met with the woman who had acted as comforter; she was just returning from accompanying the mother to her lonely habitation, and I drew from her some particulars connected with the affecting scene I had witnessed.

The parents of the deceased had resided in the village from childhood. They had inhabited one of the neatest cottages, and by various rural occupations and the assistance of a small garden, had supported themselves creditably and comfortably and led a happy and a blameless life. They had one son, who had grown up to be the staff and pride of their age. "Oh, sir!" said the good woman, "he was such a comely lad, so sweet-tempered, so kind to everyone around him, so dutiful to his parents! It did one's heart good to see him of a Sunday, dressed out in his best, so tall, so straight, so cheery, supporting his old mother to church—for she was always fonder of leaning on George's arm than on her good man's; and, poor soul, she might well be proud of him, for a finer lad there was not in the country round."

Unfortunately, the son was tempted, during a year of scarcity and agricultural hardship, to enter into the service of one of the small craft that plied on a neighboring river. He had not been long in this employ when he was entrapped by a press gang and carried off to sea. His parents received tidings of his seizure, but beyond that they could learn nothing. It was the loss of their main prop. The father, who was already infirm, grew heartless and melancholy and sunk into his grave. The widow, left lonely in her age and feebleness, could no longer support herself and came upon the parish. Still there was a kind feeling toward her throughout the village, and a certain respect as being one of the oldest inhabitants. As no one applied for the cottage in which she had passed so many happy days, she was permitted to remain in it, where she lived solitary and almost helpless. The few wants of nature were chiefly supplied from the scanty productions of her little garden, which the neighbors would now and then cultivate for her. It was but a few days before the time at which these circumstances were told me that she was gathering some vegetables for her repast when she heard the cottage door which faced the garden suddenly opened. A stranger came out and seemed to be looking eagerly and wildly around. He was dressed in seaman's clothes, was emaciated and ghastly pale, and bore the air of one broken by sickness and hardships. He saw her and hastened toward her, but his steps were faint and faltering; he sank on his knees before her and sobbed like a child. The poor woman gazed upon him with a vacant and wandering eye—"Oh, my dear, dear mother! Don't you know your son? Your poor boy, George?" It was indeed the wreck of her once noble lad, who, shattered by wounds, by sickness and foreign imprisonment, had, at length, dragged his wasted limbs homeward, to repose among the scenes of his childhood.

I will not attempt to detail the particulars of such a meeting, where joy and sorrow were so completely blended. Still he was alive! He was come home! He might yet live to comfort and cherish her old age! Nature, however, was exhausted in him, and if anything had been wanting to finish the work of fate, the desolation of his native cottage would have been sufficient. He stretched himself on the pallet on which his widowed mother had passed many a sleepless night, and he never rose from it again.

The villagers, when they heard that George Somers had returned, crowded to see him, offering every comfort and assistance that their humble means afforded. He was too weak, however, to talk—he could only look his thanks. His mother was his constant attendant, and he seemed unwilling to be helped by any other hand.

There is something in sickness that breaks down the pride of manhood, that softens the heart and brings it back to the feelings of infancy. Who that has languished, even in advanced life, in sickness and despondency, who that has pined on a weary bed in the neglect and loneliness of a foreign land but has thought on the mother "that looked on his childhood," that smoothed his pillow and administered to his helplessness? Oh! There is an enduring tenderness in the love of a mother to her son that transcends all other affections of the heart. It is neither to be chilled by selfishness, nor daunted by danger, nor weakened by worthlessness, nor stifled by ingratitude. She will sacrifice every comfort to his convenience, she will surrender every pleasure to his enjoyment, she will glory in his fame and exult in his prosperity; and, if misfortune overtake him, he will be the dearer to her from misfortune; and if disgrace settle upon his name, she will still love and cherish him in spite of his disgrace; and if all the world beside cast him off, she will be all the world to him.

Poor George Somers had known what it was to be in sickness, and none to soothe—lonely and in prison, and none to visit him. He could not endure his mother from his sight; if she moved away, his eye would follow her. She would sit for hours by his bed, watching him as he slept. Sometimes he would start from a feverish dream and look anxiously up until he saw her bending over him, when he would take her hand, lay it on his bosom, and fall asleep, with the tranquillity of a child. In this way he died.

My first impulse on hearing this humble tale of affliction was to visit the cottage of the mourner and administer pecuniary assistance and, if possible, comfort. I found, however, on inquiry that the good feelings of the villagers had prompted them to do everything that the case admitted; and as the poor know best how to console each other's sorrows, I did not venture to intrude.

The next Sunday I was at the village church when, to my surprise, I saw the poor old woman tottering down the aisle to her accustomed seat on the steps of the altar.

She had made an effort to put on something like mourning for her son; and nothing could be more touching than this struggle between pious affection and utter poverty: a black ribbon or so, a faded black handkerchief, and one or two more such humble attempts to express by outward signs that grief which passes show. When I looked around upon the storied monuments, the stately hatchments, the cold marble pomp with which grandeur mourned magnificently over departed pride, and turned to this poor widow, bowed down by age and sorrow, at the altar of her God and offering up the prayers and praises of a pious though a broken heart, I felt that this living monument of real grief was worth them all.

I related her story to some of the wealthy members of the congregation, and they were moved by it. They exerted themselves to render her situation more comfortable and to lighten her afflictions. It was, however, but smoothing a few steps to the grave. In the course of a Sunday or two after, she was missed from her usual seat at church, and before I left the neighborhood I heard, with a feeling of satisfaction, that she had quietly breathed her last and had gone to rejoin those she loved, in that world where sorrow is never known and friends are never parted.

A SUNDAY IN LONDON*

In a preceding paper I have spoken of an English Sunday in the country and its tranquilizing effect upon the landscape; but where is its sacred influence more strikingly apparent than in the very heart of that great Babel, London? On this sacred day the gigantic monster is charmed into repose. The intolerable din and struggle of the week are at an end. The shops are shut. The fires of forges and manufactories are extinguished; and the sun, no longer obscured by murky clouds of smoke, pours down a sober, yellow radiance into the quiet streets. The few pedestrians we meet, instead of hurrying forward with anxious countenances, move leisurely along; their brows are smoothed from the wrinkles of business and care; they have put on their Sunday looks and Sunday manners with their Sunday clothes, and are cleansed in mind as well as in person.

And now the melodious clangor of bells from church towers summons their several flocks to the fold. Forth issues from his mansion the family of the decent trades-man, the small children in the advance; then the citizen and his comely spouse, followed by the grown-up daughters, with small morocco-bound prayerbooks laid in the folds of their pocket handkerchiefs. The housemaid looks

*Part of a sketch omitted in the preceding editions.

after them from the window, admiring the finery of the family and receiving, perhaps, a nod and smile from her young mistresses, at whose toilet she has assisted.

Now rumbles along the carriage of some magnate of the city, peradventure an alderman or a sheriff; and now the patter of many feet announces a procession of charity scholars, in uniforms of antique cut, and each with a prayerbook under his arm.

The ringing of bells is at an end; the rumbling of the carriage has ceased; the pattering of feet is heard no more; the flocks are folded in ancient churches, cramped up in by-lanes and corners of the crowded city, where the vigilant beadle keeps watch, like the shepherd's dog, around the threshold of the sanctuary. For a time everything is hushed; but soon is heard the deep, pervading sound of the organ, rolling and vibrating through the empty lanes and courts, and the sweet chanting of the choir making them resound with melody and praise. Never have I been more sensible of the sanctifying effect of church music than when I have heard it thus poured forth, like a river of joy, through the inmost recesses of this great metropolis, elevating it, as it were, from all the sordid pollutions of the week, and bearing the poor, world-worn soul on a tide of triumphant harmony to heaven.

The morning service is at an end. The streets are again alive with the congregations returning to their homes, but soon again relapse into silence. Now comes on the Sunday dinner, which, to the city tradesman, is a meal of some importance. There is more leisure for social enjoyment at the board. Members of the family can now gather together, who are separated by the laborious occupations of the week. A schoolboy may be permitted on that day to come to the paternal home; an old friend of the family takes his accustomed Sunday seat at the board, tells over his well-known stories and rejoices young and old with his well-known jokes.

On Sunday afternoon the city pours forth its legions to breathe the fresh air and enjoy the sunshine of the parks and rural environs. Satirists may say what they please about the rural enjoyments of a London citizen on Sunday, but to me there is something delightful in beholding the poor prisoner of the crowded and dusty city enabled thus to come forth once a week and throw himself upon the green bosom of nature. He is like a child restored to the mother's breast; and they who first spread out these noble parks and magnificent pleasure grounds which surround this huge metropolis have done at least as much for its health and morality as if they had expended the amount of cost in hospitals, prisons, and penitentiaries.

THE BOAR'S HEAD TAVERN, EASTCHEAP

A SHAKESPEAREAN RESEARCH

"A tavern is the rendezvous, the exchange, the staple of good fellows. I have heard my great-grandfather tell, how his great-great-grandfather should say, that it was an old proverb when his great-grandfather was a child, that 'it was a good wind that blew a man to the wine.'"

MOTHER BOMBIE

It is a pious custom, in some Catholic countries, to honor the memory of saints by votive lights burnt before their pictures. The popularity of a saint, therefore, may be known by the number of these offerings. One, perhaps, is left to molder in the darkness of his little chapel; another may have a solitary lamp to throw its blinking rays athwart his effigy; while the whole blaze of adoration is lavished at the shrine of some beatified father of renown. The wealthy devotee brings his huge luminary of wax; the eager zealot his seven-branched candlestick; and even the mendicant pilgrim is by no means satisfied that sufficient light is thrown upon the deceased unless he hangs up his little lamp of smoking oil. The consequence is that in the eagerness to enlighten they are often apt to obscure; and I have occasionally seen an unlucky saint almost smoked out of countenance by the officiousness of his followers.

In like manner has it fared with the immortal Shakespeare. Every writer considers it his bounden duty to light up some portion of his character or works and to rescue some merit from oblivion. The commentator, opulent in words, produces vast tomes of dissertations; the common herd of editors send up mists of obscurity from their notes at the bottom of each page; and every casual scribbler brings his farthing rushlight of eulogy or research to swell the cloud of incense and of smoke.

116

As I honor all established usages of my brethren of the quill, I thought it but proper to contribute my mite of homage to the memory of the illustrious bard. I was for some time, however, sorely puzzled in what way I should discharge this duty. I found myself anticipated in every attempt at a new reading; every doubtful line had been explained a dozen different ways and perplexed beyond the reach of elucidation; and as to fine passages, they had all been amply praised by previous admirers; nay, so completely had the bard, of late, been overlarded with panegyric by a great German critic that it was difficult now to find even a fault that had not been argued into a beauty.

In this perplexity, I was one morning turning over his pages when I casually opened upon the comic scenes of *Henry IV,* and was, in a moment, completely lost in the madcap revelry of the Boar's Head Tavern. So vividly and naturally are these scenes of humor depicted and with such force and consistency are the characters sustained that they become mingled up in the mind with the facts and personages of real life. To few readers does it occur that these are all ideal creations of a poet's brain and that, in sober truth, no such knot of merry roisters ever enlivened the dull neighborhood of Eastcheap.

For my part, I love to give myself up to the illusions of poetry. A hero of fiction that never existed is just as valuable to me as a hero of history that existed a thousand years since, and, if I may be excused such an insensibility to the common ties of human nature, I would not give up fat Jack for half the great men of ancient chronicle. What have the heroes of yore done for me, or men like me? They have conquered countries of which I do not enjoy an acre, or they have gained laurels of which I do not inherit a leaf, or they have furnished examples of hair-brained prowess which I have neither the opportunity nor the inclination to follow. But old Jack Falstaff! —kind Jack Falstaff!—sweet Jack Falstaff!—has enlarged the boundaries of human enjoyment; he has added vast regions of wit and good humor in which the poorest man may revel and has bequeathed a never-failing inheritance of jolly laughter to make mankind merrier and better to the latest posterity.

A thought suddenly struck me: "I will make a pilgrimage to Eastcheap," said I, closing the book, "and see if the old Boar's Head Tavern still exists. Who knows but I may light upon some legendary traces of Dame Quickly and her guests; at any rate, there will be a kindred pleasure in treading the halls once vocal with their mirth, to that the toper enjoys in smelling to the empty cask once filled with generous wine."

The resolution was no sooner formed than put in execution. I forbear to treat of the various adventures and wonders I encountered in my travels; of the haunted regions of Cock Lane; of the faded glories of Little Britain and the parts adjacent; what perils I ran in Cateaton-street and old Jewry; of the renowned Guildhall and its two stunted giants, the pride and wonder of the city, and the terror of all unlucky urchins; and how I visited London Stone and struck my staff upon it in imitation of that arch rebel, Jack Cade.

Let it suffice to say that I at length arrived in merry Eastcheap, that ancient region of wit and wassail where the very names of the streets relished of good cheer, as Pudding Lane bears testimony even at the present day. For Eastcheap, says old Stowe, "was always famous for its convivial doings. The cookes cried hot ribbes of beef roasted, pies well baked, and other victuals: there was clattering of pewter pots, harpe, pipe, and sawtrie." Alas! How sadly is the scene changed since the roaring days of Falstaff and old Stowe! The madcap roister has given place to the plodding tradesman; the clattering of pots and the sound of "harpe and sawtrie" to the din of carts and the accursed dinging of the dustman's bell; and no song is heard save, haply, the strain of some siren from Billingsgate, chanting the eulogy of deceased mackerel.

I sought, in vain, for the ancient abode of Dame Quickly. The only relic of it is a boar's head, carved in relief in stone, which formerly served as the sign but at present is built into the parting line of two houses, which stand on the site of the renowned old tavern.

For the history of this little abode of good fellowship, I was referred to a tallow chandler's widow, opposite, who had been born and brought up on the spot, and was looked up to as the indisputable chronicler of the neighborhood. I found her seated in a little back parlor, the window of which looked out upon a yard about eight feet square, laid out as a flower garden, while a glass door opposite afforded a distant peep of the street through a vista of soap and tallow candles: the two views, which comprised, in all probability, her prospects in life, and the little world in which she had lived and moved and had her being for the better part of a century.

To be versed in the history of Eastcheap, great and little, from London Stone even unto the Monument, was doubtless, in her opinion, to be acquainted with the history of the universe. Yet, with all this, she possessed the simplicity of true wisdom and that liberal communicative disposition which I have generally remarked in intelligent old ladies knowing in the concerns of their neighborhood.

Her information, however, did not extend far back into antiquity. She could throw no light upon the history of the Boar's Head, from the time that Dame Quickly espoused the valiant Pistol until the great fire of London, when it was unfortunately burnt down. It was soon rebuilt, and continued to flourish under the old name and sign until a dying landlord, struck with remorse for double scores, bad measures, and other iniquities which are incident to the sinful race of publicans, endeavored to make his peace with heaven by bequeathing the tavern to St. Michael's Church, Crooked Lane, toward the supporting of a chaplain. For some time the vestry meetings were regularly held there; but it was observed that the old Boar never held up his head under church government. He gradually declined and finally gave his last gasp about thirty years since. The tavern was then turned into shops; but she informed me that a picture of it was still preserved in St. Michael's Church, which stood just in the rear. To get a sight of this picture was now my determination; so, having informed myself of the abode of the sexton, I took my leave of the venerable chronicler of Eastcheap, my visit having doubtless raised greatly her opinion of her legendary lore and furnished an important incident in the history of her life.

It cost me some difficulty and much curious inquiry to ferret out the humble hanger-on to the church. I had to explore Crooked Lane, and diverse little alleys, and elbows, and dark passages, with which this old city is perforated like an ancient cheese or a worm-eaten chest of drawers. At length I traced him to a corner of a small court surrounded by lofty houses, where the inhabitants enjoy about as much of the face of heaven as a community of frogs at the bottom of a well.

The sexton was a meek, acquiescing little man, of a bowing, lowly habit; yet he had a pleasant twinkling in his eye, and, if encouraged, would now and then hazard a small pleasantry, such as a man of his low estate might venture to make in the company of high churchwardens and other mighty men of the earth. I found him in company with the deputy organist, seated apart, like Milton's angels, discoursing, no doubt, on high doctrinal points and settling the affairs of the church over a friendly pot of ale—for the lower classes of English seldom deliberate on any weighty matter without the assistance of a cool tankard to clear their understandings. I arrived at the moment when they had finished their ale and their argument and were about to repair to the church to put it in order; so, having made known my wishes, I received their gracious permission to accompany them.

The church of St. Michael's, Crooked Lane, standing a short distance from Billingsgate, is enriched with the tombs of many fishmongers of renown; and as every profession has its galaxy of glory and its constellation of great men, I presume the monument of a mighty fishmonger of the olden time is regarded with as much reverence by succeeding generations of the craft as poets feel on contemplating the tomb of Virgil or soldiers the monument of a Marlborough or Turenne.

I cannot but turn aside while thus speaking of illustrious men to observe that St. Michael's, Crooked Lane, contains also the ashes of that doughty champion, William Walworth, knight, who so manfully clove down the sturdy wight, Wat Tyler, in Smithfield; a hero worthy of honorable blazon, as almost the only Lord Mayor on record famous for deeds of arms, the sovereigns of Cockney being generally renowned as the most pacific of all potentates.*

Adjoining the church, in a small cemetery, immediately under the back window of what was once the Boar's Head, stands the tombstone of Robert Preston, whilom drawer at the tavern. It is now nearly a century since this trusty drawer of good liquor closed his bustling career and was thus quietly deposited within call of his customers. As I was clearing away the weeds from his epitaph, the little sexton drew me on one side with a mysterious air and informed me in a low voice that, once upon a time, on a dark wintry night, when the wind was unruly, howling, and whistling, banging about doors and windows and twirling weathercocks so that the living were frightened out of their beds and even the dead could not sleep quietly in their graves, the ghost of honest Preston, which happened to be airing itself in the churchyard, was attracted by the well-known call of "waiter" from the Boar's Head, and made its sudden appearance in the midst of a roaring club just as the parish clerk was singing a stave from the "mirre garland of Captain Death," to the discomfiture of sundry train-band captains and the conversion of an infidel attorney, who became a zealous Christian on the spot and was never known to twist the truth afterward, except in the way of business.

*The following was the ancient inscription on the monument of this worthy, which, unhappily, was destroyed in the great conflagration.

> Hereunder lyth a man of Fame,
> William Walworth callyd by name;
> Fishmonger he was in lyfftime here,
> And twise Lord Maior, as in books appere;
> Who, with courage stout and manly myght,
> Slew Jack Straw in Kyng Richard's sight.
> For which act done, and trew entent,
> The Kyng made him knyght incontinent;
> And gave him armes, as here you see,
> To declare his fact and chivaldrie.
> He left this lyff the yere of our God
> Thirteen hundred fourscore and three odd.

An error in the foregoing inscription has been corrected by the venerable Stowe. "Whereas," saith he, "it hath been far spread abroad by vulgar opinion, that the rebel smitten down so manfully by Sir William Walworth, the then worthy Lord Maior, was named Jack Straw, and not Wat Tyler, I thought good to reconcile this rash-conceived doubt by such testimony as I find in ancient and good records. The principal leaders, or captains, of the commons, were Wat Tyler, as the first man; the second was John, or Jack, Straw," etc., etc.

STOWE'S LONDON.

I beg it may be remembered that I do not pledge myself for the authenticity of this anecdote, though it is well known that the churchyards and by-corners of this old metropolis are very much infested with perturbed spirits, and everyone must have heard of the Cock Lane ghost and the apparition that guards the regalia in the Tower, which has frightened so many bold sentinels almost out of their wits.

Be all this as it may, this Robert Preston seems to have been a worthy successor to the nimble-tongued Francis, who attended upon the revels of Prince Hal; to have been equally prompt with his "anon, anon, sir"; and to have transcended his predecessor in honesty, for Falstaff, the veracity of whose taste no man will venture to impeach, flatly accuses Francis of putting lime in his sack, whereas honest Preston's epitaph lauds him for the sobriety of his conduct, the soundness of his wine, and the fairness of his measure.* The worthy dignitaries of the church, however, did not appear much captivated by the sober virtues of the tapster; the deputy organist, who had a moist look out of the eye, made some shrewd remark on the abstemiousness of a man brought up among full hogsheads, and the little sexton corroborated his opinion by a significant wink and a dubious shake of the head.

Thus far my researches, though they threw much light on the history of tapsters, fishmongers, and Lord Mayors, yet disappointed me in the great object of my quest, the picture of the Boar's Head Tavern. No such painting was to be found in the church of St. Michael. "Marry and amen!" said I. "Here endeth my research!"

---

*As this inscription is rife with excellent morality, I transcribe it for the admonition of delinquent tapsters. It is, no doubt, the production of some choice spirit, who once frequented the Boar's Head.

> Bacchus, to give the toping world surprise,
> Produced one sober son, and here he lies.
> Though rear'd among full hogsheads, he defy'd
> The charms of wine, and every one beside.
> O reader, if to justice thou'rt inclined,
> Keep honest Preston daily in thy mind.
> He drew good wine, took care to fill his pots,
> Had sundry virtues that excused his faults.
> You that on Bacchus have the like dependence,
> Pray copy Bob in measure and attendance.

So I was giving the matter up, with the air of a baffled antiquary, when my friend the sexton, perceiving me to be curious in everything relative to the old tavern, offered to show me the choice vessels of the vestry, which had been handed down from remote times when the parish meetings were held at the Boar's Head. These were deposited in the parish clubroom, which had been transferred, on the decline of the ancient establishment, to a tavern in the neighborhood.

A few steps brought us to the house, which stands No. 12 Miles Lane, bearing the title of The Mason's Arms, and is kept by Master Edward Honeyball, the "bully-rock" of the establishment. It is one of those little taverns which abound in the heart of the city and form the center of gossip and intelligence of the neighborhood. We entered the barroom, which was narrow and darkling, for in these close lanes but few rays of reflected light are enabled to struggle down to the inhabitants, whose broad day is at best but a tolerable twilight. The room was partitioned into boxes, each containing a table spread with a clean, white cloth, ready for dinner. This showed that the guests were of the good old stamp, and divided their day equally, for it was but just one o'clock. At the lower end of the room was a clear coal fire, before which a breast of lamb was roasting. A row of bright brass candlesticks and pewter mugs glistened along the mantelpiece, and an old-fashioned clock ticked in one corner. There was something primitive in this medley of kitchen, parlor, and hall that carried me back to earlier times and pleased me. The place, indeed, was humble, but everything had that look of order and neatness which bespeaks the superintendence of a notable English housewife. A group of amphibious-looking beings, who might be either fishermen or sailors, were regaling themselves in one of the boxes. As I was a visitor of rather higher pretensions, I was ushered into a little misshapen backroom having at least nine corners. It was lighted by a skylight, furnished with antiquated leathern chairs, and ornamented with the portrait of a fat pig. It was evidently appropriated to particular customers, and I found a shabby gentleman, in a red nose and oil-cloth hat, seated in one corner, meditating on a half-empty pot of porter.

The old sexton had taken the landlady aside, and with an air of profound importance imparted to her my errand. Dame Honeyball was a likely, plump, bustling little woman, and no bad substitute for that paragon of hostesses, Dame Quickly. She seemed delighted with an opportunity to oblige, and, hurrying up stairs to the archives of her house, where the precious vessels of the parish club were deposited, she returned, smiling and courtesying, with them in her hands.

The first she presented me was a japanned iron tobacco box, of gigantic size, out of which, I was told, the vestry had smoked at their stated meetings since time immemorial, and which was never suffered to be profaned by vulgar hands or used on common occasions. I received it with becoming reverence, but what was my delight at beholding on its cover the identical painting of which I was in quest! There was displayed the outside of the Boar's Head Tavern, and before the door was to be seen the whole convivial group, at table, in full revel, pictured with that wonderful fidelity and force with which the portraits of renowned generals and commodores are illustrated on tobacco boxes for the benefit of posterity. Lest, however, there should be any mistake, the cunning limner had warily inscribed the names of Prince Hal and Falstaff on the bottoms of their chairs.

On the inside of the cover was an inscription, nearly obliterated, recording that this box was the gift of Sir Richard Gore, for the use of the vestry meetings at the Boar's Head Tavern, and that it was "repaired and beautified by his successor, Mr. John Packard, 1767." Such is a faithful description of this august and venerable relic, and I question whether the learned Scriblerius contemplated his Roman shield, or the Knights of the Round Table the long-sought Sangreal, with more exultation.

While I was meditating on it with enraptured gaze, Dame Honeyball, who was highly gratified by the interest it excited, put in my hands a drinking cup, or goblet, which also belonged to the vestry and was descended from the old Boar's Head. It bore the inscription of having been the gift of Francis Wythers, knight, and was held, she told me, in exceeding great value, being considered very "antyke." This last opinion was strengthened by the shabby gentleman in the red nose and oilcloth hat, and whom I strongly suspected of being a lineal descendant from the valiant Bardolph. He suddenly roused from his meditation on the pot of porter and, casting a knowing look at the goblet, exclaimed, "Aye, aye! The head don't ache now that made that there article!"

The great importance attached to this memento of ancient revelry by modern churchwardens at first puzzled me, but there is nothing sharpens the apprehension so much as antiquarian research, for I immediately perceived that this could be no other than the identical "parcel-gilt goblet" on which Falstaff made his loving but faithless vow to Dame Quickly, and which would, of course, be treasured up with care among the regalia of her domains as a testimony of that solemn contract.*

Mine hostess, indeed, gave me a long history how the goblet had been handed down from generation to generation. She also entertained me with many particulars concerning the worthy vestrymen who have seated themselves thus quietly on the stools of the ancient roisters of Eastcheap, and, like so many commentators, utter clouds of smoke in honor of Shakespeare. These I forbear to relate, lest my readers should not be as curious in these matters as myself. Suffice it to say, the neighbors, one and all, about Eastcheap, believe that Falstaff and his merry crew actually lived and reveled there. Nay, there are several legendary anecdotes concerning him still extant among the oldest frequenters of the Mason's Arms, which they give as transmitted down from their forefathers; and Mr. M'Kash, an Irish hairdresser whose shop stands on the site of the old Boar's Head, has several dry jokes of Fat Jack's not laid down in the books, with which he makes his customers ready to die of laughter.

I now turned to my friend the sexton to make some further inquiries, but I found him sunk in pensive meditation. His head had declined a little on one side; a deep

---

*Thou didst swear to me upon a *parcel-gilt goblet*, sitting in my Dolphin chamber, at the round table, by a sea-coal fire, on Wednesday, in Whitsunweek, when the prince broke thy head for likening his father to a singing man at Windsor; thou didst swear to me then, as I was washing thy wound, to marry me, and make me my lady, thy wife. Canst thou deny it?—*Henry IV, Part* 2.

sigh heaved from the very bottom of his stomach; and,
though I could not see a tear trembling in his eye, yet a
moisture was evidently stealing from a corner of his
mouth. I followed the direction of his eye through the
door which stood open and found it fixed wistfully on
the savory breast of lamb, roasting in dripping richness
before the fire.

I now called to mind that, in the eagerness of my rec-
ondite investigation, I was keeping the poor man from
his dinner. My bowels yearned with sympathy, and, putting in his hand a small token of my gratitude and goodness, I departed, with a hearty benediction on him,
Dame Honeyball, and the Parish Club of Crooked Lane,
not forgetting my shabby but sententious friend in the
oil-cloth hat and copper nose.

Thus have I given a "tedious brief" account of this
interesting research, for which, if it prove too short and
unsatisfactory, I can only plead my inexperience in this
branch of literature, so deservedly popular at the present day. I am aware that a more skillful illustrator of
the immortal bard would have swelled the materials I
have touched upon to a good merchantable bulk, com-
prising the biographies of William Walworth, Jack Straw,
and Robert Preston; some notice of the eminent fishmongers of St. Michael's; the history of Eastcheap, great
and little, private anecdotes of Dame Honeyball, and her
pretty daughter, whom I have not even mentioned; to say
nothing of a damsel tending the breast of lamb (and
whom, by the way, I remarked to be a comely lass, with a
neat foot and ankle)—the whole enlivened by the riots
of Wat Tyler and illuminated by the great fire of London.

All this I leave, as a rich mine, to be worked by future commentators; nor do I despair of seeing the tobacco box and the "parcel-gilt goblet," which I have thus
brought to light, the subjects of future engravings, and
almost as fruitful of voluminous dissertations and disputes as the shield of Achilles or the far-famed Portland
vase.

THE MUTABILITY OF LITERATURE

A COLLOQUY IN WESTMINSTER ABBEY

I know that all beneath the moon decays,
And what by mortals in this world is brought,
In time's great period shall return to nought.
I know that all the muse's heavenly lays,
With toil of sprite which are so dearly bought,
As idle sounds, of few or none are sought,
That there is nothing lighter than mere praise.

DRUMMOND OF HAWTHORNDEN

There are certain half-dreaming moods of mind in which we naturally steal away from noise and glare and seek some quiet haunt, where we may indulge our reveries and build our air castles undisturbed. In such a mood I was loitering about the old gray cloisters of Westminster Abbey, enjoying that luxury of wandering thought which one is apt to dignify with the name of reflection, when suddenly an interruption of madcap boys from Westminster School, playing at football, broke in upon the monastic stillness of the place, making the vaulted passages and moldering tombs echo with their merriment. I sought to take refuge from their noise by penetrating still deeper into the solitudes of the pile, and applied to one of the vergers for admission to the library. He conducted me through a portal rich with the crumbling sculpture of former ages, which opened upon a gloomy passage leading to the chapter house and the chamber in which doomsday book is deposited. Just within the passage is a small door on the left. To this the verger applied a key; it was double-locked, and opened with some difficulty, as if seldom used. We now ascended a dark, narrow staircase, and, passing through a second door, entered the library.

I found myself in a lofty antique hall, the roof supported by massive joists of old English oak. It was soberly lighted by a row of Gothic windows at a considerable height from the floor and which apparently opened upon the roofs of the cloisters. An ancient picture of some reverend dignitary of the church in his robes hung over the fireplace. Around the hall and in a small gallery were the books, arranged in carved oaken cases. They consisted principally of old polemical writers, and were much more worn by time than use. In the center of the library was a solitary table with two or three books on it, an inkstand without ink, and a few pens parched by long disuse. The place seemed fitted for quiet study and profound meditation. It was buried deep among the massive walls of the abbey and shut up from the tumult of the world. I could only hear now and then the shouts of the schoolboys faintly swelling from the cloisters and the sound of a bell tolling for prayers, echoing soberly along the roofs of the abbey. By degrees the shouts of merriment grew fainter and fainter, and at length died away; the bell ceased to toll, and a profound silence reigned through the dusky hall.

I had taken down a little thick quarto, curiously bound in parchment, with brass clasps, and seated myself at the table in a venerable elbow chair. Instead of reading, however, I was beguiled by the solemn monastic air and lifeless quiet of the place into a train of musing. As I looked around upon the old volumes in their moldering covers, thus ranged on the shelves, and apparently never disturbed in their repose, I could not but consider the library a kind of literary catacomb, where authors, like mummies, are piously entombed and left to blacken and molder in dusty oblivion.

How much, thought I, has each of these volumes, now thrust aside with such indifference, cost some aching head! How many weary days! How many sleepless nights! How have their authors buried themselves in the solitude of cells and cloisters, shut themselves up from the face of man and the still more blessed face of nature, and devoted themselves to painful research and intense reflection! And all for what? To occupy an inch of dusty shelf—to have the title of their works read now and then in a future age by some drowsy churchman or casual straggler like myself, and in another age to be lost, even to remembrance. Such is the amount of this boasted immortality. A mere temporary rumor, a local sound, like the tone of that bell which has just tolled among these towers, filling the ear for a moment—lingering transiently in echo—and then passing away like a thing that was not.

While I sat half-murmuring, half-meditating these unprofitable speculations with my head resting on my hand, I was thrumming with the other hand upon the quarto, until I accidentally loosened the clasps; when, to my utter astonishment, the little book gave two or three yawns, like one awaking from a deep sleep, then a husky hem, and at length began to talk. At first its voice was very hoarse and broken, being much troubled by a cobweb which some studious spider had woven across it, and having probably contracted a cold from long exposure to the chills and damps of the abbey. In a short time, however, it became more distinct, and I soon found it an exceedingly fluent conversable little tome. Its language, to be sure, was rather quaint and obsolete, and its pronunciation, what, in the present day, would be deemed barbarous; but I shall endeavor, as far as I am able, to render it in modern parlance.

It began with railings about the neglect of the world—about merit being suffered to languish in obscurity and other such commonplace topics of literary repining, and complained bitterly that it had not been opened for more than two centuries. That the dean only looked now and then into the library, sometimes took down a volume or two, trifled with them for a few moments, and then returned them to their shelves. "What a plague do they mean," said the little quarto, which I began to perceive was somewhat choleric, "what a plague do they mean by keeping several thousand volumes of us shut up here, and watched by a set of old vergers, like so many beauties in a harem, merely to be looked at now and then by the dean? Books were written to give pleasure and to be enjoyed; and I would have a rule passed that the dean should pay each of us a visit at least once a year; or if he is not equal to the task, let them once in a while turn loose the whole school of Westminster among us, that at any rate we may now and then have an airing."

"Softly, my worthy friend," replied I, "you are not aware how much better you are off than most books of your generation. By being stored away in this ancient library, you are like the treasured remains of those saints and monarchs, which lie enshrined in the adjoining chapels, while the remains of your contemporary mortals, left to the ordinary course of nature, have long since returned to dust."

"Sir," said the little tome, ruffling his leaves and looking big, "I was written for all the world, not for the bookworms of an abbey. I was intended to circulate from hand to hand, like other great contemporary works; but here have I been clasped up for more than two centuries, and might have silently fallen a prey to these worms that are playing the very vengeance with my intestines if you had not by chance given me an opportunity of uttering a few last words before I go to pieces."

"My good friend," rejoined I, "had you been left to the circulation of which you speak you would long ere this have been no more. To judge from your physiognomy, you are now well stricken in years; very few of your contemporaries can be at present in existence, and those few owe their longevity to being immured like yourself in old libraries, which, suffer me to add, instead of likening to harems, you might more properly and gratefully have compared to those infirmaries attached to religious establishments for the benefit of the old and decrepit and where, by quiet fostering and no employment, they often endure to an amazingly good-for-nothing old age. You talk of your contemporaries as if in circulation—where do we meet with their works? What do we hear of Robert Grosseteste, of Lincoln? No one could have toiled harder than he for immortality. He is said to have written nearly two hundred volumes. He built, as it were, a pyramid of books to perpetuate his name. But, alas! the pyramid has long since fallen, and only a few fragments are scattered in various libraries, where they are scarcely disturbed even by the antiquarian. What do we hear of Giraldus Cambrensis, the historian, antiquary, philosopher, theologian, and poet? He declined two bishoprics that he might shut himself up and write for posterity; but posterity never inquires after his labors. What of Henry of Huntingdon, who, besides a learned history of England, wrote a treatise on the contempt of the world, which the world has revenged by forgetting him? What is quoted of Joseph of Exeter, styled the miracle of his age in classical composition? Of his three great heroic poems one is lost forever, excepting a mere fragment; the others are known only to a few of the curious in literature; and as to his love verses and epigrams, they have entirely disappeared. What is in current use of John Wallis, the Franciscan, who acquired the name of the tree of life? Of William of Malmsbury; of Simeon of Durham; of Benedict of Peterborough; of John Hanvill of St. Albans, of . . ."

"Prithee, friend," cried the quarto, in a testy tone, "how old do you think me? You are talking of authors that lived long before my time, and wrote either in Latin or French, so that they in a manner expatriated themselves, and deserved to be forgotten;* but I, sir, was ushered into the world from the press of the renowned Wynkyn de Worde. I was written in my own native tongue, at a time when the language had become fixed, and indeed I was considered a model of pure and elegant English."

(I should observe that these remarks were couched in such intolerably antiquated terms that I have had infinite difficulty in rendering them into modern phraseology.)

"I cry your mercy," said I, "for mistaking your age, but it matters little; almost all the writers of your time have likewise passed into forgetfulness, and De Worde's publications are mere literary rarities among book collectors. The purity and stability of language, too, on which you found your claims to perpetuity have been the fallacious dependence of authors of every age, even back to the times of the worthy Robert of Gloucester, who

---

*In Latin and French hath many soueraine wittes had great delyte to endite, and have many noble things fulfilde, but certes there ben some that speaken their poisye in French, or which speche the Frenchmen have as good a fantasye as we have in hearying of Frenchmen's Englishe.—*Chaucer's Testament of Love.*

wrote his history in rhymes of mongrel Saxon.* Even now many talk of Spenser's 'well of pure English undefiled,' as if the language ever sprang from a well or fountainhead, and was not rather a mere confluence of various tongues, perpetually subject to changes and intermixtures. It is this which has made English literature so extremely mutable, and the reputation built upon it so fleeting. Unless thought can be committed to something more permanent and unchangeable than such a medium, even thought must share the fate of everything else and fall into decay. This should serve as a check upon the vanity and exultation of the most popular writer. He finds the language in which he has embarked his fame gradually altering, and subject to the dilapidations of time and the caprice of fashion. He looks back and beholds the early authors of his country, once the favorites of their day, supplanted by modern writers. A few short ages have covered them with obscurity, and their merits can only be relished by the quaint taste of the bookworm. And such, he anticipates, will be the fate of his own work, which, however it may be admired in its day and held up as a model of purity, will in the course of years grow antiquated and obsolete, until it shall become almost as unintelligible in its native land as an Egyptian obelisk, or one of those Runic inscriptions said to exist in the deserts of Tartary. I declare," added I, with some emotion, "when I contemplate a modern library, filled with new works, in all the bravery of rich gilding and binding, I feel disposed to sit down and weep, like the good Xerxes, when he surveyed his army, pranked out in all the splendor of military array, and reflected that in one hundred years not one of them would be in existence!"

"Ah," said the little quarto, with a heavy sigh, "I see how it is; these modern scribblers have superseded all

---

*Holinshed, in his Chronicle, observes, "afterwards, also, by deligent travell of Geffry Chaucer and of John Gowre, in the time of Richard the Second, and after them of John Scogan and John Lydgate, monke of Berrie, our said toong was brought to an excellent passe, notwithstanding that it never came unto the type of perfection until the time of Queen Elizabeth, wherein John Jewell, Bishop of Sarum, John Fox, and sundrie learned and excellent writers, have fully accomplished the ornature of the same, to their great praise and immortal commendation."

the good old authors. I suppose nothing is read nowadays but Sir Philip Sidney's *Arcadia*, Sackville's stately plays, and *Mirror for Magistrates*, or the fine-spun euphuisms of the 'unparalleled John Lyly.'"

"There you are again mistaken," said I. "The writers whom you suppose in vogue, because they happened to be so when you were last in circulation, have long since had their day. Sir Philip Sidney's *Arcadia*, the immortality of which was so fondly predicted by his admirers,* and which, in truth, is full of noble thoughts, delicate images, and graceful turns of language, is now scarcely ever mentioned. Sackville has strutted into obscurity; and even Lyly, though his writings were once the delight of a court and apparently perpetuated by a proverb, is now scarcely known even by name. A whole crowd of authors who wrote and wrangled at the time have likewise gone down, with all their writings and their controversies. Wave after wave of succeeding literature has rolled over them, until they are buried so deep that it is only now and then that some industrious diver after fragments of antiquity brings up a specimen for the gratification of the curious.

"For my part," I continued, "I consider this mutability of language a wise precaution of Providence for the benefit of the world at large, and of authors in particular. To reason from analogy, we daily behold the varied and beautiful tribes of vegetables springing up, flourishing, adorning the fields for a short time, and then fading into dust, to make way for their successors. Were not this the case, the fecundity of nature would be a grievance instead of a blessing. The earth would groan with rank and excessive vegetation, and its surface become a tangled wilderness. In like manner the works of genius and learning decline and make way for subsequent productions. Language gradually varies, and with it fade away the writings of authors who have flourished their allotted

---

*Live ever sweete booke; the simple image of his gentle witt, and the golden-pillar of his noble courage; and ever notify unto the world that thy writer was the secretary of eloquence, the breath of the muses, the honey-bee of the daintyest flowers of witt and arte, the pith of morale and intellectual virtues, the arme of Bellona in the field, the tonge of Suada in the chamber, the sprite of Practise in esse, and the paragon of excellency in print.—*Harvey Pierce's Supererogation.*

time; otherwise, the creative powers of genius would over-
stock the world and the mind would be completely bewildered in the endless mazes of literature. Formerly there
were some restraints on this excessive multiplication.
Works had to be transcribed by hand, which was a slow
and laborious operation; they were written either on
parchment, which was expensive, so that one work was
often erased to make way for another, or on papyrus,
which was fragile and extremely perishable. Authorship
was a limited and unprofitable craft, pursued chiefly by
monks in the leisure and solitude of their cloisters. The
accumulation of manuscripts was slow and costly and
confined almost entirely to monasteries. To these circumstances it may, in some measure, be owing that we have
not been inundated by the intellect of antiquity, that the
fountains of thought have not been broken up and modern
genius drowned in the deluge. But the inventions of paper
and the press have put an end to all these restraints. They
have made everyone a writer and enabled every mind
to pour itself into print and diffuse itself over the whole
intellectual world. The consequences are alarming. The
stream of literature has swollen into a torrent—augmented into a river—expanded into a sea. A few centuries
since, five or six hundred manuscripts constituted a
great library; but what would you say to libraries such as
actually exist, containing three or four hundred thousand volumes; legions of authors at the same time busy;
and the press going on with fearfully increasing activity,
to double and quadruple the number? Unless some unforeseen mortality should break out among the progeny
of the muse, now that she has become so prolific, I
tremble for posterity. I fear the mere fluctuation of
language will not be sufficient. Criticism may do much.
It increases with the increase of literature and resembles
one of those salutary checks on population spoken of
by economists. All possible encouragement, therefore,
should be given to the growth of critics, good or bad.
But I fear all will be in vain; let criticism do what it may,
writers will write, printers will print, and the world will
inevitably be overstocked with good books. It will soon
be the employment of a lifetime merely to learn their
names. Many a man of passable information, at the pres-

ent day, reads scarcely anything but reviews; and before long a man of erudition will be little better than a mere walking catalogue."

"My very good sir," said the little quarto, yawning most drearily in my face, "excuse my interrupting you, but I perceive you are rather given to prose. I would ask the fate of an author who was making some noise just as I left the world. His reputation, however, was considered quite temporary. The learned shook their heads at him, for he was a poor, half-educated varlet who knew little of Latin and nothing of Greek and had been obliged to run the country for deer stealing. I think his name was Shakespeare. I presume he soon sank into oblivion."

"On the contrary," said I, "it is owing to that very man that the literature of his period has experienced a duration beyond the ordinary term of English literature. There rise authors now and then who seem proof against the mutability of language because they have rooted themselves in the unchanging principles of human nature. They are like gigantic trees that we sometimes see on the banks of a stream, which, by their vast and deep roots, penetrating through the mere surface and laying hold on the very foundations of the earth, preserve the soil around them from being swept away by the ever-flowing current and hold up many a neighboring plant and, perhaps, worthless weed to perpetuity. Such is the case with Shakespeare, whom we behold defying the encroachments of time, retaining in modern use the language and literature of his day, and giving duration to many an indifferent author, merely from having flourished in his vicinity. But even he, I grieve to say, is gradually assuming the tint of age, and his whole form is overrun by a profusion of commentators, who, like clambering vines and creepers, almost bury the noble plant that upholds them."

Here the little quarto began to heave his sides and chuckle, until at length he broke out in a plethoric fit of laughter that had well nigh choked him, by reason of his excessive corpulency. "Mighty well!" cried he, as soon as he could recover breath. "Mighty well! And so you would persuade me that the literature of an age is to be perpetuated by a vagabond deer stealer! By a man without learning; by a poet, forsooth—a poet!" And here he wheezed forth another fit of laughter.

I confess that I felt somewhat nettled at this rudeness, which, however, I pardoned on account of his having flourished in a less polished age. I determined, nevertheless, not to give up my point.

"Yes," resumed I, positively, "a poet; for of all writers he has the best chance for immortality. Others may write from the head, but he writes from the heart, and the heart will always understand him. He is the faithful portrayer of nature, whose features are always the same and always interesting. Prose writers are voluminous and unwieldy; their pages are crowded with commonplaces and their thoughts expanded into tediousness. But with the true poet everything is terse, touching, or brilliant. He gives the choicest thoughts in the choicest language. He illustrates them by everything that he sees most striking in nature and art. He enriches them by pictures of human life, such as it is passing before him. His writings, therefore, contain the spirit, the aroma, if I may use the phrase, of the age in which he lives. They are caskets which enclose within a small compass the wealth of the language—its family jewels, which are thus transmitted in a portable form to posterity. The setting may occasionally be antiquated and require now and then to be renewed, as in the case of Chaucer; but the brilliancy and intrinsic value of the gems continue unaltered. Cast a look back over the long reach of literary history. What vast valleys of dullness, filled with monkish legends and academical controversies! What bogs of theological speculations! What dreary wastes of metaphysics! Here and there only do we behold the heaven-illuminated bards, elevated like beacons on their widely separate heights, to transmit the pure light of poetical intelligence from age to age." *

*Thorow earth and waters deepe,
  The pen by skill doth passe:
And featly nyps the worldes abuse,
  And shoes us in a glasse,
The vertu and the vice
  Of every wight alyve;
The honey comb that bee doth make
  Is not so sweet in hyve,
As are the golden leves
  That drop from poet's head!
Which doth surmount our common talke
  As farre as dross doth lead.

Churchyard

I was just about to launch forth into eulogiums upon the poets of the day when the sudden opening of the door caused me to turn my head. It was the verger, who came to inform me that it was time to close the library. I sought to have a parting word with the quarto, but the worthy little tome was silent; the clasps were closed, and it looked perfectly unconscious of all that had passed. I have been to the library two or three times since, and have endeavored to draw it into further conversation, but in vain; and whether all this rambling colloquy actually took place or whether it was another of those odd daydreams to which I am subject, I have never to this moment been able to discover.

RURAL FUNERALS

Here's a few flowers! but about midnight more:
The herbs that have on them cold dew o' the night;
Are strewings fitt'st for graves——
You were as flowers now wither'd; even so
These herblets shall, which we upon you strow.
                                        CYMBELINE

Among the beautiful and simple-hearted customs of rural
life which still linger in some parts of England are
those of strewing flowers before the funerals and planting
them at the graves of departed friends. These, it is said,
are the remains of some of the rites of the primitive
church; but they are of still higher antiquity, having been
observed among the Greeks and Romans and frequently
mentioned by their writers, and were, no doubt, the spontaneous tributes of unlettered affection, originating long
before art had tasked itself to modulate sorrow into song,
or story it on the monument. They are now only to be
met with in the most distant and retired places of the
kingdom, where fashion and innovation have not been
able to throng in and trample out all the curious and interesting traces of the olden time.

In Glamorganshire, we are told, the bed whereon the
corpse lies is covered with flowers, a custom alluded to in
one of the wild and plaintive ditties of Ophelia:

> White his shroud as the mountain snow
>   Larded all with sweet flowers;
> Which be-wept to the grave did go,
>   With true love showers.

There is also a most delicate and beautiful rite observed in some of the remote villages of the south, at the
funeral of a female who has died young and unmarried.

A chaplet of white flowers is borne before the corpse by a young girl nearest in age, size, and resemblance, and is afterward hung up in the church over the accustomed seat of the deceased. These chaplets are sometimes made of white paper, in imitation of flowers, and inside of them is generally a pair of white gloves. They are intended as emblems of the purity of the deceased and the crown of glory which she has received in heaven.

In some parts of the country, also, the dead are carried to the grave with the singing of psalms and hymns: a kind of triumph, "to show," says Bourne, "that they have finished their course with joy, and are become conquerors." This, I am informed, is observed in some of the northern counties, particularly in Northumberland, and it has a pleasing though melancholy effect, to hear, of a still evening in some lonely country scene, the mournful melody of a funeral dirge swelling from a distance, and to see the train slowly moving along the landscape.

> Thus, thus, and thus, we compass round
>   Thy harmlesse and unhaunted ground,
> And as we sing thy dirge, we will
>   The daffodill
> And other flowers lay upon
> The altar of our love, thy stone.
>   HERRICK

There is also a solemn respect paid by the traveler to the passing funeral in these sequestered places, for such spectacles, occurring among the quiet abodes of nature, sink deep into the soul. As the mourning train approaches, he pauses, uncovered, to let it go by; he then follows silently in the rear, sometimes quite to the grave, at other times for a few hundred yards, and, having paid this tribute of respect to the deceased, turns and resumes his journey.

The rich vein of melancholy which runs through the English character and gives it some of its most touching and ennobling graces is finely evidenced in these pathetic customs and in the solicitude shown by the common people for an honored and a peaceful grave. The humblest peasant, whatever may be his lowly lot while living, is anxious that some little respect may be paid to his re-

mains. Sir Thomas Overbury, describing the "faire and
happy milkmaid," observes, "thus lives she, and all her
care is, that she may die in the spring-time, to have store
of flowers stucke upon her windingsheet." The poets, too,
who always breathe the feeling of a nation, continually
advert to this fond solicitude about the grave. In *The
Maid's Tragedy*, by Beaumont and Fletcher, there is a
beautiful instance of the kind, describing the capricious
melancholy of a brokenhearted girl:

> When she sees a bank
> Stuck full of flowers, she, with a sigh, will tell
> Her servants, what a pretty place it were
> To bury lovers in; and make her maids
> Pluck 'em, and slew her over like a corse.

The custom of decorating graves was once universally
prevalent; osiers were carefully bent over them to keep
the turf uninjured, and about them were planted evergreens and flowers. "We adorn their graves," says Evelyn,
in his *Sylva*, "with flowers and redolent plants, just emblems of the life of man, which has been compared in
Holy Scriptures to those fading beauties, whose roots
being buried in dishonor, rise again in glory." This
usage has now become extremely rare in England, but it
may still be met with in the churchyards of retired
villages, among the Welsh mountains; and I recollect an
instance of it at the small town of Ruthen, which lies at
the head of the beautiful vale of Clewyd. I have been
told also by a friend, who was present at the funeral of a
young girl in Glamorganshire, that the female attendants
had their aprons full of flowers, which, as soon as the
body was interred, they stuck about the grave.

He noticed several graves which had been decorated
in the same manner. As the flowers had been merely
stuck in the ground, and not planted, they had soon
withered, and might be seen in various states of decay,
some drooping, others quite perished. They were afterward to be supplanted by holly, rosemary, and other
evergreens, which on some graves had grown to great
luxuriance and overshadowed the tombstones.

There was formerly a melancholy fancifulness in the

arrangement of these rustic offerings that had something in it truly poetical. The rose was sometimes blended with the lily, to form a general emblem of frail mortality. "This sweet flower," said Evelyn, "borne on a branch set with thorns and accompanied with the lily are natural hieroglyphics of our fugitive, umbratile, anxious, and transitory life, which, making so fair a show for a time, is not yet without its thorns and crosses." The nature and color of the flowers, and of the ribbons with which they were tied, had often a particular reference to the qualities or story of the deceased, or were expressive of the feelings of the mourner. In an old poem, entitled *Corydon's Doleful Knell,* a lover specifies the decorations he intends to use:

> A garland shall be framed
>   By art and nature's skill,
> Of sundry-color'd flowers,
>   In token of good-will.
>
> And sundry-color'd ribands
>   On it I will bestow;
> But chiefly blacke and yellowe
>   With her to grave shall go.
>
> I'll deck her tomb with flowers,
>   The rarest ever seen;
> And with my tears as showers,
>   I'll keep them fresh and green.

The white rose, we are told, was planted at the grave of a virgin; her chaplet was tied with white ribbons, in token of her spotless innocence, though sometimes black ribbons were intermingled, to bespeak the grief of the survivors. The red rose was occasionally used in remembrance of such as had been remarkable for benevolence, but roses in general were appropriated to the graves of lovers. Evelyn tells us that the custom was not altogether extinct in his time, near his dwelling in the county of Surrey, "where the maidens yearly planted and decked the graves of their defunct sweethearts with rosebushes." And Camden likewise remarks, in his *Britannia*: "Here is also a certain custom, observed time out of mind, of planting rose trees upon the graves, especially by the young men and maids who have lost their loves; so that this churchyard is now full of them."

When the deceased had been unhappy in their loves, emblems of a more gloomy character were used, such as the yew and cypress, and if flowers were strewn, they were of the most melancholy colors. Thus, in poems by Thomas Stanley, Esq. (published in 1651), is the following stanza:

> Yet strew
> Upon my dismall grave
> Such offerings as you have,
>   Forsaken cypresse and sad yewe;
> For kinder flowers can take no birth
> Or growth from such unhappy earth.

In *The Maid's Tragedy*, a pathetic little air is introduced, illustrative of this mode of decorating the funerals of females who had been disappointed in love:

> Lay a garland on my hearse.
>   Of the dismall yew,
> Maidens, willow branches wear,
>   Say I died true.
>
> My love was false, but I was firm,
>   From my hour of birth,
> Upon my buried body lie
>   Lightly, gentle earth.

The natural effect of sorrow over the dead is to refine and elevate the mind, and we have a proof of it in the purity of sentiment and the unaffected elegance of thought which pervaded the whole of these funeral observances. Thus, it was an especial precaution that none but sweet-scented evergreens and flowers should be employed. The intention seems to have been to soften the horrors of the tomb, to beguile the mind from brooding over the disgraces of perishing mortality, and to associate the memory of the deceased with the most delicate and beautiful objects in nature. There is a dismal process going on in the grave, ere dust can return to its kindred dust, which the imagination sinks from contemplating; and we seek still to think of the form we have loved with those refined associations which it awakened when blooming before us in youth and beauty. "Lay her i' the earth," sayd Laertes, of his virgin sister,

> And from her fair and unpolluted flesh
> May violets spring!

Herrick, also, in his *Dirge of Jephtha,* pours forth a fragrant flow of poetical thought and image, which in a manner embalms the dead in the recollections of the living.

> Sleep in thy peace, thy bed of spice,
> And make this place all Paradise:
> May sweets grow here! and smoke from hence
> Fat frankincense.
> Let balme and cassia send their scent
> From out thy maiden monument.
>
> * * * * * *
>
> May all shie maids at wonted hours
> Come forth to strew thy tombe with flowers!
> May virgins, when they come to mourn,
> Male incense burn
> Upon thine altar! then return
> And leave thee sleeping in thine urn.

I might crowd my pages with extracts from the older British poets who wrote when these rites were more prevalent, and delighted frequently to allude to them, but I have already quoted more than is necessary. I cannot, however, refrain from giving a passage from Shakespeare, even though it should appear trite, which illustrates the emblematical meaning often conveyed in these floral tributes, and at the same time possesses that magic of language and appositeness of imagery for which he stands pre-eminent.

> With fairest flowers,
> Whilst summer lasts, and I live here, Fidele,
> I'll sweeten thy sad grave; thou shalt not lack
> The flower that's like thy face, pale primrose; nor
> The azured harebell, like thy veins; no, nor
> The leaf of eglantine; whom not to slander,
> Outsweeten'd not thy breath.

There is certainly something more affecting in these prompt and spontaneous offerings of nature than in the most costly monuments of art; the hand strews the flower while the heart is warm and the tear falls on the grave as affection is binding the osier round the sod; but pathos expires under the slow labor of the chisel and is chilled among the cold conceits of sculptured marble.

It is greatly to be regretted that a custom so truly elegant and touching has disappeared from general use, and exists only in the most remote and insignificant villages. But it seems as if poetical custom always shuns the walks of cultivated society. In proportion as people grow polite they cease to be poetical. They talk of poetry, but they have learned to check its free impulses, to distrust its sallying emotions, and to supply its most affecting and picturesque usages by studied form and pompous ceremonial. Few pageants can be more stately and frigid than an English funeral in town. It is made up of show and gloomy parade; mourning carriages, mourning horses, mourning plumes, and hireling mourners, who make a mockery of grief. "There is a grave digged," says Jeremy Taylor, "and a solemn mourning, and a great talk in the neighborhood, and when the daies are finished, they shall be, and they shall be remembered no more." The associate in the gay and crowded city is soon forgotten; the hurrying succession of new intimates and new pleasures effaces him from our minds, and the very scenes and circles in which he moved are incessantly fluctuating. But funerals in the country are solemnly impressive. The stroke of death makes a wider space in the village circle, and is an awful event in the tranquil uniformity of rural life. The passing bell tolls its knell in every ear; it steals with its pervading melancholy over hill and vale, and saddens all the landscape.

The fixed and unchanging features of the country also perpetuate the memory of the friend with whom we once enjoyed them, who was the companion of our most retired walks, and gave animation to every lonely scene. His idea is associated with every charm of nature; we hear his voice in the echo which he once delighted to awaken; his spirit haunts the grove which he once frequented; we think of him in the wild upland solitude or

amidst the pensive beauty of the valley. In the freshness of
joyous morning, we remember his beaming smiles and
bounding gaiety; and when sober evening returns with
its gathering shadows and subduing quiet, we call to
mind many a twilight hour of gentle talk and sweet-
souled melancholy.

> Each lonely place shall him restore,
> For him the tear be duly shed;
> Belov'd, till life can charm no more;
> And mourn'd till pity's self be dead.

Another cause that perpetuates the memory of the
deceased in the country is that the grave is more immediately in sight of the survivors. They pass it on their way
to prayer, it meets their eyes when their hearts are softened by the exercises of devotion; they linger about it
on the Sabbath, when the mind is disengaged from worldly
cares and most disposed to turn aside from present
pleasures and present loves and to sit down among the
solemn mementos of the past. In North Wales the peasantry kneel and pray over the graves of their deceased
friends for several Sundays after the interment; and
where the tender rite of strewing and planting flowers is
still practiced, it is always renewed on Easter, Whitsun-
tide, and other festivals, when the season brings the companion of former festivity more vividly to mind. It is
also invariably performed by the nearest relatives and
friends; no menials nor hirelings are employed; and if a
neighbor yields assistance, it would be deemed an insult
to offer compensation.

I have dwelled upon this beautiful rural custom because, as it is one of the last, so is it one of the holiest
offices of love. The grave is the ordeal of true affection.
It is there that the divine passion of the soul manifests
its superiority to the instinctive impulse of mere animal
attachment. The latter must be continually refreshed and
kept alive by the presence of its object; but the love that
is seated in the soul can live on long remembrance.
The mere inclinations of sense languish and decline with
the charms which excited them, and turn with shuddering
disgust from the dismal precincts of the tomb; but it is

thence that truly spiritual affection rises, purified from every sensual desire, and returns, like a holy flame, to illumine and sanctify the heart of the survivor.

The sorrow for the dead is the only sorrow from which we refuse to be divorced. Every other wound we seek to heal—every other affliction to forget; but this wound we consider it a duty to keep open—this affliction we cherish and brood over in solitude. Where is the mother who would willingly forget the infant that perished like a blossom from her arms, though every recollection is a pang? Where is the child that would willingly forget the most tender of parents, though to remember be but to lament? Who, even in the hour of agony, would forget the friend over whom he mourns? Who, even when the tomb is closing upon the remains of her he most loved, when he feels his heart, as it were, crushed in the closing of its portal, would accept of consolation that must be bought by forgetfulness? No, the love which survives the tomb is one of the noblest attributes of the soul. If it has its woes, it has likewise its delights; and when the overwhelming burst of grief is calmed into the gentle tear of recollection, when the sudden anguish and the convulsive agony over the present ruins of all that we most loved are softened away into pensive meditation on all that it was in the days of its loveliness—who would root out such a sorrow from the heart? Though it may sometimes throw a passing cloud over the bright hour of gaiety, or spread a deeper sadness over the hour of gloom, yet who would exchange it even for the song of pleasure, or the burst of revelry? No, there is a voice from the tomb sweeter than song. There is a remembrance of the dead to which we turn even from the charms of the living. Oh, the grave! The grave! It buries every error—covers every defect—extinguishes every resentment! From its peaceful bosom spring none but fond regrets and tender recollections. Who can look down upon the grave even of an enemy and not feel a compunctious throb that he should ever have warred with the poor handful of earth that lies moldering before him.

But the grave of those we loved—what a place for meditation! There it is that we call up in long review the whole history of virtue and gentleness, and the thousand endearments lavished upon us almost unheeded in the daily intercourse of intimacy—there it is that we dwell upon the tenderness, the solemn, awful tenderness of the parting scene. The bed of death, with all its stifled griefs—its noiseless attendance—its mute, watchful assiduities. The last testimonies of expiring love! The feeble, fluttering, thrilling—oh! how thrilling!—pressure of the hand! The faint, faltering accents, struggling in death to give one more assurance of affection! The last fond look of the glazing eye, turned upon us even from the threshold of existence!

Ay, go to the grave of buried love and meditate! There settle the account with thy conscience for every past benefit unrequited—every past endearment unregarded, of that departed being, who can never, never, never return to be soothed by thy contrition!

If thou art a child and hast ever added a sorrow to the soul or a furrow to the silvered brow of an affectionate parent; if thou art a husband and hast ever caused the fond bosom that ventured its whole happiness in thy arms to doubt one moment of thy kindness or thy truth; if thou art a friend and hast ever wronged, in thought, or word, or deed, the spirit that generously confided in thee; if thou art a lover and hast ever given one unmerited pang to that true heart which now lies cold and still beneath thy feet—then be sure that every unkind look, every ungracious word, every ungentle action, will come thronging back upon thy memory, and knocking dolefully at thy soul—then be sure that thou wilt lie down sorrowing and repentant on the grave, and utter the unheard groan, and pour the unavailing tear, more deep, more bitter, because unheard and unavailing.

Then weave thy chaplet of flowers and strew the beauties of nature about the grave; console thy broken spirit, if thou canst, with these tender yet futile tributes of regret; but take warning by the bitterness of this thy contrite affliction over the dead, and henceforth be more faithful and affectionate in the discharge of thy duties to the living.

————————

In writing the preceding article, it was not intended to

give a full detail of the funeral customs of the English peasantry, but merely to furnish a few hints and quotations illustrative of particular rites, to be appended, by way of note, to another paper, which has been withheld. The article swelled insensibly into its present form, and this is mentioned as an apology for so brief and casual a notice of these usages, after they have been amply and learnedly investigated in other works.

I must observe, also, that I am well aware that this custom of adorning graves with flowers prevails in other countries besides England. Indeed, in some it is much more general, and is observed even by the rich and fashionable; but it is then apt to lose its simplicity, and to degenerate into affectation. Bright, in his travels in Lower Hungary, tells of monuments of marble and recesses formed for retirement, with seats placed among bowers of greenhouse plants; and that the graves generally are covered with the gayest flowers of the season. He gives a casual picture of filial piety, which I cannot but transcribe, for I trust it is as useful as it is delightful, to illustrate the amiable virtues of the sex. "When I was at Berlin," says he, "I followed the celebrated Iffland to the grave. Mingled with some pomp, you might trace much real feeling. In the midst of the ceremony, my attention was attracted by a young woman, who stood on a mound of earth, newly covered with turf, which she anxiously protected from the feet of the passing crowd. It was the tomb of her parent; and the figure of this affectionate daughter presented a monument more striking than the most costly work of art."

I will barely add an instance of sepulchral decoration that I once met with among the mountains of Switzerland. It was at the village of Gersau, which stands on the borders of the Lake of Lucerne, at the foot of Mount Rigi. It was once the capital of a miniature republic, shut up between the Alps and the lake, and accessible on the land side only by footpaths. The whole force of the republic did not exceed six hundred fighting men, and a few miles of circumference, scooped out as it were from the bosom of the mountains, comprised its territory. The village of Gersau seemed separated from the rest of the world, and retained the golden simplicity of a

purer age. It had a small church, with a burying ground
adjoining. At the heads of the graves were placed crosses
of wood or iron. On some were affixed miniatures, rudely
executed, but evidently attempts at likenesses of the deceased. On the crosses were hung chaplets of flowers,
some withering, others fresh, as if occasionally renewed.
I paused with interest at this scene; I felt that I was at
the source of poetical description, for these were the
beautiful but unaffected offerings of the heart which
poets are fain to record. In a gayer and more populous
place, I should have suspected them to have been suggested by factitious sentiment, derived from books; but
the good people of Gersau knew little of books, there
was not a novel nor a love poem in the village, and I
question whether any peasant of the place dreamt, while
he was twining a fresh chaplet for the grave of his mistress, that he was fulfilling one of the most fanciful rites
of poetical devotion, and that he was practically a poet.

THE INN KITCHEN

Shall I not take mine ease in mine inn?
                                        FALSTAFF

During a journey that I once made through the Nether-
lands I arrived one evening at the Pomme d'Or, the
principal inn of a small Flemish village. It was after the
hour of the *table d'hôte,* so that I was obliged to make
a solitary supper from the relics of its ampler board. The
weather was chilly; I was seated alone in one end of a
great gloomy dining room, and, my repast being over, I
had the prospect before me of a long dull evening without
any visible means of enlivening it. I summoned mine host,
and requested something to read; he brought me the
whole literary stock of his household, a Dutch family
Bible, an almanac in the same language, and a number
of old Paris newspapers. As I sat dozing over one of the
latter, reading old and stale criticisms, my ear was now
and then struck with bursts of laughter which seemed to
proceed from the kitchen. Everyone who has traveled on
the Continent must know how favorite a resort the kitchen
of a country inn is to the middle and inferior order of
travelers, particularly in that equivocal kind of weather
when a fire becomes agreeable toward evening. I threw
aside the newspaper and explored my way to the kitchen,
to take a peep at the group that appeared to be so merry.
It was composed partly of travelers who had arrived some
hours before in a diligence and partly of the usual attendants and hangers-on of inns. They were seated around
a great burnished stove that might have been mistaken

for an altar at which they were worshiping. It was covered with various kitchen vessels of resplendent brightness, among which steamed and hissed a huge copper teakettle. A large lamp threw a strong mass of light upon the group, bringing out many odd features in strong relief. Its yellow rays partially illumined the spacious kitchen, dying duskily away into remote corners, except where they settled in mellow radiance on the broad side of a flitch of bacon or were reflected back from well-scoured utensils that gleamed from the midst of obscurity. A strapping Flemish lass, with long golden pendants in her ears and a necklace with a golden heart suspended to it, was the presiding priestess of the temple.

Many of the company were furnished with pipes, and most of them with some kind of evening potation. I found their mirth was occasioned by anecdotes, which a little swarthy Frenchman, with a dry wizened face and large whiskers, was giving of his love adventures; at the end of each of which there was one of those bursts of honest unceremonious laughter in which a man indulges in that temple of true liberty, an inn.

As I had no better mode of getting through a tedious blustering evening, I took my seat near the stove, and listened to a variety of traveler's tales, some very extravagant and most very dull. All of them, however, have faded from my treacherous memory except one, which I will endeavor to relate. I fear, however, it derived its chief zest from the manner in which it was told, and the peculiar air and appearance of the narrator. He was a corpulent old Swiss, who had the look of a veteran traveler. He was dressed in a tarnished green traveling jacket, with a broad belt around his waist, and a pair of overalls, with buttons from the hips to the ankles. He was of a full, rubicund countenance, with a double chin, aquiline nose, and a pleasant, twinkling eye. His hair was light, and curled from under an old green velvet traveling cap stuck on one side of his head. He was interrupted more than once by the arrival of guests or the remarks of his auditors, and paused now and then to replenish his pipe, at which times he had generally a roguish leer and a sly joke for the buxom kitchen maid.

I wish my readers could imagine the old fellow lolling in a huge armchair, one arm akimbo, the other holding a curiously twisted tobacco pipe, formed of genuine *écume de mer,* decorated with silver chain and silken tassel—his head cocked on one side, and the whimsical cut of the eye occasionally, as he related the following story.

THE SPECTER BRIDEGROOM

A TRAVELER'S TALE*

> He that supper for is dight,
> He lyes full cold, I trow, this night!
> Yestreen to chamber I him led,
> This night Gray-Steel has made his bed.
> SIR EGER, SIR GRAHAME, AND SIR GRAY-STEEL

On the summit of one of the heights of the Odenwald, a wild and romantic tract of Upper Germany that lies not far from the confluence of the Main and the Rhine, there stood, many, many years since, the Castle of the Baron Von Landshort. It is now quite fallen to decay and almost buried among beech trees and dark firs, above which, however, its old watchtower may still be seen, struggling, like the former possessor I have mentioned, to carry a high head and look down upon the neighboring country.

The baron was a dry branch of the great family of Katzenellenbogen,† and inherited the relics of the property and all the pride of his ancestors. Though the war-like disposition of his predecessors had much impaired the family possessions, yet the baron still endeavored to keep up some show of former state. The times were peaceable, and the German nobles, in general, had abandoned their inconvenient old castles, perched like eagles'

---

*The erudite reader, well versed in good-for-nothing lore, will perceive that the above Tale must have been suggested to the old Swiss by a little French anecdote, a circumstance said to have taken place at Paris.

†*I.e.*, CAT'S-ELBOW. The name of a family of those parts very powerful in former times. The appellation, we are told, was given in compliment to a peerless dame of the family, celebrated for her fine arm.

nests among the mountains, and had built more convenient residences in the valleys; still the baron remained proudly drawn up in his little fortress, cherishing, with hereditary inveteracy, all the old family feuds, so that he was on ill terms with some of his nearest neighbors on account of disputes that had happened between their great-great-grandfathers.

The baron had but one child, a daughter; but nature, when she grants but one child, always compensates by making it a prodigy, and so it was with the daughter of the baron. All the nurses, gossips, and country cousins assured her father that she had not her equal for beauty in all Germany; and who should know better than they? She had, moreover, been brought up with great care under the superintendence of two maiden aunts, who had spent some years of their early life at one of the little German courts and were skilled in all the branches of knowledge necessary to the education of a fine lady. Under their instructions she became a miracle of accomplishments. By the time she was eighteen she could embroider to admiration and had worked whole histories of the saints in tapestry with such strength of expression in their countenances that they looked like so many souls in purgatory. She could read without great difficulty, and had spelled her way through several church legends and almost all the chivalric wonders of the Heldenbuch. She had even made considerable proficiency in writing, could sign her own name without missing a letter, and so legibly that her aunts could read it without spectacles. She excelled in making little elegant good-for-nothing ladylike knickknacks of all kinds; was versed in the most abstruse dancing of the day; played a number of airs on the harp and guitar; and knew all the tender ballads of the Minnelieders by heart.

Her aunts, too, having been great flirts and coquettes in their younger days, were admirably calculated to be vigilant guardians and strict censors of the conduct of their niece, for there is no duenna so rigidly prudent and inexorably decorous as a superannuated coquette. She was rarely suffered out of their sight; never went beyond the domains of the castle, unless well attended, or rather well watched; had continual lectures read to her about strict decorum and implicit obedience; and, as to the men—pah!—she was taught to hold them at such a distance, and in such absolute distrust, that, unless properly authorized, she would not have cast a glance upon the handsomest cavalier in the world—no, not if he were even dying at her feet.

The good effects of this system were wonderfully apparent. The young lady was a pattern of docility and correctness. While others were wasting their sweetness in the glare of the world and liable to be plucked and thrown aside by every hand, she was coyly blooming into fresh and lovely womanhood under the protection of those immaculate spinsters, like a rosebud blushing forth among guardian thorns. Her aunts looked upon her with pride and exultation, and vaunted that though all the other young ladies in the world might go astray, yet, thank Heaven, nothing of the kind could happen to the heiress of Katzenellenbogen.

But, however scantily the Baron Von Landshort might be provided with children, his household was by no means a small one, for Providence had enriched him with abundance of poor relations. They, one and all, possessed the affectionate disposition common to humble relatives, were wonderfully attached to the baron, and took every possible occasion to come in swarms and enliven the castle. All family festivals were commemorated by these good people at the baron's expense; and when they were filled with good cheer they would declare that there was nothing on earth so delightful as these family meetings, these jubilees of the heart.

The baron, though a small man, had a large soul, and it swelled with satisfaction at the consciousness of being the greatest man in the little world about him. He loved to tell long stories about the dark old warriors whose portraits looked grimly down from the walls around, and he found no listeners equal to those that fed at his expense. He was much given to the marvelous, and a firm believer in all those supernatural tales with which every mountain and valley in Germany abounds. The faith of his guests exceeded even his own; they listened to every tale of wonder with open eyes and mouth, and never failed to be astonished, even though repeated for the hundredth time. Thus lived the Baron Von Landshort, the oracle of his table, the absolute monarch of his little territory, and happy, above all things, in the persuasion that he was the wisest man of the age.

At the time of which my story treats there was a great family gathering at the castle, on an affair of the utmost importance: it was to receive the destined bridegroom of the baron's daughter. A negotiation had been carried on between the father and an old nobleman of Bavaria to unite the dignity of their houses by the marriage of their children. The preliminaries had been conducted with proper punctilio. The young people were betrothed without seeing each other, and the time was appointed for the marriage ceremony. The young Count Von Altenburg had been recalled from the army for the purpose, and was actually on his way to the baron's to receive his bride. Missives had even been received from him, from Würzburg, where he was accidentally detained, mentioning the day and hour when he might be expected to arrive.

The castle was in a tumult of preparation to give him a suitable welcome. The fair bride had been decked out with uncommon care. The two aunts had superintended her toilet and quarreled the whole morning about every article of her dress. The young lady had taken advantage of their contest to follow the bent of her own taste, and fortunately it was a good one. She looked as lovely as youthful bridegroom could desire, and the flutter of expectation heightened the luster of her charms.

The suffusions that mantled her face and neck, the gentle heaving of the bosom, the eye now and then lost in reverie, all betrayed the soft tumult that was going on in her little heart. The aunts were continually hovering around her, for maiden aunts are apt to take great interest in affairs of this nature. They were giving her a world of staid counsel how to deport herself, what to say, and in what manner to receive the expected lover.

The baron was no less busied in preparations. He had, in truth, nothing exactly to do, but he was naturally a fuming bustling little man, and could not remain passive when all the world was in a hurry. He worried from top to bottom of the castle with an air of infinite anxiety; he continually called the servants from their work to exhort them to be diligent; and buzzed about every hall and chamber, as idly restless and importunate as a bluebottle fly on a warm summer's day.

In the meantime the fatted calf had been killed; the forests had rung with the clamor of the huntsmen; the kitchen was crowded with good cheer; the cellars had yielded up whole oceans of *Rhein-wein* and *Ferne-wein;* and even the great Heidelberg tun had been laid under contribution. Everything was ready to receive the distinguished guest with *Saus und Braus* in the true spirit of German hospitality—but the guest delayed to make his appearance. Hour rolled after hour. The sun that had poured his downward rays upon the rich forest of the Odenwald now just gleamed along the summits of the mountains. The baron mounted the highest tower, and strained his eyes in hope of catching a distant sight of the count and his attendants. Once he thought he beheld them; the sound of horns came floating from the valley, prolonged by the mountain echoes. A number of horsemen were seen far below, slowly advancing along the road; but when they had nearly reached the foot of the mountain they suddenly struck off in a different direction. The last ray of sunshine departed—the bats began to flit by in the twilight—the road grew dimmer and dimmer to the view; and nothing appeared stirring in it but now and then a peasant lagging homeward from his labor.

While the old castle of Landshort was in this state of perplexity a very interesting scene was transacting in a different part of the Odenwald.

The young Count Von Altenburg was tranquilly pursuing his route in that sober jog-trot way, in which a man travels toward matrimony when his friends have taken all the trouble and uncertainty of courtship off his hands, and a bride is waiting for him as certainly as a dinner at the end of his journey. He had encountered at Würzburg a youthful companion in arms with whom he had seen some service on the frontiers, Herman Von Starkenfaust, one of the stoutest hands and worthiest hearts of German chivalry, who was now returning from the army.

His father's castle was not far distant from the old fortress of Landshort, although an hereditary feud rendered the families hostile and strangers to each other.

In the warmhearted moment of recognition the young friends related all their past adventures and fortunes, and the count gave the whole history of his intended nuptials with a young lady whom he had never seen but of whose charms he had received the most enrapturing descriptions.

As the route of the friends lay in the same direction, they agreed to perform the rest of their journey together; and, that they might do it the more leisurely, set off from Würzburg at an early hour, the count having given directions for his retinue to follow and overtake him.

They beguiled their wayfaring with recollections of their military scenes and adventures; but the count was apt to be a little tedious, now and then, about the reputed charms of his bride, and the felicity that awaited him.

In this way they had entered among the mountains of the Odenwald, and were traversing one of its most lonely and thickly wooded passes. It is well known that the forests of Germany have always been as much infested by robbers as its castles by specters; and at this time the former were particularly numerous, from the hordes of disbanded soldiers wandering about the country. It will not appear extraordinary, therefore, that the cavaliers were attacked by a gang of these stragglers in the midst of the forest. They defended themselves with bravery, but were nearly overpowered, when the count's retinue arrived to their assistance. At sight of them the robbers fled, but not until the count had received a mortal wound. He was slowly and carefully conveyed back to the city of Würzburg, and a friar summoned from a neighboring convent, who was famous for his skill in administering to both soul and body; but half of his skill was superfluous; the moments of the unfortunate count were numbered.

With his dying breath he entreated his friend to repair instantly to the castle of Landshort and explain the fatal cause of his not keeping his appointment with his bride. Though not the most ardent of lovers, he was one of the most punctilious of men, and appeared earnestly solicitous

that his mission should be speedily and courteously executed. "Unless this is done," said he, "I shall not sleep
quietly in my grave!" He repeated these last words with
peculiar solemnity. A request, at a moment so impressive,
admitted no hesitation. Starkenfaust endeavored to soothe
him to calmness, promised faithfully to execute his wish,
and gave him his hand in solemn pledge. The dying man
pressed it in acknowledgment, but soon lapsed into delir-
ium—raved about his bride—his engagements—his
plighted word; ordered his horse that he might ride to
the castle of Landshort; and expired in the fancied act of
vaulting into the saddle.

Starkenfaust bestowed a sigh and a soldier's tear on the
untimely fate of his comrade, and then pondered on the
awkward mission he had undertaken. His heart was heavy
and his head perplexed, for he was to present himself an
unbidden guest among hostile people, and to damp their
festivity with tidings fatal to their hopes. Still there were
certain whisperings of curiosity in his bosom to see this
far-famed beauty of Katzenellenbogen, so cautiously shut
up from the world, for he was a passionate admirer of
the sex, and there was a dash of eccentricity and enterprise in his character that made him fond of all singular
adventure.

Previous to his departure he made all due arrangements with the holy fraternity of the convent for the
funeral solemnities of his friend, who was to be buried
in the cathedral of Würzburg, near some of his illustrious
relatives; and the mourning retinue of the count took
charge of his remains.

It is now high time that we should return to the ancient family of Katzenellenbogen, who were impatient for
their guest, and still more for their dinner; and to the
worthy little baron, whom we left airing himself on the
watchtower.

Night closed in, but still no guest arrived. The baron
descended from the tower in despair. The banquet, which
had been delayed from hour to hour, could no longer be
postponed. The meats were already overdone; the cook
in an agony; and the whole household had the look of a
garrison that had been reduced by famine. The baron was
obliged reluctantly to give orders for the feast without

the presence of the guest. All were seated at table, and just on the point of commencing when the sound of a horn from without the gate gave notice of the approach of a stranger. Another long blast filled the old courts of the castle with its echoes, and was answered by the warder from the walls. The baron hastened to receive his future son-in-law.

The drawbridge had been let down, and the stranger was before the gate. He was a tall, gallant cavalier, mounted on a black steed. His countenance was pale, but he had a beaming, romantic eye, and an air of stately melancholy. The baron was a little mortified that he should have come in this simple, solitary style. His dignity for a moment was ruffled, and he felt disposed to consider it a want of proper respect for the important occasion and the important family with which he was to be connected. He pacified himself, however, with the conclusion that it must have been youthful impatience which had induced him thus to spur on sooner than his attendants.

"I am sorry," said the stranger, "to break in upon you thus unseasonably——"

Here the baron interrupted him with a world of compliments and greetings, for, to tell the truth, he prided himself upon his courtesy and eloquence. The stranger attempted, once or twice, to stem the torrent of words, but in vain, so he bowed his head and suffered it to flow on. By the time the baron had come to a pause, they had reached the inner court of the castle, and the stranger was again about to speak when he was once more interrupted by the appearance of the female part of the family, leading forth the shrinking and blushing bride. He gazed on her for a moment as one entranced; it seemed as if his whole soul beamed forth in the gaze, and rested upon that lovely form. One of the maiden aunts whispered something in her ear; she made an effort to speak; her moist blue eye was timidly raised, gave a shy glance of inquiry on the stranger, and was cast again to the ground. The words died away, but there was a sweet smile playing about her lips and a soft dimpling of the cheek that showed her glance had not been unsatisfactory. It was impossible for a girl of the fond age of eighteen, highly predisposed for love and matrimony, not to be pleased with so gallant a cavalier.

The late hour at which the guest had arrived left no time for parley. The baron was peremptory, and deferred all particular conversation until the morning, and led the way to the untasted banquet.

It was served up in the great hall of the castle. Around the walls hung the hard-favored portraits of the heroes of the house of Katzenellenbogen and the trophies which they had gained in the field and in the chase. Hacked corslets, splintered jousting spears, and tattered banners were mingled with the spoils of sylvan warfare; the jaws of the wolf and the tusks of the boar grinned horribly among cross-bows and battle-axes, and a huge pair of antlers branched immediately over the head of the youthful bridegroom.

The cavalier took but little notice of the company or the entertainment. He scarcely tasted the banquet, but seemed absorbed in admiration of his bride. He conversed in a low tone that could not be overheard—for the language of love is never loud; but where is the female ear so dull that it cannot catch the softest whisper of the lover? There was a mingled tenderness and gravity in his manner that appeared to have a powerful effect upon the young lady. Her color came and went as she listened with deep attention. Now and then she made some blushing reply, and when his eye was turned away, she would steal a sidelong glance at his romantic countenance and heave a gentle sigh of tender happiness. It was evident that the young couple were completely enamored. The aunts, who were deeply versed in the mysteries of the heart, declared that they had fallen in love with each other at first sight.

The feast went on merrily, or at least noisily, for the guests were all blessed with those keen appetites that attend upon light purses and mountain air. The baron told his best and longest stories, and never had he told them so well or with such great effect. If there was anything marvelous, his auditors were lost in astonishment; and if anything facetious, they were sure to laugh exactly in the right place. The baron, it is true, like most great men,

was too dignified to utter any joke but a dull one; it was
always enforced, however, by a bumper of excellent
Hockheimer, and even a dull joke, at one's own table,
served up with jolly old wine, is irresistible. Many good
things were said by poorer and keener wits that would
not bear repeating, except on similar occasions; many sly
speeches whispered in ladies' ears that almost convulsed
them with suppressed laughter; and a song or two roared
out by a poor but merry and broad-faced cousin of the
baron that absolutely made the maiden aunts hold up
their fans.

Amidst all this revelry, the stranger guest maintained
a most singular and unseasonable gravity. His countenance assumed a deeper cast of dejection as the evening
advanced; and, strange as it may appear, even the baron's
jokes seemed only to render him the more melancholy.
At times he was lost in thought, and at times there was
a perturbed and restless wandering of the eye that bespoke a mind but ill at ease. His conversations with
the bride became more and more earnest and mysterious.
Lowering clouds began to steal over the fair serenity of
her brow, and tremors to run through her tender frame.

All this could not escape the notice of the company.
Their gaiety was chilled by the unaccountable gloom of
the bridegroom; their spirits were infected; whispers and
glances were interchanged, accompanied by shrugs and
dubious shakes of the head. The song and the laugh grew
less and less frequent; there were dreary pauses in the
conversation, which were at length succeeded by wild tales
and supernatural legends. One dismal story produced
another still more dismal, and the baron nearly frightened
some of the ladies into hysterics with the history of the
goblin horseman that carried away the fair Leonora; a
dreadful story, which has since been put into excellent
verse, and is read and believed by all the world.

The bridegroom listened to this tale with profound
attention. He kept his eyes steadily fixed on the baron,
and, as the story drew to a close, began gradually to rise
from his seat, growing taller and taller, until, in the
baron's entranced eye, he seemed almost to tower into a
giant. The moment the tale was finished, he heaved a
deep sigh, and took a solemn farewell of the company.

They were all amazement. The baron was perfectly thunderstruck.

"What! Going to leave the castle at midnight? Why, everything was prepared for his reception; a chamber was ready for him if he wished to retire."

The stranger shook his head mournfully and mysteriously. "I must lay my head in a different chamber to-night!"

There was something in this reply and the tone in which it was uttered that made the baron's heart misgive him, but he rallied his forces and repeated his hospitable entreaties.

The stranger shook his head silently, but positively, at every offer; and, waving his farewell to the company, stalked slowly out of the hall. The maiden aunts were absolutely petrified—the bride hung her head, and a tear stole to her eye.

The baron followed the stranger to the great court of the castle, where the black charger stood pawing the earth, and snorting with impatience. When they had reached the portal, whose deep archway was dimly lighted by a cresset, the stranger paused, and addressed the baron in a hollow tone of voice, which the vaulted roof rendered still more sepulchral.

"Now that we are alone," said he, "I will impart to you the reason of my going. I have a solemn, an indispensable engagement——"

"Why," said the baron, "cannot you send someone in your place?"

"It admits of no substitute—I must attend it in person —I must away to Würzburg cathedral——"

"Ay," said the baron, plucking up spirit, "but not until tomorrow—tomorrow you shall take your bride there."

"No! no!" replied the stranger, with tenfold solemnity, "my engagement is with no bride—the worms! The worms expect me! I am a dead man—I have been slain by robbers—my body lies at Würzburg—at midnight I am to be buried—the grave is waiting for me—I must keep my appointment!"

He sprang on his black charger, dashed over the drawbridge, and the clattering of his horse's hoofs was lost in the whistling of the night blast.

The baron returned to the hall in the utmost consternation and related what had passed. Two ladies fainted outright, others sickened at the idea of having banqueted with a specter. It was the opinion of some that this might be the wild huntsman, famous in German legend. Some talked of mountain sprites, of wood demons, and of other supernatural beings, with which the good people of Germany have been so grievously harassed since time immemorial. One of the poor relations ventured to suggest that it might be some sportive evasion of the young cavalier, and that the very gloominess of the caprice seemed to accord with so melancholy a personage. This, however, drew on him the indignation of the whole company, and especially of the baron, who looked upon him as little better than an infidel, so that he was fain to abjure his heresy as speedily as possible and come into the faith of the true believers.

But whatever may have been the doubts entertained, they were completely put to an end by the arrival, next day, of regular missives, confirming the intelligence of the young count's murder, and his interment in Würzburg cathedral.

The dismay at the castle may well be imagined. The baron shut himself up in his chamber. The guests, who had come to rejoice with him, could not think of abandoning him in his distress. They wandered about the courts, or collected in groups in the hall, shaking their heads and shrugging their shoulders at the troubles of so good a man; and sat longer than ever at table, and ate and drank more stoutly than ever, by way of keeping up their spirits. But the situation of the widowed bride was the most pitiable. To have lost a husband before she had even embraced him—and such a husband! If the very specter could be so gracious and noble, what must have been the living man? She filled the house with lamentations.

On the night of the second day of her widowhood, she had retired to her chamber, accompanied by one of her aunts, who insisted on sleeping with her. The aunt, who was one of the best tellers of ghost stories in all Germany, had just been recounting one of her longest, and had fallen asleep in the very midst of it. The chamber was remote, and overlooked a small garden. The niece lay pensively gazing at the beams of the rising moon, as they trembled on the leaves of an aspen tree before the lattice. The castle clock had just tolled midnight when a soft strain of music stole up from the garden. She rose hastily from her bed, and stepped lightly to the window. A tall figure stood among the shadows of the trees. As it raised its head, a beam of moonlight fell upon the countenance. Heaven and earth! She beheld the Specter Bridegroom! A loud shriek at that moment burst upon her ear, and her aunt, who had been awakened by the music and had followed her silently to the window, fell into her arms. When she looked again, the specter had disappeared.

Of the two females, the aunt now required the more soothing, for she was perfectly beside herself with terror. As to the young lady, there was something, even in the specter of her lover, that seemed endearing. There was still the semblance of manly beauty; and though the shadow of a man is but little calculated to satisfy the affections of a lovesick girl, yet, where the substance is not to be had, even that is consoling. The aunt declared she would never sleep in that chamber again; the niece, for once, was refractory, and declared as strongly that she would sleep in no other in the castle. The consequence was that she had to sleep in it alone; but she drew a promise from her aunt not to relate the story of the specter, lest she should be denied the only melancholy pleasure left her on earth—that of inhabiting the chamber over which the guardian shade of her lover kept its nightly vigils.

How long the good old lady would have observed this promise is uncertain, for she dearly loved to talk of the marvelous, and there is a triumph in being the first to tell a frightful story; it is, however, still quoted in the neighborhood, as a memorable instance of female secrecy, that she kept it to herself for a whole week, when she was suddenly absolved from all further restraint by intelligence brought to the breakfast table one morning that the young lady was not to be found. Her room was empty—the bed had not been slept in—the window was open, and the bird had flown!

The astonishment and concern with which the intelligence was received can only be imagined by those who have witnessed the agitation which the mishaps of a great man cause among his friends. Even the poor relations paused for a moment from the indefatigable labors of the trencher, when the aunt, who had at first been struck speechless, wrung her hands, and shrieked out, "The goblin! The goblin! She's carried away by the goblin."

In a few words she related the fearful scene of the garden, and concluded that the specter must have carried off his bride. Two of the domestics corroborated the opinion, for they had heard the clattering of a horse's hoofs down the mountain about midnight, and had no doubt that it was the specter on his black charger, bearing her away to the tomb. All present were struck with the direful probability, for events of the kind are extremely common in Germany, as many well-authenticated histories bear witness.

What a lamentable situation was that of the poor baron! What a heart-rending dilemma for a fond father, and a member of the great family of Katzenellenbogen! His only daughter had either been rapt away to the grave, or he was to have some wood demon for a son-in-law, and, perchance, a troop of goblin grandchildren. As usual, he was completely bewildered, and all the castle in an uproar. The men were ordered to take horse and scour every road and path and glen of the Odenwald. The baron himself had just drawn on his jack boots, girded on his sword, and was about to mount his steed to sally forth on the doubtful quest when he was brought to a pause by a new apparition. A lady was seen approaching the castle, mounted on a palfrey, attended by a cavalier on horseback. She galloped up to the gate, sprang from her horse, and, falling at the baron's feet, embraced his knees. It was his lost daughter and her companion—the Specter Bridegroom! The baron was astounded. He looked at his daughter, then at the specter, and almost doubted the evidence of his senses. The latter, too, was wonderfully improved in his appearance since his visit to the world of spirits. His dress was splendid, and set off a noble figure of manly symmetry.

He was no longer pale and melancholy. His fine countenance was flushed with the glow of youth, and joy rioted in his large dark eye.

The mystery was soon cleared up. The cavalier (for, in truth, as you must have known all the while, he was no goblin) announced himself as Sir Herman Von Starkenfaust. He related his adventure with the young count. He told how he had hastened to the castle to deliver the unwelcome tidings, but that the eloquence of the baron had interrupted him in every attempt to tell his tale. How the sight of the bride had completely captivated him, and that to pass a few hours near her he had tacitly suffered the mistake to continue. How he had been sorely perplexed in what way to make a decent retreat, until the baron's goblin stories had suggested his eccentric exit. How, fearing the feudal hostility of the family, he had repeated his visits by stealth—had haunted the garden beneath the young lady's window—had wooed—had won—had borne away in triumph—and, in a word, had wedded the fair.

Under any other circumstances the baron would have been inflexible, for he was tenacious of paternal authority and devoutly obstinate in all family feuds; but he loved his daughter; he had lamented her as lost; he rejoiced to find her still alive; and, though her husband was of a hostile house, yet, thank Heaven, he was not a goblin. There was something, it must be acknowledged, that did not exactly accord with his notions of strict veracity, in the joke the knight had passed upon him of his being a dead man; but several old friends present, who had served in the wars, assured him that every stratagem was excusable in love, and that the cavalier was entitled to especial privilege, having lately served as a trooper.

Matters, therefore, were happily arranged. The baron pardoned the young couple on the spot. The revels at the castle were resumed. The poor relations overwhelmed this new member of the family with loving kindness; he was so gallant, so generous—and so rich. The aunts, it is true, were somewhat scandalized that their system of strict seclusion and passive obedience should be so badly exemplified, but attributed it all to their negligence in not having the windows grated. One of them was particularly mortified at having her marvelous story marred, and that the only specter she had ever seen should turn out a counterfeit; but the niece seemed perfectly happy at having found him substantial flesh and blood—and so the story ends.

WESTMINSTER ABBEY

When I behold, with deep astonishment,
To famous Westminster how there resorte
Living in brasse or stoney monument,
The princes and the worthies of all sorte;
Doe not I see reformde nobilitie,
Without contempt, or pride, or ostentation,
And looke upon offenselesse majesty,
Naked of pomp or earthly domination?
And how a play-game of a painted stone
Contents the quiet now and silent sprites,
Whome all the world which late they stood upon
Could not content or quench their appetites.
    Life is a frost of cold felicitie,
    And death the thaw of all our vanitie.
        CHRISTOLERO'S EPIGRAMS BY T. B.   1598

On one of those sober and rather melancholy days, in
the latter part of autumn, when the shadows of
morning and evening almost mingle together and throw a
gloom over the decline of the year, I passed several hours
in rambling about Westminster Abbey. There was something congenial to the season in the mournful magnificence of the old pile; and, as I passed its threshold,
seemed like stepping back into the regions of antiquity
and losing myself among the shades of former ages.

I entered from the inner court of Westminster School,
through a long, low, vaulted passage that had an almost
subterranean look, being dimly lighted in one part by
circular perforations in the massive walls. Through this
dark avenue I had a distant view of the cloisters, with
the figure of an old verger, in his black gown, moving
along their shadowy vaults, and seeming like a specter
from one of the neighboring tombs. The approach to the
abbey through these gloomy monastic remains prepares
the mind for its solemn contemplation. The cloisters still
retain something of the quiet and seclusion of former
days. The gray walls are discolored by damps and crumbling with age; a coat of hoary moss has gathered over
the inscriptions of the mural monuments and obscured
the death's heads and other funereal emblems. The sharp

touches of the chisel are gone from the rich tracery of the arches; the roses which adorned the keystones have lost their leafy beauty; everything bears marks of the gradual dilapidations of time, which yet has something touching and pleasing in its very decay.

The sun was pouring down a yellow autumnal ray into the square of the cloisters, beaming upon a scanty plot of grass in the center and lighting up an angle of the vaulted passage with a kind of dusky splendor. From between the arcades, the eye glanced up to a bit of blue sky or a passing cloud, and beheld the sun-gilt pinnacles of the abbey towering into the azure heaven.

As I paced the cloisters, sometimes contemplating this mingled picture of glory and decay, and sometimes endeavoring to decipher the inscriptions on the tombstones, which formed the pavement beneath my feet, my eye was attracted to three figures, rudely carved in relief, but nearly worn away by the footsteps of many generations. They were the effigies of three of the early abbots; the epitaphs were entirely effaced; the names alone remained, having no doubt been renewed in later times. (Vitalis Abbas. 1082, and Gislebertus Crispinus. Abbas. 1114, and Laurentius. Abbas. 1176.) I remained some little while, musing over these casual relics of antiquity, thus left like wrecks upon this distant shore of time, telling no tale but that such beings had been and had perished; teaching no moral but the futility of that pride which hopes still to exact homage in its ashes, and to live in an inscription. A little longer and even these faint records will be obliterated, and the monument will cease to be a memorial. While I was yet looking down upon these gravestones, I was roused by the sound of the abbey clock, reverberating from buttress to buttress, and echoing among the cloisters. It is almost startling to hear this warning of departed time sounding among the tombs and telling the lapse of the hour, which, like a billow, has rolled us onward toward the grave. I pursued my walk to an arched door opening to the interior of the abbey. On entering here, the magnitude of the building breaks fully upon the mind, contrasted with the vaults of the cloisters. The eyes gaze with wonder at clustered columns of gigantic dimensions, with arches springing from them to such an amazing height; and man wandering about their bases, shrunk into insignificance in comparison with his own handiwork. The spaciousness and gloom of this vast edifice produce a profound and mysterious awe. We step cautiously and softly about, as if fearful of disturbing the hallowed silence of the tomb, while every footfall whispers along the walls and chatters among the sepulchers, making us more sensible of the quiet we have interrupted.

It seems as if the awful nature of the place presses down upon the soul, and hushes the beholder into noiseless reverence. We feel that we are surrounded by the congregated bones of the great men of past times, who have filled history with their deeds and the earth with their renown.

And yet it almost provokes a smile at the vanity of human ambition to see how they are crowded together and jostled in the dust; what parsimony is observed in doling out a scanty nook, a gloomy corner, a little portion of earth, to those, whom, when alive, kingdoms could not satisfy; and how many shapes, and forms, and artifices are devised to catch the casual notice of the passenger and save from forgetfulness for a few short years a name which once aspired to occupy ages of the world's thought and admiration.

I passed some time in Poets' Corner, which occupies an end of one of the transepts or cross aisles of the abbey. The monuments are generally simple, for the lives of literary men afford no striking themes for the sculptor. Shakespeare and Addison have statues erected to their memories, but the greater part have busts, medallions, and sometimes mere inscriptions. Notwithstanding the simplicity of these memorials, I have always observed that the visitors to the abbey remained longest about them. A kinder and fonder feeling takes the place of that cold curiosity or vague admiration with which they gaze on the splendid monuments of the great and the heroic. They linger about these as about the tombs of friends and companions, for indeed there is something of companionship between the author and the reader. Other men are known to posterity only through the medium of history, which is continually growing faint and obscure; but the intercourse between the author and his fellow men is ever new, active, and immediate. He has lived for them more than for himself; he has sacrificed surrounding enjoyments and shut himself up from the delights of social life that he might the more intimately commune with distant minds and distant ages. Well may the world cherish his renown, for it has been purchased, not by deeds of violence and blood, but by the diligent dispensation of pleasure. Well may posterity be grateful to his memory, for he has left it an inheritance, not of empty names and sounding actions, but whole treasures of wisdom, bright gems of thought, and golden veins of language.

From Poets' Corner I continued my stroll toward that part of the abbey which contains the sepulchers of the kings. I wandered among what once were chapels but which are now occupied by the tombs and monuments of the great. At every turn I met with some illustrious name, or the cognizance of some powerful house renowned in history. As the eye darts into these dusky chambers of death, it catches glimpses of quaint effigies; some kneeling in niches, as if in devotion; others stretched upon the tombs, with hands piously pressed together—warriors in armor, as if reposing after battle; prelates with crosiers and miters; and nobles in robes and coronets, lying as it were in state. In glancing over this scene, so strangely populous, yet where every form is so still and silent, it seems almost as if we were treading a mansion of that fabled city, where every being had been suddenly transmuted into stone.

I paused to contemplate a tomb on which lay the effigy of a knight in complete armor. A large buckler was on one arm; the hands were pressed together in supplication upon the breast: the face was almost covered by the morion; the legs were crossed, in token of the warrior's having been engaged in the holy war. It was the tomb of a crusader, of one of those military enthusiasts who so strangely mingled religion and romance and whose exploits form the connecting link between fact and fiction, between the history and the fairy tale. There is something extremely picturesque in the tombs of these adventurers, decorated as they are with rude armorial bearings and Gothic sculpture. They comport with the antiquated chapels in which they are generally found; and in considering them the imagination is apt to kindle with the legendary associations, the romantic fiction, the chivalrous pomp and pageantry which poetry has spread over the wars for the sepulcher of Christ. They are the relics of times utterly gone by, of beings passed from recollection, of customs and manners with which ours have no affinity. They are like objects from some strange and distant land, of which we have no certain knowledge and about which all our conceptions are vague and visionary. There is something extremely solemn and awful in those effigies on Gothic tombs, extended as if in the sleep of death, or in the supplication of the dying hour. They have an effect infinitely more impressive on my feelings than the fanciful attitudes, the overwrought conceits, and allegorical groups, which abound on modern monuments. I have been struck, also, with the superiority of many of the old sepulchral inscriptions. There was a noble way, in former times, of saying things simply, and yet saying them proudly; and I do not know an epitaph that breathes a loftier consciousness of family worth and honorable lineage than one which affirms, of a noble house, that "all the brothers were brave, and all the sisters virtuous."

In the opposite transept to Poets' Corner stands a monument which is among the most renowned achievements of modern art, but which to me appears horrible rather than sublime. It is the tomb of Mrs. Nightingale, by Roubillac. The bottom of the monument is represented as throwing open its marble doors, and a sheeted skeleton is starting forth. The shroud is falling from its fleshless frame as he launches his dart at his victim. She is sinking into her affrighted husband's arms, who strives, with vain and frantic effort, to avert the blow. The whole is executed with terrible truth and spirit; we almost fancy we hear the gibbering yell of triumph bursting from the distended jaws of the specter. But why should we thus seek to clothe death with unnecessary terrors, and to spread horrors around the tomb of those we love? The grave should be surrounded by everything that might inspire tenderness and veneration for the dead, or that might win the living to virtue. It is the place, not of disgust and dismay, but of sorrow and meditation.

While wandering about these gloomy vaults and silent aisles, studying the records of the dead, the sound of busy existence from without occasionally reaches the ear— the rumbling of the passing equipage, the murmur of the multitude, or perhaps the light laugh of pleasure. The contrast is striking with the deathlike repose around, and it has a strange effect upon the feelings, thus to hear the surges of active life hurrying along, and beating against the very walls of the sepulcher.

I continued in this way to move from tomb to tomb, and from chapel to chapel. The day was gradually wearing away; the distant tread of loiterers about the abbey grew less and less frequent; the sweet-tongued bell was summoning to evening prayers; and I saw at a distance the choristers, in their white surplices, crossing the aisle and entering the choir. I stood before the entrance to Henry the Seventh's chapel. A flight of steps lead up to it, through a deep and gloomy but magnificent arch. Great gates of brass, richly and delicately wrought, turn heavily upon their hinges, as if proudly reluctant to admit the feet of common mortals into this most gorgeous of sepulchers.

On entering, the eye is astonished by the pomp of architecture and the elaborate beauty of sculptured detail. The very walls are wrought into universal ornament, encrusted with tracery, and scooped into niches, crowded with the statues of saints and martyrs. Stone seems, by the cunning labor of the chisel, to have been robbed of its weight and density, suspended aloft, as if by magic, and the fretted roof achieved with the wonderful minuteness and airy security of a cobweb.

Along the sides of the chapel are the lofty stalls of the Knights of the Bath, richly carved of oak, though with the grotesque decorations of Gothic architecture. On the pinnacles of the stalls are affixed the helmets and crests of the knights, with their scarfs and swords; and above them are suspended their banners, emblazoned with armorial bearings, and contrasting the splendor of gold and purple and crimson with the cold gray fretwork of the roof. In the midst of this grand mausoleum stands the sepulcher of its founder—his effigy, with that of his queen, extended on a sumptuous tomb, and the whole surrounded by a superbly wrought brazen railing.

There is a sad dreariness in this magnificence, this strange mixture of tombs and trophies, these emblems of living and aspiring ambition, close beside mementos which show the dust and oblivion in which all must sooner or later terminate. Nothing impresses the mind with a deeper feeling of loneliness than to tread the silent and deserted scene of former throng and pageant. On looking around on the vacant stalls of the knights and their esquires and on the rows of dusty but gorgeous banners that were once borne before them, my imagination conjured up the scene when this hall was bright with the valor and beauty of the land, glittering with the splendor of jeweled rank and military array, alive with the tread of many feet and the hum of an admiring multitude. All had passed away; the silence of death had settled again upon the place, interrupted only by the casual chirping of birds, which had found their way into the chapel and built their nests among its friezes and pendants—sure signs of solitariness and desertion.

When I read the names inscribed on the banners, they were those of men scattered far and wide about the world, some tossing upon distant seas, some under arms in distant lands, some mingling in the busy intrigues of courts and cabinets; all seeking to deserve one more distinction in this mansion of shadowy honors—the melancholy reward of a monument.

Two small aisles on each side of this chapel present a touching instance of the equality of the grave, which brings down the oppressor to a level with the oppressed, and mingles the dust of the bitterest enemies together. In one is the sepulcher of the haughty Elizabeth; in the other is that of her victim, the lovely and unfortunate Mary. Not an hour in the day but some ejaculation of pity is uttered over the fate of the latter, mingled with indignation at her oppressor. The walls of Elizabeth's sepulcher continually echo with the sighs of sympathy heaved at the grave of her rival.

A peculiar melancholy reigns over the aisle where Mary lies buried. The light struggles dimly through windows darkened by dust. The greater part of the place is in deep shadow, and the walls are stained and tinted by time and weather. A marble figure of Mary is stretched upon the tomb, around which is an iron railing, much corroded, bearing her national emblem—the thistle. I was weary with wandering, and sat down to rest myself by the monument, revolving in my mind the checkered and disastrous story of poor Mary.

The sound of casual footsteps had ceased from the abbey. I could only hear, now and then, the distant voice of the priest repeating the evening service, and the faint responses of the choir; these paused for a time, and all was hushed. The stillness, the desertion and obscurity that were gradually prevailing around gave a deeper and more solemn interest to the place:

> For in the silent grave no conversation,
> No joyful tread of friends, no voice of lovers,
> No careful father's counsel—nothing's heard,
> For nothing is, but all oblivion,
> Dust, and an endless darkness.

Suddenly the notes of the deep-laboring organ burst upon the ear, falling with doubled and redoubled intensity, and rolling, as it were, huge billows of sound. How well do their volume and grandeur accord with this mighty building! With what pomp do they swell through its vast vaults, and breathe their awful harmony through these caves of death, and make the silent sepulcher vocal! And now they rise in triumph and acclamation, heaving higher and higher their accordant notes, and piling sound on sound. And now they pause, and the soft voices of the choir break out into sweet gushes of melody; they soar aloft, and warble along the roof, and seem to play about these lofty vaults like the pure airs of heaven. Again the pealing organ heaves its thrilling thunders, compressing air into music, and rolling it forth upon the soul. What long-drawn cadences! What solemn sweeping concords! It grows more and more dense and powerful—it fills the vast pile, and seems to jar the very walls—the ear is stunned—the senses are overwhelmed. And now it is winding up in full jubilee—it is rising from the earth to heaven—the very soul seems rapt away and floated upward on this swelling tide of harmony!

I sat for some time lost in that kind of reverie which a strain of music is apt sometimes to inspire; the shadows of evening were gradually thickening around me, the monuments began to cast deeper and deeper gloom, and the distant clock again gave token of the slowly waning day.

I rose and prepared to leave the abbey. As I descended the flight of steps which lead into the body of the building, my eye was caught by the shrine of Edward the Confessor, and I ascended the small staircase that conducts to it, to take from thence a general survey of this wilderness of tombs. The shrine is elevated upon a kind of platform, and close around it are the sepulchers of various kings and queens. From this eminence the eye looks down between pillars and funeral trophies to the chapels and chambers below, crowded with tombs, where warriors, prelates, courtiers and statesmen lie moldering in their "beds of darkness." Close by me stood the great chair of coronation, rudely carved of oak, in the barbarous taste of a remote and Gothic age. The scene seemed almost as if contrived, with theatrical artifice, to produce an effect upon the beholder. Here was a type of the beginning and the end of human pomp and power; here it was literally but a step from the throne to the sepulcher. Would not one think that these incongruous mementos had been gathered together as a lesson to living greatness? —to show it, even in the moment of its proudest exaltation, the neglect and dishonor to which it must soon arrive; how soon that crown which encircles its brow must pass away, and it must lie down in the dust and disgraces of the tomb, and be trampled upon by the feet of the meanest of the multitude. For, strange to tell, even the grave is here no longer a sanctuary. There is a shocking levity in some natures which leads them to sport with awful and hallowed things; and there are base minds, which delight to revenge on the illustrious dead the abject homage and groveling servility which they pay to the living. The coffin of Edward the Confessor has been broken open, and his remains despoiled of their funereal ornaments; the scepter has been stolen from the hand of the imperious Elizabeth, and the effigy of Henry the Fifth lies headless. Not a royal monument but bears some proof how false and fugitive is the homage of mankind. Some are plundered; some mutilated; some covered with ribaldry and insult—all more or less outraged and dishonored!

The last beams of day were now faintly streaming through the painted windows in the high vaults above me; the lower parts of the abbey were already wrapped in the obscurity of twilight. The chapels and aisles grew darker and darker. The effigies of the kings faded into shadows; the marble figures of the monuments assumed strange shapes in the uncertain light; the evening breeze crept through the aisles like the cold breath of the grave; and even the distant footfall of a verger, traversing the Poets' Corner, had something strange and dreary in its sound. I slowly retraced my morning's walk, and as I passed out at the portal of the cloisters, the door, closing with a jarring noise behind me, filled the whole building with echoes.

I endeavored to form some arrangement in my mind of the objects I had been contemplating, but found they were already fallen into indistinctness and confusion. Names, inscriptions, trophies, had all become confounded in my recollection, though I had scarcely taken my foot from off the threshold. What, thought I, is this vast assemblage of sepulchers but a treasury of humiliation; a huge pile of reiterated homilies on the emptiness of renown and the certainty of oblivion! It is, indeed, the empire of death; his great shadowy palace, where he sits in state, mocking at the relics of human glory, and spreading dust and forgetfulness on the monuments of princes. How idle a boast, after all, is the immortality of a name! Time is ever silently turning over his pages; we are too much engrossed by the story of the present to think of the characters and anecdotes that gave interest to the past; and each age is a volume thrown aside to be speedily forgotten. The idol of today pushes the hero of yesterday out of our recollection, and will, in turn, be supplanted by his successor of tomorrow. "Our fathers," says Sir Thomas Brown, "find their graves in our short memories, and sadly tell us how we may be buried in our survivors." History fades into fable; fact becomes clouded

with doubt and controversy; the inscription molders from
the tablet; the statue falls from the pedestal. Columns,
arches, pyramids, what are they but heaps of sand; and
their epitaphs, but characters written in the dust? What
is the security of a tomb, or the perpetuity of an em-
balmment? The remains of Alexander the Great have
been scattered to the wind, and his empty sarcophagus
is now the mere curiosity of a museum. "The Egyptian
mummies, which Cambyses or time hath spared, avarice
now consumeth; Mizraim cures wounds, and Pharaoh is
sold for balsams."*

What then is to insure this pile which now towers
above me from sharing the fate of mightier mausoleums?
The time must come when its gilded vaults, which now
spring so loftily, shall lie in rubbish beneath the feet;
when, instead of the sound of melody and praise, the
wind shall whistle through the broken arches, and the
owl hoot from the shattered tower; when the garish sun-
beam shall break into these gloomy mansions of death,
and the ivy twine around the fallen column, and the fox-
glove hang its blossoms about the nameless urn, as if in
mockery of the dead. Thus man passes away; his name
perishes from record and recollection; his history is as a
tale that is told, and his very monument becomes a
ruin.†

*Sir T. Brown.   †For notes on Westminster Abbey, see Appendix.

CHRISTMAS

But is old, old, good old Christmas gone? Nothing but the hair of his good, gray, old head and beard left? Well, I will have that, seeing I cannot have more of him.

HUE AND CRY AFTER CHRISTMAS

A man might then behold
  At Christmas, in each hall
Good fires to curb the cold,
  And meat for great and small.
The neighbors were friendly bidden,
  And all had welcome true,
The poor from the gates were not chidden
  When this old cap was new.

OLD SONG

Nothing in England exercises a more delightful spell over my imagination than the lingerings of the holiday customs and rural games of former times. They recall the pictures my fancy used to draw in the May morning of life, when as yet I only knew the world through books, and believed it to be all that poets had painted it; and they bring with them the flavor of those honest days of yore, in which, perhaps, with equal fallacy I am apt to think the world was more homebred, social, and joyous than at present. I regret to say that they are daily growing more and more faint, being gradually worn away by time, but still more obliterated by modern fashion. They resemble those picturesque morsels of Gothic architecture, which we see crumbling in various parts of the country, partly dilapidated by the waste of ages, and partly lost in the additions and alterations of later days. Poetry, however, clings with cherishing fondness about the rural game and holiday revel from which it has derived so many of its themes—as the ivy winds its rich foliage about the Gothic arch and moldering tower, gratefully repaying their support, by clasping together their tottering remains, and, as it were, embalming them in verdure.

Of all the old festivals, however, that of Christmas awakens the strongest and most heartfelt associations.

There is a tone of solemn and sacred feeling that blends with our conviviality and lifts the spirit to a state of hallowed and elevated enjoyment. The services of the church about this season are extremely tender and inspiring. They dwell on the beautiful story of the origin of our faith, and the pastoral scenes that accompanied its announcement. They gradually increase in fervor and pathos during the season of Advent, until they break forth in full jubilee on the morning that brought peace and good will to men. I do not know a grander effect of music on the moral feelings than to hear the full choir and the pealing organ performing a Christmas anthem in a cathedral, and filling every part of the vast pile with triumphant harmony.

It is a beautiful arrangement, also, derived from days of yore, that this festival, which commemorates the announcement of the religion of peace and love, has been made the season for gathering together of family connections, and drawing closer again those bands of kindred hearts, which the cares and pleasures and sorrows of the world are continually operating to cast loose; of calling back the children of a family, who have launched forth in life, and wandered widely asunder, once more to assemble about the paternal hearth, that rallying place of the affections, there to grow young and loving again among the endearing mementos of childhood.

There is something in the very season of the year that gives a charm to the festivity of Christmas. At other times we derive a great portion of our pleasures from the mere beauties of nature. Our feelings sally forth and dissipate themselves over the sunny landscape, and we "live abroad and everywhere." The song of the bird, the murmur of the stream, the breathing fragrance of spring, the soft voluptuousness of summer, the golden pomp of autumn; earth with its mantle of refreshing green, and heaven with its deep delicious blue and its cloudy magnificence, all fill us with mute but exquisite delight and we revel in the luxury of mere sensation. But in the depth of winter, when Nature lies despoiled of every charm and wrapped in her shroud of sheeted snow, we turn for our gratifications to moral sources. The dreariness and desolation of the landscape, the short gloomy days and darksome nights, while they circumscribe our wanderings, shut in our feelings also from rambling abroad, and make us more keenly disposed for the pleasure of the social circle. Our thoughts are more concentrated, our friendly sympathies more aroused. We feel more sensibly the charm of each other's society, and are brought more closely together by dependence on each other for enjoyment. Heart calleth unto heart; and we draw our pleasures from the deep wells of loving-kindness, which lie in the quiet recesses of our bosoms, and which, when resorted to, furnish forth the pure element of domestic felicity.

The pitchy gloom without makes the heart dilate on entering the room filled with the glow and warmth of the evening fire. The ruddy blaze diffuses an artificial summer and sunshine through the room, and lights up each countenance in a kindlier welcome. Where does the honest face of hospitality expand into a broader and more cordial smile—where is the shy glance of love more sweetly eloquent—than by the winter fireside? And as the hollow blast of wintry wind rushes through the hall, claps the distant door, whistles about the casement, and rumbles down the chimney, what can be more grateful than that feeling of sober and sheltered security with which we look around upon the comfortable chamber and the scene of domestic hilarity?

The English, from the great prevalence of rural habit throughout every class of society, have always been fond of those festivals and holidays which agreeably interrupt the stillness of country life; and they were, in former days, particularly observant of the religious and social rites of Christmas. It is inspiring to read even the dry details which some antiquaries have given of the quaint humors, the burlesque pageants, the complete abandonment to mirth and good-fellowship with which this festival was celebrated. It seemed to throw open every door and unlock every heart. It brought the peasant and the peer together, and blended all ranks in one warm generous flow of joy and kindness. The old halls of castles and manor houses resounded with the harp and the Christmas carol, and their ample boards groaned under the weight of hospitality. Even the poorest cottage welcomed the festive season with green decorations of bay and holly—the cheerful fire glanced its rays through the lattice, inviting the passengers to raise the latch, and join the gossip knot huddled around the hearth, beguiling the long evening with legendary jokes and oft-told Christmas tales.

One of the least pleasing effects of modern refinement is the havoc it has made among the hearty old holiday customs. It has completely taken off the sharp touchings and spirited reliefs of these embellishments of life, and has worn down society into a more smooth and polished, but certainly a less characteristic surface. Many of the games and ceremonials of Christmas have entirely disappeared, and, like the sherris sack of old Falstaff, are become matters of speculation and dispute among commentators. They flourished in times full of spirit and lustihood, when men enjoyed life roughly, but heartily and vigorously; times wild and picturesque, which have furnished poetry with its richest materials, and the drama with its most attractive variety of characters and manners. The world has become more worldly. There is more of dissipation, and less of enjoyment. Pleasure has expanded into a broader but a shallower stream, and has forsaken many of those deep and quiet channels where it flowed sweetly through the calm bosom of domestic life. Society has acquired a more enlightened and elegant tone, but it has lost many of its strong local peculiarities, its homebred feelings, its honest fireside delights. The traditionary customs of golden-hearted antiquity, its feudal hospitalities, and lordly wassailings, have passed away with the baronial castles and stately manor houses in which they were celebrated. They comported with the shadowy hall, the great oaken gallery, and the tapestried parlor, but are unfitted to the light showy saloons and gay drawing rooms of the modern villa.

Shorn, however, as it is, of its ancient and festive honors, Christmas is still a period of delightful excitement in England. It is gratifying to see that home feeling completely aroused which holds so powerful a place in every English bosom. The preparations making on every side for the social board that is again to unite friends and kindred; the presents of good cheer passing and repassing, those tokens of regard, and quickeners of kind feelings;

the evergreens distributed about houses and churches, emblems of peace and gladness; all these have the most pleasing effect in producing fond associations and kindling benevolent sympathies. Even the sound of the Waits, rude as may be their minstrelsy, breaks upon the mid-watches of a winter night with the effect of perfect harmony. As I have been awakened by them in that still and solemn hour, "when deep sleep falleth upon man," I have listened with a hushed delight, and, connecting them with the sacred and joyous occasion, have almost fancied them into another celestrial choir, announcing peace and good will to mankind.

How delightfully the imagination, when wrought upon by these moral influences, turns everything to melody and beauty! The very crowing of the cock, heard some-times in the profound repose of the country, "telling the night watches to his feathery dames," was thought by the common people to announce the approach of this sacred festival.

> "Some say that ever 'gainst that season comes
> Wherein our Saviour's birth is celebrated,
> This bird of dawning singeth all night long;
> And then, they say, no spirit dares stir abroad;
> The nights are wholesome—then no planets strike,
> No fairy takes, no witch hath power to charm,
> So hallow'd and so gracious is the time."

Amidst the general call to happiness, the bustle of the spirits, and stir of the affections which prevail at this period, what bosom can remain insensible? It is, indeed, the season of regenerated feeling—the season for kindling, not merely the fire of hospitality in the hall, but the genial flame of charity in the heart.

The scene of early love again rises green to memory beyond the sterile waste of years; and the idea of home, fraught with the fragrance of home-dwelling joys, reanimates the drooping spirit, as the Arabian breeze will sometimes waft the freshness of the distant fields to the weary pilgrim of the desert.

Stranger and sojourner as I am in the land—though for me no social hearth may blaze, no hospitable roof throw open its doors, nor the warm grasp of friendship welcome me at the threshold—yet I feel the influence of the season beaming into my soul from the happy looks of those around me. Surely happiness is reflective, like the light of heaven; and every countenance, bright with smiles and glowing with innocent enjoyment, is a mirror transmitting to others the rays of a supreme and ever-shining benevolence. He who can turn churlishly away from contemplating the felicity of his fellow-beings and can sit down darkling and repining in his loneliness when all around is joyful may have his moments of strong excitement and selfish gratification, but he wants the genial and social sympathies which constitute the charm of a Merry Christmas.

THE STAGECOACH

Omne bené
Sine pœna
Tempus est ludendi.
Venit hora
Absque morá
Libros deponendi.

OLD HOLIDAY SCHOOL SONG

In the preceding paper I have made some general observations on the Christmas festivities of England, and am tempted to illustrate them by some anecdotes of a Christmas passed in the country, in perusing which I would most courteously invite my reader to lay aside the austerity of wisdom, and to put on that genuine holiday spirit which is tolerant of folly, and anxious only for amusement.

In the course of a December tour in Yorkshire, I rode for a long distance in one of the public coaches on the day preceding Christmas. The coach was crowded, both inside and out, with passengers, who, by their talk, seemed principally bound to the mansions of relations or friends to eat the Christmas dinner. It was loaded also with hampers of game, and baskets and boxes of delicacies; and hares hung dangling their long ears about the coachman's box, presents from distant friends for the impending feast. I had three fine rosy-cheeked boys for my fellow-passengers inside, full of the buxom health and manly spirit which I have observed in the children of this country. They were returning home for the holidays in high glee, and promising themselves a world of enjoyment. It was delightful to hear the gigantic plans of the little rogues, and the impracticable feats they were to perform during their six weeks' emancipation from the abhorred thraldom of book, birch, and pedagogue. They were full of anticipations of the meeting with the family and household, down to the very cat and dog; and of the joy they were to give their little sisters by the presents with which their pockets were crammed; but the meeting to which they seemed to look forward with the greatest impatience was with Bantam, which I found to be a pony, and, according to their talk, possessed of more virtues than any steed since the days of Bucephalus. How he could trot! How he could run! And then such leaps as he would take—there was not a hedge in the whole country that he could not clear.

They were under the particular guardianship of the coachman, to whom, whenever an opportunity presented, they addressed a host of questions, and pronounced him one of the best fellows in the world. Indeed, I could not but notice the more than ordinary air of bustle and importance of the coachman, who wore his hat a little on one side, and had a large bunch of Christmas greens stuck in the buttonhole of his coat. He is always a personage full of mighty care and business, but he is particularly so during this season, having so many commissions to execute in consequence of the great interchange of presents. And here, perhaps, it may not be unacceptable to my untraveled readers to have a sketch that may serve as a general representation of this very numerous and important class of functionaries, who have a dress, a manner, a language, an air, peculiar to themselves, and prevalent throughout the fraternity, so that, wherever an English stagecoachman may be seen, he cannot be mistaken for one of any other craft or mystery.

He has commonly a broad, full face, curiously mottled with red, as if the blood had been forced by hard feeding into every vessel of the skin; he is swelled into jolly dimensions by frequent potations of malt liquors, and his bulk is still further increased by a multiplicity of coats, in which he is buried like a cauliflower, the upper one reaching to his heels. He wears a broad-brimmed, low-crowned hat; a huge roll of colored handkerchief about his neck, knowingly knotted and tucked in at the bosom; and has in summertime a large bouquet of flowers in his buttonhole, the present, most probably, of

some enamored country lass. His waistcoat is commonly
of some bright color, striped, and his small clothes extend far below the knees, to meet a pair of jockey boots
which reach about halfway up his legs.

All this costume is maintained with much precision;
he has a pride in having his clothes of excellent materials; and, notwithstanding the seeming grossness of his
appearance, there is still discernible that neatness and
propriety of person which are almost inherent in an Englishman. He enjoys great consequence and consideration
along the road; has frequent conferences with the village
housewives, who look upon him as a man of great trust
and dependence; and he seems to have a good understanding with every bright-eyed country lass. The moment
he arrives where the horses are to be changed he throws
down the reins with something of an air, and abandons
the cattle to the care of the hostler, his duty being merely
to drive from one stage to another. When off the box, his
hands are thrust into the pockets of his greatcoat, and
he rolls about the inn yard with an air of the most absolute lordliness. Here he is generally surrounded by an admiring throng of hostlers, stable boys, shoeblacks, and
those nameless hangers-on that infest inns and taverns
and run errands and do all kinds of odd jobs for the
privilege of battening on the drippings of the kitchen
and the leakage of the taproom. These all look up to him
as to an oracle, treasure up his cant phrases, echo his
opinions about horses and other topics of jockey lore,
and, above all, endeavor to imitate his air and carriage.
Every ragamuffin that has a coat to his back thrusts his
hands in the pockets, rolls in his gait, talks slang, and is
an embryo Coachey.

Perhaps it might be owing to the pleasing serenity that
reigned in my own mind that I fanced I saw cheerfulness in every countenance throughout the journey. A
stagecoach, however, carries animation always with it,
and puts the world in motion as it whirls along. The
horn, sounded at the entrance of a village, produces a
general bustle. Some hasten forth to meet friends; some
with bundles and bandboxes to secure places, and in the
hurry of the moment can hardly take leave of the group
that accompanies them. In the meantime, the coachman

has a world of small commissions to execute. Sometimes
he delivers a hare or pheasant; sometimes jerks a small
parcel or newspaper to the door of a public house; and
sometimes, with knowing leer and words of sly import,
hands to some half-blushing, half-laughing housemaid an
odd-shaped billet-doux from some rustic admirer. As the
coach rattles through the village, everyone runs to the
window, and you have glances on every side of fresh
country faces and blooming giggling girls. At the corners
are assembled juntos of village idlers and wise men, who
take their stations there for the important purpose of
seeing company pass, but the sagest knot is generally at
the blacksmith's, to whom the passing of the coach is an
event fruitful of much speculation. The smith, with the
horse's heel in his lap, pauses as the vehicle whirls by;
the cyclops around the anvil suspend their ringing ham-
mers, and suffer the iron to grow cool; and the sooty
specter, in brown paper cap, laboring at the bellows,
leans on the handle for a moment, and permits the asth-
matic engine to heave a long-drawn sigh while he glares
through the murky smoke and sulphurous gleams of the
smithy.

Perhaps the impending holiday might have given a
more than usual animation to the country, for it seemed
to me as if everybody was in good looks and good spirits.
Game, poultry, and other luxuries of the table were in
brisk circulation in the villages; the grocers', butchers',
and fruiterers' shops were thronged with customers. The
housewives were stirring briskly about, putting their
dwellings in order; and the glossy branches of holly,
with their bright-red berries, began to appear at the windows. The scene brought to mind an old writer's account
of Christmas preparations: "Now capons and hens, beside
turkeys, geese, and ducks, with beef and mutton—must
all die—for in twelve days a multitude of people will not
be fed with a little. Now plums and spice, sugar and
honey, square it among pies and broth. Now or never
must music be in tune, for the youth must dance and
sing to get them a heat, while the aged sit by the fire.
The country maid leaves half her market, and must be
sent again if she forgets a pack of cards on Christmas
Eve. Great is the contention of holly and ivy, whether

master or dame wears the breeches. Dice and cards benefit the butler; and if the cook do not lack wit, he will sweetly lick his fingers."

I was roused from this fit of luxurious meditation by a shout from my little traveling companions. They had been looking out of the coach windows for the last few miles, recognizing every tree and cottage as they approached home, and now there was a general burst of joy. "There's John! And there's old Carlo! And there's Bantam!" cried the happy little rogues, clapping their hands.

At the end of a lane there was an old sober-looking servant in livery waiting for them; he was accompanied by a superannuated pointer, and by the redoubtable Bantam, a little old rat of a pony with a shaggy mane and long rusty tail, who stood dozing quietly by the roadside, little dreaming of the bustling times that awaited him.

I was pleased to see the fondness with which the little fellows leaped about the steady old footman, and hugged the pointer, who wriggled his whole body for joy. But Bantam was the great object of interest; all wanted to mount at once, and it was with some difficulty that John arranged that they should ride by turns, and the eldest should ride first.

Off they set at last, one on the pony, with the dog bounding and barking before him, and the others holding John's hands, both talking at once and overpowering him with questions about home and with school anecdotes. I looked after them with a feeling in which I do not know whether pleasure or melancholy predominated, for I was reminded of those days when, like them, I had neither known care nor sorrow, and a holiday was the summit of earthly felicity. We stopped a few moments afterward to water the horses, and on resuming our route, a turn of the road brought us in sight of a neat country seat. I could just distinguish the forms of a lady and two young girls in the portico, and I saw my little comrades, with Bantam, Carlo, and old John, trooping along the carriage road. I leaned out of the coach window in hopes of witnessing the happy meeting, but a grove of trees shut it from my sight.

In the evening we reached a village where I had determined to pass the night. As we drove into the great gateway of the inn, I saw on one side the light of a rousing kitchen fire beaming through a window. I entered, and admired for the hundredth time that picture of convenience, neatness, and broad honest enjoyment, the kitchen of an English inn. It was of spacious dimensions, hung around with copper and tin vessels highly polished, and decorated here and there with a Christmas green. Hams, tongues, and flitches of bacon were suspended from the ceiling; a smokejack made its ceaseless clanking beside the fireplace, and a clock ticked in one corner. A well-scoured deal table extended along one side of the kitchen, with a cold round of beef and other hearty viands upon it, over which two foaming tankards of ale seemed mounting guard. Travelers of inferior order were preparing to attack this stout repast, while others sat smoking and gossiping over their ale on two high-backed oaken settles beside the fire. Trim housemaids were hurrying backward and forward under the directions of a fresh, bustling landlady, but still seizing an occasional moment to exchange a flippant word and have a rallying laugh with the group around the fire. The scene completely realized Poor Robin's humble idea of the comforts of midwinter:

> Now trees their leafy hats do bare
> To reverence Winter's silver hair;
> A handsome hostess, merry host,
> A pot of ale now and a toast,
> Tobacco and a good coal fire,
> Are things this season doth require.*

I had not been long at the inn when a post-chaise drove up to the door. A young gentleman stepped out, and by the light of the lamps I caught a glimpse of a countenance which I thought I knew. I moved forward to get a nearer view when his eye caught mine. I was not mistaken; it was Frank Bracebridge, a sprightly good-humored young fellow with whom I had once traveled on the Continent. Our meeting was extremely cordial, for the countenance

*Poor Robin's Almanac, 1684.

of an old fellow-traveler always brings up the recollection of a thousand pleasant scenes, odd adventures, and
excellent jokes. To discuss all these in a transient interview at an inn was impossible; and finding that I was
not pressed for time and was merely making a tour of
observation, he insisted that I should give him a day or
two at his father's country seat, to which he was going
to pass the holidays and which lay at a few miles distance. "It is better than eating a solitary Christmas dinner at an inn," said he, "and I can assure you of a hearty
welcome in something of the old-fashioned style." His
reasoning was cogent, and I must confess the preparation
I had seen for universal festivity and social enjoyment
had made me feel a little impatient of my loneliness. I
closed, therefore, at once, with his invitation; the chaise
drove up to the door, and in a few moments I was on my
way to the family mansion of the Bracebridges.

CHRISTMAS EVE

Saint Francis and Saint Benedight
Blesse this house from wicked wight;
From the night-mare and the goblin,
That is hight good fellow Robin:
Keep it from all evil spirits,
Fairies, weezels, rats, and ferrets:
    From curfew time
    To the next prime.

CARTWRIGHT

It was a brilliant moonlight night, but extremely cold; our chaise whirled rapidly over the frozen ground; the postboy smacked his whip incessantly, and a part of the time his horses were on a gallop. "He knows where he is going," said my companion, laughing, "and is eager to arrive in time for some of the merriment and good cheer of the servants' hall. My father, you must know, is a bigoted devotee of the old school, and prides himself upon keeping up something of old English hospitality. He is a tolerable specimen of what you will rarely meet with nowadays in its purity, the old English country gentleman, for our men of fortune spend so much of their time in town and fashion is carried so much into the country that the strong rich peculiarities of ancient rural life are almost polished away. My father, however, from early years, took honest Peacham * for his textbook, instead of Chesterfield; he determined in his own mind that there was no condition more truly honorable and enviable than that of a country gentleman on his paternal lands, and therefore passes the whole of his time on his estate. He is a strenuous advocate for the revival of the old rural games and holiday observances, and is deeply read in the writers, ancient and

*Peacham's *The Complete Gentleman*, 1622

modern, who have treated on the subject. Indeed, his favorite range of reading is among the authors who flourished at least two centuries since, who, he insists, wrote and thought more like true Englishmen than any of their successors. He even regrets sometimes that he had not been born a few centuries earlier, when England was itself, and had its peculiar manners and customs. As he lives at some distance from the main road, in rather a lonely part of the country, without any rival gentry near him, he has that most enviable of all blessings to an Englishman, an opportunity of indulging the bent of his own humor without molestation. Being representative of the oldest family in the neighborhood, and a great part of the peasantry being his tenants, he is much looked up to, and, in general, is known simply by the appellation of 'The Squire,' a title which has been accorded to the head of the family since time immemorial. I think it best to give you these hints about my worthy old father to prepare you for any eccentricities that might otherwise appear absurd."

We had passed for some time along the wall of a park, and at length the chaise stopped at the gate. It was in a heavy magnificent old style, of iron bars, fancifully wrought at top into flourishes and flowers. The huge square columns that supported the gate were surmounted by the family crest. Close adjoining was the porter's lodge, sheltered under dark fir trees, and almost buried in shrubbery.

The postboy rang a large porter's bell, which resounded through the still frosty air and was answered by the distant barking of dogs, with which the mansion house seemed garrisoned. An old woman immediately appeared at the gate. As the moonlight fell strongly upon her, I had a full view of a little primitive dame, dressed very much in the antique taste, with a neat kerchief and stomacher, and her silver hair peeping from under a cap of snowy whiteness. She came courtesying forth, with many expressions of simple joy at seeing her young master. Her husband, it seemed, was up at the house keeping Christmas Eve in the servants' hall; they could not do without him, as he was the best hand at a song and story in the household.

My friend proposed that we should alight and walk through the park to the hall, which was at no great distance, while the chaise should follow on. Our road wound through a noble avenue of trees, among the naked branches of which the moon glittered as she rolled through the deep vault of a cloudless sky. The lawn beyond was sheeted with a slight covering of snow, which here and there sparkled as the moonbeams caught a frosty crystal; and at a distance might be seen a thin transparent vapor, stealing up from the low grounds and threatening gradually to shroud the landscape.

My companion looked around him with transport. "How often," said he, "have I scampered up this avenue, on returning home on school vacations! How often have I played under these trees when a boy! I feel a degree of filial reverence for them, as we look up to those who have cherished us in childhood. My father was always scrupulous in exacting our holidays, and having us around him on family festivals. He used to direct and superintend our games with the strictness that some parents do the studies of their children. He was very particular that we should play the old English games according to their original form, and consulted old books for precedent and authority for every 'merrie disport'; yet, I assure you, there never was pedantry so delightful. It was the policy of the good old gentleman to make his children feel that home was the happiest place in the world, and I value this delicious home feeling as one of the choicest gifts a parent could bestow."

We were interrupted by the clamor of a troop of dogs of all sorts and sizes, "mongrel, puppy, whelp and hound, and curs of low degree," that, disturbed by the ring of the porter's bell and the rattling of the chaise, came bounding, open-mouthed, across the lawn.

> "——The little dogs and all,
> Tray, Blanch, and Sweetheart, see, they bark at me!"

cried Bracebridge, laughing. At the sound of his voice, the bark was changed into a yelp of delight, and in a moment he was surrounded and almost overpowered by the caresses of the faithful animals.

We had now come in full view of the old family mansion, partly thrown in deep shadow and partly lit up by the cold moonshine. It was an irregular building of some magnitude, and seemed to be of the architecture of different periods. One wing was evidently very ancient, with heavy stone-shafted bow windows jutting out and overrun with ivy, from among the foliage of which the small diamond-shaped panes of glass glittered with the moonbeams. The rest of the house was in the French taste of Charles the Second's time, having been repaired and altered, as my friend told me, by one of his ancestors, who returned with that monarch at the Restoration. The grounds about the house were laid out in the old formal manner of artificial flower beds, clipped shrubberies, raised terraces, and heavy stone balustrades, ornamented with urns, a leaden statue or two, and a jet of water. The old gentleman, I was told, was extremely careful to preserve this obsolete finery in all its original state. He admired this fashion in gardening; it had an air of magnificence, was courtly and noble, and befitting good old family style. The boasted imitation of nature in modern gardening had sprung up with modern republican notions, but did not suit a monarchical government; it smacked of the leveling system—I could not help smiling at this introduction of politics into gardening, though I expressed some apprehension that I should find the old gentleman rather intolerant in his creed. Frank assured me, however, that it was almost the only instance in which we had ever heard his father meddle with politics, and he believed that he had got this notion from a member of parliament who once passed a few weeks with him. The squire was glad of any argument to defend his clipped yew trees and formal terraces, which had been occasionally attacked by modern landscape gardeners.

As we approached the house, we heard the sound of music and now and then a burst of laughter from one end of the building. This, Bracebridge said, must proceed from the servants' hall, where a great deal of revelry was permitted and even encouraged by the squire throughout the twelve days of Christmas, provided everything was done conformably to ancient usage. Here were

kept up the old games of hoodman blind, shoe the wild
mare, hot cockles, steal the white loaf, bob apple, and
snap dragon; the Yule clog and Christmas candle were
regularly burned, and the mistletoe, with its white berries, hung up, to the imminent peril of all the pretty
housemaids.*

So intent were the servants upon their sports that we had
to ring repeatedly before we could make ourselves heard.
On our arrival being announced, the squire came out to
receive us, accompanied by his two other sons, one a
young officer in the army, home on leave of absence, the
other an Oxonian, just from the university. The squire
was a fine, healthy-looking old gentleman, with silver
hair curling lightly round an open florid countenance, in
which the physiognomist, with the advantage, like myself,
of a previous hint or two, might discover a singular mixture of whim and benevolence.

The family meeting was warm and affectionate; as the
evening was far advanced, the squire would not permit
us to change our traveling dresses but ushered us at
once to the company, which was assembled in a large
old-fashioned hall. It was composed of different branches
of a numerous family connection, where there were the
usual proportion of old uncles and aunts, comfortable
married dames, superannuated spinsters, blooming country cousins, half-fledged striplings, and bright-eyed
boarding-school hoydens. They were variously occupied,
some at a round game of cards, others conversing around
the fireplace; at one end of the hall was a group of the
young folks, some nearly grown up, others of a more
tender and budding age, fully engrossed by a merry game;
and a profusion of wooden horses, penny trumpets, and
tattered dolls about the floor showed traces of a troop
of little fairy beings, who, having frolicked through a
happy day, had been carried off to slumber through a
peaceful night.

While the mutual greetings were going on between
young Bracebridge and his relatives, I had time to scan

*The mistletoe is still hung up in farmhouses and kitchens at
Christmas; and the young men have the privilege of kissing the girls
under it, plucking each time a berry from the bush. When the berries
are all plucked, the privilege ceases.

the apartment. I have called it a hall, for so it had certainly been in old times, and the squire had evidently endeavored to restore it to something of its primitive state. Over the heavy projecting fireplace was suspended a picture of a warrior in armor, standing by a white horse, and on the opposite wall hung a helmet, buckler, and lance. At one end an enormous pair of antlers were inserted in the wall, the branches serving as hooks on which to suspend hats, whips, and spurs; and in the corners of the apartment were fowling pieces, fishing rods, and other sporting implements. The furniture was of the cumbrous workmanship of former days, though some articles of modern convenience had been added, and the oaken floor had been carpeted, so that the whole presented an odd mixture of parlor and hall.

The grate had been removed from the wide overwhelming fireplace to make way for a fire of wood, in the midst of which was an enormous log glowing and blazing, and sending forth a vast volume of light and heat. This I understood was the Yule clog, which the squire was particular in having brought in and illumined on a Christmas Eve, according to ancient custom.*

It was really delightful to see the old squire seated in his hereditary elbow chair, by the hospitable fireside of

---

*The *Yule clog* is a great log of wood, sometimes the root of a tree, brought into the house with great ceremony, on Christmas Eve, laid in the fireplace, and lighted with the brand of last year's clog. While it lasted, there was great drinking, singing, and telling of tales. Sometimes it was accompanied by Christmas candles; but in the cottages the only light was from the ruddy blaze of the great wood fire. The Yule clog was to burn all night; if it went out, it was considered a sign of ill luck.

Herrick mentions it in one of his songs:

> Come, bring with a noise,
> My merrie, merrie boyes,
> The Christmas log to the firing;
> While my good dame, she
> Bids ye all be free,
> And drink to your hearts desiring.

The Yule clog is still burned in many farmhouses and kitchens in England, particularly in the north, and there are several superstitions connected with it among the peasantry. If a squinting person comes to the house while it is burning, or a person barefooted, it is considered an ill omen. The brand remaining from the Yule clog is carefully put away to light the next year's Christmas fire.

his ancestors, and looking around him like the sun of a system, beaming warmth and gladness to every heart. Even the very dog that lay stretched at his feet, as he lazily shifted his position and yawned, would look fondly up in his master's face, wag his tail against the floor, and stretch himself again to sleep, confident of kindness and protection. There is an emanation from the heart in genuine hospitality which cannot be described but is immediately felt and puts the stranger at once at his ease. I had not been seated many minutes by the comfortable hearth of the worthy old cavalier before I found myself as much at home as if I had been one of the family.

Supper was announced shortly after our arrival. It was served up in a spacious oaken chamber, the panels of which shone with wax and around which were several family portraits decorated with holly and ivy. Besides the accustomed lights, two great wax tapers called Christmas candles, wreathed with greens, were placed on a highly polished buffet among the family plate. The table was abundantly spread with substantial fare, but the squire made his supper of frumenty, a dish made of wheat cakes boiled in milk, with rich spices, being a standing dish in old times for Christmas Eve.

I was happy to find my old friend, mince pie, in the retinue of the feast; and finding him to be perfectly orthodox, and that I need not be ashamed of my predilection, I greeted him with all the warmth wherewith we usually greet an old and very genteel acquaintance.

The mirth of the company was greatly promoted by the humors of an eccentric personage whom Mr. Bracebridge always addressed with the quaint appellation of Master Simon. He was a tight brisk little man, with the air of an arrant old bachelor. His nose was shaped like the bill of a parrot; his face slightly pitted with the smallpox, with a dry perpetual bloom on it, like a frostbitten leaf in autumn. He had an eye of great quickness and vivacity, with a drollery and lurking waggery of expression that were irresistible. He was evidently the wit of the family, dealing very much in sly jokes and innuendoes with the ladies, and making infinite merriment by harping upon old themes, which, unfortunately, my ignorance of the family chronicles did not permit me to enjoy. It seemed to be his great delight during supper to keep a young girl next him in a continual agony of stifled laughter, in spite of her awe of the reproving looks of her mother, who sat opposite. Indeed, he was the idol of the younger part of the company, who laughed at everything he said or did, and at every turn of his countenance; I could not wonder at it, for he must have been a miracle of accomplishments in their eyes. He could imitate Punch and Judy, make an old woman of his hand, with the assistance of a burnt cork and pocket handkerchief, and cut an orange into such a ludicrous caricature that the young folks were ready to die with laughing.

I was let briefly into his history by Frank Bracebridge. He was an old bachelor, of a small independent income, which, by careful management, was sufficient for all his wants. He revolved through the family system like a vagrant comet in its orbit, sometimes visiting one branch, and sometimes another quite remote, as is often the case with gentlemen of extensive connections and small fortunes in England. He had a chirping buoyant disposition, always enjoying the present moment, and his frequent change of scene and company prevented his acquiring those rusty unaccommodating habits with which old bachelors are so uncharitably charged. He was a complete family chronicle, being versed in the genealogy, history, and intermarriages of the whole house of Bracebridge, which made him a great favorite with the old folks; he was a beau of all the elder ladies and superannuated spinsters, among whom he was habitually considered rather a young fellow; and he was master of the revels among the children, so that there was not a more popular being in the sphere in which he moved than Mr. Simon Bracebridge. Of late years he had resided almost entirely with the squire, to whom he had become a factotum, and whom he particularly delighted by jumping with his humor in respect to old times, and by having a scrap of an old song to suit every occasion. We had presently a specimen of his last-mentioned talent, for no sooner was supper removed and spiced wines and other beverages peculiar to the season introduced than Master Simon was called on for a good old Christmas song. He bethought himself for a moment, and then, with a sparkle of the eye and a voice that was by no means bad, excepting that it ran occasionally into a falsetto, like the notes of a split reed, he quavered forth a quaint old ditty.

> Now Christmas is come,
> Let us beat up the drum,
> And call all our neighbors together,
> And when they appear,
> Let us make them such cheer,
> As will keep out the wind and the weather, etc.

The supper had disposed everyone to gaiety, and an old harper was summoned from the servants' hall, where he had been strumming all the evening, and to all appearance comforting himself with some of the squire's home-brewed. He was a kind of hanger-on, I was told, of the establishment, and, though ostensibly a resident of the village, was oftener to be found in the squire's kitchen than his own home, the old gentleman being fond of the sound of "harp in hall."

The dance, like most dances after supper, was a merry one; some of the older folks joined in it, and the squire himself figured down several couple with a partner, with whom he affirmed he had danced at every Christmas for nearly half a century. Master Simon, who seemed to be a kind of connecting link between the old times and the new, and to be withal a little antiquated in the taste of his accomplishments, evidently piqued himself on his dancing, and was endeavoring to gain credit by the heel and toe, rigadoon, and other graces of the ancient school, but he had unluckily assorted himself with a little romping girl from boarding school, who by her wild vivacity kept him continually on the stretch, and defeated all his sober attempts at elegance. Such are the ill-assorted matches to which antique gentlemen are unfortunately prone!

The young Oxonian, on the contrary, had led out one of his maiden aunts, on whom the rogue played a thousand little knaveries with impunity; he was full of practical jokes, and his delight was to tease his aunts and cousins, yet, like all madcap youngsters, he was a universal favorite among the women. The most interesting couple in the dance was the young officer and a ward of the squire's, a beautiful blushing girl of seventeen. From several shy glances which I had noticed in the course of the evening, I suspected there was a little kindness growing up between them; and, indeed, the young soldier was just the hero to captivate a romantic girl. He was tall, slender, and handsome, and, like most young British officers of late years, had picked up various small accomplishments on the Continent—he could talk French and Italian, draw landscapes, sing very tolerably, dance divinely; but, above all, he had been wounded at Waterloo: what girl of seventeen, well read in poetry and romance, could resist such a mirror of chivalry and perfection!

The moment the dance was over, he caught up a guitar, and, lolling against the old marble fireplace, in an attitude which I am half inclined to suspect was studied, began the little French air of the Troubadour. The squire, however, exclaimed against having anything on Christmas Eve but good old English; upon which the young minstrel, casting up his eyes for a moment as if in an effort of memory, struck into another strain, and, with a charming air of gallantry, gave Herrick's *Night Piece to Julia*.

> Her eyes the glow-worm lend thee,
> The shooting stars attend thee,
>   And the elves also,
>   Whose little eyes glow
> Like the sparks of fire, befriend thee.
>
> No Will o' the Wisp mislight thee;
> Nor snake nor slow-worm bite thee;
>   But on, on thy way,
>   Not making a stay,
> Since ghost there is none to affright thee.
>
> Then let not the dark thee cumber;
> What though the moon does slumber,
>   The stars of the night
>   Will lend thee their light,
> Like tapers clear without number.
>
> Then, Julia, let me woo thee,
> Thus, thus to come unto me,
>   And when I shall meet
>   Thy silvery feet,
> My soul I'll pour into thee.

The song might or might not have been intended in compliment to the fair Julia, for so I found his partner was called; she, however, was certainly unconscious of any such application, for she never looked at the singer, but kept her eyes cast upon the floor. Her face was suffused, it is true, with a beautiful blush, and there was a gentle heaving of the bosom, but all that was doubtless caused by the exercise of the dance; indeed, so great was her indifference that she amused herself with plucking to pieces a choice bouquet of hothouse flowers, and by the time the song was concluded the nosegay lay in ruins on the floor.

The party now broke up for the night with the kind-hearted old custom of shaking hands. As I passed through the hall on my way to my chamber, the dying embers of the Yule clog still sent forth a dusky glow, and had it not been the season when "no spirit dares stir abroad," I should have been half tempted to steal from my room at midnight and peep whether the fairies might not be at their revels about the hearth.

My chamber was in the old part of the mansion, the ponderous furniture of which might have been fabricated in the days of the giants. The room was paneled with cornices of heavy carved work in which flowers and grotesque faces were strangely intermingled, and a row of black-looking portraits stared mournfully at me from the walls. The bed was of rich though faded damask, with a lofty tester, and stood in a niche opposite a bow window. I had scarcely got into bed when a strain of music seemed to break forth in the air just below the window. I listened, and found it proceeded from a band, which I concluded to be the waits from some neighboring village. They went around the house, playing under the windows. I drew aside the curtains to hear them more distinctly. The moonbeams fell through the upper part of the casement, partially lighting up the antiquated apartment. The sounds, as they receded, became more soft and aerial, and seemed to accord with the quiet and moonlight. I listened and listened—they became more and more tender and remote, and, as they gradually died away, my head sunk upon the pillow and I fell asleep.

CHRISTMAS DAY

Dark and dull night, flie hence away,
And give the honor to this day
That sees December turn'd to May.

*   *   *   *   *

Why does the chilling winter's morne
Smile like a field beset with corn?
Or smell like to a meade new-shorne,
Thus on the sudden?—Come and see
The cause why things thus fragrant be.

HERRICK

When I woke the next morning, it seemed as if all the events of the preceding evening had been a dream, and nothing but the identity of the ancient chamber convinced me of their reality. While I lay musing on my pillow, I heard the sound of little feet pattering outside of the door, and a whispering consultation. Presently a choir of small voices chanted forth an old Christmas carol, the burden of which was—

Rejoice, our Saviour he was born
On Christmas Day in the morning.

I rose softly, slipped on my clothes, opened the door suddenly, and beheld one of the most beautiful little fairy groups that a painter could imagine. It consisted of a boy and two girls, the eldest not more than six, and lovely as seraphs. They were going the rounds of the house, and singing at every chamber door, but my sudden appearance frightened them into mute bashfulness. They remained for a moment playing on their lips with their fingers, and now and then stealing a shy glance from under their eyebrows, until, as if by one impulse, they scampered away, and as they turned an angle of the gallery I heard them laughing in triumph at their escape. Everything conspired to produce kind and happy feel-

ings in this stronghold of old-fashioned hospitality. The
window of my chamber looked out upon what in summer
would have been a beautiful landscape. There was a sloping lawn, a fine stream winding at the foot of it, and a
track of park beyond, with noble clumps of trees and
herds of deer. At a distance was a neat hamlet, with the
smoke from the cottage chimneys hanging over it, and a
church with its dark spire in strong relief against the
clear, cold sky. The house was surrounded with evergreens, according to the English custom, which would
have given almost an appearance of summer; but the
morning was extremely frosty, the light vapor of the
preceding evening had been precipitated by the cold, and
covered all the trees and every blade of grass with its
fine crystallizations. The rays of a bright morning sun
had a dazzling effect among the glittering foliage. A
robin, perched upon the top of a mountain ash that hung
its clusters of red berries just before my window, was
basking himself in the sunshine, and piping a few querulous notes, and a peacock was displaying all the glories
of his train and strutting with the pride and gravity of a
Spanish grandee on the terrace walk below.

I had scarcely dressed myself when a servant appeared to invite me to family prayers. He showed me the
way to a small chapel in the old wing of the house,
where I found the principal part of the family already
assembled in a kind of gallery, furnished with cushions,
hassocks, and large prayerbooks; the servants were
seated on benches below. The old gentleman read
prayers from a desk in front of the gallery, and Master
Simon acted as clerk, and made the responses; and I
must do him the justice to say that he acquitted himself
with great gravity and decorum.

The service was followed by a Christmas carol, which
Mr. Bracebridge himself had constructed from a poem of
his favorite author, Herrick; and it had been adapted to
an old church melody by Master Simon. As there were
several good voices among the household, the effect was
extremely pleasing, but I was particularly gratified by
the exaltation of heart and sudden sally of grateful feeling with which the worthy squire delivered one stanza,

his eye glistening, and his voice rambling out of all the
bounds of time and tune:

> " 'Tis thou that crown'st my glittering hearth
>   With guiltlesse mirth,
> And giv'st me Wassaile bowles to drink
>   Spiced to the brink:
> Lord, 'tis thy plenty-dropping hand
>   That soiles my land:
> And giv'st me for my bushell sowne,
>   Twice ten for one."

I afterward understood that early morning service was
read on every Sunday and saints' day throughout the
year, either by Mr. Bracebridge or by some member of
the family. It was once almost universally the case at
the seats of the nobility and gentry of England, and it is
much to be regretted that the custom is falling into neglect, for the dullest observer must be sensible of the order
and serenity prevalent in those households where the occasional exercise of a beautiful form of worship in the
morning gives, as it were, the keynote to every temper
for the day and attunes every spirit to harmony.

Our breakfast consisted of what the squire denominated true old English fare. He indulged in some bitter
lamentations over modern breakfasts of tea and toast,
which he censured as among the causes of modern effeminacy and weak nerves, and the decline of old English
heartiness; and though he admitted them to his table to
suit the palates of his guests, yet there was a brave display of cold meats, wine, and ale on the sideboard.

After breakfast I walked about the grounds with Frank
Bracebridge and Master Simon, or, Mr. Simon, as he was
called by everybody but the squire. We were escorted
by a number of gentlemanlike dogs that seemed loungers
about the establishment, from the frisking spaniel to the
steady old staghound, the last of which was of a race
that had been in the family time out of mind; they were
all obedient to a dog whistle which hung to Master Simon's buttonhole, and in the midst of their gambols
would glance an eye occasionally upon a small switch he
carried in his hand.

The old mansion had a still more venerable look in the yellow sunshine than by pale moonlight, and I could not but feel the force of the squire's idea that the formal terraces, heavily molded balustrades, and clipped yew trees carried with them an air of proud aristocracy. There appeared to be an unusual number of peacocks about the place, and I was making some remarks upon what I termed a flock of them that were basking under a sunny wall when I was gently corrected in my phraseology by Master Simon, who told me that, according to the most ancient and approved treatise on hunting, I must say a *muster* of peacocks. "In the same way," added he, with a slight air of pedantry, "we say a flight of doves or swallows, a bevy of quails, a herd of deer, of wrens, or cranes, a skulk of foxes, or a building of rooks." He went on to inform me that, according to Sir Anthony Fitzherbert, we ought to ascribe to this bird "both understanding and glory; for, being praised, he will presently set up his tail, chiefly against the sun, to the intent you may the better behold the beauty thereof. But at the fall of the leaf, when his tail falleth, he will mourn and hide himself in corners, till his tail come again as it was."

I could not help smiling at this display of small erudition on so whimsical a subject; but I found that the peacocks were birds of some consequence at the hall, for Frank Bracebridge informed me that they were great favorites with his father, who was extremely careful to keep up the breed, partly because they belonged to chivalry and were in great request at the stately banquets of the olden time, and partly because they had a pomp and magnificence about them highly becoming an old family mansion. Nothing, he was accustomed to say, had an air of greater state and dignity than a peacock perched upon an antique stone balustrade.

Master Simon had now to hurry off, having an appointment at the parish church with the village choristers, who were to perform some music of his selection. There was something extremely agreeable in the cheerful flow of animal spirits of the little man, and I confess I had been somewhat surprised at his apt quotations from authors who certainly were not in the range of everyday reading.

I mentioned this last circumstance to Frank Bracebridge, who told me with a smile that Master Simon's whole stock of erudition was confined to some half a dozen old authors, which the squire had put into his hands, and which he read over and over whenever he had a studious fit, as he sometimes had on a rainy day, or a long winter evening. Sir Anthony Fitzherbert's *Book of Husbandry*, Markham's *Country Contentments*, the *Tretyse of Hunting* by Sir Thomas Cockayne, Knight, Izaak Walton's *Angler*, and two or three more such ancient worthies of the pen were his standard authorities; and, like all men who know but a few books, he looked up to them with a kind of idolatry and quoted them on all occasions. As to his songs, they were chiefly picked out of old books in the squire's library, and adapted to tunes that were popular among the choice spirits of the last century. His practical application of scraps of literature, however, had caused him to be looked upon as a prodigy of book knowledge by all the grooms, huntsmen, and small sportsmen of the neighborhood.

While we were talking we heard the distant tolling of the village bell, and I was told that the squire was a little particular in having his household at church on a Christmas morning, considering it a day of pouring out of thanks and rejoicing, for, as old Tusser observed,

"At Christmas be merry, *and thankful withal*,
  And feast thy poor neighbors, the great with the small."

"If you are disposed to go to church," said Frank Bracebridge, "I can promise you a specimen of my cousin Simons' musical achievements. As the church is destitute of an organ, he has formed a band from the village amateurs, and established a musical club for their improvement; he has also sorted a choir, as he sorted my father's pack of hounds, according to the directions of Jervaise Markham in his *Country Contentments*; for the bass he has sought out all the 'deep, solemn mouths,' and for the tenor the 'loud-ringing mouths' among the country bumpkins, and for 'sweet mouths' he has culled with curious taste among the prettiest lasses in the neighborhood,

though these last, he affirms, are the most difficult to keep
in tune, your pretty female singer being exceedingly way-
ward and capricious, and very liable to accident."

As the morning, though frosty, was remarkably fine
and clear, the most of the family walked to the church,
which was a very old building of gray stone, and stood
near a village, about half a mile from the park gate.
Adjoining it was a low snug parsonage, which seemed
coeval with the church. The front of it was perfectly
matted with a yew tree that had been trained against
its walls, through the dense foliage of which, apertures
had been formed to admit light into the small antique
lattices. As we passed this sheltered nest, the parson issued forth and preceded us.

I had expected to see a sleek well-conditioned pastor,
such as is often found in a snug living in the vicinity of a
rich patron's table, but I was disappointed. The parson
was a little, meager, black-looking man, with a grizzled
wig that was too wide, and stood off from each ear, so
that his head seemed to have shrunk away within it, like
a dried filbert in its shell. He wore a rusty coat, with
great skirts and pockets that would have held the
church Bible and prayerbook; and his small legs seemed
still smaller from being planted in large shoes decorated
with enormous buckles.

I was informed by Frank Bracebridge that the parson
had been a chum of his father's at Oxford, and had received this living shortly after the latter had come to
his estate. He was a complete black-letter hunter, and
would scarcely read a work printed in the Roman character. The editions of Caxton and Wynkin de Worde were
his delight; and he was indefatigable in his researches after
such old English writers as have fallen into oblivion from
their worthlessness. In deference, perhaps, to the notions
of Mr. Bracebridge, he had made diligent investigations
into the festive rites and holiday customs of former
times, and had been as zealous in the inquiry as if he had
been a boon companion, but it was merely with that plodding spirit with which men of adust temperament follow
up any track of study, merely because it is denominated
learning, indifferent to its intrinsic nature, whether it be
the illustration of the wisdom or of the ribaldry and

obscenity of antiquity. He had pored over these old volumes so intensely that they seemed to have been reflected in his countenance; which, if the face be indeed an index of the mind, might be compared to a title page of black-letter.

On reaching the church porch, we found the parson rebuking the gray-headed sexton for having used mistletoe among the greens with which the church was decorated. It was, he observed, an unholy plant, profaned by having been used by the Druids in their mystic ceremonies; and though it might be innocently employed in the festive ornamenting of halls and kitchens, yet it had been deemed by the Fathers of the Church as unhallowed and totally unfit for sacred purposes. So tenacious was he on this point that the poor sexton was obliged to strip down a great part of the humble trophies of his taste before the parson would consent to enter upon the service of the day.

The interior of the church was venerable but simple; on the walls were several mural monuments of the Brace-bridges, and just beside the altar was a tomb of ancient workmanship, on which lay the effigy of a warrior in armor, with his legs crossed, a sign of his having been a crusader. I was told it was one of the family who had signalized himself in the Holy Land, and the same whose picture hung over the fireplace in the hall.

During service Master Simon stood up in the pew, and repeated the responses very audibly, evincing that kind of ceremonious devotion punctually observed by a gentleman of the old school and a man of old family connections. I observed too that he turned over the leaves of a folio prayerbook with something of a flourish, possibly to show off an enormous seal ring which enriched one of his fingers and which had the look of a family relic. But he was evidently most solicitous about the musical part of the service, keeping his eye fixed intently on the choir, and beating time with much gesticulation and emphasis.

The orchestra was in a small gallery, and presented a most whimsical grouping of heads, piled one above the other, among which I particularly noticed that of the village tailor, a pale fellow with a retreating forehead and chin, who played on the clarinet, and seemed to have blown his face to a point; and there was another, a short pursy man, stooping and laboring at a bass viol, so as to show nothing but the top of a round bald head, like the egg of an ostrich. There were two or three pretty faces among the female singers, to which the keen air of a frosty morning had given a bright rosy tint; but the gentlemen choristers had evidently been chosen, like old Cremona fiddles, more for tone than looks; and as several had to sing from the same book, there were clusterings of odd physiognomies not unlike those groups of cherubs we sometimes see on country tombstones.

The usual services of the choir were managed tolerably well, the vocal parts generally lagging a little behind the instrumental, and some loitering fiddler now and then making up for lost time by traveling over a passage with prodigious celerity and clearing more bars than the keenest fox hunter to be in at the death. But the great trial was an anthem that had been prepared and arranged by Master Simon, and on which he had founded great expectation. Unluckily there was a blunder at the very outset; the musicians became flurried; Master Simon was in a fever; everything went on lamely and irregularly until they came to a chorus beginning "Now let us sing with one accord," which seemed to be a signal for parting company: all became discord and confusion; each shifted for himself, and got to the end as well, or, rather, as soon as he could, excepting one old chorister in a pair of horn spectacles, bestriding and pinching a long sonorous nose, who happened to stand a little apart, and, being wrapped up in his own melody, kept on a quavering course, wriggling his head, ogling his book, and winding all up by a nasal solo of at least three bars' duration.

The parson gave us a most erudite sermon on the rites and ceremonies of Christmas and the propriety of observing it not merely as a day of thanksgiving, but of rejoicing, supporting the correctness of his opinions by the earliest usages of the church and enforcing them by the authorities of Theophilus of Caesarea, St. Cyprian, St. Chrysostom, St. Augustine, and a cloud more of saints and fathers, from whom he made copious quotations. I was a little at a loss to perceive the necessity of such a mighty array of forces to maintain a point which no one present seemed inclined to dispute; but I soon found that the good man had a legion of ideal adversaries to contend with, having, in the course of his researches on the subject of Christmas, got completely embroiled in the sectarian controversies of the Revolution, when the Puritans made such a fierce assault upon the ceremonies of the church, and poor old Christmas was driven out of the land by proclamation of Parliament.* The worthy parson lived but with times past, and knew but little of the present.

Shut up among worm-eaten tomes in the retirement of his antiquated little study, the pages of old times were to him as the gazettes of the day, while the era of the Revolution was mere modern history. He forgot that nearly two centuries had elapsed since the fiery persecution of poor mince pie throughout the land, when plum porridge was denounced as "mere popery," and roast beef as anti-Christian, and that Christmas had been brought in again triumphantly with the merry court of King Charles at the Restoration. He kindled into warmth with the ardor of his contest and the host of imaginary foes with whom he had to combat; he had a stubborn conflict with old Prynne and two or three other forgotten champions of the Round Heads on the subject of Christmas festivity, and concluded by urging his hearers, in the most solemn and affecting manner, to stand to the traditional customs of their fathers, and feast and make merry on this joyful anniversary of the Church.

I have seldom known a sermon attended apparently with more immediate effects, for on leaving the church the congregation seemed one and all possessed with the gaiety of spirit so earnestly enjoined by their pastor.

*From the *Flying Eagle*, a small gazette, published December 24, 1652—"The House spent much time this day about the business of the Navy, for settling the affairs at sea, and before they rose, were presented with a terrible remonstrance against Christmas day, grounded upon divine Scriptures, 2 Cor. v. 16; 1 Cor. xv. 14, 17; and in honor of the Lord's Day, grounded upon these Scriptures, John xx. 1; Rev. i. 10; Psalm cxviii. 24; Lev. xxiii. 7, 11; Mark xv. 8; Psalm lxxxiv. 10, in which Christmas is called Anti-christ's masse, and those Massemongers and Papists who observe it, etc. In consequence of which Parliament spent some time in consultation about the abolition of Christmas day, passed orders to that effect, and resolved to sit on the following day, which was commonly called Christmas day."

The elder folks gathered in knots in the churchyard, greeting and shaking hands, and the children ran about crying Ule! Ule! and repeating some uncouth rhymes,* which the parson, who had joined us, informed me had been handed down from days of yore. The villagers doffed their hats to the squire as he passed, giving him the good wishes of the season with every appearance of heartfelt sincerity, and were invited by him to the hall, to take something to keep out the cold of the weather; and I heard blessings uttered by several of the poor, which convinced me that, in the midst of his enjoyments, the worthy old cavalier had not forgotten the true Christmas virtue of charity.

On our way homeward his heart seemed overflowed with generous and happy feelings. As we passed over a rising ground which commanded something of a prospect, the sounds of rustic merriment now and then reached our ears; the squire paused for a few moments, and looked around with an air of inexpressible benignity. The beauty of the day was of itself sufficient to inspire philanthropy. Notwithstanding the frostiness of the morning, the sun in his cloudless journey had acquired sufficient power to melt away the thin covering of snow from every southern declivity, and to bring out the living green which adorns an English landscape even in midwinter. Large tracts of smiling verdure contrasted with the dazzling whiteness of the shaded slopes and hollows. Every sheltered bank on which the broad rays rested yielded its silver rill of cold and limpid water, glittering through the dripping grass, and sent up slight exhalations to contribute to the thin haze that hung just above the surface of the earth. There was something truly cheering in this triumph of warmth and verdure over the frosty thraldom of winter; it was, as the squire observed, an emblem of Christmas hospitality, breaking through the chills of ceremony and selfishness, and thawing every heart into a flow. He pointed with pleasure to the indications of good cheer reeking from the chimneys of the comfortable farmhouses

*"Ule! Ule!
Three puddings in a pule
Crack nuts and cry ule!"

and low thatched cottages. "I love," said he, "to see this day well kept by rich and poor; it is a great thing to have one day in the year, at least, when you are sure of being welcome wherever you go, and of having, as it were, the world thrown all open to you; and I am almost disposed to join with Poor Robin, in his malediction on every churlish enemy to this honest festival—

> "Those who at Christmas do repine
> And would fain hence dispatch him,
> May they with old Duke Humphry dine,
> Or else may Squire Ketch catch 'em."

The squire went on to lament the deplorable decay of the games and amusements which were once prevalent at this season among the lower orders, and countenanced by the higher, when the old halls of the castles and manor houses were thrown open at daylight, when the tables were covered with brawn, and beef, and humming ale, when the harp and the carol resounded all day long, and when rich and poor were alike welcome to enter and make merry.* "Our old games and local customs," said he, "had a great effect in making the peasant fond of his home, and the promotion of them by the gentry made him fond of his lord. They made the times merrier, and kinder, and better, and I can truly say, with one of our old poets:

> "I like them well—the curious preciseness
> And all-pretended gravity of those
> That seek to banish hence these harmless sports,
> Have thrust away much ancient honesty.'

"The nation," continued he, "is altered; we have almost lost our simple truehearted peasantry. They have broken

---

*"An English gentleman, at the opening of the great day, i. e. on Christmas day in the morning, had all his tenants and neighbors enter his hall by daybreak. The strong beer was broached, and the blackjacks went plentifully about with toast, sugar and nutmeg, and good Cheshire cheese. The Hackin (the great sausage) must be boiled by daybreak, or else two young men must take the maiden (i. e. the cook) by the arms, and run her round the market-place till she is shamed of her laziness."—*Round about Our Sea-Coal Fire.*

asunder from the higher classes, and seem to think their interests are separate. They have become too knowing, and begin to read newspapers, listen to ale-house politicians, and talk of reform. I think one mode to keep them in good humor in these hard times would be for the nobility and gentry to pass more time on their estates, mingle more among the country people, and set the merry old English games going again."

Such was the good squire's project for mitigating public discontent; and, indeed, he had once attempted to put his doctrine in practice, and a few years before had kept open house during the holidays in the old style. The country people, however, did not understand how to play their parts in the scene of hospitality; many uncouth circumstances occurred; the manor was overrun by all the vagrants of the country, and more beggars drawn into the neighborhood in one week than the parish officers could get rid of in a year. Since then he had contented himself with inviting the decent part of the neighboring peasantry to call at the hall on Christmas Day, and with distributing beef and bread and ale among the poor, that they might make merry in their own dwellings.

We had not been long home when the sound of music was heard from a distance. A band of country lads, without coats, their shirt sleeves fancifully tied with ribbons, their hats decorated with greens, and clubs in their hands, was seen advancing up the avenue, followed by a large number of villagers and peasantry. They stopped before the hall door, where the music struck up a peculiar air, and the lads performed a curious and intricate dance, advancing, retreating, and striking their clubs together, keeping exact time to the music, while one, whimsically crowned with a fox's skin, the tail of which flaunted down his back, kept capering around the skirts of the dance, and rattling a Christmas box with many antic gesticulations.

The squire eyed this fanciful exhibition with great interest and delight, and gave me a full account of its origin, which he traced to the times when the Romans held possession of the island, plainly proving that this was a lineal descendant of the sword dance of the ancients. "It was now," he said, "nearly extinct, but he had accidentally met with traces of it in the neighborhood, and had encouraged its revival; though, to tell the truth, it was too apt to be followed up by the rough cudgel play, and broken heads in the evening."

After the dance was concluded, the whole party was entertained with brawn and beef and stout home-brewed. The squire himself mingled among the rustics, and was received with awkward demonstrations of deference and regard. It is true I perceived two or three of the younger peasants, as they were raising their tankards to their mouths, when the squire's back was turned, making something of a grimace, and giving each other the wink; but the moment they caught my eye they pulled grave faces, and were exceedingly demure. With Master Simon, however, they all seemed more at their ease. His varied occupations and amusements had made him well known throughout the neighborhood. He was a visitor at every farmhouse and cottage; gossiped with the farmers and their wives; romped with their daughters; and, like that type of a vagrant bachelor, the humblebee, tolled the sweets from all the rosy lips of the country round.

The bashfulness of the guests soon gave way before good cheer and affability. There is something genuine and affectionate in the gaiety of the lower orders when they are excited by the bounty and familiarity of those above them; the warm glow of gratitude enters into their mirth, and a kind word or a small pleasantry frankly uttered by a patron gladdens the heart of the dependent more than oil and wine. When the squire had retired, the merriment increased, and there was much joking and laughter, particularly between Master Simon and a hale, ruddy-faced, white-headed farmer who appeared to be the wit of the village, for I observed all his companions to wait with open mouths for his retorts and burst into a gratuitous laugh before they could well understand them.

The whole house indeed seemed abandoned to merriment; as I passed to my room to dress for dinner I heard the sound of music in a small court, and looking through a window that commanded it, I perceived a band of wandering musicians, with pandean pipes and tambourine; a pretty coquettish housemaid was dancing a jig with a smart country lad, while several of the other servants were looking on. In the midst of her sport the girl caught a glimpse of my face at the window, and, coloring up, ran off with an air of roguish affected confusion.

THE CHRISTMAS DINNER

> Lo, now is come our joyful'st feast!
>   Let every man be jolly,
> Eache roome with yvie leaves is drest,
>   And every post with holly.
> Now all our neighbours' chimneys smoke,
>   And Christmas blocks are burning;
> Their ovens they with bak't meats choke
>   And all their spits are turning.
>   Without the door let sorrow lie,
>   And if, for cold, it hap to die,
>   Wee'le bury 't in a Christmas pye,
>   And evermore be merry.
>   WITHERS' JUVENILIA

I had finished my toilet and was loitering with Frank Bracebridge in the library when we heard a distant thwacking sound, which he informed me was a signal for the serving up of the dinner. The squire kept up old customs in kitchen as well as hall; and the rolling pin, struck upon the dresser by the cook, summoned the servants to carry in the meats.

> Just in this nick the cook knock'd thrice,
> And all the waiters in a trice
>   His summons did obey;
> Each serving man, with dish in hand,
> March'd boldly up, like our train band,
>   Presented, and away.*

The dinner was served up in the great hall, where the squire always held his Christmas banquet. A blazing crackling fire of logs had been heaped on to warm the spacious apartment, and the flame went sparkling and wreathing up the wide-mouthed chimney. The great picture of the crusader and his white horse had been profusely decorated with greens for the occasion, and holly and ivy had likewise been wreathed around the helmet and weapons on the opposite wall, which I understood were the arms of the same warrior. I must own, by the

---

*Sir John Suckling.

by, I had strong doubts about the authenticity of the painting and armor as having belonged to the crusader, they certainly having the stamp of more recent days; but I was told that the painting had been so considered time out of mind, and that, as to the armor, it had been found in a lumber room and elevated to its present situation by the squire, who at once determined it to be the armor of the family hero, and as he was absolute authority on all such subjects in his own household, the matter had passed into current acceptation. A sideboard was set out just under this chivalric trophy, on which was a display of plate that might have vied (at least in variety) with Belshazzar's parade of the vessels of the temple: "flagons, cans, cups, beakers, goblets, basins, and ewers," the gorgeous utensils of good companionship that had gradually accumulated through many generations of jovial housekeepers. Before these stood the two Yule candles, beaming like two stars of the first magnitude; other lights were distributed in branches, and the whole array glittered like a firmament of silver.

We were ushered into this banqueting scene with the sound of minstrelsy, the old harper being seated on a stool beside the fireplace and twanging his instrument with a vast deal more power than melody. Never did Christmas board display a more goodly and gracious assemblage of countenances; those who were not handsome were, at least, happy, and happiness is a rare improver of your hard-favored visage. I always consider an old English family as well worth studying as a collection of Holbein's portraits or Albrecht Dürer's prints. There is much antiquarian lore to be acquired, much knowledge of the physiognomies of former times. Perhaps it may be from having continually before their eyes those rows of old family portraits, with which the mansions of this country are stocked; certain it is that the quaint features of antiquity are often most faithfully perpetuated in these ancient lines, and I have traced an old family nose through a whole picture gallery, legitimately handed down from generation to generation, almost from the time of the Conquest. Something of the kind was to be observed in the worthy company around me. Many of their faces had evidently originated in a Gothic age, and been merely copied by succeeding generations; and there was one little girl in particular, of staid demeanor, with a high Roman nose, and an antique vinegar aspect, who was a great favorite of the squire's, being, as he said, a Bracebridge all over, and the very counterpart of one of his ancestors who figured in the court of Henry VIII.

The parson said grace, which was not a short familiar one, such as is commonly addressed to the Deity in these unceremonious days, but a long, courtly, well-worded one of the ancient school. There was now a pause, as if something was expected, when suddenly the butler entered the hall with some degree of bustle; he was attended by a servant on each side with a large wax light, and bore a silver dish, on which was an enormous pig's head, decorated with rosemary, with a lemon in its mouth, which was placed with great formality at the head of the table. The moment this pageant made its appearance, the harper struck up a flourish, at the conclusion of which the young Oxonian, on receiving a hint from the squire, gave, with an air of the most comic gravity, an old carol, the first verse of which was as follows:

> Caput apri defero
> Reddens laudes Domino.
> The boar's head in hand bring I,
> With garlands gay and rosemary.
> I pray you all synge merrily
> Qui estis in convivio.

Though prepared to witness many of these little eccentricities, from being apprised of the peculiar hobby of mine host, yet, I confess, the parade with which so odd a dish was introduced somewhat perplexed me, until I gathered from the conversation of the squire and the parson that it was meant to represent the bringing in of the boar's head, a dish formerly served up with much ceremony and the sound of minstrelsy and song, at great tables, on Christmas Day. "I like the old custom," said the squire, "not merely because it is stately and pleasing in itself, but because it was observed at the college at Oxford at which I was educated. When I hear the old song chanted, it brings to mind the time when I was young and gamesome—and the noble old college hall—and my fellow-students loitering about in their black gowns, many of whom, poor lads, are now in their graves!"

The parson, however, whose mind was not haunted by such associations and who was always more taken up with the text than the sentiment, objected to the Oxonian's version of the carol, which he affirmed was different from that sung at college. He went on, with the dry perseverance of a commentator, to give the college reading, accompanied by sundry annotations, addressing himself at first to the company at large; but finding their attention gradually diverted to other talk and other objects, he lowered his tone as his number of auditors diminished, until he concluded his remarks in an under voice, to a fat-headed old gentleman next him, who was silently engaged in the discussion of a huge plateful of turkey.*

> The boar's head in hand bear I,
> Bedeck'd with bays and rosemary;
> And I pray you, my masters, be merry
>   Quot estis in convivio.
>   Caput apri defero,
>   Reddens laudes domino.
>
> The boar's head, as I understand,
> Is the rarest dish in all this land,
> Which thus bedeck'd with a gay garland
>   Let us servire cantico.
>   Caput apri defero, etc.
>
> Our steward hath provided this
> In honor of the king of Bliss,
> Which on this day to be served is
>   In Reginensi Atrio.
>   Caput apri defero,
>   etc., etc., etc.

The table was literally loaded with good cheer, and presented an epitome of country abundance, in this season of overflowing larders. A distinguished post was allotted to "ancient sirloin," as mine host termed it, being,

*The old ceremony of serving up the boar's head on Christmas Day is still observed in the hall of Queen's College, Oxford. I was favored by the parson with a copy of the carol as now sung, and as it may be acceptable to such of my readers as are curious in these grave and learned matters, I give it entire.

as he added, "the standard of old English hospitality, and a joint of goodly presence, and full of expectation." There were several dishes quaintly decorated, and which had evidently something traditional in their embellishments, but about which, as I did not like to appear over-curious, I asked no questions.

I could not, however, but notice a pie, magnificently decorated with peacock's feathers, in imitation of the tail of that bird, which overshadowed a considerable tract of the table. This, the squire confessed, with some little hesitation, was a pheasant pie, though a peacock pie was certainly the most authentical; but there had been such a mortality among the peacocks this season that he could not prevail upon himself to have one killed.*

It would be tedious, perhaps, to my wiser readers, who may not have that foolish fondness for odd and obsolete things to which I am a little given, were I to mention the other makeshifts of this worthy old humorist, by which he was endeavoring to follow up, though at humble distance, the quaint customs of antiquity. I was pleased, however, to see the respect shown to his whims by his children and relatives, who, indeed, entered readily into the full spirit of them, and seemed all well versed in their parts, having doubtless been present at many a rehearsal. I was amused, too, at the air of profound gravity with which the butler and other servants executed the duties assigned them, however eccentric. They had an old-fashioned look, having, for the most part, been brought up in the household, and grown into keeping with the antiquated

*The peacock was anciently in great demand for stately entertainments. Sometimes it was made into a pie, at one end of which the head appeared above the crust in all its plumage, with the beak richly gilt; at the other end the tail was displayed. Such pies were served up at the solemn banquets of chivalry, when knights-errant pledged themselves to undertake any perilous enterprise, whence came the ancient oath, used by Justice Shallow, "by cock and pie."

The peacock was also an important dish for the Christmas feast; and Massinger, in his *City Madam*, gives some idea of the extravagance with which this, as well as other dishes, was prepared for the gorgeous revels of the olden times:—

Men may talk of Country Christmasses,
Their thirty pound butter'd eggs, their pies of carps' tongues;
Their pheasants drench'd with ambergris; *the carcases of three fat wethers bruised for gravy to make sauce for a single peacock.*

mansion, and the humors of its lord, and most probably looked upon all his whimsical regulations as the established laws of honorable housekeeping.

When the cloth was removed, the butler brought in a huge silver vessel of rare and curious workmanship, which he placed before the squire. Its appearance was hailed with acclamation, being the Wassail Bowl, so renowned in Christmas festivity. The contents had been prepared by the squire himself, for it was a beverage in the skillful mixture of which he particularly prided himself, alleging that it was too abstruse and complex for the comprehension of an ordinary servant. It was a potation, indeed, that might well make the heart of a toper leap within him, being composed of the richest and raciest wines, highly spiced and sweetened, with roasted apples bobbing about the surface.*

The old gentleman's whole countenance beamed with a serene look of indwelling delight as he stirred this mighty bowl. Having raised it to his lips with a hearty wish of a merry Christmas to all present, he sent it brimming around the board, for everyone to follow his example, according to the primitive style, pronouncing it "the ancient fountain of good feeling, where all hearts met together." †

There was much laughing and rallying as the honest emblem of Christmas joviality circulated, and was kissed rather coyly by the ladies. When it reached Master Simon, he raised it in both hands, and with the air of a boon companion struck up an old Wassail chanson.

---

*The Wassail Bowl was sometimes composed of ale instead of wine, with nutmeg, sugar, toast, ginger, and roasted crabs; in this way the nut-brown beverage is still prepared in some old families, and around the hearths of substantial farmers at Christmas. It is also called Lamb's Wool, and is celebrated by Herrick in his *Twelfth Night:*

> Next crowne the bowle full
> With gentle Lamb's Wool;
> Add sugar, nutmeg, and ginger
> With store of ale too;
> And thus ye must doe
> To make the Wassaile a swinger.

†"The custom of drinking out of the same cup gave place to each having his cup. When the steward came to the doore with the Wassel, he was to cry three times, *Wassel, Wassel, Wassel,* and then the chappell (chaplein) was to answer with a song."—ARCHÆOLOGIA.

The brown bowle,
The merry brown bowle,
As it goes round about-a,
     Fill
     Still,
Let the world say what it will,
And drink your fill all out-a.

The deep canne,
The merry deep canne,
As thou dost freely quaff-a,
     Sing
     Fling,
Be as merry as a king,
And sound a lusty laugh-a.*

Much of the conversation during dinner turned upon
family topics, to which I was a stranger. There was,
however, a great deal of rallying of Master Simon about
some gay widow, with whom he was accused of having a
flirtation. This attack was commenced by the ladies; but
it was continued throughout the dinner by the fat-headed
old gentleman next the parson, with the persevering
assiduity of a slow hound, being one of those long-
winded jokers, who, though rather dull at starting game,
are unrivaled for their talents in hunting it down. At
every pause in the general conversation he renewed his
bantering in pretty much the same terms, winking hard
at me with both eyes whenever he gave Master Simon
what he considered a home thrust. The latter, indeed,
seemed fond of being teased on the subject, as old bachelors are apt to be; and he took occasion to inform me,
in an undertone, that the lady in question was a pro-
digiously fine woman, and drove her own curricle.

The dinnertime passed away in this flow of innocent
hilarity, and, though the old hall may have resounded in
its time with many a scene of broader rout and revel,
yet I doubt whether it ever witnessed more honest and
genuine enjoyment. How easy it is for one benevolent
being to diffuse pleasure around him; and how truly is a
kind heart a fountain of gladness, making everything in

*From Poor Robin's Almanac.

its vicinity to freshen into smiles! The joyous disposition of the worthy squire was perfectly contagious; he was happy himself, and disposed to make all the world happy, and the little eccentricities of his humor did but season, in a manner, the sweetness of his philanthropy.

When the ladies had retired, the conversation, as usual, became still more animated; many good things were broached which had been thought of during dinner, but which would not exactly do for a lady's ear; and though I cannot positively affirm that there was much wit uttered, yet I have certainly heard many contests of rare wit produce much less laughter. Wit, after all, is a mighty tart, pungent ingredient, and much too acid for some stomachs; but honest good humor is the oil and wine of a merry meeting, and there is no jovial companionship equal to that where the jokes are rather small, and the laughter abundant.

The squire told several long stories of early college pranks and adventures, in some of which the parson had been a sharer; though in looking at the latter, it required some effort of imagination to figure such a little dark anatomy of a man into the perpetrator of a madcap gambol. Indeed, the two college chums presented pictures of what men may be made by their different lots in life. The squire had left the university to live lustily on his paternal domains, in the vigorous enjoyment of prosperity and sunshine, and had flourished on to a hearty and florid old age; while the poor parson, on the contrary, had dried and withered away, among dusty tomes, in the silence and shadows of his study. Still there seemed to be a spark of almost extinguished fire, feebly glimmering in the bottom of his soul; and as the squire hinted at a sly story of the parson and a pretty milkmaid, whom they once met on the banks of the Isis, the old gentleman made an "alphabet of faces," which, as far as I could decipher his physiognomy, I verily believe was indicative of laughter; indeed, I have rarely met with an old gentleman that took absolute offense at the imputed gallantries of his youth.

I found the tide of wine and wassail fast gaining on the dry land of sober judgment. The company grew merrier and louder as their jokes grew duller. Master Simon was in as chirping a humor as a grasshopper filled with dew; his old songs grew of a warmer complexion, and he began to talk maudlin about the widow. He even gave a long song about the wooing of a widow, which he informed me he had gathered from an excellent black-letter work, entitled *Cupid's Solicitor for Love,* containing store of good advice for bachelors, and which he promised to lend me. The first verse was to this effect:

> He that will woo a widow must not dally,
> He must make hay while the sun doth shine;
> He must not stand with her, shall I, shall I,
> But boldly say Widow, thou must be mine.

This song inspired the fat-headed old gentleman, who made several attempts to tell a rather broad story out of Joe Miller that was pat to the purpose; but he always stuck in the middle, everybody recollecting the latter part excepting himself. The parson, too, began to show the effects of good cheer, having gradually settled down into a doze, and his wig sitting most suspiciously on one side. Just at this juncture we were summoned to the drawing room, and, I suspect, at the private instigation of mine host, whose joviality seemed always tempered with a proper love of decorum.

After the dinner table was removed, the hall was given up to the younger members of the family, who, prompted to all kind of noisy mirth by the Oxonian and Master Simon, made its old walls ring with their merriment as they played at romping games. I delight in witnessing the gambols of children, and particularly at this happy holiday season, and could not help stealing out of the drawing room on hearing one of their peals of laughter. I found them at the game of blindman's buff. Master Simon, who was the leader of their revels, and seemed on all occasions to fulfill the office of that ancient potentate, the Lord of Misrule,* was blinded in the midst of

---

*At Christmasse there was in the Kinge's house, wheresoever hee was lodged, a lorde of misrule, or mayster of merie disportes, and the like had ye in the house of every nobleman of honor, or good worshippe, were he spirituall or temporall.—STOWE.

the hall. The little beings were as busy about him as the mock fairies about Falstaff, pinching him, plucking at the skirts of his coat, and tickling him with straws. One fine blue-eyed girl of about thirteen, with her flaxen hair all in beautiful confusion, her frolic face in a glow, her frock half torn off her shoulders, a complete picture of a romp, was the chief tormentor; and, from the slyness with which Master Simon avoided the smaller game, and hemmed this wild little nymph in corners, and obliged her to jump shrieking over chairs, I suspected the rogue of being not a whit more blinded than was convenient.

When I returned to the drawing room, I found the company seated around the fire, listening to the parson, who was deeply ensconced in a high-backed oaken chair, the work of some cunning artificer of yore, which had been brought from the library for his particular accommodation. From this venerable piece of furniture, with which his shadowy figure and dark weazen face so admirably accorded, he was dealing out strange accounts of the popular superstitions and legends of the surrounding country, with which he had become acquainted in the course of his antiquarian researches. I am half inclined to think that the old gentleman was himself somewhat tinctured with superstition, as men are very apt to be who live a recluse and studious life in a sequestered part of the country, and pore over black-letter tracts, so often filled with the marvelous and supernatural. He gave us several anecdotes of the fancies of the neighboring peasantry, concerning the effigy of the crusader, which lay on the tomb by the church altar. As it was the only monument of the kind in that part of the country, it had always been regarded with feelings of superstition by the good wives of the village. It was said to get up from the tomb and walk the rounds of the churchyard in stormy nights, particularly when it thundered; and one old woman, whose cottage bordered on the churchyard, had seen it through the windows of the church, when the moon shone, slowly pacing up and down the aisles. It was the belief that some wrong had been left unredressed by the deceased, or some treasure hidden, which kept the spirit in a state of trouble and restlessness. Some talked of gold and jewels buried in the tomb, over which the

specter kept watch; and there was a story current of a
sexton in old times, who endeavored to break his way to
the coffin at night, but, just as he reached it, received a
violent blow from the marble hand of the effigy, which
stretched him senseless on the pavement. These tales
were often laughed at by some of the sturdier among the
rustics, yet, when night came on, there were many of
the stoutest unbelievers that were shy of venturing alone
in the footpath that led across the churchyard.

From these and other anecdotes that followed, the
crusader appeared to be the favorite hero of ghost stories
throughout the vicinity. His picture, which hung up in
the hall, was thought by the servants to have something
supernatural about it, for they remarked that, in whatever part of the hall you went, the eyes of the warrior
were still fixed on you. The old porter's wife, too, at the
lodge, who had been born and brought up in the family,
and was a great gossip among the maidservants, affirmed
that in her young days she had often heard say that on
Midsummer Eve, when it was well known all kinds of
ghosts, goblins, and fairies become visible and walk
abroad, the crusader used to mount his horse, come
down from his picture, ride about the house, down the
avenue, and so to the church to visit the tomb, on which
occasion the church door most civilly swung open of
itself; not that he needed it, for he rode through closed
gates and even stone walls, and had been seen by one of
the dairy maids to pass between two bars of the great
park gate, making himself as thin as a sheet of paper.

All these superstitions I found had been very much
countenanced by the squire, who, though not superstitious
himself, was very fond of seeing others so. He listened to
every goblin tale of the neighboring gossips with infinite
gravity, and held the porter's wife in high favor on account of her talent for the marvelous. He was himself a
great reader of old legends and romances, and often
lamented that he could not believe in them, for a superstitious person, he thought, must live in a kind of fairyland.

While we were all attention to the parson's stories,
our ears were suddenly assailed by a burst of heterogeneous sounds from the hall, in which were mingled

something like the clang of rude minstrelsy with the uproar of many small voices and girlish laughter. The door suddenly flew open, and a train came trooping into the room that might almost have been mistaken for the breaking up of the court of Fairy. That indefatigable spirit, Master Simon, in the faithful discharge of his duties as lord of misrule, had conceived the idea of a Christmas mummery or masking, and having called in to his assistance the Oxonian and the young officer, who were equally ripe for anything that should occasion romping and merriment, they had carried it into instant effect. The old housekeeper had been consulted; the antique clothes presses and wardrobes rummaged and made to yield up the relics of finery that had not seen the light for several generations; the younger part of the company had been privately convened from the parlor and hall, and the whole had been bedizened out, into a burlesque imitation of an antique mask.*

Master Simon led the van, as "Ancient Christmas," quaintly appareled in a ruff, a short cloak, which had very much the aspect of one of the old housekeeper's petticoats, and a hat that might have served for a village steeple, and must indubitably have figured in the days of the Covenanters. From under this his nose curved boldly forth, flushed with a frostbitten bloom that seemed the very trophy of a December blast. He was accompanied by the blue-eyed romp, dished up as "Dame Mince Pie," in the venerable magnificence of a faded brocade, long stomacher, peaked hat, and high-heeled shoes. The young officer appeared as Robin Hood, in a sporting dress of Kendal green and a foraging cap with a gold tassel.

The costume, to be sure, did not bear testimony to deep research, and there was an evident eye to the picturesque, natural to a young gallant in the presence of his mistress. The fair Julia hung on his arm in a pretty rustic dress, as "Maid Marian." The rest of the train had been metamorphosed in various ways; the girls trussed

---

*Maskings or mummeries were favorite sports at Christmas in old times; and the wardrobes at halls and manor houses were often laid under contribution to furnish dresses and fantastic disguisings. I strongly suspect Master Simon to have taken the idea of his from Ben Jonson's Masque of Christmas.

up in the finery of the ancient belles of the Bracebridge line, and the striplings bewhiskered with burned cork, and gravely clad in broad skirts, hanging sleeves, and full-bottomed wigs, to represent the character of Roast Beef, Plum Pudding, and other worthies celebrated in ancient maskings. The whole was under the control of the Oxonian, in the appropriate character of Misrule, and I observed that he exercised rather a mischievous sway with his wand over the smaller personages of the pageant.

The irruption of this motley crew, with beat of drum, according to ancient custom, was the consummation of uproar and merriment. Master Simon covered himself with glory by the stateliness with which, as Ancient Christmas, he walked a minuet with the peerless, though giggling, Dame Mince Pie. It was followed by a dance of all the characters, which from its medley of costumes seemed as though the old family portraits had skipped down from their frames to join in the sport. Different centuries were figuring at cross hands and right and left; the Dark Ages were cutting pirouettes and rigadoons; and the days of Queen Bess jigging merrily down the middle, through a line of succeeding generations.

The worthy squire contemplated these fantastic sports and this resurrection of his old wardrobe with the simple relish of childish delight. He stood chuckling and rubbing his hands, and scarcely hearing a word the parson said, notwithstanding that the latter was discoursing most authentically on the ancient and stately dance at the Paon, or peacock,* from which he conceived the minuet to be derived.* For my part, I was in a continual excitement from the varied scenes of whim and innocent gaiety passing before me. It was inspiring to see wild-eyed frolic and warmhearted hospitality breaking out from among the chills and glooms of winter, and old age throwing off his apathy and catching once more the freshness of youthful enjoyment. I felt also an interest in the scene

---

*Sir John Hawkins, speaking of the dance called the Pavon, from pavo, a peacock, says, "It is a grave and majestic dance; the method of dancing it anciently was by gentlemen dressed with caps and swords, by those of the long robe in their gowns, by the peers in their mantles, and by the ladies in gowns with long trains, the motion whereof, in dancing, resembled that of a peacock."—*History of Music.*

from the consideration that these fleeting customs were posting fast into oblivion, and that this was, perhaps, the only family in England in which the whole of them was still punctiliously observed. There was a quaintness, too, mingled with all this revelry that gave it a peculiar zest: it was suited to the time and place; and as the old manor house almost reeled with mirth and wassail it seemed echoing back the joviality of long departed years.*

But enough of Christmas and its gambols; it is time for me to pause in this garrulity. Methinks I hear the questions asked by my graver readers, "To what purpose is all this—how is the world to be made wiser by this talk?" Alas! Is there not wisdom enough extant for the instruction of the world? And if not, are there not thousands of abler pens laboring for its improvement? It is so much pleasanter to please than to instruct—to play the companion rather than the preceptor.

What, after all, is the mite of wisdom that I could throw into the mass of knowledge; or how am I sure that my sagest deductions may be safe guides for the opinions of others? But in writing to amuse, if I fail, the only evil is in my own disappointment. If, however, I can by any lucky chance, in these days of evil, rub out one wrinkle from the brow of care, or beguile the heavy heart of one moment of sorrow; if I can now and then penetrate through the gathering film of misanthropy, prompt a benevolent view of human nature, and make my reader more in good humor with his fellow beings and himself, surely, surely, I shall not then have written entirely in vain.

---

*At the time of the first publication of this paper, the picture of an old-fashioned Christmas in the country was pronounced by some as out of date. The author had afterward an opportunity of witnessing almost all the customs above described, existing in unexpected vigor in the skirts of Derbyshire and Yorkshire, where he passed the Christmas holidays. The reader will find some notice of them in the author's account of his sojourn at Newstead Abbey.

LONDON ANTIQUES

>   ——I do walk
> Methinks like Guido Vaux, with my dark lanthorn,
> Stealing to set the town o' fire; i' th' country
> I should be taken for William o' the Wisp,
> Or Robin Goodfellow.
>
> FLETCHER

I am somewhat of an antiquity hunter, and am fond of exploring London in quest of the relics of old times. These are principally to be found in the depths of the city, swallowed up and almost lost in a wilderness of brick and mortar, but deriving poetical and romantic interest from the commonplace prosaic world around them. I was struck with an instance of the kind in the course of a recent summer ramble into the city, for the city is only to be explored to advantage in summertime, when free from the smoke and fog and rain and mud of winter. I had been buffeting for some time against the current of population setting through Fleet Street. The warm weather had unstrung my nerves, and made me sensitive to every jar and jostle and discordant sound. The flesh was weary, the spirit faint, and I was getting out of humor with the bustling busy throng through which I had to struggle, when in a fit of desperation I tore my way through the crowd, plunged into a by-lane, and after passing through several obscure nooks and angles, emerged into a quaint and quiet court with a grass plot in the center, overhung by elms and kept perpetually fresh and green by a fountain with its sparkling jet of water. A student with book in hand was seated on a stone bench, partly reading, partly meditating on the movements of two or three trim nursery maids with their infant charges.

I was like an Arab who had suddenly come upon an oasis amid the panting sterility of the desert. By degrees the quiet and coolness of the place soothed my nerves and refreshed my spirit. I pursued my walk, and came, hard by, to a very ancient chapel, with a low-browed Saxon portal of massive and rich architecture. The interior was circular and lofty, and lighted from above. Around were monumental tombs of ancient date, on which were extended the marble effigies of warriors in armor. Some had the hands devoutly crossed upon the breast; others grasped the pommel of the sword, menacing hostility even in the tomb!—while the crossed legs of several indicated soldiers of the Faith who had been on crusades to the Holy Land.

I was, in fact, in the chapel of the Knights Templars, strangely situated in the very center of sordid traffic; and I do not know a more impressive lesson for the man of the world than thus suddenly to turn aside from the highway of busy money-seeking life and sit down among these shadowy sepulchers, where all is twilight, dust, and forgetfulness.

In a subsequent tour of observation, I encountered another of these relics of a "foregone world" locked up in the heart of the city. I had been wandering for some time through dull monotonous streets, destitute of anything to strike the eye or excite the imagination, when I beheld before me a Gothic gateway of moldering antiquity. It opened into a spacious quadrangle forming the courtyard of a stately Gothic pile, the portal of which stood invitingly open.

It was apparently a public edifice, and as I was antiquity hunting, I ventured in, though with dubious steps. Meeting no one either to oppose or rebuke my intrusion, I continued on until I found myself in a great hall, with a lofty arched roof and oaken gallery, all of Gothic architecture. At one end of the hall was an enormous fireplace, with wooden settles on each side; at the other end was a raised platform, or dais, the seat of state, above which was the portrait of a man in antique garb, with a long robe, a ruff, and a venerable gray beard.

The whole establishment had an air of monastic quiet and seclusion, and what gave it a mysterious charm was that I had not met with a human being since I had passed the threshold.

Encouraged by this loneliness, I seated myself in a recess of a large bow window, which admitted a broad flood of yellow sunshine, checkered here and there by tints from panes of colored glass, while an open casement let in the soft summer air. Here, leaning my head on my hand and my arm on an old oaken table, I indulged in a sort of reverie about what might have been the ancient uses of this edifice. It had evidently been of monastic origin, perhaps one of those collegiate establishments built of yore for the promotion of learning, where the patient monk, in the ample solitude of the cloister, added page to page and volume to volume, emulating in the productions of his brain the magnitude of the pile he inhabited.

As I was seated in this musing mood, a small paneled door in an arch at the upper end of the hall was opened, and a number of gray-headed old men, clad in long black cloaks, came forth one by one, proceeding in that manner through the hall, without uttering a word, each turning a pale face on me as he passed and disappearing through a door at the lower end.

I was singularly struck with their appearance; their black cloaks and antiquated air comported with the style of this most venerable and mysterious pile. It was as if the ghosts of the departed years, about which I had been musing, were passing in review before me. Pleasing myself with such fancies, I set out, in the spirit of romance, to explore what I pictured to myself a realm of shadows, existing in the very center of substantial realities.

My ramble led me through a labyrinth of interior courts and corridors and dilapidated cloisters, for the main edifice had many additions and dependencies, built at various times and in various styles; in one open space a number of boys, who evidently belonged to the establishment, were at their sports, but everywhere I observed those mysterious old gray men in black mantles, sometimes sauntering alone, sometimes conversing in groups; they appeared to be the pervading genii of the place. I now called to mind what I had read of certain colleges in old times, where judicial astrology, geomancy, necro-

mancy, and other forbidden and magical sciences were
taught. Was this an establishment of the kind, and were
these black-cloaked old men really professors of the
black art?

These surmises were passing through my mind as my
eye glanced into a chamber, hung round with all kinds of
strange and uncouth objects—implements of savage warfare, strange idols and stuffed alligators, bottled serpents
and monsters decorated the mantelpiece, while on the
high tester of an old-fashioned bedstead grinned a human
skull, flanked on each side by a dried cat.

I approached to regard more narrowly this mystic
chamber, which seemed a fitting laboratory for a nec-
romancer, when I was startled at beholding a human
countenance staring at me from a dusky corner. It was
that of a small, shriveled old man, with thin cheeks,
bright eyes, and gray wiry projecting eyebrows. I at first
doubted whether it were not a mummy curiously preserved, but it moved, and I saw that it was alive. It was
another of those black-cloaked old men, and, as I regarded his quaint physiognomy, his obsolete garb, and the
hideous and sinister objects by which he was surrounded,
I began to persuade myself that I had come upon the
arch mago who ruled over this magical fraternity.

Seeing me pausing before the door, he rose and invited
me to enter. I obeyed with singular hardihood, for how
did I know whether a wave of his wand might not meta-
morphose me into some strange monster, or conjure me
into one of the bottles on his mantelpiece? He proved,
however, to be anything but a conjurer, and his simple
garrulity soon dispelled all the magic and mystery with
which I had enveloped this antiquated pile and its no less
antiquated inhabitants.

It appeared that I had made my way into the center of
an ancient asylum for superannuated tradesmen and decayed householders, with which was connected a school
for a limited number of boys. It was founded upward
of two centuries since on an old monastic establishment,
and retained somewhat of the conventual air and character. The shadowy line of old men in black mantles who
had passed before me in the hall, and whom I had ele-

vated into magi, turned out to be the pensioners returning from morning service in the chapel.

John Hallum, the little collector of curiosities whom I had made the arch magician, had been for six years a resident of the place, and had decorated this final nestling place of his old age with relics and rarities picked up in the course of his life. According to his own account he had been somewhat of a traveler, having been once in France, and very near making a visit to Holland. He regretted not having visited the latter country, "as then he might have said he had been there." He was evidently a traveler of the simplest kind.

He was aristocratical too in his notions, keeping aloof, as I found, from the ordinary run of pensioners. His chief associates were a blind man who spoke Latin and Greek, of both which languages Hallum was profoundly ignorant, and a broken-down gentleman who had run through a fortune of forty thousand pounds, left him by his father, and ten thousand pounds, the marriage portion of his wife. Little Hallum seemed to consider it an indubitable sign of gentle blood as well as of lofty spirit to be able to squander such enormous sums.

P. S. The picturesque remnant of old times into which I have thus beguiled the reader is what is called the Charter House, originally the Chartreuse. It was founded in 1611, on the remains of an ancient convent, by Sir Thomas Sutton, being one of those noble charities set on foot by individual munificence, and kept up with the quaintness and sanctity of ancient times amidst the modern changes and innovations of London. Here eighty broken-down men, who have seen better days, are provided, in their old age, with food, clothing, fuel, and a yearly allowance for private expenses. They dine together as did the monks of old, in the hall which had been the refectory of the original convent. Attached to the establishment is a school for forty-four boys.

Stow, whose work I have consulted on the subject, speaking of the obligations of the gray-headed pensioners, says, "They are not to intermeddle with any business touching the affairs of the hospital, but to attend only to the service of God, and take thankfully what is provided for them, without muttering, murmuring, or grudging. None to wear weapon, long hair, colored boots, spurs or colored shoes, feathers in their hats, or any ruffian-like or unseemly apparel, but such as becomes hospital men to wear." "And in truth," adds Stow, "happy are they that are so taken from the cares and sorrows of the world, and fixed in so good a place as these old men are; having nothing to care for, but the good of their souls, to serve God and to live in brotherly love."

For the amusement of such as have been interested by the preceding sketch, taken down from my own observation, and who may wish to know a little more about the mysteries of London, I subjoin a modicum of local history, put into my hands by an odd-looking old gentleman in a small brown wig and a snuff-colored coat with whom I became acquainted shortly after my visit to the Charter House. I confess I was a little dubious at first, whether it was not one of those apocryphal tales often passed off upon inquiring travelers like myself, and which have brought our general character for veracity into such unmerited reproach. On making proper inquiries, however, I have received the most satisfactory assurances of the author's probity; and, indeed, have been told that he is actually engaged in a full and particular account of the very interesting region in which he resides, of which the following may be considered merely as a foretaste.

LITTLE BRITAIN

What I write is most true * * * * I have a whole booke
of cases lying by me which if I should sette foorth, some grave
auntients (within the hearing of Bow bell) would be out of
charity with me.

NASHE

In the center of the great city of London lies a small
neighborhood, consisting of a cluster of narrow streets
and courts, of very venerable and debilitated houses,
which goes by the name of LITTLE BRITAIN. Christ Church
School and St. Bartholomew's Hospital bound it on the
west; Smithfield and Long Lane on the north; Aldersgate
Street, like an arm of the sea, divides it from the eastern
part of the city; while the yawning gulf of Bull and Mouth
Street separates it from Butcher Lane and the regions of
Newgate. Over this little territory, thus bounded and designated, the great dome of St. Paul's, swelling above the
intervening houses of Paternoster Row, Amen Corner,
and Ave Maria Lane, looks down with an air of motherly
protection.

This quarter derives its appellation from having been,
in ancient times, the residence of the Dukes of Brittany.
As London increased, however, rank and fashion rolled
off to the west, and trade creeping on at their heels took
possession of their deserted abodes. For some time Little Britain became the great mart of learning, and was
peopled by the busy and prolific race of booksellers;
these also gradually deserted it, and emigrating beyond
the great strait of Newgate Street, settled down in Paternoster Row and St. Paul's Church Yard, where they continue to increase and multiply even at the present day.

But though thus fallen into decline, Little Britain still bears traces of its former splendor. There are several houses ready to tumble down, the fronts of which are magnificently enriched with old oaken carvings of hideous faces, unknown birds, beasts, and fishes, and fruits and flowers which it would perplex a naturalist to classify. There are also, in Aldersgate Street, certain remains of what were once spacious and lordly family mansions, but which have in latter days been subdivided into several tenements. Here may often be found the family of a petty tradesman, with its trumpery furniture burrowing among the relics of antiquated finery in great rambling time-stained apartments, with fretted ceilings, gilded cornices, and enormous marble fireplaces. The lanes and courts also contain many smaller houses, not on so grand a scale, but, like your small ancient gentry, sturdily maintaining their claims to equal antiquity. These have their gable ends to the street, great bow windows, with diamond panes set in lead, grotesque carvings, and low arched doorways.*

In this most venerable and sheltered little nest have I passed several quiet years of existence, comfortably lodged in the second floor of one of the smallest but oldest edifices. My sitting room is an old wainscoted chamber, with small panels, and set off with a miscellaneous array of furniture. I have a particular respect for three or four high-backed claw-footed chairs, covered with tarnished brocade, which bear the marks of having seen better days and have doubtless figured in some of the old palaces of Little Britain. They seem to me to keep together and to look down with sovereign contempt upon their leathern-bottomed neighbors, as I have seen decayed gentry carry a high head among the plebeian society with which they were reduced to associate. The whole front of my sitting room is taken up with a bow window, on the panes of which are recorded the names of previous occupants for many generations, mingled with scraps of very indifferent gentlemanlike poetry, written in

---

*It is evident that the author of this interesting communication has included, in his general title of Little Britain, many of those little lanes and courts that belong immediately to Cloth Fair.

characters which I can scarcely decipher, and which extol
the charms of many a beauty of Little Britain, who has
long, long since bloomed, faded, and passed away. As I
am an idle personage with no apparent occupation and
pay my bill regularly every week, I am looked upon as the
only independent gentleman of the neighborhood; and,
being curious to learn the internal state of a community
so apparently shut up within itself, I have managed to
work my way into all the concerns and secrets of the
place.

Little Britain may truly be called the heart's core of
the city, the stronghold of true John Bullism. It is a fragment of London as it was in its better days, with its
antiquated folks and fashions. Here flourish in great
preservation many of the holiday games and customs of
yore. The inhabitants most religiously eat pancakes on
Shrove Tuesday, hot cross buns on Good Friday, and
roast goose at Michaelmas; they send love letters on
Valentine's Day, burn the pope on the fifth of November,
and kiss all the girls under the mistletoe at Christmas.
Roast beef and plum pudding are also held in superstitious veneration, and port and sherry maintain their
grounds as the only true English wines, all others being
considered vile outlandish beverages.

Little Britain has its long catalogue of city wonders,
which its inhabitants consider the wonders of the world,
such as the great bell of St. Paul's, which sours all the
beer when it tolls; the figures that strike the hours at
St. Dunstan's clock; the Monument; the lions in the
Tower; and the wooden giants in Guildhall. They still
believe in dreams and fortune-telling, and an old woman
that lives in Bull and Mouth Street makes a tolerable
subsistence by detecting stolen goods, and promising the
girls good husbands. They are apt to be rendered uncom-
fortable by comets and eclipses; and if a dog howls
dolefully at night it is looked upon as a sure sign of a
death in the place. There are even many ghost stories
current, particularly concerning the old mansion houses,
in several of which it is said strange sights are sometimes seen. Lords and ladies, the former in full-bottomed
wigs, hanging sleeves, and swords, the latter in lappets,
stays, hoops, and brocade, have been seen walking up

and down the great waste chambers on moonlight nights, and are supposed to be the shades of the ancient proprietors in their court dresses.

Little Britain has likewise its sages and great men. One of the most important of the former is a tall, dry old gentleman, of the name of Skryme, who keeps a small apothecary's shop. He has a cadaverous countenance, full of cavities and projections, with a brown circle around each eye, like a pair of horn spectacles. He is much thought of by the old women, who consider him as a kind of conjurer because he has two or three stuffed alligators hanging up in his shop and several snakes in bottles. He is a great reader of almanacs and newspapers, and is much given to pore over alarming accounts of plots, conspiracies, fires, earthquakes, and volcanic eruptions, which last phenomena he considers as signs of the times. He has always some dismal tale of the kind to deal out to his customers with their doses, and thus at the same time puts both soul and body into an uproar. He is a great believer in omens and predictions, and has the prophecies of Robert Nixon and Mother Shipton by heart. No man can make so much out of an eclipse, or even an unusually dark day; and he shook the tail of the last comet over the heads of his customers and disciples until they were nearly frightened out of their wits. He has lately got hold of a popular legend or prophecy, on which he has been unusually eloquent. There has been a saying current among the ancient sibyls, who treasure up these things, that when the grasshopper on the top of the Exchange shook hands with the dragon on the top of Bow Church steeple, fearful events would take place. This strange conjunction, it seems, has as strangely come to pass. The same architect has been engaged lately on the repairs of the cupola of the Exchange, and the steeple of Bow Church; and, fearful to relate, the dragon and the grasshopper actually lie, cheek by jowl, in the yard of his workshop.

"Others," as Mr. Skryme is accustomed to say, "may go star-gazing, and look for conjunctions in the heavens, but here is a conjunction on the earth, near at home, and under our own eyes, which surpasses all the signs and calculations of astrologers." Since these portentous weathercocks have thus laid their heads together, wonderful events had already occurred. The good old king, notwithstanding that he had lived eighty-two years, had all at once given up the ghost; another king had mounted the throne; a royal duke had died suddenly—another, in France, had been murdered; there had been radical meetings in all parts of the kingdom; the bloody scenes at Manchester; the great plot in Cato Street; and, above all, the Queen had returned to England! All these sinister events are recounted by Mr. Skryme with a mysterious look and a dismal shake of the head; and being taken with his drugs, and associated in the minds of his auditors with stuffed sea monsters, bottled serpents, and his own visage, which is a title page of tribulation, they have spread great gloom through the minds of the people of Little Britain. They shake their heads whenever they go by Bow Church, and observe that they never expected any good to come of taking down that steeple, which in old times told nothing but glad tidings, as the history of Whittington and his Cat bears witness.

The rival oracle of Little Britain is a substantial cheesemonger, who lives in a fragment of one of the old family mansions, and is as magnificently lodged as a round-bellied mite in the midst of one of his own Cheshires. Indeed he is a man of no little standing and importance, and his renown extends through Huggin Lane, and Lad Lane, and even unto Aldermanbury. His opinion is very much taken in affairs of state, having read the Sunday papers for the last half century, together with the *Gentleman's Magazine,* Rapin's *History of England,* and the *Naval Chronicle*. His head is stored with invaluable maxims which have borne the test of time and use for centuries. It is his firm opinion that "it is a moral impossible," so long as England is true to herself, that anything can shake her; and he has much to say on the subject of the national debt, which, somehow or other, he proves to be a great national bulwark and blessing. He passed the greater part of his life in the purlieus of Little Britain, until of late years, when, having become rich and grown into the dignity of a Sunday cane, he begins to take his pleasure and see the world. He has therefore made several excursions to Hampstead, Highgate, and other neighboring towns, where he has passed whole afternoons in looking back upon the metropolis through a telescope, and endeavoring to descry the steeple of St. Bartholomew's. Not a stage coachman of Bull and Mouth Street but touches his hat as he passes; and he is considered quite a patron at the coach office of the Goose and Gridiron, St. Paul's Church Yard. His family have been very urgent for him to make an expedition to Margate, but he has great doubts of those new gimcracks, the steamboats, and indeed thinks himself too advanced in life to undertake sea voyages.

Little Britain has occasionally its factions and divisions, and party spirit ran very high at one time in consequence of two rival "Burial Societies" being set up in the place. One held its meeting at the Swan and Horse Shoe, and was patronized by the cheesemonger; the other at the Cock and Crown, under the auspices of the apothecary: it is needless to say that the latter was the most flourishing. I have passed an evening or two at each, and have acquired much valuable information as to the best mode of being buried, the comparative merits of churchyards, together with diverse hints on the subject of patent-iron coffins. I have heard the question discussed in all its bearings as to the legality of prohibiting the latter on account of their durability. The feuds occasioned by these societies have happily died of late; but they were for a long time prevailing themes of controversy, the people of Little Britain being extremely solicitous of funereal honors and of lying comfortably in their graves.

Besides these two funeral societies there is a third of quite a different cast, which tends to throw the sunshine of good humor over the whole neighborhood. It meets once a week at a little old-fashioned house kept by a jolly publican of the name of Wagstaff, and bearing for insignia a resplendent half-moon with a most seductive bunch of grapes. The old edifice is covered with inscriptions to catch the eye of the thirsty wayfarer, such as "Truman, Hanbury, and Co.'s Entire," "Wine, Rum, and Brandy Vaults," "Old Tom, Rum and Compounds, etc." This indeed has been a temple of Bacchus and Momus from time immemorial. It has always been in the family of the Wagstaffs, so that its history is tolerably pre-

served by the present landlord. It was much frequented
by the gallants and cavalieros of the reign of Elizabeth,
and was looked into now and then by the wits of Charles
the Second's day. But what Wagstaff principally prides
himself upon is that Henry the Eighth, in one of his
nocturnal rambles, broke the head of one of his ancestors with his famous walking staff. This, however, is considered as rather a dubious and vainglorious boast of the
landlord.

The club which now holds its weekly sessions here
goes by the name of "The Roaring Lads of Little Britain."
They abound in old catches, glees, and choice stories
that are traditional in the place and not to be met with
in any other part of the metropolis. There is a madcap
undertaker who is inimitable at a merry song; but the
life of the club, and indeed the prime wit of Little Britain,
is bully Wagstaff himself. His ancestors were all wags before him, and he has inherited with the inn a large stock
of songs and jokes, which go with it from generation to
generation as heirlooms. He is a dapper little fellow, with
bandy legs and pot belly, a red face, with a moist merry
eye, and a little shock of gray hair behind. At the opening of
every club night he is called in to sing his "Confession of
Faith," which is the famous old drinking trowl from
Gammer Gurton's Needle. He sings it, to be sure, with
many variations, as he received it from his father's lips,
for it has been a standing favorite at the Half-Moon and
Bunch of Grapes ever since it was written; nay, he affirms
that his predecessors have often had the honor of singing
it before the nobility and gentry at Christmas mummeries, when Little Britain was in all its glory.*

---

*As mine host of the Half-Moon's "Confession of Faith" may not
be familiar to the majority of readers, and as it is a specimen of the
current songs of Little Britain, I subjoin it in its original orthography.
I would observe, that the whole club always join in the chorus with a
fearful thumping on the table and clattering of pewter pots.

> I cannot eate but lytle meate,
> My stomacke is not good,
> But sure I thinke that I can drinke
> With him that weares a hood.
> Though I go bare, take ye no care,
> I nothing am a colde,
> I stuff my skyn so full within,
> Of joly good ale and olde.

It would do one's heart good to hear, on a club night, the shouts of merriment, the snatches of song, and now and then the choral bursts of half a dozen discordant voices which issue from this jovial mansion. At such times the street is lined with listeners, who enjoy a delight equal to that of gazing into a confectioner's window or snuffing up the steams of a cookshop.

There are two annual events which produce great stir and sensation in Little Britain; these are St. Bartholomew's fair, and the Lord Mayor's day. During the time of the fair, which is held in the adjoining regions of Smithfield, there is nothing going on but gossiping and gadding about. The late quiet streets of Little Britain are overrun with an irruption of strange figures and faces; every tavern is a scene of rout and revel. The fiddle and the song are heard from the taproom morning, noon, and

Chorus.   Backe and syde go bare, go bare,
       Booth foote and hand go colde,
   But belly, God send thee good ale ynoughe
       Whether it be new or olde.

I have no rost, but a nut brawne toste,
   And a crab laid in the fyre;
A little breade shall do me steade,
   Much breade I not desyre.
No frost nor snow, nor winde, I trowe,
   Can hurte mee, if I wolde,
I am so wrapt and throwly lapt
   Of joly good ale and olde.
Chorus.   Backe and syde go bare, go bare, etc.

And Tyb my wife, that, as her lyfe,
   Loveth well good ale to seeke,
Full oft drynkes shee, tyll ye may see,
   The teares run downe her cheeke.
Then doth she trowle to me the bowle,
   Even as a mault-worme sholde,
And sayth, sweete harte, I tooke my parte
   Of this joly good ale and olde.
Chorus.   Backe and syde go bare, go bare, etc.

Now let them drynke, tyll they nod and winke,
   Even as goode fellowes sholde doe,
They shall not mysse to have the blisse,
   Good ale doth bring men to;
And all poore soules that have scowred bowles,
   Or have them lustily trolde,
God save the lyves of them and their wives,
   Whether they be yonge or olde.
Chorus.   Backe and syde go bare, go bare, etc.

night; and at each window may be seen some group of boon companions, with half-shut eyes, hats on one side, pipe in mouth, and tankard in hand, fondling, and prosing, and singing maudlin songs over their liquor. Even the sober decorum of private families, which I must say is rigidly kept up at other times among my neighbors, is no proof against this Saturnalia. There is no such thing as keeping maidservants within doors. Their brains are absolutely set madding with Punch and the Puppet Show; the Flying Horses, Signior Polito, the Fire-Eater, the celebrated Mr. Paap, and the Irish Giant. The children too lavish all their holiday money in toys and gilt gingerbread, and fill the house with the Lilliputian din of drums, trumpets, and penny whistles.

But the Lord Mayor's day is the great anniversary. The Lord Mayor is looked up to by the inhabitants of Little Britain as the greatest potentate upon earth, his gilt coach with six horses as the summit of human splendor, and his procession, with all the Sheriffs and Aldermen in his train, as the grandest of earthly pageants. How they exult in the idea that the King himself dare not enter the city without first knocking at the gate of Temple Bar and asking permission of the Lord Mayor, for if he did, heaven and earth! There is no knowing what might be the consequences. The man in armor who rides before the Lord Mayor, and is the city champion, has orders to cut down everybody that offends against the dignity of the city; and then there is the little man with a velvet porringer on his head who sits at the window of the state coach and holds the city sword, as long as a pike staff—Odd's blood! If he once draws that sword, Majesty itself is not safe!

Under the protection of this mighty potentate, therefore, the good people of Little Britain sleep in peace. Temple Bar is an effectual barrier against all interior foes; and as to foreign invasion, the Lord Mayor has but to throw himself into the Tower, call in the train bands, and put the standing army of Beefeaters under arms, and he may bid defiance to the world!

Thus wrapped up in its own concerns, its own habits, and its own opinions, Little Britain has long flourished as a sound heart to this great fungous metropolis. I have pleased myself with considering it as a chosen spot, where the principles of sturdy John Bullism were garnered up, like seed corn, to renew the national character, when it had run to waste and degeneracy. I have rejoiced also in the general spirit of harmony that prevailed throughout it, for though there might now and then be a few clashes of opinion between the adherents of the cheesemonger and the apothecary, and an occasional feud between the burial societies, yet these were but transient clouds, and soon passed away. The neighbors met with good will, parted with a shake of the hand, and never abused each other except behind their backs.

I could give rare descriptions of snug junketing parties at which I have been present, where we played at All-Fours, Pope Joan, Tom-come-tickle-me, and other choice old games, and where we sometimes had a good old English country dance to the tune of Sir Roger de Coverley. Once a year also the neighbors would gather together, and go on a gypsy party to Epping Forest. It would have done any man's heart good to see the merriment that took place here as we banqueted on the grass under the trees. How we made the woods ring with bursts of laughter at the songs of little Wagstaff and the merry undertaker! After dinner, too, the young folks would play at blind-man's buff and hide-and-seek; and it was amusing to see them tangled among the briers, and to hear a fine romping girl now and then squeak from among the bushes. The elder folks would gather around the cheesemonger and the apothecary to hear them talk politics, for they generally brought out a newspaper in their pockets to pass away time in the country. They would now and then, to be sure, get a little warm in argument; but their disputes were always adjusted by reference to a worthy old umbrella maker in a double chin, who, never exactly comprehending the subject, managed somehow or other to decide in favor of both parties.

All empires, however, says some philosopher or historian, are doomed to changes and revolutions. Luxury and innovation creep in; factions arise; and families now and then spring up whose ambition and intrigues throw the whole system into confusion. Thus in latter days has the tranquillity of Little Britain been grievously disturbed, and its golden simplicity of manners threatened with total subversion by the aspiring family of a retired butcher.

The family of the Lambs had long been among the most thriving and popular in the neighborhood; the Miss Lambs were the belles of Little Britain, and everybody was pleased when Old Lamb had made money enough to shut up shop and put his name on a brass plate on his door. In an evil hour, however, one of the Miss Lambs had the honor of being a lady in attendance on the Lady Mayoress, at her grand annual ball, on which occasion she wore three towering ostrich feathers on her head. The family never got over it; they were immediately smitten with a passion for high life, set up a one-horse carriage, put a bit of gold lace around the errand boy's hat, and have been the talk and detestation of the whole neighborhood ever since. They could no longer be induced to play at Pope Joan or blind-man's buff; they could endure no dances but quadrilles, which nobody had ever heard of in Little Britain; and they took to reading novels, talking bad French, and playing upon the piano. Their brother, too, who had been articled to an attorney, set up for a dandy and a critic, characters hitherto unknown in these parts, and he confounded the worthy folks exceedingly by talking about Kean, the opera, and the *Edinburgh Review*.

What was still worse, the Lambs gave a grand ball, to which they neglected to invite any of their old neighbors; but they had a great deal of genteel company from Theobald's Road, Red Lion Square, and other parts toward the west. There were several beaux of their brother's acquaintance from Gray's Inn Lane and Hatton Garden, and not less than three Aldermen's ladies with their daughters. This was not to be forgotten or forgiven. All Little Britain was in an uproar with the smacking of whips, the lashing of miserable horses, and the rattling and the jingling of hackney coaches. The gossips of the neighborhood might be seen popping their nightcaps out at every window, watching the crazy vehicles rumble by; and there was a knot of virulent old cronies that kept a lookout from a house just opposite the retired butcher's, and scanned and criticized everyone that knocked at the door.

This dance was a cause of almost open war, and the whole neighborhood declared they would have nothing more to say to the Lambs. It is true that Mrs. Lamb, when she had no engagements with her quality acquaintance, would give little humdrum tea junketings to some of her old cronies, "quite," as she would say, "in a friendly way"; and it is equally true that her invitations were always accepted, in spite of all previous vows to the contrary. Nay, the good ladies would sit and be delighted with the music of the Miss Lambs, who would condescend to strum an Irish melody for them on the piano, and they would listen with wonderful interest to Mrs. Lamb's anecdotes of Alderman Plunket's family, of Portsokenward, and the Miss Timberlakes, the rich heiresses of Crutched Friars; but then they relieved their consciences and averted the reproaches of their confederates by canvassing at the next gossiping convocation everything that had passed, and pulling the Lambs and their rout all to pieces.

The only one of the family that could not be made fashionable was the retired butcher himself. Honest Lamb, in spite of the meekness of his name, was a rough, hearty old fellow, with the voice of a lion, a head of black hair like a shoe brush, and a broad face mottled like his own beef. It was in vain that the daughters always spoke of him as "the old gentleman," addressed him as "papa" in tones of infinite softness, and endeavored to coax him into a dressing gown and slippers and other gentlemanly habits. Do what they might, there was no keeping down the butcher. His sturdy nature would break through all their glozings. He had a hearty, vulgar good humor that was irrepressible. His very jokes made his sensitive daughters shudder; and he persisted in wearing his blue cotton coat of a morning, dining at two o'clock, and having a "bit of sausage with his tea."

He was doomed, however, to share the unpopularity of his family. He found his old comrades gradually growing cold and civil to him, no longer laughing at his jokes, and now and then throwing out a fling at "some people," and a hint about "quality binding." This both nettled and perplexed the honest butcher; and his wife and daughters, with the consummate policy of the shrewder sex, taking advantage of the circumstance, at length prevailed upon

him to give up his afternoon's pipe and tankard at
Wagstaff's, to sit after dinner by himself, and take his pint
of port—a liquor he detested—and to nod in his chair in
solitary and dismal gentility.

The Miss Lambs might now be seen flaunting along
the streets in French bonnets, with unknown beaux, and
talking and laughing so loud that it distressed the nerves
of every good lady within hearing. They even went so
far as to attempt patronage, and actually induced a French
dancing master to set up in the neighborhood; but the
worthy folks of Little Britain took fire at it, and did so
persecute the poor Gaul that he was fain to pack up
fiddle and dancing pumps and decamp with such precipitation that he absolutely forgot to pay for his lodgings.

I had flattered myself, at first, with the idea that all this
fiery indignation on the part of the community was merely
the overflowing of their zeal for good old English manners,
and their horror of innovation; and I applauded the silent
contempt they were so vociferous in expressing for upstart pride, French fashions, and the Miss Lambs. But
I grieve to say that I soon perceived the infection had
taken hold, and that my neighbors, after condemning,
were beginning to follow their example. I overheard my
landlady importuning her husband to let their daughters
have one quarter at French and music, and that they
might take a few lessons in quadrille. I even saw, in the
course of a few Sundays, no less than five French bonnets,
precisely like those of the Miss Lambs, parading about
Little Britain.

I still had my hopes that all this folly would gradually
die away, that the Lambs might move out of the neighborhood, might die, or might run away with attorneys'
apprentices, and that quiet and simplicity might be again
restored to the community. But unluckily a rival power
arose. An opulent oilman died, and left a widow with a
large jointure and a family of buxom daughters. The
young ladies had long been repining in secret at the parsimony of a prudent father, which kept down all their
elegant aspirings. Their ambition, being now no longer
restrained, broke out into a blaze, and they openly took
the field against the family of the butcher. It is true that
the Lambs, having had the first start, had naturally an

advantage of them in the fashionable career. They could speak a little bad French, play the piano, dance quadrilles, and had formed high acquaintances; but the Trotters were not to be distanced. When the Lambs appeared with two feathers in their hats, the Miss Trotters mounted four, and of twice as fine colors. If the Lambs gave a dance, the Trotters were sure not to be behindhand; and though they might not boast of as good company, yet they had double the number, and were twice as merry.

The whole community has at length divided itself into fashionable factions, under the banners of these two families. The old games of Pope Joan and Tom-come-tickle-me are entirely discarded; there is no such thing as getting up an honest country dance; and on my attempting to kiss a young lady under the mistletoe last Christmas, I was indignantly repulsed, the Miss Lambs having pronounced it "shocking vulgar." Bitter rivalry has also broken out as to the most fashionable part of Little Britain, the Lambs standing up for the dignity of Cross Keys Square and the Trotters for the vicinity of St. Bartholomew's.

Thus is this little territory torn by factions and internal dissensions, like the great empire whose name it bears; and what will be the result would puzzle the apothecary himself, with all his talent at prognostics, to determine, though I apprehend that it will terminate in the total downfall of genuine John Bullism.

The immediate effects are extremely unpleasant to me. Being a single man, and, as I observed before, rather an idle good-for-nothing personage, I have been considered the only gentleman by profession in the place. I stand therefore in high favor with both parties, and have to hear all their cabinet councils and mutual backbitings. As I am too civil not to agree with the ladies on all occasions, I have committed myself most horribly with both parties by abusing their opponents. I might manage to reconcile this to my conscience, which is a truly accommodating one, but I cannot to my apprehension—if the Lambs and Trotters ever come to a reconciliation and compare notes I am ruined!

I have determined, therefore, to beat a retreat in time, and am actually looking out for some other nest in this great city, where old English manners are still kept up, where French is neither eaten, drunk, danced, nor spoken, and where there are no fashionable families of retired tradesmen. This found, I will, like a veteran rat, hasten away before I have an old house about my ears; bid a long, though a sorrowful adieu to my present abode, and leave the rival factions of the Lambs and the Trotters to divide the distracted empire of LITTLE BRITAIN.

STRATFORD ON AVON

Thou soft-flowing Avon, by thy silver stream
Of things more than mortal sweet Shakespeare would dream;
The fairies by moonlight dance round his green bed,
For hallow'd the turf is which pillow'd his head.

GARRICK

To a homeless man, who has no spot on this wide world which he can truly call his own, there is a momentary feeling of something like independence and territorial consequence when, after a weary day's travel, he kicks off his boots, thrusts his feet into slippers, and stretches himself before an inn fire. Let the world without go as it may; let kingdoms rise or fall, so long as he has the wherewithal to pay his bill, he is, for the time being, the very monarch of all he surveys. The armchair is his throne, the poker his scepter, and the little parlor, some twelve feet square, his undisputed empire. It is a morsel of certainty, snatched from the midst of the uncertainties of life; it is a sunny moment gleaming out kindly on a cloudy day, and he who has advanced some way on the pilgrimage of existence knows the importance of husbanding even morsels and moments of enjoyment. "Shall I not take mine ease in mine inn?" thought I, as I gave the fire a stir, lolled back in my elbow chair, and cast a complacent look about the little parlor of the Red Horse, at Stratford on Avon.

The words of sweet Shakespeare were just passing through my mind as the clock struck midnight from the tower of the church in which he lies buried. There was a gentle tap at the door, and a pretty chambermaid, putting in her smiling face, inquired, with a hesitating air, whether I had rung. I understood it as a modest hint that it was time to retire. My dream of absolute dominion was at an end; so abdicating my throne, like a prudent potentate, to avoid being deposed, and putting the Stratford *Guide Book* under my arm as a pillow companion I went to bed, and dreamed all night of Shakespeare, the jubilee, and David Garrick.

The next morning was one of those quickening mornings which we sometimes have in early spring, for it was about the middle of March. The chills of a long winter had suddenly given way; the north wind had spent its last gasp; and a mild air came stealing from the west, breathing the breath of life into nature, and wooing every bud and flower to burst forth into fragrance and beauty.

I had come to Stratford on a poetical pilgrimage. My first visit was to the house where Shakespeare was born, and where, according to tradition, he was brought up to his father's craft of wool-combing. It is a small, mean-looking edifice of wood and plaster, a true nestling place of genius, which seems to delight in hatching its off-spring in by-corners. The walls of its squalid chambers are covered with names and inscriptions in every language, by pilgrims of all nations, ranks, and conditions, from the prince to the peasant, and present a simple but striking instance of the spontaneous and universal homage of mankind to the great poet of nature.

The house is shown by a garrulous old lady, in a frosty red face, lighted up by a cold blue anxious eye, and garnished with artificial locks of flaxen hair, curling from under an exceedingly dirty cap. She was peculiarly assiduous in exhibiting the relics with which this, like all other celebrated shrines, abounds. There was the shattered stock of the very match lock with which Shakespeare shot the deer on his poaching exploits. There, too, was his tobacco box, which proves that he was a rival smoker of Sir Walter Raleigh; the sword also with which he played Hamlet; and the identical lantern with which Friar Laurence discovered Romeo and Juliet at the tomb! There was an ample supply also of Shakespeare's mulberry tree, which seems to have as extraordinary powers of self-multiplication as the wood of the true cross, of which there is enough extant to build a ship of the line.

The most favorite object of curiosity, however, is Shakespeare's chair. It stands in the chimney nook of a small gloomy chamber, just behind what was his father's shop. Here he may many a time have sat when a boy, watching the slowly revolving spit with all the longing of an urchin, or of an evening, listening to the cronies and gossips of Stratford dealing forth churchyard tales and legendary anecdotes of the troublesome times of England. In this chair it is the custom of everyone that visits the house to sit: whether this be done with the hope of inbibing any of the inspiration of the bard I am at a loss to say, I merely mention the fact; and mine hostess privately assured me that, though built of solid oak, such was the fervent zeal of devotees that the chair had to be new bottomed at least once in three years. It is worthy of notice also, in the history of this extraordinary chair, that it partakes something of the volatile nature of the Santa Casa of Loretto, or the flying chair of the Arabian enchanter, for though sold some few years since to a northern princess, yet, strange to tell, it has found its way back again to the old chimney corner.

I am always of easy faith in such matters, and am ever willing to be deceived where the deceit is pleasant and costs nothing. I am therefore a ready believer in relics, legends, and local anecdotes of goblins and great men, and would advise all travelers who travel for their gratification to be the same. What is it to us whether these stories be true or false, so long as we can persuade ourselves into the belief of them, and enjoy all the charm of the reality? There is nothing like resolute good-humored credulity in these matters; and on this occasion I went even so far as willingly to believe the claims of mine hostess to a lineal descent from the poet, when, luckily, for my faith, she put into my hands a play of her own composition, which set all belief in her consanguinity at defiance.

From the birthplace of Shakespeare a few paces brought me to his grave. He lies buried in the chancel of the parish church, a large and venerable pile, moldering with age, but richly ornamented. It stands on the banks of the Avon, on an embowered point, and separated by adjoining gardens from the suburbs of the town.

Its situation is quiet and retired; the river runs murmuring at the foot of the churchyard, and the elms which grow upon its banks droop their branches into its clear bosom. An avenue of limes, the boughs of which are curiously interlaced so as to form in summer an arched way of foliage, leads up from the gate of the yard to the church porch. The graves are overgrown with grass; the gray tombstones, some of them nearly sunk into the earth, are half covered with moss, which has likewise tinted the reverend old building. Small birds have built their nests among the cornices and fissures of the walls, and keep up a continual flutter and chirping; and rooks are sailing and cawing about its lofty gray spire.

In the course of my rambles I met with the gray-headed sexton, Edmonds, and accompanied him home to get the key of the church. He had lived in Stratford, man and boy, for eighty years, and seemed still to consider himself a vigorous man, with the trivial exception that he had nearly lost the use of his legs for a few years past. His dwelling was a cottage looking out upon the Avon and its bordering meadows, and was a picture of that neatness, order, and comfort which pervade the humblest dwellings in this country. A low white-washed room with a stone floor carefully scrubbed served for parlor, kitchen, and hall. Rows of pewter and earthen dishes glittered along the dresser. On an old oaken table, well rubbed and polished, lay the family Bible and prayer-book, and the drawer contained the family library, composed of about half a score of well-thumbed volumes. An ancient clock, that important article of cottage furniture, ticked on the opposite side of the room, with a bright warming pan hanging on one side of it, and the old man's horn-handled Sunday cane on the other. The fireplace, as usual, was wide and deep enough to admit a gossip knot within its jambs. In one corner sat the old man's granddaughter sewing, a pretty blue-eyed girl—and in the opposite corner was a superannuated crony, whom he addressed by the name of John Ange, and who, I found, had been his companion from childhood. They had played together in infancy; they had worked together in manhood; they were now tottering about and gossiping away the evening of life; and in a short time they will probably be buried together in the neighboring churchyard. It is not often that we see two streams of existence running thus evenly and tranquilly side by side; it is only in such quiet "bosom scenes" of life that they are to be met with.

I had hoped to gather some traditionary anecdotes of the bard from these ancient chroniclers, but they had nothing new to impart. The long interval during which Shakespeare's writings lay in comparative neglect has spread its shadow over his history, and it is his good or evil lot that scarcely anything remains to his biographers but a scanty handful of conjectures.

The sexton and his companion had been employed as carpenters on the preparations for the celebrated Stratford jubilee, and they remembered Garrick, the prime mover of the fete, who superintended the arrangements, and who, according to the sexton, was "a short punch man, very lively and bustling." John Ange had assisted also in cutting down Shakespeare's mulberry tree, of which he had a morsel in his pocket for sale, no doubt a sovereign quickener of literary conception.

I was grieved to hear these two worthy wights speak very dubiously of the eloquent dame who shows the Shakespeare house. John Ange shook his head when I mentioned her valuable collection of relics, particularly her remains of the mulberry tree, and the old sexton even expressed a doubt as to Shakespeare having been born in her house. I soon discovered that he looked upon her mansion with an evil eye, as a rival to the poet's tomb, the latter having comparatively but few visitors. Thus it is that historians differ at the very outset, and mere pebbles make the stream of truth diverge into different channels even at the fountainhead.

We approached the church through the avenue of limes, and entered by a Gothic porch, highly ornamented, with carved doors of massive oak. The interior is spacious, and the architecture and embellishments superior to those of most country churches. There are several ancient monuments of nobility and gentry, over some of which hang funeral escutcheons, and banners dropping piecemeal from the walls. The tomb of Shakespeare is in the chancel. The place is solemn and sepulchral. Tall elms wave before the pointed windows, and the Avon, which runs at a short distance from the walls, keeps up a low perpetual murmur. A flat stone marks the spot where the bard is buried. There are four lines inscribed on it, said to have been written by himself, and which have in them something extremely awful. If they are indeed his own, they show that solicitude about the quiet of the grave which seems natural to fine sensibilities and thoughtful minds.

> Good friend, for Jesus' sake forbeare
> To dig the dust enclosed here.
> Blessed be he that spares these stones,
> And curst be he that moves my bones.

Just over the grave, in a niche of the wall, is a bust of Shakespeare, put up shortly after his death, and considered as a resemblance. The aspect is pleasant and serene, with a finely arched forehead, and I thought I could read in it clear indications of that cheerful, social disposition by which he was as much characterized among his contemporaries as by the vastness of his genius. The inscription mentions his age at the time of his decease—fifty-three years; an untimely death for the world, for what fruit might not have been expected from the golden autumn of such a mind, sheltered as it was from the stormy vicissitudes of life and flourishing in the sunshine of popular and royal favor.

The inscription on the tombstone has not been without its effect. It has prevented the removal of his remains from the bosom of his native place to Westminster Abbey, which was at one time contemplated. A few years since also, as some laborers were digging to make an adjoining vault, the earth caved in, so as to leave a vacant space almost like an arch, through which one might have reached into his grave. No one, however, presumed to meddle with his remains so awfully guarded by a malediction; and lest any of the idle or the curious or any collector of relics should be tempted to commit depredations, the old sexton kept watch over the place for two days until the vault was finished and the aperture closed again. He told me that he had made bold to look in at the hole, but could see neither coffin nor bones; nothing but dust. It was something, I thought, to have seen the dust of Shakespeare.

Next to this grave are those of his wife, his favorite daughter, Mrs. Hall, and others of his family. On a tomb close by, also, is a full-length effigy of his old friend John Combe of usurious memory, on whom he is said to have written a ludicrous epitaph. There are other monuments around, but the mind refuses to dwell on anything that is not connected with Shakespeare. His idea pervades the place; the whole pile seems but as his mausoleum. The feelings, no longer checked and thwarted by doubt, here indulge in perfect confidence; other traces of him may be false or dubious, but here is palpable evidence and absolute certainty. As I trod the sounding pavement there was something intense and thrilling in the idea that, in very truth, the remains of Shakespeare were moldering beneath my feet. It was a long time before I could prevail upon myself to leave the place; and as I passed through the churchyard I plucked a branch from one of the yew trees, the only relic that I have brought from Stratford.

I had now visited the usual objects of a pilgrim's devotion, but I had a desire to see the old family seat of the Lucys, at Charlecot, and to ramble through the park where Shakespeare, in company with some of the roysters of Stratford, committed his youthful offence of deer stealing. In this harebrained exploit we are told that he was taken prisoner and carried to the keeper's lodge, where he remained all night in doleful captivity. When brought into the presence of Sir Thomas Lucy, his treatment must have been galling and humiliating, for it so wrought upon his spirit as to produce a rough pasquinade, which was affixed to the park gate at Charlecot.*

---

*The following is the only stanza extant of this lampoon:

A parliament member, a justice of peace,
At home a poor scarecrow, at London an asse,
If lowsie is Lucy, as some volke miscalle it,
Then Lucy is lowsie, whatever befall it.
    He thinks himself great;
    Yet an asse in his state,
We allow by his ears but with asses to mate,
If Lucy is lowsie, as some volke miscalle it,
Then sing lowsie Lucy whatever befall it.

This flagitious attack upon the dignity of the knight so incensed him that he applied to a lawyer at Warwick to put the severity of the laws in force against the rhyming deer stalker. Shakespeare did not wait to brave the united puissance of a knight of the shire and a country attorney. He forthwith abandoned the pleasant banks of the Avon and his paternal trade, wandered away to London, became a hanger-on to the theaters, then an actor, and, finally, wrote for the stage; and thus, through the persecution of Sir Thomas Lucy, Stratford lost an indifferent wool comber and the world gained an immortal poet. He retained, however, for a long time a sense of the harsh treatment of the Lord of Charlecot, and revenged himself in his writings, but in the sportive way of a good-natured mind. Sir Thomas is said to be the original Justice Shallow, and the satire is slyly fixed upon him by the justice's armorial bearings, which, like those of the knight, had white luces * in the quarterings.

Various attempts have been made by his biographers to soften and explain away this early transgression of the poet, but I look upon it as one of those thoughtless exploits natural to his situation and turn of mind. Shakespeare, when young, had doubtless all the wildness and irregularity of an ardent, undisciplined, and undirected genius. The poetic temperament has naturally something in it of the vagabond. When left to itself it runs loosely and wildly, and delights in everything eccentric and licentious. It is often a turn-up of a die, in the gambling freaks of fate, whether a natural genius shall turn out a great rogue or a great poet; and had not Shakespeare's mind fortunately taken a literary bias, he might have as daringly transcended all civil as he has all dramatic laws.

I have little doubt that, in early life, when running, like an unbroken colt, about the neighborhood of Stratford, he was to be found in the company of all kinds of odd anomalous characters, that he associated with all the madcaps of the place, and was one of those unlucky urchins at mention of whom old men shake

---

*The luce is a pike or jack, and abounds in the Avon about Charlecot.

their heads and predict that they will one day come to the gallows. To him the poaching in Sir Thomas Lucy's park was doubtless like a foray to a Scottish knight, and struck his eager and as yet untamed imagination as something delightfully adventurous.*

The old mansion of Charlecot and its surrounding park still remain in the possession of the Lucy family, and are peculiarly interesting from being connected with this whimsical but eventful circumstance in the scanty history of the bard. As the house stood but little more than three miles' distance from Stratford, I resolved to pay it a pedestrian visit, that I might stroll leisurely through some of those scenes from which Shakespeare must have derived his earliest ideas of rural imagery.

The country was yet naked and leafless, but English scenery is always verdant, and the sudden change in the temperature of the weather was surprising in its quickening effects upon the landscape. It was inspiring and animating to witness this first awakening of spring, to feel its warm breath stealing over the senses, to see the

---

*A proof of Shakespeare's random habits and associates in his youthful days may be found in a traditionary anecdote, picked up at Stratford by the elder Ireland, and mentioned in his *Picturesque Views on the Avon.*

About seven miles from Stratford lies the thirsty little market town of Bedford, famous for its ale. Two societies of the village yeomanry used to meet, under the appellation of the Bedford topers, and to challenge the lovers of good ale of the neighboring villages to a contest of drinking. Among others, the people of Stratford were called out to prove the strength of their heads; and in the number of the champions was Shakespeare, who, in spite of the proverb that "they who drink beer will think beer," was as true to his ale as Falstaff to his sack. The chivalry of Stratford was staggered at the first onset, and sounded a retreat while they had yet legs to carry them off the field. They had scarcely marched a mile when, their legs failing them, they were forced to lie down under a crabtree, where they passed the night. It is still standing, and goes by the name of Shakespeare's tree.

In the morning his companions awaked the bard, and proposed returning to Bedford, but he declined, saying he had had enough, having drank with

> Piping Pebworth, Dancing Marston,
> Haunted Hilbro', Hungry Grafton,
> Dudging Exhall, Papist Wicksford,
> Beggarly Broom, and Drunken Bedford.

"The villages here alluded to," says Ireland, "still bear the epithets thus given them: the people of Pebworth are still famed for their skill on the pipe and tabor; Hilborough is now called Haunted Hilborough; and Grafton is famous for the poverty of its soil."

moist mellow earth beginning to put forth the green sprout and the tender blade, and the trees and shrubs, in their reviving tints and bursting buds, giving the promise of returning foliage and flower. The cold snowdrop, that little borderer on the skirts of winter, was to be seen with its chaste white blossoms in the small gardens before the cottages. The bleating of the new-dropped lambs was faintly heard from the fields. The sparrow twittered about the thatched eaves and budding hedges; the robin threw a livelier note into his late querulous wintry strain; and the lark, springing up from the reeking bosom of the meadow, towered away into the bright fleecy cloud, pouring forth torrents of melody. As I watched the little songster, mounting up higher and higher until his body was a mere speck on the white bosom of the cloud, while the ear was still filled with his music, it called to mind Shakespeare's exquisite little song in *Cymbeline*:

> Hark! hark! the lark at heaven's gate sings,
>   And Phœbus 'gins arise,
> His steeds to water at those springs,
>   On chaliced flowers that lies.
>
> And winking mary-buds begin
>   To ope their golden eyes;
> With every thing that pretty bin,
>   My lady sweet arise!

Indeed the whole country about here is poetic ground: everything is associated with the idea of Shakespeare. Every old cottage that I saw, I fancied into some resort of his boyhood, where he had acquired his intimate knowledge of rustic life and manners, and heard those legendary tales and wild superstitions which he has woven like witchcraft into his dramas. For in his time, we are told, it was a popular amusement in winter evenings "to sit round the fire, and tell merry tales of errant knights, queens, lovers, lords, ladies, giants, dwarfs, thieves, cheaters, witches, fairies, goblins, and friars." *

---

*Scott, in his *Discoverie of Witchcraft*, enumerates a host of these fireside fancies. "And they have so fraid us with bull-beggars, spirits, witches, urchins, elves, hags, fairies, satyrs, pans, faunes, syrens, kit with the can sticke, tritons, centaurs, dwarfes, giantes, imps, calcars,

My route for a part of the way lay in sight of the Avon, which made a variety of the most fancy doublings and windings through a wide and fertile valley, sometimes glittering from among willows which fringed its borders, sometimes disappearing among groves or beneath green banks, and sometimes rambling out into full view, and making an azure sweep around a slope of meadow land. This beautiful bosom of country is called the Vale of the Red Horse. A distant line of undulating blue hills seems to be its boundary, while all the soft intervening landscape lies in a manner enchained in the silver links of the Avon.

After pursuing the road for about three miles, I turned off into a footpath which led along the borders of fields and under hedgerows to a private gate of the park; there was a stile, however, for the benefit of the pedestrian, there being a public right of way through the grounds. I delight in these hospitable estates, in which everyone has a kind of property—at least as far as the footpath is concerned. It in some measure reconciles a poor man to his lot, and, what is more, to the better lot of his neighbor thus to have parks and pleasure grounds thrown open for his recreation. He breathes the pure air as freely and lolls as luxuriously under the shade as the lord of the soil; and if he has not the privilege of calling all that he sees his own, he has not, at the same time, the trouble of paying for it and keeping it in order.

I now found myself among noble avenues of oaks and elms, whose vast size bespoke the growth of centuries. The wind sounded solemnly among their branches, and the rooks cawed from their hereditary nests in the tree tops. The eye ranged through a long lessening vista, with nothing to interrupt the view but a distant statue, and a vagrant deer stalking like a shadow across the opening.

There is something about these stately old avenues that has the effect of Gothic architecture, not merely from the pretended similarity of form, but from their

---

conjurors, nymphes, changelings, incubus, Robin-good-fellow, the spoorne, the mare, the man in the oke, the hell-waine, the fier-drake, the puckle, Tom Thombe, hobgoblins, Tom Tumbler, boneless, and such other bugs, that we were afraid of our own shadowes."

bearing the evidence of long duration, and of having had their origin in a period of time with which we associate ideas of romantic grandeur. They betoken also the long-settled dignity and proudly concentrated independence of an ancient family; and I have heard a worthy but aristocratic old friend observe, when speaking of the sumptuous palaces of modern gentry, that "money could do much with stone and mortar, but, thank Heaven, there was no such thing as suddenly building up an avenue of oaks."

It was from wandering in early life among this rich scenery and about the romantic solitudes of the adjoining park of Fullbroke, which then formed a part of the Lucy estate, that some of Shakespeare's commentators have supposed he derived his noble forest meditations of Jaques, and the enchanting woodland pictures in *As You Like It*. It is in lonely wanderings through such scenes that the mind drinks deep but quiet drafts of inspiration, and becomes intensely sensible of the beauty and majesty of nature. The imagination kindles into reverie and rapture; vague but exquisite images and ideas keep breaking upon it; and we revel in a mute and almost incommunicable luxury of thought. It was in some such mood, and perhaps under one of those very trees before me which threw their broad shades over the grassy banks and quivering waters of the Avon that the poet's fancy may have sallied forth into that little song which breathes the very soul of a rural voluptuary:

> Under the greenwood tree,
> Who loves to lie with me,
> And tune his merry throat
> Unto the sweet bird's note,
> Come hither, come hither, come hither.
> Here shall he see
> No enemy,
> But winter and rough weather.

I had now come in sight of the house. It is a large building of brick, with stone quoins, and is in the Gothic style of Queen Elizabeth's day, having been built in the first year of her reign. The exterior remains very nearly in its original state, and may be considered a fair speci-

men of the residence of a wealthy country gentleman of
those days. A great gateway opens from the park into a
kind of courtyard in front of the house, ornamented with
a grass plot, shrubs, and flower beds. The gateway is in
imitation of the ancient barbacan, being a kind of outpost
and flanked by towers, though evidently for mere ornament instead of defence. The front of the house is completely in the old style, with stone-shafted casements, a
great bow window of heavy stonework, and a portal with
armorial bearings over it, carved in stone. At each corner
of the building is an octagon tower, surmounted by a
gilt ball and weathercock.

The Avon, which winds through the park, makes a
bend just at the foot of a gently sloping bank, which
sweeps down from the rear of the house. Large herds of
deer were feeding or reposing upon its borders, and
swans were sailing majestically upon its bosom. As I
contemplated the venerable old mansion, I called to mind
Falstaff's encomium on Justice Shallow's abode, and the
affected indifference and real vanity of the latter:

> "*Falstaff*. You have a goodly dwelling and a rich.
> *Shallow*. Barren, barren, barren; beggars all, beggars all,
> Sir John:—marry, good air."

What may have been the joviality of the old mansion
in the days of Shakespeare, it had now an air of stillness
and solitude. The great iron gateway that opened into the
courtyard was locked; there was no show of servants
bustling about the place; the deer gazed quietly at me as
I passed, being no longer harried by the moss troopers of
Stratford. The only sign of domestic life that I met with
was a white cat, stealing with wary look and stealthy
pace toward the stables, as if on some nefarious expedition. I must not omit to mention the carcass of a scoundrel crow which I saw suspended against the barn wall,
as it shows that the Lucys still inherit that lordly ab-
horrence of poachers and maintain that rigorous exercise of territorial power which was so strenuously mani-
fested in the case of the bard.

After prowling about for some time, I at length found
my way to a lateral portal, which was the everyday en-

trance to the mansion. I was courteously received by a worthy old housekeeper, who, with the civility and communicativeness of her order, showed me the interior of the house. The greater part has undergone alterations and been adapted to modern tastes and modes of living; there is a fine old oaken staircase, and the great hall, that noble feature in an ancient manor house, still retains much of the appearance it must have had in the days of Shakespeare. The ceiling is arched and lofty, and at one end is a gallery in which stands an organ. The weapons and trophies of the chase, which formerly adorned the hall of a country gentleman, have made way for family portraits. There is a wide hospitable fireplace, calculated for an ample old-fashioned wood fire, formerly the rallying place of winter festivity. On the opposite side of the hall is the huge Gothic bow window, with stone shafts, which looks out upon the courtyard. Here are emblazoned in stained glass the armorial bearings of the Lucy family for many generations, some being dated in 1558. I was delighted to observe in the quarterings the three *white luces,* by which the character of Sir Thomas was first identified with that of Justice Shallow. They are mentioned in the first scene of *The Merry Wives of Windsor,* where the Justice is in a rage with Falstaff for having "beaten his men, killed his deer, and broken into his lodge." The poet had no doubt the offenses of himself and his comrades in mind at the time, and we may suppose the family pride and vindictive threats of the puissant Shallow to be a caricature of the pompous indignation of Sir Thomas.

"*Shallow.* Sir Hugh, persuade me not: I will make a Star-Chamber matter of it; if he were twenty John Falstaffs, he shall not abuse Sir Robert Shallow, Esq.
Slender. In the county of Gloster, justice of peace, and *coram.*
Shallow. Ay, cousin Slender, and *custalorum.*
Slender. Ay, and *ratalorum* too, and a gentleman born, master parson; who writes himself *Armigero* in any bill, warrant, quittance, or obligation, *Armigero.*
Shallow. Ay, that I do; and have done any time these three hundred years.
Slender. All his successors gone before him have done't,

and all his ancestors that come after him may; they may
give the dozen *white luces* in their coat.*****

Shallow. The council shall hear it; it is a riot.

Evans. It is not meet the council hear of a riot; there is
no fear of Got in a riot; the council, hear you, shall desire
to hear the fear of Got, and not to hear a riot; take your
vizaments in that.

Shallow. Ha! o' my life, if I were young again, the sword
should end it!"

Near the window thus emblazoned hung a portrait by
Sir Peter Lely, of one of the Lucy family, a great beauty
of the time of Charles the Second; the old housekeeper
shook her head as she pointed to the picture, and informed me that this lady had been sadly addicted to cards,
and had gambled away a great portion of the family
estate, among which was that part of the park where
Shakespeare and his comrades had killed the deer. The
lands thus lost had not been entirely regained by the
family even at the present day. It is but justice to this
recreant dame to confess that she had a surpassingly fine
hand and arm.

The picture which most attracted my attention was a
great painting over the fireplace, containing likenesses of
Sir Thomas Lucy and his family, who inhabited the
hall in the latter part of Shakespeare's lifetime. I at first
thought that it was the vindictive knight himself, but the
housekeeper assured me that it was his son, the only
likeness extant of the former being an effigy upon his
tomb in the church of the neighboring hamlet of Charlecot.* The picture gives a lively idea of the costume and

---

*This effigy is in white marble, and represents the knight in complete
armor. Near him lies the effigy of his wife, and on her tomb is the
following inscription, which, if really composed by her husband, places
him quite above the intellectual level of Master Shallow:

Here lyeth the Lady Joyce Lucy wife of Sir Thomas Lucy of
Charlecot in ye county of Warwick, Knight, Daughter and heir of
Thomas Acton of Sutton in ye county of Worcester Esquire who departed out of this wretched world to her heavenly kingdom ye 10 day
of February in ye yeare of our Lord God 1595 and of her age 60
and three. All the time of her lyfe a true and faythful servant of her
good God, never detected of any cryme or vice. In religion most
sounde, in love to her husband most faythful and true. In friendship
most constant; to what in trust was committed unto her most secret.
In wisdom excelling. In governing of her house, bringing up of youth
in ye fear of God that did converse with her moste rare and singular.

manners of the time. Sir Thomas is dressed in ruff and doublet, white shoes with roses in them, and has a peaked yellow, or, as Master Slender would say, "a cane-colored beard." His lady is seated on the opposite side of the picture, in wide ruff and long stomacher, and the children have a most venerable stiffness and formality of dress. Hounds and spaniels are mingled in the family group; a hawk is seated on his perch in the foreground, and one of the children holds a bow—all intimating the knight's skill in hunting, hawking, and archery, so indispensable to an accomplished gentleman in those days.*

I regretted to find that the ancient furniture of the hall had disappeared, for I had hoped to meet with the stately elbow chair of carved oak in which the country squire of former days was wont to sway the scepter of empire over his rural domains, and in which it might be presumed the redoubted Sir Thomas sat enthroned in awful state when the recreant Shakespeare was brought before him. As I like to deck out pictures for my own entertainment, I pleased myself with the idea that this very hall had been the scene of the unlucky bard's examination on the morning after his captivity in the lodge. I fancied to myself the rural potentate, surrounded by his bodyguard of butler, pages, and blue-coated servingmen, with their badges, while the luckless culprit was brought in, forlorn and chopfallen, in the custody of gamekeepers, huntsmen, and whippers-in, and followed by a rabble

---

A great maintayner of hospitality. Greatly esteemed of her betters; misliked of none unless of the envyous. When all is spoken that can be saide a woman so garnished with virtue as not to be bettered and hardly to be equalled by any. As shee lived most virtuously so shee died most Godly. Set downe by him yt best did knowe what hath byn written to be true. Thomas Lucye.

*Bishop Earle, speaking of the country gentleman of his time, observes, "his housekeeping is seen much in the different families of dogs, and servingmen attendant on their kennels; and the deepness of their throats is the depth of his discourse. A hawk he esteems the true burden of nobility, and is exceedingly ambitious to seem delighted with the sport, and have his fist gloved with his jesses." And Gilpin, in his description of a Mr. Hastings, remarks, "he kept all sorts of hounds that run buck, fox, hare, otter, and badger; and had hawks of all kinds both long and short winged. His great hall was commonly strewed with marrow bones, and full of hawk perches, hounds, spaniels, and terriers. On a broad hearth, paved with brick, lay some of the choicest terriers, hounds, and spaniels."

rout of country clowns. I fancied bright faces of curious housemaids peeping from the half-opened doors, while from the gallery the fair daughters of the knight leaned gracefully forward, eying the youthful prisoner with that pity "that dwells in womanhood." Who would have thought that this poor varlet, thus trembling before the brief authority of a country squire, and the sport of rustic boors, was soon to become the delight of princes, the theme of all tongues and ages, the dictator to the human mind, and was to confer immortality on his oppressor by a caricature and a lampoon!

I was now invited by the butler to walk into the garden, and I felt inclined to visit the orchard and arbor where the justice treated Sir John Falstaff and Cousin Silence "to a last year's pippin of his own grafting, with a dish of caraways"; but I had already spent so much of the day in my ramblings that I was obliged to give up any further investigations. When about to take my leave I was gratified by the civil entreaties of the housekeeper and butler that I would take some refreshment, an instance of good old hospitality which, I grieve to say, we castle hunters seldom meet with in modern days. I make no doubt it is a virtue which the present representative of the Lucys inherits from his ancestors, for Shakespeare, even in his caricature, makes Justice Shallow importunate in this respect, as witness his pressing instances to Falstaff.

"By cock and pye, sir, you shall not away to-night * * * I will not excuse you; you shall not be excused; excuses shall not be admitted; there is no excuse shall serve; you shall not be excused * * *. Some pigeons, Davy; a couple of short-legged hens; a joint of mutton; and any pretty little tiny kickshaws, tell William Cook."

I now bade a reluctant farewell to the old hall. My mind had become so completely possessed by the imaginary scenes and characters connected with it that I seemed to be actually living among them. Everything brought them as it were before my eyes, and as the door of the dining room opened I almost expected to hear the feeble voice of Master Silence quavering forth his favorite ditty:

> " 'Tis merry in hall, when beards wag all,
>   And welcome merry shrove-tide!"

On returning to my inn, I could not but reflect on the singular gift of the poet; to be able thus to spread the magic of his mind over the very face of nature; to give to things and places a charm and character not their own, and to turn this "working-day world" into a perfect fairyland. He is indeed the true enchanter, whose spell operates, not upon the senses, but upon the imagination and the heart. Under the wizard influence of Shakespeare I had been walking all day in a complete delusion. I had surveyed the landscape through the prism of poetry, which tinged every object with the hues of the rainbow. I had been surrounded with fancied beings, with mere airy nothings, conjured up by poetic power, yet which, to me, had all the charm of reality. I had heard Jaques soliloquize beneath his oak; had beheld the fair Rosalind and her companion adventuring through the woodlands; and, above all, had been once more present in spirit with fat Jack Falstaff and his contemporaries, from the august Justice Shallow, down to the gentle Master Slender and the sweet Anne Page. Ten thousand honors and blessings on the bard who has thus gilded the dull realities of life with innocent illusions; who has spread exquisite and unbought pleasures in my checkered path; and beguiled my spirit in many a lonely hour with all the cordial and cheerful sympathies of social life!

As I crossed the bridge over the Avon on my return, I paused to contemplate the distant church in which the poet lies buried, and could not but exult in the malediction which has kept his ashes undisturbed in its quiet and hallowed vaults. What honor could his name have derived from being mingled in dusty companionship with the epitaphs and escutcheons and venal eulogiums of a titled multitude? What would a crowded corner in Westminster Abbey have been, compared with this reverend pile, which seems to stand in beautiful loneliness as his sole mausoleum! The solicitude about the grave may be but the offspring of an overwrought sensibility; but human nature is made up of foibles and prejudices, and its best and tenderest affections are mingled with these factitious feelings. He who has sought renown about the world and has reaped a full harvest of worldly favor will find, after all, that there is no love, no admiration, no applause, so sweet to the soul as that which springs up in his native place. It is there that he seeks to be gathered in peace and honor among his kindred and his early friends. And when the weary heart and failing head begin to warn him that the evening of life is drawing on, he turns as fondly as does the infant to the mother's arms, to sink to sleep in the bosom of the scene of his childhood.

How would it have cheered the spirit of the youthful bard when, wandering forth in disgrace upon a doubtful world, he cast back a heavy look upon his paternal home, could he have foreseen that, before many years, he should return to it covered with renown; that his name should become the boast and glory of his native place; that his ashes should be religiously guarded as its most precious treasure; and that its lessening spire, on which his eyes were fixed in tearful contemplation, should one day become the beacon, towering amidst the gentle landscape, to guide the literary pilgrim of every nation to his tomb!

TRAITS OF INDIAN CHARACTER

"I appeal to any white man if ever he entered Logan's cabin hungry, and he gave him not to eat; if ever he came cold and naked, and he clothed him not."

SPEECH OF AN INDIAN CHIEF

There is something in the character and habits of the North American savage, taken in connection with the scenery over which he is accustomed to range, its vast lakes, boundless forests, majestic rivers, and trackless plains, that is, to my mind, wonderfully striking and sublime. He is formed for the wilderness as the Arab is for the desert. His nature is stern, simple, and enduring; fitted to grapple with difficulties, and to support privations. There seems but little soil in his heart for the support of the kindly virtues, and yet, if we would but take the trouble to penetrate through that proud stoicism and habitual taciturnity which lock up his character from casual observation we should find him linked to his fellow-man of civilized life by more of those sympathies and affections than are usually ascribed to him.

It has been the lot of the unfortunate aborigines of America, in the early periods of colonization, to be doubly wronged by the white men. They have been dispossessed of their hereditary possessions by mercenary and frequently wanton warfare, and their characters have been traduced by bigoted and interested writers. The colonist often treated them like beasts of the forest, and the author has endeavored to justify him in his outrages. The former found it easier to exterminate than to civilize, the latter to vilify than to discriminate. The appellations of savage and pagan were deemed sufficient to sanction the hostilities of both; and thus the poor wanderers of the forest were persecuted and defamed, not because they were guilty, but because they were ignorant.

The rights of the savage have seldom been properly appreciated or respected by the white man. In peace he has too often been the dupe of artful traffic; in war he has been regarded as a ferocious animal whose life or death was a question of mere precaution and convenience. Man is cruelly wasteful of life when his own safety is endangered, and he is sheltered by impunity; and little mercy is to be expected from him when he feels the sting of the reptile and is conscious of the power to destroy.

The same prejudices, which were indulged thus early, exist in common circulation at the present day. Certain learned societies have, it is true, with laudable diligence endeavored to investigate and record the real characters and manners of the Indian tribes; the American government, too, has wisely and humanely exerted itself to inculcate a friendly and forbearing spirit toward them and to protect them from fraud and injustice.* The current opinion of the Indian character, however, is too apt to be formed from the miserable hordes which infest the frontiers and hang on the skirts of the settlements. These are too commonly composed of degenerate beings, corrupted and enfeebled by the vices of society without being benefited by its civilization. That proud independence, which formed the main pillar of savage virtue, has been shaken down, and the whole moral fabric lies in ruins. Their spirits are humiliated and debased by a sense of inferiority, and their native courage cowed and daunted by the superior knowledge and power of their enlightened neighbors. Society has advanced upon them like one of those withering airs that will sometimes breed desolation over a whole region of fertility. It has enervated their

---

*The American government has been indefatigable in its exertions to ameliorate the situation of the Indians, and to introduce among them the arts of civilization, and civil and religious knowledge. To protect them from the frauds of the white traders, no purchase of land from them by individuals is permitted; nor is any person allowed to receive lands from them as a present, without the express sanction of government. These precautions are strictly enforced.

strength, multiplied their diseases, and superinduced upon their original barbarity the low vices of artificial life. It has given them a thousand superfluous wants, while it has diminished their means of mere existence. It has driven before it the animals of the chase, who fly from the sound of the axe and the smoke of the settlement and seek refuge in the depths of remoter forests and yet untrodden wilds. Thus do we too often find the Indians on our frontiers to be the mere wrecks and remnants of once powerful tribes who have lingered in the vicinity of the settlements and sunk into precarious and vagabond existence. Poverty, repining and hopeless poverty, a canker of the mind unknown in savage life, corrodes their spirits and blights every free and noble quality of their natures. They become drunken, indolent, feeble, thievish, and pusillanimous. They loiter like vagrants about the settlements, among spacious dwellings replete with elaborate comforts which only render them sensible of the comparative wretchedness of their own condition. Luxury spreads its ample board before their eyes; but they are excluded from the banquet. Plenty revels over the fields; but they are starving in the midst of its abundance: the whole wilderness has blossomed into a garden; but they feel as reptiles that infest it.

How different was their state while yet the undisputed lords of the soil! Their wants were few, and the means of gratification within their reach. They saw everyone around them sharing the same lot, enduring the same hardships, feeding on the same aliments, arrayed in the same rude garments. No roof then rose but was open to the homeless stranger; no smoke curled among the trees but he was welcome to sit down by its fire and join the hunter in his repast. "For," says an old historian of New England, "their life is so void of care, and they are so loving also that they make use of those things they enjoy as common goods, and are therein so compassionate that rather than one should starve through want, they would starve all; thus they pass their time merrily, not regarding our pomp, but are better content with their own, which some men esteem so meanly of." Such were the Indians while in the pride and energy of their primitive natures; they resembled those wild plants which thrive best in the shades of the forest but shrink from the hand of cultivation and perish beneath the influence of the sun.

In discussing the savage character, writers have been too prone to indulge in vulgar prejudice and passionate exaggeration, instead of the candid temper of true philosophy. They have not sufficiently considered the peculiar circumstances in which the Indians have been placed, and the peculiar principles under which they have been educated. No being acts more rigidly from rule than the Indian. His whole conduct is regulated according to some general maxims early implanted in his mind. The moral laws that govern him are, to be sure, but few, but then he conforms to them all; the white man abounds in laws of religion, morals, and manners, but how many does he violate?

A frequent ground of accusation against the Indians is their disregard of treaties, and the treachery and wantonness with which, in time of apparent peace, they will suddenly fly to hostilities. The intercourse of the white men with the Indians, however, is too apt to be cold, distrustful, oppressive, and insulting. They seldom treat them with that confidence and frankness which are indispensable to real friendship; nor is sufficient caution observed not to offend against those feelings of pride or superstition which often prompt the Indian to hostility quicker than mere considerations of interest. The solitary savage feels silently, but acutely. His sensibilities are not diffused over so wide a surface as those of the white man, but they run in steadier and deeper channels. His pride, his affections, his superstitions, are all directed toward fewer objects; but the wounds inflicted on them are proportionably severe, and furnish motives of hostility which we cannot sufficiently appreciate. Where a community is also limited in number, and forms one great patriarchal family, as in an Indian tribe, the injury of an individual is the injury of the whole, and the sentiment of vengeance is almost instantaneously diffused. One council fire is sufficient for the discussion and arrangement of a plan of hostilities. Here all the fighting men and sages assemble. Eloquence and superstition combine to inflame the minds of the warriors. The orator awakens their martial ardor, and they are wrought up to a kind of religious desperation by the visions of the prophet and the dreamer.

An instance of one of those sudden exasperations, arising from a motive peculiar to the Indian character, is extant in an old record of the early settlement of Massachusetts. The planters of Plymouth had defaced the monuments of the dead at Passonagessit, and had plundered the grave of the Sachem's mother of some skins with which it had been decorated. The Indians are remarkable for the reverence which they entertain for the sepulchers of their kindred. Tribes that have passed generations exiled from the abodes of their ancestors, when by chance they have been traveling in the vicinity, have been known to turn aside from the highway, and, guided by wonderfully accurate tradition, have crossed the country for miles to some tumulus, buried perhaps in woods, where the bones of their tribe were anciently deposited, and there have passed hours in silent meditation. Influenced by this sublime and holy feeling, the Sachem, whose mother's tomb had been violated, gathered his men together, and addressed them in the following beautifully simple and pathetic harangue, a curious specimen of Indian eloquence and an affecting instance of filial piety in a savage.

"When last the glorious light of all the sky was underneath this globe, and birds grew silent, I began to settle, as my custom is, to take repose. Before mine eyes were fast closed, methought I saw a vision, at which my spirit was much troubled; and trembling at that doleful sight, a spirit cried aloud, 'Behold, my son, whom I have cherished, see the breasts that gave thee suck, the hands that lapped thee warm, and fed thee oft. Canst thou forget to take revenge of those wild people who have defaced my monument in a despiteful manner, disdaining our antiquities and honorable customs? See, now, the Sachem's grave lies like the common people, defaced by an ignoble race. Thy mother doth complain, and implore thy aid against this thievish people, who have newly intruded on our land. If this be suffered, I shall not rest quiet in my everlasting habitation.' This said, the spirit vanished, and

I, all in a sweat, not able scarce to speak, began to get some strength, and recollect my spirits that were fled, and determined to demand your counsel and assistance."

I have adduced this anecdote at some length, as it tends to show how these sudden acts of hostility, which have been attributed to caprice and perfidy, may often arise from deep and generous motives, which our inattention to Indian character and customs prevents our properly appreciating.

Another ground of violent outcry against the Indians is their barbarity to the vanquished. This had its origin partly in policy and partly in superstition. The tribes, though sometimes called nations, were never so formidable in their numbers but that the loss of several warriors was sensibly felt; this was particularly the case when they had frequently been engaged in warfare; and many an instance occurs in Indian history where a tribe that had long been formidable to its neighbors has been broken up and driven away by the capture and massacre of its principal fighting men. There was a strong temptation, therefore, to the victor to be merciless, not so much to gratify any cruel revenge as to provide for future security. The Indians had also the superstitious belief, frequent among barbarous nations and prevalent also among the ancients, that the manes of their friends who had fallen in battle were soothed by the blood of the captives. The prisoners, however, who are not thus sacrificed are adopted into their families in the place of the slain and are treated with the confidence and affection of relatives and friends; nay, so hospitable and tender is their entertainment that when the alternative is offered them, they will often prefer to remain with their adopted brethren rather than return to the home and the friends of their youth.

The cruelty of the Indians toward their prisoners has been heightened since the colonization of the whites. What was formerly a compliance with policy and superstition has been exasperated into a gratification of vengeance. They cannot but be sensible that the white men are the usurpers of their ancient dominion, the cause of their degradation, and the gradual destroyers of their race. They go forth to battle, smarting with injuries and indignities which they have individually suffered, and they are driven to madness and despair by the wide-spreading desolation and the overwhelming ruin of European warfare. The whites have too frequently set them an example of violence by burning their villages and laying waste their slender means of subsistence; and yet they wonder that savages do not show moderation and magnanimity toward those who have left them nothing but mere existence and wretchedness.

We stigmatize the Indians, also, as cowardly and treacherous, because they use stratagem in warfare in preference to open force; but in this they are fully justified by their rude code of honor. They are early taught that stratagem is praiseworthy; the bravest warrior thinks it no disgrace to lurk in silence and take every advantage of his foe: he triumphs in the superior craft and sagacity by which he has been enabled to surprise and destroy an enemy. Indeed, man is naturally more prone to subtilty than open valor, owing to his physical weakness in comparison with other animals. They are endowed with natural weapons of defense: with horns, with tusks, with hoofs, and talons; but man has to depend on his superior sagacity. In all his encounters with these, his proper enemies, he resorts to stratagem; and when he perversely turns his hostility against his fellow-man, he at first continues the same subtle mode of warfare.

The natural principle of war is to do the most harm to our enemy with the least harm to ourselves, and this of course is to be effected by stratagem. That chivalrous courage which induces us to despise the suggestions of prudence and to rush in the face of certain danger is the offspring of society and produced by education. It is honorable because it is in fact the triumph of lofty sentiment over an instinctive repugnance to pain and over those yearnings after personal ease and security which society has condemned as ignoble. It is kept alive by pride and the fear of shame; and thus the dread of real evil is overcome by the superior dread of an evil which exists but in the imagination. It has been cherished and stimulated also by various means. It has been the theme of spirit-stirring song and chivalrous story. The poet and minstrel have delighted to shed round it the splendors of fiction; and even the historian has forgotten the sober gravity of narration and broken forth into enthusiasm and rhapsody in its praise. Triumphs and gorgeous pageants have been its reward: monuments, on which art has exhausted its skill and opulence its treasures, have been erected to perpetuate a nation's gratitude and admiration. Thus artificially excited, courage has risen to an extraordinary and factitious degree of heroism; and arrayed in all the glorious "pomp and circumstance of war," this turbulent quality has even been able to eclipse many of those quiet but invaluable virtues which silently ennoble the human character and swell the tide of human happiness.

But if courage intrinsically consists in the defiance of danger and pain, the life of the Indian is a continual exhibition of it. He lives in a state of perpetual hostility and risk. Peril and adventure are congenial to his nature, or rather seem necessary to arouse his faculties and to give an interest to his existence. Surrounded by hostile tribes, whose mode of warfare is by ambush and surprisal, he is always prepared for fight, and lives with his weapons in his hands. As the ship careers in fearful singleness through the solitudes of ocean; as the bird mingles among clouds and storms, and wings its way, a mere speck, across the pathless fields of air; so the Indian holds his course, silent, solitary, but undaunted, through the boundless bosom of the wilderness. His expeditions may vie in distance and danger with the pilgrimage of the devotee, or the crusade of the knight-errant. He traverses vast forests, exposed to the hazards of lonely sickness, of lurking enemies, and pining famine. Stormy lakes, those great inland seas, are no obstacles to his wanderings; in his light canoe of bark he sports, like a feather, on their waves, and darts, with the swiftness of an arrow, down the roaring rapids of the rivers. His very subsistence is snatched from the midst of toil and peril. He gains his food by the hardships and dangers of the chase; he wraps himself in the spoils of the bear, the panther, and the buffalo, and sleeps among the thunders of the cataract.

No hero of ancient or modern days can surpass the Indian in his lofty contempt of death, and the fortitude with which he sustains its cruelest infliction. Indeed we here behold him rising superior to the white man, in consequence of his peculiar education. The latter rushes to glorious death at the cannon's mouth; the former calmly contemplates its approach, and triumphantly endures it, amid the varied torments of surrounding foes and the protracted agonies of fire. He even takes a pride in taunting his persecutors and provoking their ingenuity of torture; and as the devouring flames prey on his very vitals, and the flesh shrinks from the sinews, he raises his last song of triumph, breathing the defiance of an unconquered heart and invoking the spirits of his fathers to witness that he dies without a groan.

Notwithstanding the obloquy with which the early historians have overshadowed the characters of the unfortunate natives, some bright gleams occasionally break through, which throw a degree of melancholy luster on their memories. Facts are occasionally to be met with in the rude annals of the eastern provinces, which, though recorded with the coloring of prejudice and bigotry, yet speak for themselves, and will be dwelt on with applause and sympathy when prejudice shall have passed away.

In one of the homely narratives of the Indian wars in New England, there is a touching account of the desolation carried into the tribe of the Pequod Indians. Humanity shrinks from the cold-blooded detail of indiscriminate butchery. In one place we read of the surprisal of an Indian fort in the night, when the wigwams were wrapped in flames, and the miserable inhabitants shot down and slain in attempting to escape, "all being despatched and ended in the course of an hour." After a series of similar transactions, "our soldiers," as the historian piously observes, "being resolved by God's assistance to make a final destruction of them," the unhappy savages being hunted from their homes and fortresses and pursued with fire and sword, a scanty but gallant band, the sad remnant of the Pequod warriors, with their wives and children, took refuge in a swamp.

Burning with indignation and rendered sullen by despair, with hearts bursting with grief at the destruction of their tribe and spirits galled and sore at the fancied ignominy of their defeat, they refused to ask their lives at the hands of an insulting foe, and preferred death to submission.

As the night drew on they were surrounded in their dismal retreat, so as to render escape impracticable. Thus situated, their enemy "plied them with shot all the time, by which means many were killed and buried in the mire." In the darkness and fog that preceded the dawn of day some few broke through the besiegers and escaped into the woods; "the rest were left to the conquerors, of which many were killed in the swamp, like sullen dogs who would rather, in their self-willedness and madness, sit still and be shot through, or cut to pieces," than implore for mercy. When the day broke upon this handful of forlorn but dauntless spirits, the soldiers, we are told, entering the swamp, "saw several heaps of them sitting close together, upon whom they discharged their pieces, laden with ten or twelve pistol bullets at a time, putting the muzzles of the pieces under the boughs, within a few yards of them; so as, besides those that were found dead, many more were killed and sunk into the mire, and never were minded more by friend or foe."

Can anyone read this plain unvarnished tale without admiring the stern resolution, the unbending pride, the loftiness of spirit that seemed to nerve the hearts of these self-taught heroes and to raise them above the instinctive feelings of human nature? When the Gauls laid waste the city of Rome, they found the senators clothed in their robes, and seated with stern tranquillity in their curule chairs; in this manner they suffered death without resistance or even supplication. Such conduct was, in them, applauded as noble and magnanimous; in the hapless Indian it was reviled as obstinate and sullen! How truly are we the dupes of show and circumstance! How different is virtue, clothed in purple and enthroned in state, from virtue, naked and destitute, and perishing obscurely in a wilderness!

But I forbear to dwell on these gloomy pictures. The eastern tribes have long since disappeared; the forests that sheltered them have been laid low, and scarce any traces remain of them in the thickly settled states of New

England, excepting here and there the Indian name of a village or a stream. And such must, sooner or later, be the fate of those other tribes which skirt the frontiers, and have occasionally been inveigled from their forests to mingle in the wars of white men. In a little while, and they will go the way that their brethren have gone before. The few hordes which still linger about the shores of Huron and Superior and the tributary streams of the Mississippi will share the fate of those tribes that once spread over Massachusetts and Connecticut and lorded it along the proud banks of the Hudson, of that gigantic race said to have existed on the borders of the Susquehanna, and of those various nations that flourished about the Potomac and the Rappahannock and that peopled the forests of the vast valley of Shenandoah. They will vanish like a vapor from the face of the earth; their very history will be lost in forgetfulness, and "the places that now know them will know them no more for ever." Or if, perchance, some dubious memorial of them should survive, it may be in the romantic dreams of the poet, to people in imagination his glades and groves, like the fauns and satyrs and sylvan deities of antiquity. But should he venture upon the dark story of their wrongs and wretchedness; should he tell how they were invaded, corrupted, despoiled, driven from their native abodes and the sepulchers of their fathers, hunted like wild beasts about the earth, and sent down with violence and butchery to the grave, posterity will either turn with horror and incredulity from the tale, or blush with indignation at the inhumanity of their forefathers. "We are driven back," said an old warrior, "until we can retreat no farther—our hatchets are broken, our bows are snapped, our fires are nearly extinguished: a little longer and the white man will cease to persecute us—for we shall cease to exist!"

PHILIP OF POKANOKET

AN INDIAN MEMOIR

As monumental bronze unchanged his look:
A soul that pity touch'd but never shook:
Train'd from his tree-rock'd cradle to his bier,
The fierce extremes of good and ill to brook
Impassive—fearing but the shame of fear—
A stoic of the woods—a man without a tear.

CAMPBELL

It is to be regretted that those early writers who treated of the discovery and settlement of America have not given us more particular and candid accounts of the remarkable characters that flourished in savage life. The scanty anecdotes which have reached us are full of peculiarity and interest; they furnish us with nearer glimpses of human nature, and show what man is in a comparatively primitive state, and what he owes to civilization. There is something of the charm of discovery in lighting upon these wild and unexplored tracts of human nature, in witnessing, as it were, the native growth of moral sentiment, and perceiving those generous and romantic qualities which have been artificially cultivated by society, vegetating in spontaneous hardihood and rude magnificence.

In civilized life, where the happiness, and indeed almost the existence, of man depends so much upon the opinion of his fellow-men, he is constantly acting a studied part. The bold and peculiar traits of native character are refined away or softened down by the leveling influence of what is termed good breeding; and he practices so many petty deceptions and affects so many generous sentiments for the purposes of popularity that it is difficult to distinguish his real from his artificial character. The Indian, on the contrary, free from the restraints and refinements of polished life, and, in a great degree, a solitary and independent being, obeys the impulses of his inclination or the dictates of his judgment, and thus the attributes of his nature, being freely indulged, grow singly great and striking. Society is like a lawn, where every roughness is smoothed, every bramble eradicated, and where the eye is delighted by the smiling verdure of a velvet surface; he, however, who would study nature in its wildness and variety must plunge into the forest, must explore the glen, must stem the torrent, and dare the precipice.

These reflections arose on casually looking through a volume of early colonial history, wherein are recorded, with great bitterness, the outrages of the Indians, and their wars with the settlers of New England. It is painful to perceive even from these partial narratives how the footsteps of civilization may be traced in the blood of the aborigines; how easily the colonists were moved to hostility by the lust of conquest; how merciless and exterminating was their warfare. The imagination shrinks at the idea, how many intellectual beings were hunted from the earth, how many brave and noble hearts, of nature's sterling coinage, were broken down and trampled in the dust!

Such was the fate of PHILIP OF POKANOKET, an Indian warrior, whose name was once a terror throughout Massachusetts and Connecticut. He was the most distinguished of a number of contemporary Sachems who reigned over the Pequods, the Narragansets, the Wampanoags, and the other eastern tribes at the time of the first settlement of New England; a band of native untaught heroes, who made the most generous struggle of which human nature is capable, fighting to the last gasp in the cause of their country, without a hope of victory or a thought of renown. Worthy of an age of poetry and fit subjects for local story and romantic fiction, they have left scarcely any authentic traces on the page of history, but stalk, like gigantic shadows, in the dim twilight of tradition.*

---

*While correcting the proof sheets of this article, the author is informed that a celebrated English poet has nearly finished an heroic poem on the story of Philip of Pokanoket.

When the pilgrims, as the Plymouth settlers are called by their descendants, first took refuge on the shores of the New World from the religious persecutions of the Old, their situation was to the last degree gloomy and disheartening. Few in number, and that number rapidly perishing away through sickness and hardships, surrounded by a howling wilderness and savage tribes, exposed to the rigors of an almost arctic winter and the vicissitudes of an ever-shifting climate, their minds were filled with doleful forebodings, and nothing preserved them from sinking into despondency but the strong excitement of religious enthusiasm. In this forlorn situation they were visited by Massasoit, chief Sagamore of the Wampanoags, a powerful chief who reigned over a great extent of country. Instead of taking advantage of the scanty number of the strangers, and expelling them from his territories, into which they had intruded, he seemed at once to conceive for them a generous friendship, and extended toward them the rites of primitive hospitality. He came early in the spring to their settlement of New Plymouth, attended by a mere handful of followers, entered into a solemn league of peace and amity; sold them a portion of the soil, and promised to secure for them the good will of his savage allies. Whatever may be said of Indian perfidy, it is certain that the integrity and good faith of Massasoit have never been impeached. He continued a firm and magnanimous friend of the white men, suffering them to extend their possessions and to strengthen themselves in the land, and betraying no jealousy of their increasing power and prosperity. Shortly before his death he came once more to New Plymouth, with his son Alexander, for the purpose of renewing the covenant of peace, and of securing it to his posterity.

At this conference he endeavored to protect the religion of his forefathers from the encroaching zeal of the missionaries, and stipulated that no further attempt should be made to draw off his people from their ancient faith; but, finding the English obstinately opposed to any such condition, he mildly relinquished the demand. Almost the last act of his life was to bring his two sons, Alexander and Philip (as they had been named by the

English), to the residence of a principal settler, recommending mutual kindness and confidence, and entreating that the same love and amity which had existed between the white men and himself might be continued afterward with his children. The good old Sachem died in peace, and was happily gathered to his fathers before sorrow came upon his tribe; his children remained behind to experience the ingratitude of white men.

His eldest son, Alexander, succeeded him. He was of a quick and impetuous temper, and proudly tenacious of his hereditary rights and dignity. The intrusive policy and dictatorial conduct of the strangers excited his indignation, and he beheld with uneasiness their exterminating wars with the neighboring tribes. He was doomed soon to incur their hostility, being accused of plotting with the Narragansets to rise against the English and drive them from the land. It is impossible to say whether this accusation was warranted by facts or was grounded on mere suspicion. It is evident, however, by the violent and overbearing measures of the settlers that they had by this time begun to feel conscious of the rapid increase of their power, and to grow harsh and inconsiderate in their treatment of the natives. They despatched an armed force to seize upon Alexander, and to bring him before their courts. He was traced to his woodland haunts, and surprised at a hunting house, where he was reposing with a band of his followers, unarmed, after the toils of the chase. The suddenness of his arrest and the outrage offered to his sovereign dignity so preyed upon the irascible feelings of this proud savage as to throw him into a raging fever. He was permitted to return home, on condition of sending his son as a pledge for his reappearance; but the blow he had received was fatal, and before he had reached his home he fell a victim to the agonies of a wounded spirit.

The successor of Alexander was Metacomet, or King Philip, as he was called by the settlers, on account of his lofty spirit and ambitious temper. These, together with his well-known energy and enterprise, had rendered him an object of great jealousy and apprehension, and he was accused of having always cherished a secret and implacable hostility toward the whites. Such may very probably, and very naturally, have been the case. He considered them as originally but mere intruders into the country, who had presumed upon indulgence, and were extending an influence baneful to savage life. He saw the whole race of his countrymen melting before them from the face of the earth, their territories slipping from their hands, and their tribes becoming feeble, scattered and dependent. It may be said that the soil was originally purchased by the settlers; but who does not know the nature of Indian purchases, in the early periods of colonization? The Europeans always made thrifty bargains through their superior adroitness in traffic; and they gained vast accessions of territory by easily provoked hostilities. An uncultivated savage is never a nice inquirer into the refinements of law, by which an injury may be gradually and legally inflicted. Leading facts are all by which he judges; and it was enough for Philip to know that before the intrusion of the Europeans his countrymen were lords of the soil, and that now they were becoming vagabonds in the land of their fathers.

But whatever may have been his feelings of general hostility, and his particular indignation at the treatment of his brother, he suppressed them for the present, renewed the contract with the settlers, and resided peaceably for many years at Pokanoket, or, as it was called by the English, Mount Hope,* the ancient seat of dominion of his tribe. Suspicions, however, which were at first but vague and indefinite began to acquire form and substance; and he was at length charged with attempting to instigate the various Eastern tribes to rise at once, and, by a simultaneous effort, to throw off the yoke of their oppressors. It is difficult at this distant period to assign the proper credit due to these early accusations against the Indians. There was a proneness to suspicion and an aptness to acts of violence on the part of the whites that gave weight and importance to every idle tale. Informers abounded where talebearing met with countenance and reward; and the sword was readily unsheathed when its success was certain, and it carved out empire.

*Now Bristol, Rhode Island.

The only positive evidence on record against Philip is the accusation of one Sausaman, a renegade Indian, whose natural cunning had been quickened by a partial education which he had received among the settlers. He changed his faith and his allegiance two or three times with a facility that evinced the looseness of his principles. He had acted for some time as Philip's confidential secretary and counselor, and had enjoyed his bounty and protection. Finding, however, that the clouds of adversity were gathering around his patron, he abandoned his service and went over to the whites; and, in order to gain their favor, charged his former benefactor with plotting against their safety. A rigorous investigation took place. Philip and several of his subjects submitted to be examined, but nothing was proved against them. The settlers, however, had now gone too far to retract; they had previously determined that Philip was a dangerous neighbor; they had publicly evinced their distrust and had done enough to insure his hostility; according, therefore, to the usual mode of reasoning in these cases, his destruction had become necessary to their security. Sausaman, the treacherous informer, was shortly afterward found dead, in a pond, having fallen a victim to the vengeance of his tribe. Three Indians, one of whom was a friend and counselor of Philip, were apprehended and tried, and, on the testimony of one very questionable witness, were condemned and executed as murderers.

This treatment of his subjects and ignominious punishment of his friend outraged the pride and exasperated the passions of Philip. The bolt which had fallen thus at his very feet awakened him to the gathering storm, and he determined to trust himself no longer in the power of the white men. The fate of his insulted and brokenhearted brother still rankled in his mind; and he had a further warning in the tragical story of Miantonimo, a great Sachem of the Narragansets, who, after manfully facing his accusers before a tribunal of the colonists, exculpating himself from a charge of conspiracy, and receiving assurances of amity, had been perfidiously despatched at their instigation. Philip, therefore, gathered his fighting men about him, persuaded all strangers that he could to join his cause, sent the women and children to the Narragansets for safety, and wherever he appeared was continually surrounded by armed warriors.

When the two parties were thus in a state of distrust and irritation, the least spark was sufficient to set them in a flame. The Indians, having weapons in their hands, grew mischievous, and committed various petty depredations. In one of their maraudings a warrior was fired on and killed by a settler. This was the signal for open hostilities, the Indians pressed to revenge the death of their comrade, and the alarm of war resounded through the Plymouth colony.

In the early chronicles of these dark and melancholy times we meet with many indications of the diseased state of the public mind. The gloom of religious abstraction and the wildness of their situation among trackless forests and savage tribes had disposed the colonists to superstitious fancies, and had filled their imaginations with the frightful chimeras of witchcraft and spectrology. They were much given also to a belief in omens. The troubles with Philip and his Indians were preceded, we are told, by a variety of those awful warnings which forerun great and public calamities. The perfect form of an Indian bow appeared in the air at New Plymouth, which was looked upon by the inhabitants as a "prodigious apparition." At Hadley, Northampton, and other towns in their neighborhood, "was heard the report of a great piece of ordnance, with a shaking of the earth and a considerable echo." * Others were alarmed on a still, sunshiny morning by the discharge of guns and muskets; bullets seemed to whistle past them, and the noise of drums resounded in the air, seeming to pass away to the westward; others fancied that they heard the galloping of horses over their heads; and certain monstrous births, which took place about the time, filled the superstitious in some towns with doleful forebodings. Many of these portentous sights and sounds may be ascribed to natural phenomena: to the northern lights which occur vividly in those latitudes; the meteors which explode in the air; the casual rushing of a blast through the top branches of the forest; the crash

*The Rev. Increase Mather's history.

of fallen trees or disrupted rocks; and to those other uncouth sounds and echoes which will sometimes strike the ear so strangely amidst the profound stillness of woodland solitudes. These may have startled some melancholy imaginations, may have been exaggerated by the love of the marvelous, and listened to with that avidity with which we devour whatever is fearful and mysterious. The universal currency of these superstitious fancies, and the grave record made of them by one of the learned men of the day, are strongly characteristic of the times.

The nature of the contest that ensued was such as too often distinguishes the warfare between civilized men and savages. On the part of the whites it was conducted with superior skill and success, but with a wastefulness of the blood and a disregard of the natural rights of their antagonists; on the part of the Indians it was waged with the desperation of men fearless of death, and who had nothing to expect from peace but humiliation, dependence, and decay.

The events of the war are transmitted to us by a worthy clergyman of the time, who dwells with horror and indignation on every hostile act of the Indians, however justifiable, while he mentions with applause the most sanguinary atrocities of the whites. Philip is reviled as a murderer and a traitor, without considering that he was a true-born prince, gallantly fighting at the head of his subjects to avenge the wrongs of his family, to retrieve the tottering power of his line, and to deliver his native land from the oppression of usurping strangers.

The project of a wide and simultaneous revolt, if such had really been formed, was worthy of a capacious mind, and, had it not been prematurely discovered, might have been overwhelming in its consequences. The war that actually broke out was but a war of detail, a mere succession of casual exploits and unconnected enterprises. Still it sets forth the military genius and daring prowess of Philip; and wherever, in the prejudiced and passionate narrations that have been given of it, we can arrive at simple facts, we find him displaying a vigorous mind, a fertility of expedients, a contempt of suffering and hardship, and an unconquerable resolution that command our sympathy and applause.

Driven from his paternal domains at Mount Hope, he threw himself into the depths of those vast and trackless forests that skirted the settlements and were almost impervious to anything but a wild beast or an Indian. Here he gathered together his forces, like the storm accumulating its stores of mischief in the bosom of the thundercloud, and would suddenly emerge at a time and place least expected, carrying havoc and dismay into the villages. There were now and then indications of these impending ravages that filled the minds of the colonists with awe and apprehension. The report of a distant gun would perhaps be heard from the solitary woodland, where there was known to be no white man; the cattle which had been wandering in the woods would sometimes return home wounded; or an Indian or two would be seen lurking about the skirts of the forests, and suddenly disappearing, as the lightning will sometimes be seen playing silently about the edge of the cloud that is brewing up the tempest.

Though sometimes pursued and even surrounded by the settlers, yet Philip as often escaped almost miraculously from their toils, and, plunging into the wilderness, would be lost to all search or inquiry until he again emerged at some far distant quarter, laying the country desolate. Among his strongholds were the great swamps or morasses which extend in some parts of New England, composed of loose bogs of deep black mud, perplexed with thickets, brambles, rank weeds, the shattered and moldering trunks of fallen trees, overshadowed by lugubrious hemlocks. The uncertain footing and the tangled mazes of these shaggy wilds rendered them almost impracticable to the white man, though the Indian could thrid their labyrinths with the agility of a deer. Into one of these, the great swamp of Pocasset Neck, was Philip once driven with a band of his followers. The English did not dare to pursue him, fearing to venture into these dark and frightful recesses, where they might perish in fens and miry pits or be shot down by lurking foes. They therefore invested the entrance to the Neck, and began to build a fort, with the thought of starving out the foe; but Philip and his warriors wafted themselves on a raft over an arm of the sea, in the dead of night, leaving the women and children behind, and escaped away to the westward, kindling the flames of war among the tribes of Massachusetts and the Nipmuck country, and threatening the colony of Connecticut.

In this way Philip became a theme of universal apprehension. The mystery in which he was enveloped exaggerated his real terrors. He was an evil that walked in darkness, whose coming none could foresee, and against which none knew when to be on the alert. The whole country abounded with rumors and alarms. Philip seemed almost possessed of ubiquity, for, in whatever part of the widely extended frontier an irruption from the forest took place, Philip was said to be its leader. Many superstitious notions also were circulated concerning him. He was said to deal in necromancy, and to be attended by an old Indian witch or prophetess, whom he consulted and who assisted him by her charms and incantations. This indeed was frequently the case with Indian chiefs, either through their own credulity or to act upon that of their followers; and the influence of the prophet and the dreamer over Indian superstition has been fully evidenced in recent instances of savage warfare.

At the time that Philip effected his escape from Pocasset, his fortunes were in a desperate condition. His forces had been thinned by repeated fights, and he had lost almost the whole of his resources. In this time of adversity he found a faithful friend in Canonchet, chief Sachem of all the Narragansets. He was the son and heir of Miantonimo, the great Sachem, who, as already mentioned, after an honorable acquittal of the charge of conspiracy, had been privately put to death at the perfidious instigations of the settlers. "He was the heir," says the old chronicler, "of all his father's pride and insolence, as well as of his malice toward the English"; he certainly was the heir of his insults and injuries, and the legitimate avenger of his murder. Though he had forborne to take an active part in this hopeless war, yet he received Philip and his broken forces with open arms, and gave them the most generous countenance and support. This at once drew upon him the hostility of the English; and it was determined to strike a signal blow that should involve both the Sachems in one common ruin. A great force was, therefore, gathered together from

Massachusetts, Plymouth, and Connecticut, and was sent into the Narraganset country in the depth of winter, when the swamps, being frozen and leafless, could be traversed with comparative facility, and would no longer afford dark and impenetrable fastnesses to the Indians.

Apprehensive of attack, Canonchet had conveyed the greater part of his stores, together with the old, the infirm, the women and children of his tribe, to a strong fortress, where he and Philip had likewise drawn up the flower of their forces. This fortress, deemed by the Indians impregnable, was situated upon a rising mound or kind of island, of five or six acres, in the midst of a swamp; it was constructed with a degree of judgment and skill vastly superior to what is usually displayed in Indian fortification, and indicative of the martial genius of these two chieftains.

Guided by a renegade Indian, the English penetrated, through December snows, to this stronghold, and came upon the garrison by surprise. The fight was fierce and tumultuous. The assailants were repulsed in their first attack, and several of their bravest officers were shot down in the act of storming the fortress sword in hand. The assault was renewed with greater success. A lodgment was effected. The Indians were driven from one post to another. They disputed their ground inch by inch, fighting with the fury of despair. Most of their veterans were cut to pieces; and after a long and bloody battle, Philip and Canonchet, with a handful of surviving warriors, retreated from the fort, and took refuge in the thickets of the surrounding forest.

The victors set fire to the wigwams and the fort; the whole was soon in a blaze; many of the old men, the women and the children perished in the flames. This last outrage overcame even the stoicism of the savage. The neighboring woods resounded with the yells of rage and despair uttered by the fugitive warriors as they beheld the destruction of their dwellings and heard the agonizing cries of their wives and offspring. "The burning of the wigwams," says a contemporary writer, "the shrieks and cries of the women and children, and the yelling of the warriors, exhibited a most horrible and affecting scene, so that it greatly moved some of the soldiers." The same writer cautiously adds, "they were in *much doubt* then, and afterward seriously inquired whether burning their enemies alive could be consistent with humanity, and the benevolent principles of the Gospel." *

The fate of the brave and generous Canonchet is worthy of particular mention: the last scene of his life is one of the noblest instances on record of Indian magnanimity.

Broken down in his power and resources by this signal defeat, yet faithful to his ally and to the hapless cause which he had espoused, he rejected all overtures of peace, offered on condition of betraying Philip and his followers, and declared that "he would fight it out to the last man, rather than become a servant to the English." His home being destroyed, his country harassed and laid waste by the incursions of the conquerors, he was obliged to wander away to the banks of the Connecticut, where he formed a rallying point to the whole body of western Indians and laid waste several of the English settlements.

Early in the spring he departed on a hazardous expedition, with only thirty chosen men, to penetrate to Seaconck, in the vicinity of Mount Hope, and to procure seed corn to plant for the sustenance of his troops. This little band of adventurers had passed safely through the Pequod country, and were in the center of the Narraganset, resting at some wigwams near Pawtucket River, when an alarm was given of an approaching enemy. Having but seven men by him at the time, Canonchet despatched two of them to the top of a neighboring hill to bring intelligence of the foe.

Panic-stricken by the appearance of a troop of English and Indians rapidly advancing, they fled in breathless terror past their chieftain without stopping to inform him of the danger. Canonchet sent another scout, who did the same. He then sent two more, one of whom, hurrying back in confusion and affright, told him that the whole British army was at hand. Canonchet saw there was no choice but immediate flight. He attempted to es-

*MS of the Rev. W. Ruggles.

cape around the hill, but was perceived and hotly pursued by the hostile Indians and a few of the fleetest of the English. Finding the swiftest pursuer close upon his heels, he threw off, first his blanket, then his silver-laced coat and belt of peag, by which his enemies knew him to be Canonchet, and redoubled the eagerness of pursuit.

At length, in dashing through the river, his foot slipped upon a stone, and he fell so deep as to wet his gun. This accident so struck him with despair that, as he afterward confessed, "his heart and his bowels turned within him, and he became like a rotten stick, void of strength."

To such a degree was he unnerved, that, being seized by a Pequod Indian within a short distance of the river, he made no resistance, though a man of great vigor of body and boldness of heart. But on being made prisoner the whole pride of his spirit arose within him; and from that moment, we find, in the anecdotes given by his enemies, nothing but repeated flashes of elevated and princelike heroism. Being questioned by one of the English who first came up with him, and who had not attained his twenty-second year, the proud-hearted warrior, looking with lofty contempt upon his youthful countenance, replied, "You are a child—you cannot understand matters of war—let your brother or your chief come—him will I answer."

Though repeated offers were made to him of his life on condition of submitting with his nation to the English, yet he rejected them with disdain, and refused to send any proposals of the kind to the great body of his subjects, saying that he knew none of them would comply. Being reproached with his breach of faith toward the whites, his boast that he would not deliver up a Wampanoag nor the paring of a Wampanoag's nail, and his threat that he would burn the English alive in their houses, he disdained to justify himself, haughtily answering that others were as forward for the war as himself, and "he desired to hear no more thereof."

So noble and unshaken a spirit, so true a fidelity to his cause and his friend might have touched the feelings of the generous and the brave; but Canonchet was an Indian, a being toward whom war had no courtesy, humanity no law, religion no compassion—he was con-

demned to die. The last words of him that are recorded
are worthy the greatness of his soul. When sentence of
death was passed upon him, he observed "that he liked
it well, for he should die before his heart was soft, or he
had spoken any thing unworthy of himself." His enemies
gave him the death of a soldier, for he was shot at
Stoningham by three young Sachems of his own rank.

The defeat at the Narraganset fortress and the death
of Canonchet were fatal blows to the fortunes of King
Philip. He made an ineffectual attempt to raise a head of
war by stirring up the Mohawks to take arms; but though
possessed of the native talents of a statesman, his arts
were counteracted by the superior arts of his enlightened enemies, and the terror of their warlike skill began
to subdue the resolution of the neighboring tribes. The
unfortunate chieftain saw himself daily stripped of power
and his ranks rapidly thinning around him. Some were
suborned by the whites; others fell victims to hunger
and fatigue and to the frequent attacks by which they
were harassed. His stores were all captured; his chosen
friends were swept away from before his eyes; his uncle
was shot down by his side; his sister was carried into
captivity; and in one of his narrow escapes he was compelled to leave his beloved wife and only son to the
mercy of the enemy. "His ruin," says the historian, "being
thus gradually carried on, his misery was not prevented,
but augmented thereby; being himself made acquainted
with the sense and experimental feeling of the captivity
of his children, loss of friends, slaughter of his subjects,
bereavement of all family relations, and being stripped of
all outward comforts, before his own life should be taken
away."

To fill up the measure of his misfortunes, his own followers began to plot against his life, that by sacrificing
him they might purchase dishonorable safety. Through
treachery a number of his faithful adherents, the subjects
of Wetamoe, an Indian princess of Pocasset, a near kins-
woman and confederate of Philip, were betrayed into the
hands of the enemy. Wetamoe was among them at the
time, and attempted to make her escape by crossing a
neighboring river; either exhausted by swimming or
starved by cold and hunger she was found dead and

naked near the water side. But persecution ceased not at the grave. Even death, the refuge of the wretched, where the wicked commonly cease from troubling, was no protection to this outcast female whose great crime was affectionate fidelity to her kinsman and her friend. Her corpse was the object of unmanly and dastardly vengeance; the head was severed from the body and set upon a pole, and was thus exposed at Taunton, to the view of her captive subjects. They immediately recognized the features of their unfortunate queen, and were so affected at this barbarous spectacle that we are told they broke forth into the "most horrible and diabolical lamentations."

However Philip had borne up against the complicated miseries and misfortunes that surrounded him, the treachery of his followers seemed to wring his heart and reduce him to despondency. It is said that "he never rejoiced afterward, nor had success in any of his designs." The spring of hope was broken—the ardor of enterprise was extinguished—he looked around, and all was danger and darkness; there was no eye to pity, nor any arm that could bring deliverance. With a scanty band of followers who still remained true to his desperate fortunes, the unhappy Philip wandered back to the vicinity of Mount Hope, the ancient dwelling of his fathers. Here he lurked about, like a specter, among the scenes of former power and prosperity, now bereft of home, of family and friend. There needs no better picture of his destitute and piteous situation than that furnished by the homely pen of the chronicler, who is unwarily enlisting the feelings of the reader in favor of the hapless warrior whom he reviles. "Philip," he says, "like a savage wild beast, having been hunted by the English forces through the woods, above a hundred miles backward and forward, at last was driven to his own den upon Mount Hope, where he retired, with a few of his best friends, into a swamp, which proved but a prison to keep him fast till the messengers of death came by divine permission to execute vengeance upon him."

Even in this last refuge of desperation and despair, a sullen grandeur gathers around his memory. We picture him to ourselves seated among his care-worn followers, brooding in silence over his blasted fortunes, and acquiring a savage sublimity from the wildness and dreariness of his lurking place. Defeated, but not dismayed—crushed to the earth, but not humiliated—he seemed to grow more haughty beneath disaster, and to experience a fierce satisfaction in draining the last dregs of bitterness. Little minds are tamed and subdued by misfortune, but great minds rise above it. The very idea of submission awakened the fury of Philip, and he smote to death one of his followers who proposed an expedient of peace. The brother of the victim made his escape, and in revenge betrayed the retreat of his chieftain. A body of white men and Indians were immediately despatched to the swamp where Philip lay crouched, glaring with fury and despair. Before he was aware of their approach, they had begun to surround him. In a little while he saw five of his trustiest followers laid dead at his feet; all resistance was vain; he rushed forth from his covert and made a headlong attempt to escape, but was shot through the heart by a renegade Indian of his own nation.

Such is the scanty story of the brave but unfortunate King Philip; persecuted while living, slandered and dishonored when dead. If, however, we consider even the prejudiced anecdotes furnished us by his enemies, we may perceive in them traces of amiable and lofty character sufficient to awaken sympathy for his fate and respect for his memory. We find that, amidst all the harassing cares and ferocious passions of constant warfare, he was alive to the softer feelings of connubial love and paternal tenderness, and to the generous sentiment of friendship. The captivity of his "beloved wife and only son" is mentioned with exultation as causing him poignant misery; the death of any near friend is triumphantly recorded as a new blow on his sensibilities; but the treachery and desertion of many of his followers, in whose affections he had confided, are said to have desolated his heart and to have bereaved him of all further comfort. He was a patriot attached to his native soil—a prince true to his subjects, and indignant of their wrongs—a soldier, daring in battle, firm in adversity, patient of fatigue, of hunger, of every variety of bodily suffering, and ready to perish in the cause he had espoused. Proud of heart and with an untamable love of natural liberty, he preferred to enjoy it among the beasts of the forests or in the dismal and famished recesses of swamps and morasses rather than bow his haughty spirit to submission and live dependent and despised in the ease and luxury of the settlements. With heroic qualities and bold achievements that would have graced a civilized warrior and have rendered him the theme of the poet and the historian, he lived a wanderer and a fugitive in his native land, and went down, like a lonely bark foundering amid darkness and tempest—without a pitying eye to weep his fall or a friendly hand to record his struggle.

JOHN BULL

An old song, made by an aged old pate,
Of an old worshipful gentleman who had a great estate,
That kept a brave old house at a bountiful rate,
And an old porter to relieve the poor at his gate.
With an old study fill'd full of learned old books,
With an old reverend chaplain, you might know him by his looks,
With an old buttery hatch worn quite off the hooks,
And an old kitchen that maintained half-a-dozen old cooks.
          Like an old courtier, etc.

                                        OLD SONG

There is no species of humor in which the English more excel than that which consists in caricaturing and giving ludicrous appellations, or nicknames. In this way they have whimsically designated, not merely individuals, but nations; and, in their fondness for pushing a joke, they have not spared even themselves. One would think that, in personifying itself, a nation would be apt to picture something grand, heroic, and imposing; but it is characteristic of the peculiar humor of the English, and of their love for what is blunt, comic, and familiar that they have embodied their national oddities in the figure of a sturdy, corpulent old fellow, with a three-cornered hat, red waistcoat, leather breeches, and stout oaken cudgel. Thus they have taken a singular delight in exhibiting their most private foibles in a laughable point of view, and have been so successful in their delineations that there is scarcely a being in actual existence more absolutely present to the public mind than that eccentric personage, John Bull.

Perhaps the continual contemplation of the character thus drawn of them has contributed to fix it upon the nation, and thus to give reality to what at first may have been painted in a great measure from the imagination. Men are apt to acquire peculiarities that are continually ascribed to them. The common orders of English seem wonderfully captivated with the *beau ideal* which they have formed of John Bull, and endeavor to act up to the broad caricature that is perpetually before their eyes. Unluckily, they sometimes make their boasted Bull-ism an apology for their prejudice or grossness; and this I have especially noticed among those truly homebred and genuine sons of the soil who have never migrated beyond the sound of Bow bells. If one of these should be a little uncouth in speech, and apt to utter impertinent truths, he confesses that he is a real John Bull, and always speaks his mind. If he now and then flies into an unreasonable burst of passion about trifles, he observes that John Bull is a choleric old blade, but then his passion is over in a moment, and he bears no malice. If he betrays a coarseness of taste, and an insensibility to foreign refinements, he thanks heaven for his ignorance—he is a plain John Bull, and has no relish for frippery and nicknacks. His very proneness to be gulled by strangers and to pay extravagantly for absurdities is excused under the plea of munificence—for John is always more generous than wise.

Thus, under the name of John Bull, he will contrive to argue every fault into a merit, and will frankly convict himself of being the honestest fellow in existence.

However little, therefore, the character may have suited in the first instance, it has gradually adapted itself to the nation, or rather they have adapted themselves to each other; and a stranger who wishes to study English peculiarities may gather much valuable information from the innumerable portraits of John Bull as exhibited in the windows of the caricature shops. Still, however, he is one of those fertile humorists that are continually throwing out new portraits, and presenting different aspects from different points of view; and, often as he has been described, I cannot resist the temptation to give a slight sketch of him, such as he has met my eye.

John Bull, to all appearance, is a plain downright matter-of-fact fellow, with much less of poetry about him than rich prose. There is little of romance in his nature, but a vast deal of strong natural feeling. He excels in humor more than in wit; is jolly rather than gay; melancholy rather than morose; can easily be moved to a sud-

den tear, or surprised into a broad laugh; but he loathes
sentiment, and has no turn for light pleasantry. He is
a boon companion if you allow him to have his humor
and to talk about himself; and he will stand by a friend
in a quarrel, with life and purse, however soundly he
may be cudgeled.

In this last respect, to tell the truth, he has a propensity to be somewhat too ready. He is a busy-minded personage, who thinks not merely for himself and family,
but for all the country around, and is most generously disposed to be everybody's champion. He is continually vol-
unteering his services to settle his neighbors' affairs, and
takes it in great dudgeon if they engage in any matter
of consequence without asking his advice, though he seldom engages in any friendly office of the kind without
finishing by getting into a squabble with all parties, and
then railing bitterly at their ingratitude. He unluckily took
lessons in his youth in the noble science of defense, and
having accomplished himself in the use of his limbs and
his weapons, and become a perfect master at boxing and
cudgel play, he has had a troublesome life of it ever since.
He cannot hear of a quarrel between the most distant of
his neighbors but he begins incontinently to fumble with
the head of his cudgel and consider whether his interest
or honor does not require that he should meddle in the
broil. Indeed he has extended his relations of pride and
policy so completely over the whole country that no
event can take place without infringing some of his finely
spun rights and dignities. Couched in his little domain,
with these filaments stretching forth in every direction, he
is like some choleric, bottle-bellied old spider, who has
woven his web over a whole chamber, so that a fly
cannot buzz nor a breeze blow without startling his repose and causing him to sally forth wrathfully from his
den.

Though really a goodhearted, good-tempered old fellow at bottom, yet he is singularly fond of being in the
midst of contention. It is one of his peculiarities, however,
that he only relishes the beginning of an affray; he always goes into a fight with alacrity, but comes out of it
grumbling even when victorious; and though no one
fights with more obstinacy to carry a contested point,

yet, when the battle is over and he comes to the reconciliation, he is so much taken up with the mere shaking of hands that he is apt to let his antagonist pocket all that they have been quarreling about. It is not, therefore, fighting that he ought so much to be on his guard against as making friends. It is difficult to cudgel him out of a farthing; but put him in a good humor, and you may bargain him out of all the money in his pocket. He is like a stout ship which will weather the roughest storm uninjured but roll its masts overboard in the succeeding calm.

He is a little fond of playing the magnifico abroad; of pulling out a long purse; flinging his money bravely about at boxing matches, horse races, cockfights, and carrying a high head among "gentlemen of the fancy:" but immediately after one of these fits of extravagance he will be taken with violent qualms of economy; stop short at the most trivial expenditure; talk desperately of being ruined and brought upon the parish; and, in such moods, will not pay the smallest tradesman's bill without violent altercation. He is in fact the most punctual and discontented paymaster in the world, drawing his coin out of his breeches pocket with infinite reluctance, paying to the uttermost farthing, but accompanying every guinea with a growl.

With all his talk of economy, however, he is a bountiful provider, and a hospitable housekeeper. His economy is of a whimsical kind, its chief object being to devise how he may afford to be extravagant, for he will begrudge himself a beefsteak and pint of port one day that he may roast an ox whole, broach a hogshead of ale, and treat all his neighbors on the next.

His domestic establishment is enormously expensive, not so much from any great outward parade as from the great consumption of solid beef and pudding, the vast number of followers he feeds and clothes, and his singular disposition to pay hugely for small services. He is a most kind and indulgent master, and, provided his servants humor his peculiarities, flatter his vanity a little now and then, and do not peculate grossly on him before his face, they may manage him to perfection. Everything that lives on him seems to thrive and grow fat. His house

servants are well paid, and pampered, and have little to
do. His horses are sleek and lazy, and prance slowly before his state carriage, and his house dogs sleep quietly
about the door, and will hardly bark at a housebreaker.

His family mansion is an old castellated manor house,
gray with age, and of a most venerable though weather-
beaten appearance. It has been built upon no regular
plan, but is a vast accumulation of parts, erected in various tastes and ages. The center bears evident traces of
Saxon architecture, and is as solid as ponderous stone
and old English oak can make it. Like all the relics of
that style, it is full of obscure passages, intricate mazes,
and dusky chambers; and though these have been partially lighted up in modern days, yet there are many
places where you must still grope in the dark. Additions have been made to the original edifice from time to
time, and great alterations have taken place; towers and
battlements have been erected during wars and tumults,
wings built in time of peace; and outhouses, lodges, and
offices run up according to the whim or convenience of
different generations, until it has became one of the most
spacious, rambling tenements imaginable. An entire wing
is taken up with the family chapel, a reverend pile that
must have been exceedingly sumptuous, and, indeed, in
spite of having been altered and simplified at various periods, has still a look of solemn religious pomp. Its walls
within are stored with the monuments of John's ancestors; and it is snugly fitted up with soft cushions and
well-lined chairs, where such of his family as are inclined to church services may doze comfortably in the discharge of their duties.

To keep up this chapel has cost John much money;
but he is stanch in his religion, and piqued in his zeal,
from the circumstance that many dissenting chapels
have been erected in his vicinity, and several of his neighbors, with whom he has had quarrels, are strong
papists.

To do the duties of the chapel he maintains, at a large
expense, a pious and portly family chaplain. He is a
most learned and decorous personage, and a truly well-
bred Christian, who always backs the old gentleman in his
opinions, winks discreetly at his little peccadilloes, re-

bukes the children when refractory, and is of great use in exhorting the tenants to read their Bibles, say their prayers, and, above all, to pay their rents punctually, and without grumbling.

The family apartments are in a very antiquated taste, somewhat heavy, and often inconvenient, but full of the solemn magnificence of former times, fitted up with rich though faded tapestry, unwieldy furniture, and loads of massy gorgeous old plate. The vast fireplaces, ample kitchens, extensive cellars, and sumptuous banqueting halls, all speak of the roaring hospitality of days of yore, of which the modern festivity at the manor house is but a shadow. There are, however, complete suites of rooms apparently deserted and time-worn, and towers and turrets that are tottering to decay, so that in high winds there is danger of their tumbling about the ears of the household.

John has frequently been advised to have the old edifice thoroughly overhauled, and to have some of the useless parts pulled down, and the others strengthened with their materials; but the old gentleman always grows testy on this subject. He swears the house is an excellent house—that it is tight and weatherproof, and not to be shaken by tempests—that it has stood for several hundred years, and, therefore, is not likely to tumble down now—that as to its being inconvenient, his family is accustomed to the inconveniences, and would not be comfortable without them—that as to its unwieldy size and irregular construction, these result from its being the growth of centuries, and being improved by the wisdom of every generation—that an old family like his requires a large house to dwell in; new, upstart families may live in modern cottages and snug boxes, but an old English family should inhabit an old English manor house. If you point out any part of the building as superfluous, he insists that it is material to the strength or decoration of the rest and the harmony of the whole, and swears that the parts are so built into each other that if you pull down one you run the risk of having the whole about your ears.

The secret of the matter is that John has a great disposition to protect and patronize. He thinks it indispensable to the dignity of an ancient and honorable family to be bounteous in its appointments, and to be eaten up by dependents; and so, partly from pride and partly from kindheartedness, he makes it a rule always to give shelter and maintenance to his superannuated servants.

The consequence is that, like many other venerable family establishments, his manor is encumbered by old retainers whom he cannot turn off, and an old style which he cannot lay down. His mansion is like a great hospital of invalids, and, with all its magnitude, is not a whit too large for its inhabitants. Not a nook or corner but is of use in housing some useless personage. Groups of veteran beefeaters, gouty pensioners, and retired heroes of the buttery and the larder are seen lolling about its walls, crawling over its lawns, dozing under its trees, or sunning themselves upon the benches at its doors. Every office and outhouse is garrisoned by these supernumeraries and their families, for they are amazingly prolific, and when they die off are sure to leave John a legacy of hungry mouths to be provided for. A mattock cannot be struck against the most moldering tumble-down tower but out pops, from some cranny or loophole, the gray pate of some superannuated hanger-on, who has lived at John's expense all his life, and makes the most grievous outcry at their pulling down the roof from over the head of a worn-out servant of the family. This is an appeal that John's honest heart never can withstand, so that a man who has faithfully eaten his beef and pudding all his life is sure to be rewarded with a pipe and tankard in his old days.

A great part of his park, also, is turned into paddocks, where his broken-down chargers are turned loose to graze undisturbed for the remainder of their existence—a worthy example of grateful recollection, which if some of his neighbors were to imitate, would not be to their discredit. Indeed, it is one of his great pleasures to point out these old steeds to his visitors, to dwell on their good qualities, extol their past services, and boast, with some little vainglory, of the perilous adventures and hardy exploits through which they have carried him.

He is given, however, to indulge his veneration for family usages, and family incumbrances, to a whimsical extent. His manor is infested by gangs of gypsies;

yet he will not suffer them to be driven off because they have infested the place time out of mind, and been regular poachers upon every generation of the family. He will scarcely permit a dry branch to be lopped from the great trees that surround the house, lest it should molest the rooks that have bred there for centuries. Owls have taken possession of the dovecote; but they are hereditary owls, and must not be disturbed. Swallows have nearly choked up every chimney with their nests; martins build in every frieze and cornice; crows flutter about the towers, and perch on every weathercock; and old gray-headed rats may be seen in every quarter of the house, running in and out of their holes undauntedly in broad daylight. In short, John has such a reverence for everything that has been long in the family that he will not hear even of abuses being reformed, because they are good old family abuses.

All those whims and habits have concurred woefully to drain the old gentleman's purse; and as he prides himself on punctuality in money matters, and wishes to maintain his credit in the neighborhood, they have caused him great perplexity in meeting his engagements. This, too, has been increased by the altercations and heartburnings which are continually taking place in his family. His children have been brought up to different callings, and are of different ways of thinking; and as they have always been allowed to speak their minds freely, they do not fail to exercise the privilege most clamorously in the present posture of his affairs. Some stand up for the honor of the race, and are clear that the old establishment should be kept up in all its state, whatever may be the cost; others, who are more prudent and considerate, entreat the old gentleman to retrench his expenses, and to put his whole system of housekeeping on a more moderate footing. He has, indeed, at times, seemed inclined to listen to their opinions, but their wholesome advice has been completely defeated by the obstreperous conduct of one of his sons. This is a noisy, rattle-pated fellow of rather low habits who neglects his business to frequent alehouses—is the orator of village clubs, and a complete oracle among the poorest of his father's tenants. No sooner does he hear any of his brothers mention reform or retrenchment than up he jumps, takes the words out of their mouths, and roars out for an overturn. When his tongue is once going nothing can stop it. He rants about the room; hectors the old man about his spendthrift practices; ridicules his tastes and pursuits; insists that he shall turn the old servants out of doors; give the broken-down horses to the hounds; send the fat chaplain packing, and take a field preacher in his place—nay, that the whole family mansion shall be leveled with the ground, and a plain one of brick and mortar built in its place. He rails at every social entertainment and family festivity, and skulks away growling to the alehouse whenever an equipage drives up to the door. Though constantly complaining of the emptiness of his purse, yet he scruples not to spend all his pocket money in these tavern convocations, and even runs up scores for the liquor over which he preaches about his father's extravagance.

It may readily be imagined how little such thwarting agrees with the old cavalier's fiery temperament. He has become so irritable from repeated crossings that the mere mention of retrenchment or reform is a signal for a brawl between him and the tavern oracle. As the latter is too sturdy and refractory for paternal discipline, having grown out of all fear of the cudgel, they have frequent scenes of wordy warfare, which at times run so high that John is fain to call in the aid of his son Tom, an officer who has served abroad, but is at present living at home on half-pay. This last is sure to stand by the old gentleman, right or wrong; likes nothing so much as a racketing, roystering life; and is ready at a wink or nod to out saber, and flourish it over the orator's head if he dares to array himself against paternal authority.

These family dissensions, as usual, have got abroad, and are rare food for scandal in John's neighborhood. People begin to look wise, and shake their heads whenever his affairs are mentioned. They all "hope that matters are not so bad with him as represented; but when a man's own children begin to rail at his extravagance, things must be badly managed. They understand he is mortgaged over head and ears, and is continually dabbling with money lenders. He is certainly an openhanded old gentleman, but they fear he has lived too fast; indeed, they never knew any good come of this fondness for hunting, racing, reveling and prize fighting. In short, Mr. Bull's estate is a very fine one, and has been in the family a long time; but, for all that, they have known many finer estates come to the hammer."

What is worst of all is the effect which these pecuniary embarrassments and domestic feuds have had on the poor man himself. Instead of that jolly round corporation and smug rosy face which he used to present, he has of late become as shriveled and shrunk as a frostbitten apple. His scarlet gold-laced waistcoat, which bellied out so bravely in those prosperous days when he sailed before the wind, now hangs loosely about him like a mainsail in a calm. His leather breeches are all in folds and wrinkles, and apparently have much ado to hold up the boots that yawn on both sides of his once sturdy legs.

Instead of strutting about as formerly, with his three-cornered hat on one side, flourishing his cudgel and bringing it down every moment with a hearty thump upon the ground, looking everyone sturdily in the face and trolling out a stave of a catch or a drinking song, he now goes about whistling thoughtfully to himself, with his head drooping down, his cudgel tucked under his arm, and his hands thrust to the bottom of his breeches pockets, which are evidently empty.

Such is the plight of honest John Bull at present; yet for all this the old fellow's spirit is as tall and as gallant as ever. If you drop the least expression of sympathy or concern, he takes fire in an instant, swears that he is the richest and stoutest fellow in the country, talks of laying out large sums to adorn his house or buy another estate, and with a valiant swagger and grasping of his cudgel longs exceedingly to have another bout at quarterstaff.

Though there may be something rather whimsical in all this, yet I confess I cannot look upon John's situation without strong feelings of interest. With all his odd humors and obstinate prejudices, he is a sterling-hearted old blade. He may not be so wonderfully fine a fellow as he thinks himself, but he is at least twice as good as his neighbors represent him. His virtues are all his own; all plain, homebred, and unaffected. His very faults smack of the raciness of his good qualities. His extravagance savors of his generosity; his quarrelsomeness of his courage; his credulity of his open faith; his vanity of his pride; and his bluntness of his sincerity. They are all the redundancies of a rich and liberal character. He is like his own oak, rough without, but sound and solid within, whose bark abounds with excrescences in proportion to the growth and grandeur of the timber, and whose branches make a fearful groaning and murmuring in the least storm from their very magnitude and luxuriance. There is something, too, in the appearance of his old family mansion that is extremely poetical and picturesque; and, as long as it can be rendered comfortably habitable, I should almost tremble to see it meddled with during the present conflict of tastes and opinions. Some of his advisers are no doubt good architects that might be of service; but many, I fear, are mere levelers, who, when they had once got to work with their mattocks on this venerable edifice, would never stop until they had brought it to the ground, and perhaps buried themselves among the ruins. All that I wish is that John's present troubles may teach him more prudence in future. That he may cease to distress his mind about other people's affairs; that he may give up the fruitless attempt to promote the good of his neighbors and the peace and happiness of the world by dint of the cudgel; that he may remain quietly at home; gradually get his house into repair; cultivate his rich estate according to his fancy; husband his income—if he thinks proper; bring his unruly children into order—if he can; renew the jovial scenes of ancient prosperity; and long enjoy, on his paternal lands, a green, an honorable, and a merry old age.

THE PRIDE OF THE VILLAGE

> May no wolfe howle; no screech owle stir
> A wing about thy sepulchre!
> No boysterous winds or stormes come hither,
>   To starve or wither
> Thy soft sweet earth! but, like a spring,
> Love kept it ever flourishing.
>
> HERRICK

In the course of an excursion through one of the remote counties of England, I had struck into one of those crossroads that lead through the more secluded parts of the country, and stopped one afternoon at a village, the situation of which was beautifully rural and retired. There was an air of primitive simplicity about its inhabitants, not to be found in the villages which lie on the great coach roads. I determined to pass the night there, and, having taken an early dinner, strolled out to enjoy the neighboring scenery.

My ramble, as is usually the case with travelers, soon led me to the church, which stood at a little distance from the village. Indeed, it was an object of some curiosity, its old tower being completely overrun with ivy, so that only here and there a jutting buttress, an angle of gray wall, or a fantastically carved ornament peered through the verdant covering. It was a lovely evening. The early part of the day had been dark and showery, but in the afternoon it had cleared up; and though sullen clouds still hung overhead, yet there was a broad tract of golden sky in the west from which the setting sun gleamed through the dripping leaves, and lit up all nature with a melancholy smile. It seemed like the parting hour of a good Christian, smiling on the sins and sorrows of the world, and giving, in the serenity of his decline, an assurance that he will rise again in glory.

311

I had seated myself on a half-sunken tombstone, and was musing, as one is apt to do at this sober-thoughted hour, on past scenes and early friends—on those who were distant and those who were dead—and indulging in that kind of melancholy fancying which has in it something sweeter even than pleasure. Every now and then the stroke of a bell from the neighboring tower fell on my ear; its tones were in unison with the scene, and, instead of jarring, chimed in with my feelings, and it was some time before I recollected that it must be tolling the knell of some new tenant of the tomb.

Presently I saw a funeral train moving across the village green; it wound slowly along a lane, was lost, and reappeared through the breaks of the hedges, until it passed the place where I was sitting. The pall was supported by young girls, dressed in white; and another, about the age of seventeen, walked before, bearing a chaplet of white flowers, a token that the deceased was a young and unmarried female. The corpse was followed by the parents. They were a venerable couple of the better order of peasantry. The father seemed to repress his feelings, but his fixed eye, contracted brow, and deeply-furrowed face showed the struggle that was passing within. His wife hung on his arm, and wept aloud with the convulsive bursts of a mother's sorrow.

I followed the funeral into the church. The bier was placed in the center aisle, and the chaplet of white flowers, with a pair of white gloves, were hung over the seat which the deceased had occupied.

Everyone knows the soul-subduing pathos of the funeral service, for who is so fortunate as never to have followed someone he has loved to the tomb? But when performed over the remains of innocence and beauty, thus laid low in the bloom of existence—what can be more affecting? At that simple but most solemn consignment of the body to the grave—"Earth to earth—ashes to ashes—dust to dust!"—the tears of the youthful companions of the deceased flowed unrestrained. The father still seemed to struggle with his feelings, and to comfort himself with the assurance that the dead are blessed which die in the Lord; but the mother only thought of her child as a flower of the field cut down and withered in the midst of its sweetness; she was like Rachel, "mourning over her children, and would not be comforted."

On returning to the inn, I learned the whole story of the deceased. It was a simple one, and such as has often been told. She had been the beauty and pride of the village. Her father had once been an opulent farmer, but was reduced in circumstances. This was an only child, and brought up entirely at home, in the simplicity of rural life. She had been the pupil of the village pastor, the favorite lamb of his little flock. The good man watched over her education with paternal care; it was limited, and suitable to the sphere in which she was to move, for he only sought to make her an ornament to her station in life, not to raise her above it. The tenderness and indulgence of her parents and the exemption from all ordinary occupations had fostered a natural grace and delicacy of character that accorded with the fragile loveliness of her form. She appeared like some tender plant of the garden, blooming accidentally amid the hardier natives of the fields.

The superiority of her charms was felt and acknowledged by her companions, but without envy, for it was surpassed by the unassuming gentleness and winning kindness of her manners. It might be truly said of her:

> This is the prettiest low-born lass, that ever
> Ran on the green-sward; nothing she does or seems,
> But smacks of something greater than herself;
> Too noble for this place.

The village was one of those sequestered spots which still retain some vestiges of old English customs. It had its rural festivals and holiday pastimes, and still kept up some faint observance of the once-popular rites of May. These, indeed, had been promoted by its present pastor, who was a lover of old customs and one of those simple Christians that think their mission fulfilled by promoting joy on earth and good will among mankind. Under his auspices the Maypole stood from year to year in the center of the village green; on May Day it was decorated with garlands and streamers, and a queen or lady of the May was appointed, as in former times, to preside at the

sports and distribute the prizes and rewards. The picturesque situation of the village and the fancifulness of its
rustic fetes would often attract the notice of casual visitors. Among these, on one May Day, was a young officer
whose regiment had been recently quartered in the neighborhood. He was charmed with the native taste that pervaded this village pageant, but, above all, with the dawning
loveliness of the queen of May. It was the village
favorite, who was crowned with flowers, and blushing
and smiling in all the beautiful confusion of girlish diffidence and delight. The artlessness of rural habits enabled
him readily to make her acquaintance; he gradually
won his way into her intimacy; and paid his court to her
in that unthinking way in which young officers are too apt
to trifle with rustic simplicity.

There was nothing in his advances to startle or alarm.
He never even talked of love; but there are modes of
making it more eloquent than language, and which con-
vey it subtilely and irresistibly to the heart. The beam of
the eye, the tone of voice, the thousand tendernesses
which emanate from every word and look and action—
these form the true eloquence of love, and can always
be felt and understood, but never described. Can we wonder that they should readily win a heart, young, guileless,
and susceptible? As to her, she loved almost unconsciously;
she scarcely inquired what was the growing passion
that was absorbing every thought and feeling, or what
were to be its consequences. She, indeed, looked not to
the future. When present, his looks and words occupied
her whole attention; when absent, she thought but of
what had passed at their recent interview. She would
wander with him through the green lanes and rural
scenes of the vicinity. He taught her to see new beauties
in nature; he talked in the language of polite and cultivated life, and breathed into her ear the witcheries of
romance and poetry.

Perhaps there could not have been a passion between
the sexes more pure than this innocent girl's. The gallant
figure of her youthful admirer and the splendor of his
military attire might at first have charmed her eye; but
it was not these that had captivated her heart. Her attachment had something in it of idolatry. She looked up to

him as to a being of a superior order. She felt in his society the enthusiasm of a mind naturally delicate and poetical, and now first awakened to a keen perception of the beautiful and grand. Of the sordid distinctions of rank and fortune she thought nothing; it was the difference of intellect, of demeanor, of manners from those of the rustic society to which she had been accustomed that elevated him in her opinion. She would listen to him with charmed ear and downcast look of mute delight, and her cheek would mantle with enthusiasm; or if ever she ventured a shy glance of timid admiration, it was as quickly withdrawn, and she would sigh and blush at the idea of her comparative unworthiness.

Her lover was equally impassioned; but his passion was mingled with feelings of a coarser nature. He had begun the connection in levity, for he had often heard his brother officers boast of their village conquests, and thought some triumph of the kind necessary to his reputation as a man of spirit. But he was too full of youthful fervor. His heart had not yet been rendered sufficiently cold and selfish by a wandering and a dissipated life; it caught fire from the very flame it sought to kindle, and before he was aware of the nature of his situation he became really in love.

What was he to do? There were the old obstacles which so incessantly occur in these heedless attachments. His rank in life—the prejudices of titled connections— his dependence upon a proud and unyielding father—all forbade him to think of matrimony: but when he looked down upon this innocent being, so tender and confiding, there was a purity in her manners, a blamelessness in her life, and a beseeching modesty in her looks that awed down every licentious feeling. In vain did he try to fortify himself by a thousand heartless examples of men of fashion, and to chill the glow of generous sentiment with that cold derisive levity with which he had heard them talk of female virtue; whenever he came into her presence, she was still surrounded by that mysterious but impassive charm of virgin purity in whose hallowed sphere no guilty thought can live.

The sudden arrival of orders for the regiment to repair to the continent completed the confusion of his mind.

He remained for a short time in a state of the most painful irresolution; he hesitated to communicate the tidings until the day for marching was at hand, when he gave her the intelligence in the course of an evening ramble.

The idea of parting had never before occurred to her. It broke in at once upon her dream of felicity; she looked upon it as a sudden and insurmountable evil, and wept with the guileless simplicity of a child. He drew her to his bosom, and kissed the tears from her soft cheek; nor did he meet with a repulse, for there are moments of mingled sorrow and tenderness which hallow the caresses of affection. He was naturally impetuous; and the sight of beauty, apparently yielding in his arms, the confidence of his power over her, and the dread of losing her for ever, all conspired to overwhelm his better feelings—he ventured to propose that she should leave her home and be the companion of his fortunes.

He was quite a novice in seduction, and blushed and faltered at his own baseness; but so innocent of mind was his intended victim that she was at first at a loss to comprehend his meaning; and why she should leave her native village, and the humble roof of her parents. When at last the nature of his proposal flashed upon her pure mind, the effect was withering. She did not weep—she did not break forth into reproach—she said not a word—but she shrunk back aghast as from a viper; gave him a look of anguish that pierced to his very soul; and, clasping her hands in agony, fled, as if for refuge, to her father's cottage.

The officer retired, confounded, humiliated, and repentant. It is uncertain what might have been the result of the conflict of his feelings had not his thoughts been diverted by the bustle of departure. New scenes, new pleasures, and new companions soon dissipated his self-reproach and stifled his tenderness; yet, amidst the stir of camps, the revelries of garrisons, the array of armies, and even the din of battles, his thoughts would sometimes steal back to the scenes of rural quiet and village simplicity—the white cottage—the footpath along the silver brook and up the hawthorn hedge, and the little village maid loitering along it, leaning on his arm, and listening to him with eyes beaming with unconscious affection.

The shock which the poor girl had received, in the destruction of all her ideal world, had indeed been cruel. Faintings and hysterics had at first shaken her tender frame, and were succeeded by a settled and pining melancholy. She had beheld from her window the march of the departing troops. She had seen her faithless lover borne off, as if in triumph, amidst the sound of drum and trumpet and the pomp of arms. She strained a last aching gaze after him, as the morning sun glittered about his figure, and his plume waved in the breeze; he passed away like a bright vision from her sight, and left her all in darkness.

It would be trite to dwell on the particulars of her after story. It was, like other tales of love, melancholy. She avoided society, and wandered out alone in the walks she had most frequented with her lover. She sought, like the stricken deer, to weep in silence and loneliness, and brood over the barbed sorrow that rankled in her soul. Sometimes she would be seen late of an evening sitting in the porch of the village church; and the milkmaids, returning from the fields, would now and then overhear her singing some plaintive ditty in the hawthorn walk. She became fervent in her devotions at church; and as the old people saw her approach, so wasted away, yet with a hectic bloom, and that hallowed air which melancholy diffuses around the form, they would make way for her, as for something spiritual, and, looking after her, would shake their heads in gloomy foreboding.

She felt a conviction that she was hastening to the tomb, but looked forward to it as a place of rest. The silver cord that had bound her to existence was loosed, and there seemed to be no more pleasure under the sun. If ever her gentle bosom had entertained resentment against her lover, it was extinguished. She was incapable of angry passions; and in a moment of saddened tenderness, she penned him a farewell letter. It was couched in the simplest language, but touching from its very simplicity. She told him that she was dying, and did not conceal from him that his conduct was the cause. She even depicted the sufferings which she had experienced, but concluded with saying that she could not die in peace until she had sent him her forgiveness and her blessing.

By degrees her strength declined, that she could no longer leave the cottage. She could only totter to the window, where, propped up in her chair, it was her enjoyment to sit all day and look out upon the landscape. Still she uttered no complaint, nor imparted to anyone the malady that was preying on her heart. She never even mentioned her lover's name, but would lay her head on her mother's bosom and weep in silence. Her poor parents hung, in mute anxiety, over this fading blossom of their hopes, still flattering themselves that it might again revive to freshness, and that the bright unearthly bloom which sometimes flushed her cheek might be the promise of returning health.

In this way she was seated between them one Sunday afternoon; her hands were clasped in theirs, the lattice was thrown open, and the soft air that stole in brought with it the fragrance of the clustering honeysuckle which her own hands had trained around the window.

Her father had just been reading a chapter in the Bible; it spoke of the vanity of worldly things, and of the joys of heaven; it seemed to have diffused comfort and serenity through her bosom. Her eye was fixed on the distant village church; the bell had tolled for the evening service; the last villager was lagging into the porch; and everything had sunk into that hallowed stillness peculiar to the day of rest. Her parents were gazing on her with yearning hearts. Sickness and sorrow, which pass so roughly over some faces, had given to hers the expression of a seraph's. A tear trembled in her soft blue eye. Was she thinking of her faithless lover? Or were her thoughts wandering to that distant churchyard, into whose bosom she might soon be gathered?

Suddenly the clang of hoofs was heard—a horseman galloped to the cottage—he dismounted before the window—the poor girl gave a faint exclamation, and sank back in her chair: it was her repentant lover! He rushed into the house and flew to clasp her to his bosom; but her wasted form—her deathlike countenance—so wan, yet so lovely in its desolation—smote him to the soul, and he threw himself in agony at her feet. She was too faint to rise—she attempted to extend her trembling hand —her lips moved as if she spoke, but no word was articulated—she looked down upon him with a smile of unutterable tenderness—and closed her eyes for ever!

Such are the particulars which I gathered of this village story. They are but scanty, and I am conscious have little novelty to recommend them. In the present rage also for strange incident and high-seasoned narrative they may appear trite and insignificant, but they interested me strongly at the time; and, taken in connection with the affecting ceremony which I had just witnessed, left a deeper impression on my mind than many circumstances of a more striking nature. I have passed through the place since, and visited the church again, from a better motive than mere curiosity. It was a wintry evening; the trees were stripped of their foliage; the churchyard looked naked and mournful, and the wind rustled coldly through the dry grass. Evergreens, however, had been planted about the grave of the village favorite, and osiers were bent over it to keep the turf uninjured.

The church door was open, and I stepped in. There hung the chaplet of flowers and the gloves, as on the day of the funeral; the flowers were withered, it is true, but care seemed to have been taken that no dust should soil their whiteness. I have seen many monuments where art has exhausted its powers to awaken the sympathy of the spectator, but I have met with none that spoke more touchingly to my heart than this simple but delicate memento of departed innocence.

THE ANGLER

This day dame Nature seem'd in love,
The lusty sap began to move,
Fresh juice did stir th' embracing vines
And birds had drawn their valentines.
The jealous trout that low did lie,
Rose at a well-dissembled flie.
There stood my friend, with patient skill.
Attending of his trembling quill.

SIR H. WOTTON

It is said that many an unlucky urchin is induced to run away from his family, and betake himself to a seafaring life, from reading the history of Robinson Crusoe; and I suspect that, in like manner, many of those worthy gentlemen who are given to haunt the sides of pastoral streams with angle rods in hand may trace the origin of their passion to the seductive pages of honest Izaak Walton. I recollect studying his *Compleat Angler* several years since, in company with a knot of friends in America, and moreover that we were all completely bitten with the angling mania. It was early in the year; but as soon as the weather was auspicious, and that the spring began to melt into the verge of summer, we took rod in hand and sallied into the country, as stark mad as was ever Don Quixote from reading books of chivalry.

One of our party had equaled the Don in the fullness of his equipments, being attired cap-a-pie for the enterprise. He wore a broad-skirted fustian coat perplexed with half a hundred pockets; a pair of stout shoes, and leathern gaiters; a basket slung on one side for fish; a patent rod, a landing net, and a score of other inconveniences only to be found in the true angler's armory. Thus harnessed for the field, he was as great a matter of stare and wonderment among the country folk, who had never seen a regular angler, as was the steel-clad hero of

La Mancha among the goatherds of the Sierra Morena.

Our first essay was along a mountain brook, among the highlands of the Hudson, a most unfortunate place for the execution of those piscatory tactics which had been invented along the velvet margins of quiet English rivulets. It was one of those wild streams that lavish among our romantic solitudes unheeded beauties, enough to fill the sketch book of a hunter of the picturesque. Sometimes it would leap down rocky shelves, making small cascades, over which the trees threw their broad balancing sprays, and long nameless weeds hung in fringes from the impending banks, dripping with diamond drops. Sometimes it would brawl and fret along a ravine in the matted shade of a forest, filling it with murmurs; and, after this termagant career, would steal forth into open day with the most placid demure face imaginable, as I have seen some pestilent shrew of a housewife, after filling her home with uproar and ill-humor, come dimpling out of doors, swimming and courtesying, and smiling upon all the world.

How smoothly would this vagrant brook glide, at such times, through some bosom of green meadow land among the mountains, where the quiet was only interrupted by the occasional tinkling of a bell from the lazy cattle among the clover, or the sound of a woodcutter's axe from the neighboring forest.

For my part, I was always a bungler at all kinds of sport that required either patience or adroitness, and had not angled above half an hour before I had completely "satisfied the sentiment," and convinced myself of the truth of Izaak Walton's opinion that angling is something like poetry—a man must be born to it. I hooked myself instead of the fish; tangled my line in every tree; lost my bait; broke my rod; until I gave up the attempt in despair, and passed the day under the trees, reading old Izaak, satisfied that it was his fascinating vein of honest simplicity and rural feeling that had bewitched me and not the passion for angling. My companions, however, were more persevering in their delusion. I have them at this moment before my eyes, stealing along the border of the brook, where it lay open to the day or was merely fringed by shrubs and bushes. I see the bittern rising with hollow scream as they break in upon his rarely invaded haunt; the kingfisher watching them suspiciously from his dry tree that overhangs the deep black millpond, in the gorge of the hills; the tortoise letting himself slip sideways from off the stone or log on which he is sunning himself; and the panic-struck frog plumping in headlong as they approach, and spreading an alarm throughout the watery world around.

I recollect also, that, after toiling and watching and creeping about for the greater part of a day with scarcely any success in spite of all our admirable apparatus, a lubberly country urchin came down from the hills with a rod made from a branch of a tree, a few yards of twine, and, as Heaven shall help me, I believe, a crooked pin for a hook, baited with a vile earthworm—and in half an hour caught more fish than we had nibbles throughout the day!

But, above all, I recollect the "good, honest, wholesome, hungry" repast which we made under a beech tree, just by a spring of pure sweet water that stole out of the side of a hill; and how, when it was over, one of the party read old Izaak Walton's scene with the milkmaid, while I lay on the grass and built castles in a bright pile of clouds until I fell asleep. All this may appear like mere egotism; yet I cannot refrain from uttering these recollections, which are passing like a strain of music over my mind, and have been called up by an agreeable scene which I witnessed not long since.

In a morning's stroll along the banks of the Alun, a beautiful little stream which flows down from the Welsh hills and throws itself into the Dee, my attention was attracted to a group seated on the margin. On approaching, I found it to consist of a veteran angler and two rustic disciples. The former was an old fellow with a wooden leg, with clothes very much but very carefully patched, betokening poverty, honestly come by, and decently maintained. His face bore the marks of former storms but present fair weather; its furrows had been worn into an habitual smile; his iron-gray locks hung about his ears, and he had altogether the good-humored air of a constitutional philosopher who was disposed to take the world as it went. One of his companions was a ragged wight, with the skulking look of an arrant poacher, and I'll warrant could find his way to any gentleman's fish pond in the neighborhood in the darkest night. The other was a tall, awkward country lad, with a lounging gait, and apparently somewhat of a rustic beau. The old man was busy in examining the maw of a trout which he had just killed, to discover by its contents what insects were seasonable for bait, and was lecturing on the subject to his companions, who appeared to listen with infinite deference. I have a kind feeling toward all "brothers of the angle" ever since I read Izaak Walton. They are men, he affirms, of a "mild, sweet, and peaceable spirit"; and my esteem for them has been increased since I met with an old *Tretyse of Fishing with the Angle,* in which are set forth many of the maxims of their inoffensive fraternity. "Take good hede," sayeth this honest little tretyse, "that in going about your disportes ye open no man's gates but that ye shet them again. Also ye shall not use this forsayd crafti disport for no covetousness to the encreasing and sparing of your money only, but principally for your solace, and to cause the helth of your body and specyally of your soule." *

I thought that I could perceive in the veteran angler before me an exemplification of what I had read, and there was a cheerful contentedness in his looks that quite drew me toward him. I could not but remark the gallant manner in which he stumped from one part of the brook to another, waving his rod in the air to keep the line from dragging on the ground or catching among the bushes, and the adroitness with which he would throw his fly to any particular place, sometimes skimming it lightly along a little rapid, sometimes casting it into one of those dark holes made by a twisted root or overhanging bank, in which the large trout are apt to lurk. In the meanwhile he was giving instructions to his two disciples, showing

---

*From this same treatise, it would appear that angling is a more industrious and devout employment than it is generally considered. "For when ye purpose to go on your disportes in fishynge ye will not desyre greatlye many persons with you, which might let you of your game. And that ye may serve God devoutly in sayinge effectually your customable prayers. And thus doying, ye shall eschew and also avoyde many vices, as ydelnes, which is principall cause to induce man to many other vices, as it is right well known."

them the manner in which they should handle their rods, fix their flies, and play them along the surface of the stream. The scene brought to my mind the instructions of the sage Piscator to his scholar. The country around was of that pastoral kind which Walton is fond of describing. It was a part of the great plain of Cheshire, close by the beautiful vale of Gessford, and just where the inferior Welsh hills begin to swell up from among fresh-smelling meadows. The day, too, like that recorded in his work, was mild and sunshiny, with now and then a soft-dropping shower that sowed the whole earth with diamonds.

I soon fell into conversation with the old angler, and was so much entertained that, under pretext of receiving instructions in his art, I kept company with him almost the whole day, wandering along the banks of the stream and listening to his talk. He was very communicative, having all the easy garrulity of cheerful old age, and I fancy was a little flattered by having an opportunity of displaying his piscatory lore, for who does not like now and then to play the sage?

He had been much of a rambler in his day, and had passed some years of his youth in America, particularly in Savannah, where he had entered into trade, and had been ruined by the indiscretion of a partner. He had afterward experienced many ups and downs in life, until he got into the navy, where his leg was carried away by a cannon ball at the battle of Camperdown. This was the only stroke of real good fortune he had ever experienced, for it got him a pension, which, together with some small paternal property, brought him in a revenue of nearly forty pounds. On this he retired to his native village, where he lived quietly and independently, and devoted the remainder of his life to the "noble art of angling."

I found that he had read Izaak Walton attentively, and he seemed to have imbibed all his simple frankness and prevalent good humor. Though he had been sorely buffeted about the world, he was satisfied that the world, in itself, was good and beautiful. Though he had been as roughly used in different countries as a poor sheep that is fleeced by every hedge and thicket, yet he spoke of every nation with candor and kindness, appearing to look only

on the good side of things; and, above all, he was almost
the only man I had ever met with who had been an
unfortunate adventurer in America, and had honesty and
magnanimity enough to take the fault to his own door,
and not to curse the country. The lad that was receiving
his instructions, I learned, was the son and heir apparent
of a fat old widow who kept the village inn, and of course
a youth of some expectation, and much courted by the
idle gentlemanlike personages of the place. In taking him
under his care, therefore, the old man had probably an
eye to a privileged corner in the taproom, and an occasional cup of cheerful ale free of expense.

There is certainly something in angling (if we could
forget, which anglers are apt to do, the cruelties and tor-
tures inflicted on worms and insects) that tends to produce a gentleness of spirit, and a pure serenity of mind.
As the English are methodical, even in their recreations,
and are the most scientific of sportsmen, it has been reduced among them to perfect rule and system. Indeed it
is an amusement peculiarly adapted to the mild and highly
cultivated scenery of England, where every roughness
has been softened away from the landscape. It is delightful
to saunter along those limpid streams which wander,
like veins of silver, through the bosom of this beautiful
country, leading one through a diversity of small home
scenery, sometimes winding through ornamented grounds,
sometimes brimming along through rich pasturage where
the fresh green is mingled with sweet-smelling flowers,
sometimes venturing in sight of villages and hamlets, and
then running capriciously away into shady retirements. The
sweetness and serenity of nature and the quiet watch-
fulness of the sport gradually bring on pleasant fits of
musing, which are now and then agreeably interrupted
by the song of a bird, the distant whistle of the
peasant, or perhaps the vagary of some fish, leaping out of the still water and skimming transiently about
its glassy surface. "When I would beget content," says
Izaak Walton, "and increase confidence in the power and
wisdom and providence of Almighty God, I will walk
the meadows by some gliding stream, and there contemplate the lilies that take no care, and those very many other
little living creatures that are not only created, but

fed (man knows not how) by the goodness of the God of nature, and therefore trust in him."

I cannot forbear to give another quotation from one of those ancient champions of angling, which breathes the same innocent and happy spirit:

> Let me live harmlessly, and near the brink
>   Of Trent or Avon have a dwelling-place,
> Where I may see my quill, or cork, down sink,
>   With eager bite of pike, or bleak, or dace;
> And on the world and my Creator think:
>   Whilst some men strive ill-gotten goods t' embrace;
> And others spend their time in base excess
>   Of wine, or worse, in war, or wantonness.
>
> Let them that will, these pastimes still pursue,
>   And on such pleasing fancies feed their fill;
> So I the fields and meadows green may view,
>   And daily by fresh rivers walk at will,
> Among the daisies and the violets blue,
>   Red hyacinth and yellow daffodil.*

On parting with the old angler I inquired after his place of abode, and happening to be in the neighborhood of the village a few evenings afterward, I had the curiosity to seek him out. I found him living in a small cottage, containing only one room, but a perfect curiosity in its method and arrangement. It was on the skirts of the village, on a green bank, a little back from the road, with a small garden in front, stocked with kitchen herbs, and adorned with a few flowers. The whole front of the cottage was overrun with a honeysuckle. On the top was a ship for a weathercock. The interior was fitted up in a truly nautical style, his ideas of comfort and convenience having been acquired on the berth deck of a man-of-war. A hammock was slung from the ceiling, which, in the daytime, was lashed up so as to take but little room. From the center of the chamber hung a model of a ship, of his own workmanship. Two or three chairs, a table, and a large sea chest formed the principal movables. About the wall were stuck up naval ballads, such as *Admiral Hosier's Ghost*, *All in the Downs*, and *Tom Bowline*, intermingled with pictures of sea fights, among which the

*J. Davors.

battle of Camperdown held a distinguished place. The mantelpiece was decorated with seashells, over which hung a quadrant, flanked by two woodcuts of most bitter-looking naval commanders. His implements for angling were carefully disposed on nails and hooks about the room. On a shelf was arranged his library, containing a work on angling, much worn, a Bible covered with canvas, an odd volume or two of voyages, a nautical almanac, and a book of songs.

His family consisted of a large black cat with one eye, and a parrot which he had caught and tamed and educated himself, in the course of one of his voyages, and which uttered a variety of sea phrases with the hoarse brattling tone of a veteran boatswain. The establishment reminded me of that of the renowned Robinson Crusoe; it was kept in neat order, everything being "stowed away" with the regularity of a ship of war; and he informed me that he "scoured the deck every morning, and swept it between meals."

I found him seated on a bench before the door, smoking his pipe in the soft evening sunshine. His cat was purring soberly on the threshold, and his parrot describing some strange evolutions in an iron ring that swung in the center of his cage. He had been angling all day, and gave me a history of his sport with as much minuteness as a general would talk over a campaign, being particularly animated in relating the manner in which he had taken a large trout, which had completely tasked all his skill and wariness, and which he had sent as a trophy to mine hostess of the inn.

How comforting it is to see a cheerful and contented old age; and to behold a poor fellow, like this, after being tempest-tossed through life, safely moored in a snug and quiet harbor in the evening of his days! His happiness, however, sprung from within himself, and was independent of external circumstances; for he had that inexhaustible good nature, which is the most precious gift of Heaven, spreading itself like oil over the troubled sea of thought and keeping the mind smooth and equable in the roughest weather.

On inquiring further about him, I learned that he was a universal favorite in the village, and the oracle of the taproom, where he delighted the rustics with his songs, and, like Sinbad, astonished them with his stories of strange lands, and shipwrecks, and sea fights. He was much noticed too by gentlemen sportsmen of the neighborhood; had taught several of them the art of angling; and was a privileged visitor to their kitchens. The whole tenor of his life was quiet and inoffensive, being principally passed about the neighboring streams, when the weather and season were favorable; and at other times he employed himself at home, preparing his fishing tackle for the next campaign, or manufacturing rods, nets, and flies for his patrons and pupils among the gentry.

He was a regular attendant at church on Sundays, though he generally fell asleep during the sermon. He had made it his particular request that when he died he should be buried in a green spot, which he could see from his seat in church, and which he had marked out ever since he was a boy, and had thought of when far from home on the raging sea, in danger of being food for the fishes—it was the spot where his father and mother had been buried.

I have done, for I fear that my reader is growing weary, but I could not refrain from drawing the picture of this worthy "brother of the angle," who has made me more than ever in love with the theory, though I fear I shall never be adroit in the practice of his art; and I will conclude this rambling sketch in the words of honest Izaak Walton, by craving the blessing of St. Peter's master upon my reader, "and upon all that are true lovers of virtue; and dare trust in his providence; and be quiet; and go a angling."

THE LEGEND OF SLEEPY HOLLOW

FOUND AMONG THE PAPERS OF THE LATE DIEDRICH
KNICKERBOCKER

> A pleasing land of drowsy head it was,
>   Of dreams that wave before the half-shut eye;
> And of gay castles in the clouds that pass,
>   For ever flushing round a summer sky.
>   CASTLE OF INDOLENCE

In the bosom of one of those spacious coves which in-
dent the eastern shore of the Hudson, at that broad ex-
pansion of the river denominated by the ancient Dutch
navigators the Tappan Zee, and where they always
prudently shortened sail, and implored the protection of
St. Nicholas when they crossed, there lies a small market town or rural port, which by some is called Greens-
burgh, but which is more generally and properly known
by the name of Tarry Town. This name was given, we
are told, in former days, by the good housewives of the
adjacent country, from the inveterate propensity of their
husbands to linger about the village tavern on market
days. Be that as it may, I do not vouch for the fact, but
merely advert to it, for the sake of being precise and authentic. Not far from this village, perhaps about two
miles, there is a little valley, or rather lap of land,
among high hills, which is one of the quietest places in
the whole world. A small brook glides through it, with just
murmur enough to lull one to repose; and the occasional
whistle of a quail or tapping of a woodpecker is almost
the only sound that ever breaks in upon the uniform tranquillity.

I recollect that, when a stripling, my first exploit in
squirrel shooting was in a grove of tall walnut trees that
shades one side of the valley. I had wandered into it at

noontime, when all nature is peculiarly quiet, and was startled by the roar of my own gun, as it broke the Sabbath stillness around, and was prolonged and reverberated by the angry echoes. If ever I should wish for a retreat, whither I might steal from the world and its distractions and dream quietly away the remnant of a troubled life, I know of none more promising than this little valley.

From the listless repose of the place, and the peculiar character of its inhabitants, who are descendants from the original Dutch settlers, this sequestered glen has long been known by the name of SLEEPY HOLLOW, and its rustic lads are called the Sleepy Hollow Boys throughout all the neighboring country. A drowsy, dreamy influence seems to hang over the land, and to pervade the very atmosphere. Some say that the place was bewitched by a high German doctor during the early days of the settlement; others, that an old Indian chief, the prophet or wizard of his tribe, held his powwows there before the country was discovered by Master Hendrick Hudson. Certain it is, the place still continues under the sway of some witching power that holds a spell over the minds of the good people, causing them to walk in a continual reverie. They are given to all kinds of marvelous beliefs, are subject to trances and visions, and frequently see strange sights, and hear music and voices in the air. The whole neighborhood abounds with local tales, haunted spots, and twilight superstitions; stars shoot and meteors glare oftener across the valley than in any other part of the country, and the nightmare, with her whole ninefold, seems to make it the favorite scene of her gambols.

The dominant spirit, however, that haunts this enchanted region and seems to be commander-in-chief of all the powers of the air is the apparition of a figure on horseback without a head. It is said by some to be the ghost of a Hessian trooper, whose head had been carried away by a cannon ball, in some nameless battle during the Revolutionary War, and who is ever and anon seen by the country folk, hurrying along in the gloom of night, as if on the wings of the wind. His haunts are not confined to the valley, but extend at times to the adjacent roads, and especially to the vicinity of a church at no great distance. Indeed, certain of the most authentic historians of those parts, who have been careful in collecting and collating the floating facts concerning this specter, allege that the body of the trooper, having been buried in the churchyard, the ghost rides forth to the scene of battle in nightly quest of his head; and that the rushing speed with which he sometimes passes along the Hollow, like a midnight blast, is owing to his being belated, and in a hurry to get back to the churchyard before daybreak.

Such is the general purport of this legendary superstition, which has furnished materials for many a wild story in that region of shadows; and the specter is known, at all the country firesides, by the name of the Headless Horseman of Sleepy Hollow.

It is remarkable that the visionary propensity I have mentioned is not confined to the native inhabitants of the valley, but is unconsciously imbibed by everyone who resides there for a time. However wide awake they may have been before they entered that sleepy region, they are sure, in a little time, to inhale the witching influence of the air, and begin to grow imaginative—to dream dreams and see apparitions.

I mention this peaceful spot with all possible laud; for it is in such little retired Dutch valleys, found here and there embosomed in the great State of New York, that population, manners, and customs remain fixed; while the great torrent of migration and improvement, which is making such incessant changes in other parts of this restless country, sweeps by them unobserved. They are like those little nooks of still water which border a rapid stream, where we may see the straw and bubble riding quietly at anchor, or slowly revolving in their mimic harbor, undisturbed by the rush of the passing current. Though many years have elapsed since I trod the drowsy shades of Sleepy Hollow, yet I question whether I should not still find the same trees and the same families vegetating in its sheltered bosom.

In this by-place of nature there abode, in a remote period of American history, that is to say, some thirty years since, a worthy wight of the name of Ichabod Crane, who sojourned, or, as he expressed it, "tarried," in Sleepy

Hollow, for the purpose of instructing the children of the vicinity. He was a native of Connecticut, a State which supplies the Union with pioneers for the mind as well as for the forest, and sends forth yearly its legions of frontier woodsmen and country schoolmasters. The cognomen of Crane was not inapplicable to his person. He was tall, but exceedingly lank, with narrow shoulders, long arms and legs, hands that dangled a mile out of his sleeves, feet that might have served for shovels, and his whole frame most loosely hung together. His head was small, and flat at top, with huge ears, large green glassy eyes, and a long snipe nose, so that it looked like a weathercock, perched upon his spindle neck, to tell which way the wind blew. To see him striding along the profile of a hill on a windy day, with his clothes bagging and fluttering about him, one might have mistaken him for the genius of famine descending upon the earth, or some scarecrow eloped from a cornfield.

His schoolhouse was a low building of one large room, rudely constructed of logs, the windows partly glazed, and partly patched with leaves of old copybooks. It was most ingeniously secured at vacant hours by a withe twisted in the handle of the door and stakes set against the window shutters, so that, though a thief might get in with perfect ease, he would find some embarrassment in getting out; an idea most probably borrowed by the architect, Yost Van Houten, from the mystery of an eel pot. The schoolhouse stood in a rather lonely but pleasant situation, just at the foot of a woody hill, with a brook running close by, and a formidable birch tree growing at one end of it. From hence the low murmur of his pupils' voices, conning over their lessons, might be heard in a drowsy summer's day, like the hum of a beehive, interrupted now and then by the authoritative voice of the master, in the tone of menace or command, or, peradventure, by the appalling sound of the birch, as he urged some tardy loiterer along the flowery path of knowledge. Truth to say, he was a conscientious man, and ever bore in mind the golden maxim, "Spare the rod and spoil the child." Ichabod Crane's scholars certainly were not spoiled.

I would not have it imagined, however, that he was

one of those cruel potentates of the school who joy in
the smart of their subjects; on the contrary, he administered justice with discrimination rather than severity, taking the burthen off the backs of the weak, and laying it
on those of the strong. Your mere puny stripling that
winced at the least flourish of the rod was passed by
with indulgence; but the claims of justice were satisfied
by inflicting a double portion on some little, tough,
wrong-headed, broad-skirted Dutch urchin, who sulked
and swelled and grew dogged and sullen beneath the
birch. All this he called "doing his duty by their parents";
and he never inflicted a chastisement without following it
by the assurance, so consolatory to the smarting urchin,
that "he would remember it, and thank him for it the
longest day he had to live."

When school hours were over, he was even the companion and playmate of the larger boys; and on holiday
afternoons would convoy some of the smaller ones home,
who happened to have pretty sisters, or good housewives
for mothers, noted for the comforts of the cupboard. Indeed it behooved him to keep on good terms with his
pupils. The revenue arising from his school was small,
and would have been scarcely sufficient to furnish him
with daily bread, for he was a huge feeder, and though
lank, had the dilating powers of an anaconda; but to help
out his maintenance, he was, according to country custom
in those parts, boarded and lodged at the houses of the
farmers whose children he instructed. With these he lived
successively a week at a time; thus going the rounds of
the neighborhood, with all his worldly effects tied up in
a cotton handkerchief.

That all this might not be too onerous on the purses of
his rustic patrons, who are apt to consider the costs of
schooling a grievous burden and schoolmasters as mere
drones, he had various ways of rendering himself both
useful and agreeable. He assisted the farmers occasionally in the lighter labors of their farms, helped to make
hay, mended the fences, took the horses to water, drove
the cows from pasture, and cut wood for the winter fire.
He laid aside, too, all the dominant dignity and absolute
sway with which he lorded it in his little empire, the
school, and became wonderfully gentle and ingratiating.

He found favor in the eyes of the mothers by petting the
children, particularly the youngest; and like the lion bold,
which whilom so magnanimously the lamb did hold, he
would sit with a child on one knee, and rock a cradle
with his foot for whole hours together.

In addition to his other vocations, he was the singing
master of the neighborhood, and picked up many
bright shillings by instructing the young folks in psalmody. It was a matter of no little vanity to him, on Sundays,
to take his station in front of the church gallery, with a
band of chosen singers; where, in his own mind, he completely carried away the palm from the parson. Certain
it is, his voice resounded far above all the rest of the
congregation; and there are peculiar quavers still to be
heard in that church, and which may even be heard half
a mile off, quite to the opposite side of the millpond, on
a still Sunday morning, which are said to be legitimately
descended from the nose of Ichabod Crane. Thus, by
diverse little makeshifts in that ingenious way which is
commonly denominated "by hook and by crook," the
worthy pedagogue got on tolerably enough, and was
thought, by all who understood nothing of the labor of
headwork, to have a wonderfully easy life of it.

The schoolmaster is generally a man of some importance in the female circle of a rural neighborhood, being considered a kind of idle gentlemanlike personage, of
vastly superior taste and accomplishments to the rough
country swains, and, indeed, inferior in learning only to
the parson. His appearance, therefore, is apt to occasion some little stir at the tea table of a farmhouse, and
the addition of a supernumerary dish of cakes or sweet-
meats, or, peradventure, the parade of a silver teapot.
Our man of letters, therefore, was peculiarly happy in
the smiles of all the country damsels. How he would
figure among them in the churchyard, between services on
Sundays! gathering grapes for them from the wild vines
that overrun the surrounding trees, reciting for their
amusement all the epitaphs on the tombstones, or sauntering, with a whole bevy of them, along the banks of
the adjacent millpond, while the more bashful country
bumpkins hung sheepishly back, envying his superior elegance and address.

From his half-itinerant life, also, he was a kind of traveling gazette, carrying the whole budget of local gossip from house to house, so that his appearance was always greeted with satisfaction. He was, moreover, esteemed by the women as a man of great erudition, for he had read several books quite through, and was a perfect master of Cotton Mather's *History of New England Witchcraft,* in which, by the way, he most firmly and potently believed.

He was, in fact, an odd mixture of small shrewdness and simple credulity. His appetite for the marvelous, and his powers of digesting it, were equally extraordinary; and both had been increased by his residence in this spellbound region. No tale was too gross or monstrous for his capacious swallow. It was often his delight, after his school was dismissed in the afternoon, to stretch himself on the rich bed of clover, bordering the little brook that whimpered by his schoolhouse, and there con over old Mather's direful tales, until the gathering dusk of the evening made the printed page a mere mist before his eyes. Then, as he wended his way, by swamp and stream and awful woodland, to the farmhouse where he happened to be quartered, every sound of nature, at that witching hour, fluttered his excited imagination: the moan of the whippoorwill * from the hillside; the boding cry of the tree toad, that harbinger of storm; the dreary hooting of the screech owl, or the sudden rustling in the thicket of birds frightened from their roost. The fireflies, too, which sparkled most vividly in the darkest places, now and then startled him, as one of uncommon brightness would stream across his path; and if, by chance, a huge blockhead of a beetle came winging his blundering flight against him, the poor varlet was ready to give up the ghost, with the idea that he was struck with a witch's token. His only resource on such occasions, either to drown thought or drive away evil spirits, was to sing psalm tunes; and the good people of Sleepy Hollow, as they sat by their doors of an evening, were often filled with awe, at hearing his nasal melody, "in linked sweet-

---

*The whippoorwill is a bird which is only heard at night. It receives its name from its note, which is thought to resemble those words.

ness long drawn out," floating from the distant hill or
along the dusky road.

Another of his sources of fearful pleasure was to pass
long winter evenings with the old Dutch wives as they
sat spinning by the fire, with a row of apples roasting
and spluttering along the hearth, and listen to their marvelous tales of ghosts and goblins, and haunted fields,
and haunted brooks, and haunted bridges, and haunted
houses, and particularly of the headless horseman, or
galloping Hessian of the Hollow, as they sometimes called
him. He would delight them equally by his anecdotes of
witchcraft, and of the direful omens and portentous
sights and sounds in the air, which prevailed in the
earlier times of Connecticut; and would frighten them
woefully with speculations upon comets and shooting
stars, and with the alarming fact that the world did
absolutely turn around, and that they were half the time
topsy-turvy!

But if there was a pleasure in all this, while snugly cud-
dling in the chimney corner of a chamber that was all of
a ruddy glow from the crackling wood fire, and where, of
course, no specter dared to show his face, it was dearly
purchased by the terrors of his subsequent walk home-
wards. What fearful shapes and shadows beset his path
amidst the dim and ghastly glare of a snowy night! With
what wistful look did he eye every trembling ray of light
streaming across the waste fields from some distant window! How often was he appalled by some shrub covered
with snow, which, like a sheeted specter, beset his very
path! How often did he shrink with curdling awe at the
sound of his own steps on the frosty crust beneath his
feet; and dread to look over his shoulder, lest he should
behold some uncouth being tramping close behind him!
And how often was he thrown into complete dismay
by some rushing blast, howling among the trees, in the
idea that it was the Galloping Hessian on one of his
nightly scourings!

All these, however, were mere terrors of the night,
phantoms of the mind that walk in darkness; and though
he had seen many specters in his time, and been more
than once beset by Satan in diverse shapes, in his
lonely perambulations, yet daylight put an end to all

these evils; and he would have passed a pleasant life of it, in despite of the devil and all his works, if his path had not been crossed by a being that causes more perplexity to mortal man than ghosts, goblins, and the whole race of witches put together, and that was—a woman.

Among the musical disciples who assembled, one evening in each week, to receive his instructions in psalmody, was Katrina Van Tassel, the daughter and only child of a substantial Dutch farmer. She was a blooming lass of fresh eighteen, plump as a partridge, ripe and melting and rosy-cheeked as one of her father's peaches, and universally famed, not merely for her beauty, but her vast expectations. She was withal a little of a coquette, as might be perceived even in her dress, which was a mixture of ancient and modern fashions, as most suited to set off her charms. She wore the ornaments of pure yellow gold, which her great-great-grandmother had brought over from Saardam; the tempting stomacher of the olden time; and withal a provokingly short petticoat, to display the prettiest foot and ankle in the country around.

Ichabod Crane had a soft and foolish heart toward the sex; and it is not to be wondered at that so tempting a morsel soon found favor in his eyes, more especially after he had visited her in her paternal mansion. Old Baltus Van Tassel was a perfect picture of a thriving, contented, liberal-hearted farmer. He seldom, it is true, sent either his eyes or his thoughts beyond the boundaries of his own farm; but within those everything was snug, happy, and well-conditioned. He was satisfied with his wealth, but not proud of it; and piqued himself upon the hearty abundance, rather than the style in which he lived. His stronghold was situated on the banks of the Hudson, in one of those green, sheltered, fertile nooks, in which the Dutch farmers are so fond of nestling. A great elm tree spread its broad branches over it, at the foot of which bubbled up a spring of the softest and sweetest water, in a little well, formed of a barrel, and then stole sparkling away through the grass, to a neighboring brook that bubbled along among alders and dwarf willows. Hard by the farmhouse was a vast barn that might have served for a church; every window and crevice of which seemed bursting forth with the treasures of the farm; the flail was busily resounding within it from morning to night; swallows and martins skimmed twittering about the eaves; and rows of pigeons, some with one eye turned up, as if watching the weather, some with their heads under their wings, or buried in their bosoms, and others swelling, and cooing, and bowing about their dames, were enjoying the sunshine on the roof. Sleek unwieldy porkers were grunting in the repose and abundance of their pens; whence sallied forth, now and then, troops of sucking pigs, as if to snuff the air. A stately squadron of snowy geese were riding in an adjoining pond, convoying whole fleets of ducks; regiments of turkeys were gobbling through the farmyard, and guinea fowls fretting about it, like ill-tempered housewives, with their peevish discontented cry. Before the barn door strutted the gallant cock, that pattern of a husband, a warrior, and a fine gentleman, clapping his burnished wings and crowing in the pride and gladness of his heart—sometimes tearing up the earth with his feet, and then generously calling his ever-hungry family of wives and children to enjoy the rich morsel which he had discovered.

The pedagogue's mouth watered as he looked upon this sumptuous promise of luxurious winter fare. In his devouring mind's eye he pictured to himself every roasting pig running about with a pudding in his belly and an apple in his mouth; the pigeons were snugly put to bed in a comfortable pie, and tucked in with a coverlet of crust; the geese were swimming in their own gravy; and the ducks pairing cozily in dishes, like snug married couples, with a decent competency of onion sauce. In the porkers he saw carved out the future sleek side of bacon, and juicy relishing ham; not a turkey but he beheld daintily trussed up, with its gizzard under its wing, and, peradventure, a necklace of savory sausages; and even bright chanticleer himself lay sprawling on his back, in a sidedish, with uplifted claws, as if craving that quarter which his chivalrous spirit disdained to ask while living.

As the enraptured Ichabod fancied all this, and as he rolled his great green eyes over the fat meadow lands, the rich fields of wheat, of rye, of buckwheat, and

Indian corn, and the orchards burthened with ruddy fruit, which surrounded the warm tenement of Van Tassel, his heart yearned after the damsel who was to inherit these domains, and his imagination expanded with the idea how they might be readily turned into cash, and the money invested in immense tracts of wild land, and shingle palaces in the wilderness. Nay, his busy fancy already realized his hopes, and presented to him the blooming Katrina, with a whole family of children, mounted on the top of a wagon loaded with household trumpery, with pots and kettles dangling beneath; and he beheld himself bestriding a pacing mare, with a colt at her heels, setting out for Kentucky, Tennessee, or the Lord knows where.

When he entered the house the conquest of his heart was complete. It was one of those spacious farmhouses, with high-ridged, but lowly sloping roofs, built in the style handed down from the first Dutch settlers, the low projecting eaves forming a piazza along the front, capable of being closed up in bad weather. Under this were hung flails, harness, various utensils of husbandry, and nets for fishing in the neighboring river. Benches were built along the sides for summer use; and a great spinning wheel at one end, and a churn at the other, showed the various uses to which this important porch might be devoted. From this piazza the wondering Ichabod entered the hall, which formed the center of the mansion and the place of usual residence. Here, rows of resplendent pewter, ranged on a long dresser, dazzled his eyes. In one corner stood a huge bag of wool ready to be spun; in another a quantity of linsey-woolsey just from the loom; ears of Indian corn and strings of dried apples and peaches hung in gay festoons along the walls, mingled with the gaud of red peppers; and a door left ajar gave him a peep into the best parlor, where the claw-footed chairs and dark mahogany tables shone like mirrors; and irons, with their accompanying shovel and tongs, glistened from their covert of asparagus tops; mock oranges and conch shells decorated the mantelpiece; strings of various colored birds' eggs were suspended above it; a great ostrich egg was hung from the center of the room, and a corner cupboard, knowingly left open, displayed immense treasures of old silver and well-mended china.

From the moment Ichabod laid his eyes upon these regions of delight, the peace of his mind was at an end, and his only study was how to gain the affections of the peerless daughter of Van Tassel. In this enterprise, however, he had more real difficulties than generally fell to the lot of a knight-errant of yore, who seldom had anything but giants, enchanters, fiery dragons, and such like easily conquered adversaries to contend with; and had to make his way merely through gates of iron and brass, and walls of adamant, to the castle keep, where the lady of his heart was confined; all which he achieved as easily as a man would carve his way to the center of a Christmas pie; and then the lady gave him her hand as a matter of course. Ichabod, on the contrary, had to win his way to the heart of a country coquette, beset with a labyrinth of whims and caprices, which were forever presenting new difficulties and impediments; and he had to encounter a host of fearful adversaries of real flesh and blood, the numerous rustic admirers, who beset every portal to her heart, keeping a watchful and angry eye upon each other, but ready to fly out in the common cause against any new competitor.

Among these the most formidable was a burly, roaring, roystering blade, of the name of Abraham, or, according to the Dutch abbreviation, Brom Van Brunt, the hero of the country round, which rang with his feats of strength and hardihood. He was broad-shouldered and double-jointed, with short curly black hair, and a bluff but not unpleasant countenance, having a mingled air of fun and arrogance. From his Herculean frame and great powers of limb, he had received the nickname of BROM BONES, by which he was universally known. He was famed for great knowledge and skill in horsemanship, being as dexterous on horseback as a Tartar. He was foremost at all races and cockfights; and, with the ascendency which bodily strength acquires in rustic life, was the umpire in all disputes, setting his hat on one side and giving his decisions with an air and tone admitting of no gainsay or appeal. He was always ready for either a fight or a frolic; but had more mischief than ill will in his composition, and, with all his overbearing roughness, there was a strong dash of waggish good humor at bottom. He had three or four boon companions, who regarded him as their model and at the head of whom he scoured the country, attending every scene of feud or merriment for miles around. In cold weather he was distinguished by a fur cap, surmounted with a flaunting fox's tail; and when the folks at a country gathering descried this well-known crest at a distance, whisking about among a squad of hard riders, they always stood by for a squall. Sometimes his crew would be heard dashing along past the farmhouses at midnight, with whoop and halloo, like a troop of Don Cossacks; and the old dames, startled out of their sleep, would listen for a moment till the hurry-scurry had clattered by, and then exclaim, "Ay, there goes Brom Bones and his gang!" The neighbors looked upon him with a mixture of awe, admiration, and good will; and when any madcap prank or rustic brawl occurred in the vicinity, always shook their heads and warranted Brom Bones was at the bottom of it.

This rantipole hero had for some time singled out the blooming Katrina for the object of his uncouth gallantries, and though his amorous toyings were something like the gentle caresses and endearments of a bear, yet it was whispered that she did not altogether discourage his hopes. Certain it is, his advances were signals for rival candidates to retire, who felt no inclination to cross a lion in his amours; insomuch, that when his horse was seen tied to Van Tassel's paling, on a Sunday night, a sure sign that his master was courting, or, as it is termed, "sparking," within, all other suitors passed by in despair, and carried the war into other quarters.

Such was the formidable rival with whom Ichabod Crane had to contend, and, considering all things, a stouter man than he would have shrunk from the competition, and a wiser man would have despaired. He had, however, a happy mixture of pliability and perseverance in his nature; he was in form and spirit like a supple jack—yielding, but tough; though he bent, he never broke; and though he bowed beneath the slightest pressure, yet, the moment it was away—jerk! he was as erect, and carried his head as high as ever.

To have taken the field openly against his rival would have been madness, for he was not a man to be thwarted in his amours, any more than that stormy lover Achilles. Ichabod, therefore, made his advances in a quiet and gently insinuating manner. Under cover of his character of singing master, he made frequent visits to the farmhouse; not that he had anything to apprehend from the meddlesome interference of parents, which is so often a stumbling block in the path of lovers. Balt Van Tassel was an easy indulgent soul; he loved his daughter better even than his pipe, and, like a reasonable man and an excellent father, let her have her way in everything. His notable little wife, too, had enough to do to attend to her housekeeping and manage her poultry; for, as she sagely observed, ducks and geese are foolish things, and must be looked after, but girls can take care of themselves. Thus while the busy dame bustled about the house, or plied her spinning wheel at one end of the piazza, honest Balt would sit smoking his evening pipe at the other, watching the achievements of a little wooden warrior, who, armed with a sword in each hand, was most valiantly fighting the wind on the pinnacle of the barn. In the meantime, Ichabod would carry on his suit with the daughter by the side of the spring under the great elm, or sauntering along in the twilight, that hour so favorable to the lover's eloquence.

I profess not to know how women's hearts are wooed and won. To me they have always been matters of riddle and admiration. Some seem to have but one vulnerable point, or door of access, while others have a thousand avenues, and may be captured in a thousand different ways. It is a great triumph of skill to gain the former, but a still greater proof of generalship to maintain possession of the latter, for the man must battle for his fortress at every door and window. He who wins a thousand common hearts is therefore entitled to some renown; but he who keeps undisputed sway over the heart of a coquette is indeed a hero. Certain it is, this was not the case with the redoubtable Brom Bones; and from the moment Ichabod Crane made his advances, the interests of the former evidently declined; his horse was no longer seen tied at the palings on Sunday nights, and a deadly

feud gradually arose between him and the preceptor of
Sleepy Hollow.

Brom, who had a degree of rough chivalry in his nature,
would fain have carried matters to open warfare, and
have settled their pretensions to the lady according to
the mode of those most concise and simple reasoners,
the knights-errant of yore—by single combat; but Ichabod was too conscious of the superior might of his ad-
versary to enter the lists against him. He had overheard a
boast of Bones that he would "double the schoolmaster
up, and lay him on a shelf of his own schoolhouse," and
he was too wary to give him an opportunity. There was
something extremely provoking in this obstinately pacific
system; it left Brom no alternative but to draw upon the
funds of rustic waggery in his disposition, and to play off
boorish practical jokes upon his rival. Ichabod became
the object of whimsical persecution to Bones and his gang
of rough riders. They harried his hitherto peaceful domains; smoked out his singing school by stopping up the
chimney; broke into the schoolhouse at night, in spite of
its formidable fastenings of withe and window stakes, and
turned everything topsy-turvy, so that the poor schoolmaster began to think all the witches in the country
held their meetings there. But what was still more an-
noying, Brom took all opportunities of turning him into
ridicule in presence of his mistress, and had a scoundrel
dog whom he taught to whine in the most ludicrous manner, and introduced as a rival of Ichabod's to instruct her
in psalmody.

In this way matters went on for sometime, without
producing any material effect on the relative situation of
the contending powers. On a fine autumnal afternoon,
Ichabod, in pensive mood, sat enthroned on the lofty
stool whence he usually watched all the concerns of his
little literary realm. In his hand he swayed a ferule, that
scepter of despotic power; the birch of justice reposed on
three nails, behind the throne, a constant terror to evil-
doers; while on the desk before him might be seen sundry
contraband articles and prohibited weapons, detected
upon the persons of idle urchins, such as half-munched
apples, popguns, whirligigs, fly cages, and whole legions
of rampant little paper gamecocks. Apparently there had

been some appalling act of justice recently inflicted, for his scholars were all busily intent upon their books, or slyly whispering behind them with one eye kept upon the master; and a kind of buzzing stillness reigned throughout the schoolroom. It was suddenly interrupted by the appearance of a Negro, in tow-cloth jacket and trousers, a round-crowned fragment of a hat, like the cap of Mercury, and mounted on the back of a ragged, wild, half-broken colt, which he managed with a rope by way of halter. He came clattering up to the school door with an invitation to Ichabod to attend a merrymaking or "quilting frolic" to be held that evening at Mynheer Van Tassel's; and having delivered his message with that air of importance and effort at fine language which a Negro is apt to display on petty embassies of the kind, he dashed over the brook and was seen scampering away up the hollow, full of the importance and hurry of his mission.

All was now bustle and hubbub in the late quiet schoolroom. The scholars were hurried through their lessons, without stopping at trifles; those who were nimble skipped over half with impunity, and those who were tardy had a smart application now and then in the rear to quicken their speed or help them over a tall word. Books were flung aside without being put away on the shelves, inkstands were overturned, benches thrown down, and the whole school was turned loose an hour before the usual time, bursting forth like a legion of young imps, yelping and racketing about the green, in joy at their early emancipation.

The gallant Ichabod now spent at least an extra half hour at his toilet, brushing and furbishing up his best and indeed only suit of rusty black, and arranging his looks by a bit of broken looking glass that hung up in the schoolhouse. That he might make his appearance before his mistress in the true style of a cavalier he borrowed a horse from the farmer with whom he was domiciliated, a choleric old Dutchman of the name of Hans Van Ripper, and, thus gallantly mounted, issued forth, like a knight-errant in quest of adventures. But it is meet I should, in the true spirit of romantic story, give some account of the looks and equipments of my hero and his steed. The animal he bestrode was a broken-down plow horse that had outlived almost everything but his viciousness. He was gaunt and shagged, with a ewe neck and a head like a hammer; his rusty mane and tail were tangled and knotted with burrs; one eye had lost its pupil and was glaring and spectral, but the other had the gleam of a genuine devil in it. Still he must have had fire and mettle in his day, if we may judge from the name he bore of Gunpowder. He had, in fact, been a favorite steed of his master's, the choleric Van Ripper, who was a furious rider, and had infused, very probably, some of his own spirit into the animal, for, old and broken-down as he looked, there was more of the lurking devil in him than in any young filly in the country.

Ichabod was a suitable figure for such a steed. He rode with short stirrups, which brought his knees nearly up to the pommel of the saddle; his sharp elbows stuck out like grasshoppers'; he carried his whip perpendicularly in his hand, like a scepter, and, as his horse jogged on, the motion of his arms was not unlike the flapping of a pair of wings. A small wool hat rested on the top of his nose, for so his scanty strip of forehead might be called; and the skirts of his black coat fluttered out almost to the horse's tail. Such was the appearance of Ichabod and his steed, as they shambled out of the gate of Hans Van Ripper, and it was altogether such an apparition as is seldom to be met with in broad daylight.

It was, as I have said, a fine autumnal day, the sky was clear and serene, and nature wore that rich and golden livery which we always associate with the idea of abundance. The forests had put on their sober brown and yellow, while some trees of the tenderer kind had been nipped by the frosts into brilliant dyes of orange, purple, and scarlet. Streaming files of wild ducks began to make their appearance high in the air; the bark of the squirrel might be heard from the groves of beech and hickory nuts, and the pensive whistle of the quail at intervals from the neighboring stubble field.

The small birds were taking their farewell banquets. In the fullness of their revelry, they fluttered, chirping and frolicking, from bush to bush, and tree to tree, capricious from the very profusion and variety around

them. There was the honest cock robin, the favorite game
of stripling sportsmen, with its loud querulous note; and
the twittering blackbirds flying in sable clouds; and the
golden-winged woodpecker, with his crimson crest, his
broad black gorget, and splendid plumage; and the cedar
bird, with its red-tipped wings and yellow-tipped tail, and
its little monteiro cap of feathers; and the blue jay,
that noisy coxcomb, in his gay light-blue coat and white
underclothes; screaming and chattering, nodding and bobbing and bowing, and pretending to be on good terms
with every songster of the grove.

As Ichabod jogged slowly on his way, his eye, ever
open to every symptom of culinary abundance, ranged
with delight over the treasures of jolly autumn. On all
sides he beheld vast store of apples, some hanging in oppressive opulence on the trees, some gathered into baskets
and barrels for the market, others heaped up in rich piles
for the cider press. Farther on he beheld great fields of
Indian corn, with its golden ears peeping from their leafy
coverts and holding out the promise of cakes and hasty
pudding; and the yellow pumpkins lying beneath them,
turning up their fair round bellies to the sun, and giving
ample prospects of the most luxurious of pies; and anon
he passed the fragrant buckwheat fields, breathing the
odor of the beehive, and as he beheld them, soft anticipations stole over his mind of dainty slapjacks, well buttered
and garnished with honey or treacle, by the delicate little
dimpled hand of Katrina Van Tassel.

Thus feeding his mind with many sweet thoughts and
"sugared suppositions," he journeyed along the sides of
a range of hills which look out upon some of the good-
liest scenes of the mighty Hudson. The sun gradually
wheeled his broad disk down into the west. The wide
bosom of the Tappan Zee lay motionless and glassy, excepting that here and there a gentle undulation waved
and prolonged the blue shadow of the distant mountain.
A few amber clouds floated in the sky, without a breath of
air to move them. The horizon was of a fine golden tint,
changing gradually into a pure apple green, and from
that into the deep blue of the mid-heaven. A slanting ray
lingered on the woody crests of the precipices that overhung some parts of the river, giving greater depth to the

dark-gray and purple of their rocky sides. A sloop was loitering in the distance, dropping slowly down with the tide, her sail hanging uselessly against the mast; and as the reflection of the sky gleamed along the still water, it seemed as if the vessel was suspended in the air.

It was toward evening that Ichabod arrived at the castle of the Heer Van Tassel, which he found thronged with the pride and flower of the adjacent country. Old farmers, a spare leathern-faced race, in homespun coats and breeches, blue stockings, huge shoes, and magnificent pewter buckles. Their brisk withered little dames, in close-crimped caps, long-waisted short gowns, homespun petticoats, with scissors and pincushions and gay calico pockets hanging on the outside. Buxom lasses, almost as antiquated as their mothers, excepting where a straw hat, a fine ribbon, or perhaps a white frock gave symptoms of city innovation. The sons, in short square-skirted coats with rows of stupendous brass buttons, and their hair generally queued in the fashion of the times, especially if they could procure an eel skin for the purpose, it being esteemed throughout the country as a potent nourisher and strengthener of the hair.

Brom Bones, however, was the hero of the scene, having come to the gathering on his favorite steed Dare-devil, creature, like himself, full of mettle and mischief, and which no one but himself could manage. He was, in fact, noted for preferring vicious animals, given to all kinds of tricks, which kept the rider in constant risk of his neck, for he held a tractable well-broken horse as unworthy of a lad of spirit.

Fain would I pause to dwell upon the world of charms that burst upon the enraptured gaze of my hero as he entered the state parlor of Van Tassel's mansion. Not those of the bevy of buxom lasses, with their luxurious display of red and white, but the ample charms of a genuine Dutch country tea table, in the sumptuous time of autumn. Such heaped-up platters of cakes of various and almost indescribable kinds, known only to experienced Dutch housewives! There was the doughty doughnut, the tenderer oly koek, and the crisp and crumbling cruller; sweet cakes and shortcakes, ginger cakes and honey cakes, and the whole family of cakes. And then there were apple pies and peach pies and pumpkin pies; besides slices of ham and smoked beef; and moreover delectable dishes of preserved plums, and peaches, and pears, and quinces; not to mention broiled shad and roasted chickens; together with bowls of milk and cream, all mingled higgledy-piggledy, pretty much as I have enumerated them, with the motherly teapot sending up its clouds of vapor from the midst—Heaven bless the mark! I want breath and time to discuss this banquet as it deserves, and am too eager to get on with my story. Happily, Ichabod Crane was not in so great a hurry as his historian, but did ample justice to every dainty.

He was a kind and thankful creature whose heart dilated in proportion as his skin was filled with good cheer, and whose spirits rose with eating as some men's do with drink. He could not help, too, rolling his large eyes around him as he ate, and chuckling with the possibility that he might one day be lord of all this scene of almost unimaginable luxury and splendor. Then, he thought, how soon he'd turn his back upon the old schoolhouse; snap his fingers in the face of Hans Van Ripper, and every other niggardly patron, and kick any itinerant pedagogue out of doors that should dare to call him comrade!

Old Baltus Van Tassel moved about among his guests with a face dilated with content and good humor, round and jolly as the harvest moon. His hospitable attentions were brief, but expressive, being confined to a shake of the hand, a slap on the shoulder, a loud laugh, and a pressing invitation to "fall to, and help themselves."

And now the sound of the music from the common room, or hall, summoned to the dance. The musician was an old gray-headed Negro, who had been the itinerant orchestra of the neighborhood for more than half a century. His instrument was as old and battered as himself. The greater part of the time he scraped on two or three strings, accompanying every movement of the bow with a motion of the head; bowing almost to the ground and stamping with his foot whenever a fresh couple were to start.

Ichabod prided himself upon his dancing as much as upon his vocal powers. Not a limb, not a fiber about him was idle; and to have seen his loosely hung frame in full

motion, and clattering about the room, you would have
thought Saint Vitus himself, that blessed patron of the
dance, was figuring before you in person. He was the
admiration of all the Negroes, who, having gathered, of
all ages and sizes, from the farm and the neighborhood,
stood forming a pyramid of shining black faces at every
door and window, gazing with delight at the scene, rolling
their white eyeballs, and showing grinning rows of ivory
from ear to ear. How could the flogger of urchins be
otherwise than animated and joyous? The lady of his
heart was his partner in the dance, and smiling graciously
in reply to all his amorous oglings, while Brom Bones,
sorely smitten with love and jealousy, sat brooding by
himself in one corner.

When the dance was at an end, Ichabod was attracted
to a knot of the sager folks, who, with old Van Tassel,
sat smoking at one end of the piazza, gossiping over former times, and drawing out long stories about the war.

This neighborhood, at the time of which I am speaking, was one of those highly favored places which abound
with chronicle and great men. The British and American
line had run near it during the war; it had, therefore, been
the scene of marauding, and infested with refugees, cow-
boys, and all kinds of border chivalry. Just sufficient
time had elapsed to enable each storyteller to dress up
his tale with a little becoming fiction, and, in the indistinctness of his recollection, to make himself the hero of every
exploit.

There was the story of Doffue Martling, a large
blue-bearded Dutchman, who had nearly taken a British frigate with an old iron nine-pounder from a mud
breastwork, only that his gun burst at the sixth discharge.
And there was an old gentleman who shall be nameless,
being too rich a mynheer to be lightly mentioned, who, in
the Battle of White Plains, being an excellent master of
defense, parried a musket ball with a small sword, insomuch that he absolutely felt it whiz around the blade and
glance off at the hilt, in proof of which he was ready at
any time to show the sword, with the hilt a little bent.
There were several more that had been equally great
in the field, not one of whom but was persuaded that he

had a considerable hand in bringing the war to a happy termination.

But all these were nothing to the tales of ghosts and apparitions that succeeded. The neighborhood is rich in legendary treasures of the kind. Local tales and superstitions thrive best in these sheltered long-settled retreats, but are trampled under foot by the shifting throng that forms the population of most of our country places. Besides, there is no encouragement for ghosts in most of our villages, for they have scarcely had time to finish their first nap and turn themselves in their graves before their surviving friends have traveled away from the neighborhood; so that when they turn out at night to walk their rounds they have no acquaintance left to call upon. This is perhaps the reason why we so seldom hear of ghosts except in our long-established Dutch communities.

The immediate cause, however, of the prevalence of supernatural stories in these parts was doubtless owing to the vicinity of Sleepy Hollow. There was a contagion in the very air that blew from that haunted region; it breathed forth an atmosphere of dreams and fancies infecting all the land. Several of the Sleepy Hollow people were present at Van Tassel's, and, as usual, were doling out their wild and wonderful legends. Many dismal tales were told about funeral trains, and mourning cries and wailings heard and seen about the great tree where the unfortunate Major André was taken, and which stood in the neighborhood. Some mention was made also of the woman in white that haunted the dark glen at Raven Rock, and was often heard to shriek on winter nights before a storm, having perished there in the snow. The chief part of the stories, however, turned upon the favorite specter of Sleepy Hollow, the headless horseman, who had been heard several times of late, patrolling the country, and, it was said, tethered his horse nightly among the graves in the churchyard.

The sequestered situation of this church seems always to have made it a favorite haunt of troubled spirits. It stands on a knoll, surrounded by locust trees and lofty elms, from among which its decent whitewashed walls shine modestly forth, like Christian purity beaming through the shades of retirement. A gentle slope descends from it to a silver sheet of water, bordered by high trees, between which peeps may be caught at the blue hills of the Hudson. To look upon its grass-grown yard, where the sunbeams seem to sleep so quietly, one would think that there at least the dead might rest in peace. On one side of the church extends a wide woody dell, along which raves a large brook among broken rocks and trunks of fallen trees. Over a deep black part of the stream, not far from the church, was formerly thrown a wooden bridge; the road that led to it, and the bridge itself, were thickly shaded by overhanging trees, which cast a gloom about it, even in the daytime, but occasioned a fearful darkness at night. This was one of the favorite haunts of the headless horseman, and the place where he was most frequently encountered. The tale was told of old Brouwer, a most heretical disbeliever in ghosts, how he met the horseman returning from his foray into Sleepy Hollow, and was obliged to get up behind him; how they galloped over bush and brake, over hill and swamp, until they reached the bridge, when the horseman suddenly turned into a skeleton, threw old Brouwer into the brook, and sprang away over the treetops with a clap of thunder.

This story was immediately matched by a thrice marvelous adventure of Brom Bones, who made light of the galloping Hessian as an arrant jockey. He affirmed that, on returning one night from the neighboring village of Sing Sing, he had been overtaken by this midnight trooper; that he had offered to race with him for a bowl of punch, and should have won it too, for Daredevil beat the goblin horse all hollow, but, just as they came to the church bridge, the Hessian bolted and vanished in a flash of fire.

All these tales, told in that drowsy undertone with which men talk in the dark, the countenances of the listeners only now and then receiving a casual gleam from the glare of a pipe, sank deep in the mind of Ichabod. He repaid them in kind with large extracts from his invaluable author, Cotton Mather, and added many marvelous events that had taken place in his native State of

Connecticut, and fearful sights which he had seen in his nightly walks about Sleepy Hollow.

The revel now gradually broke up. The old farmers gathered together their families in their wagons, and were heard for some time rattling along the hollow roads and over the distant hills. Some of the damsels mounted on pillions behind their favorite swains, and their lighthearted laughter, mingling with the clatter of hoofs, echoed along the silent woodlands, sounding fainter and fainter until they gradually died away—and the late scene of noise and frolic was all silent and deserted. Ichabod only lingered behind, according to the custom of country lovers, to have a tête-à-tête with the heiress, fully convinced that he was now on the high road to success. What passed at this interview I will not pretend to say, for in fact I do not know. Something, however, I fear me, must have gone wrong, for he certainly sallied forth, after no very great interval, with an air quite desolate and chopfallen. Oh these women! these women! Could that girl have been playing off any of her coquettish tricks? Was her encouragement of the poor pedagogue all a mere sham to secure her conquest of his rival? Heaven only knows, not I! Let it suffice to say, Ichabod stole forth with the air of one who had been sacking a hen roost rather than a fair lady's heart. Without looking to the right or left to notice the scene of rural wealth, on which he had so often gloated, he went straight to the stable, and with several hearty cuffs and kicks roused his steed most uncourteously from the comfortable quarters in which he was soundly sleeping, dreaming of mountains of corn and oats, and whole valleys of timothy and clover.

It was the very witching time of night that Ichabod, heavyhearted and crestfallen, pursued his travel homeward, along the sides of the lofty hills which rise above Tarry Town, and which he had traversed so cheerily in the afternoon. The hour was as dismal as himself. Far below him, the Tappan Zee spread its dusky and indistinct waste of waters, with here and there the tall mast of a sloop, riding quietly at anchor under the land. In the dead hush of midnight he could even hear the barking of the watchdog from the opposite shore of the Hudson, but it was so vague and faint as only to give an idea of his distance from this faithful companion of man. Now and then, too, the long-drawn crowing of a cock, accidentally awakened, would sound far, far off, from some farmhouse away among the hills—but it was like a dreaming sound in his ear. No signs of life occurred near him, but occasionally the melancholy chirp of a cricket, or perhaps the guttural twang of a bullfrog, from a neighboring marsh, as if sleeping uncomfortably and turning suddenly in his bed.

All the stories of ghosts and goblins that he had heard in the afternoon now came crowding upon his recollection. The night grew darker and darker; the stars seemed to sink deeper in the sky, and driving clouds occasionally hid them from his sight. He had never felt so lonely and dismal. He was, moreover, approaching the very place where many of the scenes of the ghost stories had been laid. In the center of the road stood an enormous tulip tree, which towered like a giant above all the other trees of the neighborhood and formed a kind of landmark. Its limbs were gnarled and fantastic, large enough to form trunks for ordinary trees, twisting down almost to the earth and rising again into the air. It was connected with the tragical story of the unfortunate André, who had been taken prisoner hard by; and was universally known by the name of Major André's tree. The common people regarded it with a mixture of respect and superstition, partly out of sympathy for the fate of its ill-starred namesake, and partly from the tales of strange sights and doleful lamentations told concerning it.

As Ichabod approached this fearful tree, he began to whistle; he thought his whistle was answered—it was but a blast sweeping sharply through the dry branches. As he approached a little nearer, he thought he saw something white hanging in the midst of the tree—he paused and ceased whistling; but on looking more narrowly, perceived that it was a place where the tree had been scathed by lightning and the white wood laid bare. Suddenly he heard a groan—his teeth chattered and his knees smote against the saddle; it was but the rubbing of one huge bough upon another as they were swayed about by the breeze. He passed the tree in safety, but new perils lay before him.

About two hundred yards from the tree a small brook crossed the road and ran into a marshy and thickly wooded glen, known by the name of Wiley's swamp. A few rough logs, laid side by side, served for a bridge over this stream. On that side of the road where the brook entered the wood, a group of oaks and chestnuts, matted thick with wild grapevines, threw a cavernous gloom over it. To pass this bridge was the severest trial. It was at this identical spot that the unfortunate André was captured, and under the covert of those chestnuts and vines were the sturdy yeomen concealed who surprised him. This has ever since been considered a haunted stream, and fearful are the feelings of the schoolboy who has to pass it alone after dark.

As he approached the stream his heart began to thump; he summoned up, however, all his resolution, gave his horse half a score of kicks in the ribs, and attempted to dash briskly across the bridge; but instead of starting forward, the perverse old animal made a lateral movement and ran broadside against the fence. Ichabod, whose fears increased with the delay, jerked the reins on the other side, and kicked lustily with the contrary foot; it was all in vain; his steed started, it is true, but it was only to plunge to the opposite side of the road into a thicket of brambles and alder bushes. The schoolmaster now bestowed both whip and heel upon the starveling ribs of old Gunpowder, who dashed forward, snuffling and snorting, but came to a stand just by the bridge with a suddenness that had nearly sent his rider sprawling over his head. Just at this moment a plashy tramp by the side of the bridge caught the sensitive ear of Ichabod. In the dark shadow of the grove, on the margin of the brook, he beheld something huge, misshapen, black and towering. It stirred not, but seemed gathered up in the gloom, like some gigantic monster ready to spring upon the traveler.

The hair of the affrighted pedagogue rose upon his head with terror. What was to be done? To turn and fly was now too late; and besides, what chance was there of escaping ghost or goblin, if such it was, which could ride upon the wings of the wind? Summoning up, therefore, a show of courage, he demanded in stammering accents—"Who are you?" He received no reply. He repeated his demand in a still more agitated voice. Still there was no answer. Once more he cudgeled the sides of the inflexible Gunpowder, and, shutting his eyes, broke forth with involuntary fervor into a psalm tune. Just then the shadowy object of alarm put itself in motion, and, with a scramble and a bound, stood at once in the middle of the road. Though the night was dark and dismal, yet the form of the unknown might now in some degree be ascertained. He appeared to be a horseman of large dimensions, and mounted on a black horse of powerful frame. He made no offer of molestation or sociability, but kept aloof on one side of the road, jogging along on the blind side of old Gunpowder, who had now got over his fright and waywardness.

Ichabod, who had no relish for this strange midnight companion, and bethought himself of the adventure of Brom Bones with the Galloping Hessian, now quickened his steed, in hopes of leaving him behind. The stranger, however, quickened his horse to an equal pace. Ichabod pulled up, and fell into a walk, thinking to lag behind—the other did the same. His heart began to sink within him; he endeavored to resume his psalm tune, but his parched tongue clove to the roof of his mouth, and he could not utter a stave. There was something in the moody and dogged silence of this pertinacious companion that was mysterious and appalling. It was soon fearfully accounted for. On mounting a rising ground, which brought the figure of his fellow-traveler in relief against the sky, gigantic in height, and muffled in a cloak, Ichabod was horror-struck on perceiving that he was headless! But his horror was still more increased on observing that the head, which should have rested on his shoulders, was carried before him on the pommel of the saddle. His terror rose to desperation; he rained a shower of kicks and blows upon Gunpowder, hoping, by a sudden movement, to give his companion the slip—but the specter started full jump with him. Away then they dashed, through thick and thin, stones flying and sparks flashing at every bound. Ichabod's flimsy garments fluttered in the air as he stretched his long lank body away over his horse's head, in the eagerness of his flight.

They had now reached the road which turns off to Sleepy Hollow; but Gunpowder, who seemed possessed with a demon, instead of keeping up it, made an opposite turn, and plunged headlong downhill to the left. This road leads through a sandy hollow, shaded by trees for about a quarter of a mile, where it crosses the bridge famous in goblin story, and just beyond swells the green knoll on which stands the whitewashed church.

As yet the panic of the steed had given his unskillful rider an apparent advantage in the chase; but just as he had got halfway through the hollow, the girths of the saddle gave way, and he felt it slipping from under him. He seized it by the pommel and endeavored to hold it firm, but in vain; and had just time to save himself by clasping old Gunpowder around the neck when the saddle fell to the earth, and he heard it trampled under foot by his pursuer. For a moment the terror of Hans Van Ripper's wrath passed across his mind—for it was his Sunday saddle; but this was no time for petty fears; the goblin was hard on his haunches, and (unskillful rider that he was!) he had much ado to maintain his seat, sometimes slipping on one side, sometimes on the other, and sometimes jolted on the high ridge of his horse's backbone with a violence that he verily feared would cleave him asunder.

An opening in the trees now cheered him with the hopes that the church bridge was at hand. The wavering reflection of a silver star in the bosom of the brook told him that he was not mistaken. He saw the walls of the church dimly glaring under the trees beyond. He recollected the place where Brom Bones's ghostly competitor had disappeared. "If I can but reach that bridge," thought Ichabod, "I am safe." Just then he heard the black steed panting and blowing close behind him; he even fancied that he felt his hot breath. Another convulsive kick in the ribs and old Gunpowder sprang upon the bridge; he thundered over the resounding planks; he gained the opposite side; and now Ichabod cast a look behind to see if his pursuer should vanish, according to rule, in a flash of fire and brimstone. Just then he saw the goblin rising in his stirrups, and in the very act of hurling his head at him. Ichabod endeavored to dodge the horrible missile, but too late. It encountered his cranium with a tremendous crash—he was tumbled headlong into the dust, and Gunpowder, the black steed, and the goblin rider, passed by like a whirlwind.

The next morning the old horse was found without his saddle, and with the bridle under his feet, soberly cropping the grass at his master's gate. Ichabod did not make his appearance at breakfast—dinner hour came, but no Ichabod. The boys assembled at the schoolhouse, and strolled idly about the banks of the brook; but no schoolmaster. Hans Van Ripper now began to feel some uneasiness about the fate of poor Ichabod, and his saddle. An inquiry was set on foot, and after diligent investigation they came upon his traces. In one part of the road leading to the church was found the saddle trampled in the dirt; the tracks of horses' hoofs deeply dented in the road, and evidently at furious speed, were traced to the bridge, beyond which, on the bank of a broad part of the brook, where the water ran deep and black, was found the hat of the unfortunate Ichabod, and close beside it a shattered pumpkin.

The brook was searched, but the body of the schoolmaster was not to be discovered. Hans Van Ripper, as executor of his estate, examined the bundle which contained all his worldly effects. They consisted of two shirts and a half, two stocks for the neck, a pair or two of worsted stockings, an old pair of corduroy small clothes, a rusty razor, a book of psalm tunes full of dogs' ears, and a broken pitchpipe. As to the books and furniture of the schoolhouse, they belonged to the community, excepting Cotton Mather's *History of Witchcraft, a New England Almanac,* and a book of dreams and fortune-telling; in which last was a sheet of foolscap much scribbled and blotted in several fruitless attempts to make a copy of verses in honor of the heiress of Van Tassel. These magic books and the poetic scrawl were forthwith consigned to the flames by Hans Van Ripper, who from that time forward determined to send his children no more to school, observing that he never knew any good come of this same reading and writing. What-

ever money the schoolmaster possessed, and he had received his quarter's pay but a day or two before, he must
have had about his person at the time of his disappearance.

The mysterious event caused much speculation at the
church on the following Sunday. Knots of gazers and gossips were collected in the churchyard, at the bridge, and
at the spot where the hat and pumpkin had been found.
The stories of Brouwer, of Bones, and a whole budget of
others were called to mind; and when they had diligently
considered them all and compared them with the symptoms of the present case, they shook their heads and
came to the conclusion that Ichabod had been carried off
by the galloping Hessian. As he was a bachelor and in nobody's debt, nobody troubled his head any more about
him. The school was removed to a different quarter of
the hollow, and another pedagogue reigned in his
stead.

It is true an old farmer, who had been down to New
York on a visit several years after, and from whom this
account of the ghostly adventure was received, brought
home the intelligence that Ichabod Crane was still alive;
that he had left the neighborhood, partly through fear of
the goblin and Hans Van Ripper, and partly in mortifica-
tion at having been suddenly dismissed by the heiress;
that he had changed his quarters to a distant part of the
country, had kept school and studied law at the same
time, had been admitted to the bar, turned politician,
electioneered, written for the newspapers, and finally
been made a justice of the Ten Pound Court. Brom Bones
too, who shortly after his rival's disappearance conducted the blooming Katrina in triumph to the altar,
was observed to look exceedingly knowing whenever the
story of Ichabod was related, and always burst into a
hearty laugh at the mention of the pumpkin, which led
some to suspect that he knew more about the matter than
he chose to tell.

The old country wives, however, who are the best
judges of these matters, maintain to this day that Ichabod was spirited away by supernatural means; and it is
a favorite story often told about the neighborhood around
the winter evening fire. The bridge became more than

ever an object of superstitious awe, and that may be the reason why the road has been altered of late years, so as to approach the church by the border of the millpond. The schoolhouse, being deserted, soon fell to decay, and was reported to be haunted by the ghost of the unfortunate pedagogue; and the plowboy, loitering homeward of a still summer evening, has often fancied his voice at a distance, chanting a melancholy psalm tune among the tranquil solitudes of Sleepy Hollow.

POSTSCRIPT

FOUND IN THE HANDWRITING OF MR. KNICKERBOCKER

THE preceding Tale is given, almost in the precise words in which I heard it related at a Corporation meeting of the ancient city of Manhattoes, at which were present many of its sagest and most illustrious burghers. The narrator was a pleasant, shabby, gentlemanly old fellow, in pepper-and-salt clothes, with a sadly humorous face, and one whom I strongly suspected of being poor—he made such efforts to be entertaining. When his story was concluded, there was much laughter and approbation, particularly from two or three deputy aldermen, who had been asleep a greater part of the time. There was, however, one tall, dry-looking old gentleman with beetling eyebrows, who maintained a grave and rather severe face throughout, now and then folding his arms, inclining his head, and looking down upon the floor, as if turning a doubt over in his mind. He was one of your wary men, who never laugh but upon good grounds—when they have reason and the law on their side. When the mirth of the rest of the company had subsided and silence was restored, he leaned one arm on the elbow of his chair, and, sticking the other akimbo, demanded, with a slight but exceedingly sage motion of the head, and contraction of the brow, what was the moral of the story, and what it went to prove?

The storyteller, who was just putting a glass of wine to his lips as a refreshment after his toils, paused for a moment, looked at his inquirer with an air of infinite deference, and, lowering the glass slowly to the table, observed that the story was intended most logically to prove:

"That there is no situation in life but has its advantages and pleasures—provided we will but take a joke as we find it.

"That, therefore, he that runs races with goblin troopers is likely to have rough riding of it.

"Ergo, for a country schoolmaster to be refused the hand of a Dutch heiress is a certain step to high preferment in the state."

The cautious old gentleman knit his brows tenfold closer after this explanation, being sorely puzzled by the ratiocination of the syllogism; while, methought, the one in pepper-and-salt eyed him with something of a triumphant leer. At length, he observed, that all this was very well, but still he thought the story a little on the extravagant—there were one or two points on which he had his doubts.

"Faith, sir," replied the storyteller, "as to that matter, I don't believe one-half of it myself."

D. K.

L'ENVOI*

Go, little booke, God send thee good passage,
And specially let this be thy prayere,
Unto them all that thee will read or hear,
Where thou art wrong, after their help to call,
Thee to correct in any part of all.
                    CHAUCER'S *Belle Dame sans Merci*

In concluding a second volume of *The Sketch Book*, the
Author cannot but express his deep sense of the indulgence with which his first has been received, and of the
liberal disposition that has been evinced to treat him with
kindness as a stranger. Even the critics, whatever may be
said of them by others, he has found to be a singularly
gentle and good-natured race; it is true that each has in
turn objected to some one or two articles, and that
these individual exceptions, taken in the aggregate, would
amount almost to a total condemnation of his work; but
then he has been consoled by observing that what one
has particularly censured, another has as particularly
praised; and thus, the encomiums being set off against
the objections, he finds his work, upon the whole, com-
mended far beyond its deserts.

He is aware that he runs a risk of forfeiting much of
this kind favor by not following the counsel that has
been liberally bestowed upon him; for where abundance
of valuable advice is given gratis, it may seem a man's
own fault if he should go astray. He can only say, in his
vindication, that he faithfully determined, for a time, to
govern himself in his second volume by the opinions
passed upon his first; but he was soon brought to a

*Closing the second volume of the London edition.

stand by the contrariety of excellent counsel. One kindly advised him to avoid the ludicrous; another to shun the pathetic; a third assured him that he was tolerable at description, but cautioned him to leave narrative alone; while a fourth declared that he had a very pretty knack at turning a story, and was really entertaining when in a pensive mood, but was grievously mistaken if he imagined himself to possess a spirit of humor.

Thus perplexed by the advice of his friends, who each in turn closed some particular path but left him all the world beside to range in, he found that to follow all their counsels would, in fact, be to stand still. He remained for a time sadly embarrassed; when, all at once, the thought struck him to ramble on as he had begun; that his work being miscellaneous, and written for different humors, it could not be expected that anyone would be pleased with the whole, but that if it should contain something to suit each reader, his end would be completely answered. Few guests sit down to a varied table with an equal appetite for every dish. One has an elegant horror of a roasted pig; another holds a curry or a devil in utter abomination; a third cannot tolerate the ancient flavor of venison and wildfowl; and a fourth, of truly masculine stomach, looks with sovereign contempt on those knickknacks, here and there dished up for the ladies. Thus each article is condemned in its turn; and yet, amidst this variety of appetites, seldom does a dish go away from the table without being tasted and relished by some one or other of the guests.

With these considerations he ventures to serve up this second volume in the same heterogeneous way with his first; simply requesting the reader, if he should find here and there something to please him, to rest assured that it was written expressly for intelligent readers like himself, but entreating him, should he find anything to dislike, to tolerate it as one of those articles which the author has been obliged to write for readers of a less refined taste.

To be serious. The author is conscious of the numerous faults and imperfections of his work, and well aware how little he is disciplined and accomplished in the arts of authorship. His deficiencies are also increased by a diffidence arising from his peculiar situation. He finds himself writing in a strange land, and appearing before a public which he has been accustomed, from childhood, to regard with the highest feelings of awe and reverence. He is full of solicitude to deserve their approbation, yet finds that very solicitude continually embarrassing his powers and depriving him of that ease and confidence which are necessary to successful exertion. Still the kindness with which he is treated encourages him to go on, hoping that in time he may acquire a steadier footing; and thus he proceeds, half venturing, half shrinking, surprised at his own good fortune, and wondering at his own temerity.

APPENDIX

NOTES CONCERNING WESTMINSTER ABBEY

TOWARD the end of the sixth century, when Britain, under the dominion of the Saxons, was in a state of barbarism and idolatry, Pope Gregory the Great, struck with the beauty of some Anglo-Saxon youths exposed for sale in the market place at Rome, conceived a fancy for the race, and determined to send missionaries to preach the gospel among these comely but benighted islanders. He was encouraged to this by learning that Ethelbert, King of Kent, and the most potent of the Anglo-Saxon princes, had married Bertha, a Christian princess, only daughter of the king of Paris, and that she was allowed by stipulation the full exercise of her religion.

The shrewd Pontiff knew the influence of the sex in matters of religious faith. He forthwith despatched Augustine, a a Roman monk, with forty associates, to the court of Ethelbert at Canterbury, to effect the conversion of the king and to obtain through him a foothold in the island.

Ethelbert received them warily, and held a conference in the open air, being distrustful of foreign priestcraft, and fearful of spells and magic. They ultimately succeeded in making him as good a Christian as his wife; the conversion of the king of course produced the conversion of his loyal subjects. The zeal and success of Augustine were rewarded by his being made Archbishop of Canterbury, and being endowed with authority over all the British churches.

One of the most prominent converts was Segebert or Sebert, king of the East Saxons, a nephew of Ethelbert. He reigned at London, of which Mellitus, one of the Roman monks who had come over with Augustine, was made bishop.

Sebert, in 605, in his religious zeal, founded a monastery by the river side to the west of the city, on the ruins of a temple of Apollo, being, in fact, the origin of the present pile of Westminster Abbey. Great preparations were made for the consecration of the church, which was to be dedicated to St. Peter. On the morning of the appointed day, Mellitus, the bishop, proceeded with great pomp and solemnity to perform the ceremony. On approaching the edifice he was met by a fisherman, who informed him that it was needless to proceed, as the ceremony was over. The bishop stared with surprise, when the fisherman went on to relate that the night before, as he was in his boat on the Thames, St. Peter appeared to him, and told him that he intended to consecrate the church himself, that very night. The apostle accordingly went into the church, which suddenly became illuminated. The ceremony was performed in sumptuous style, accompanied by strains of heavenly music and clouds of fragrant incense. After this, the apostle came into the boat and ordered the fisherman to cast his net. He did so, and had a miraculous draft of fishes, one of which he was commanded to present to the bishop, and to signify to him that the apostle had relieved him from the necessity of consecrating the church.

Mellitus was a wary man, slow of belief, and required confirmation of the fisherman's tale. He opened the church doors, and beheld wax candles, crosses, holy water, oil sprinkled in various places, and various other traces of a grand ceremonial. If he had still any lingering doubts, they were completely removed on the fisherman's producing the identical fish which he had been ordered by the apostle to present to him. To resist this would have been to resist ocular demonstration. The good bishop accordingly was convinced that the church had actually been consecrated by St. Peter in person, so he reverently abstained from proceeding further in the business.

The foregoing tradition is said to be the reason why King Edward the Confessor chose this place as the site of a religious house which he meant to endow. He pulled down the old church and built another in its place in 1045. In this his remains were deposited in a magnificent shrine.

The sacred edifice again underwent modifications, if not a reconstruction, by Henry III, in 1220, and began to assume its present appearance.

Under Henry VIII it lost its conventual character, that monarch turning the monks away, and seizing upon the revenues.

RELICS OF EDWARD THE CONFESSOR

A curious narrative was printed in 1688 by one of the choristers of the cathedral, who appears to have been the Paul Pry of the sacred edifice, giving an account of his rummaging among the bones of Edward the Confessor after they had quietly reposed in their sepulcher upward of six hundred years, and of his drawing forth the crucifix and golden chain of the deceased monarch. During eighteen years that he had officiated in the choir, it had been a common tradition, he says, among his brother choristers and the gray-headed servants of the abbey that the body of King Edward was deposited in a kind of chest or coffin, which was indistinctly seen in the upper part of the shrine erected to his memory. None of the abbey gossips, however, had ventured upon a nearer inspection, until the worthy narrator, to gratify his curiosity, mounted to the coffin by the aid of a ladder, and found it to be made of wood, apparently very strong and firm, being secured by bands of iron.

Subsequently, in 1685, on taking down the scaffolding used in the coronation of James II, the coffin was found to be broken, a hole appearing in the lid, probably made, through accident, by the workmen. No one ventured, however, to meddle with the sacred depository of royal dust, until, several weeks afterward, the circumstance came to the knowledge of the aforesaid chorister. He forthwith repaired to the abbey in company with two friends, of congenial tastes, who were desirous of inspecting the tombs. Procuring a ladder, he again mounted to the coffin, and found, as had been represented, a hole in the lid about six inches long and four inches broad, just in front of the left breast. Thrusting in his hand, and groping among the bones, he drew from underneath the shoulder a crucifix, richly adorned and enameled, affixed to a gold chain twenty-four inches long. These he showed to his inquisitive friends, who were equally surprised with himself.

"At the time," says he, "when I took the cross and chain out of the coffin, *I drew the head to the hole and viewed it,* being very sound and firm, with the upper and nether jaws whole and full of teeth, and a list of gold above an inch broad, in the nature of a coronet, surrounding the temples. There was also in the coffin, white linen and gold-colored flowered silk that looked indifferent fresh; but the least stress put thereto showed it was well nigh perished. There were all his bones, and much dust likewise, which I left as I found."

It is difficult to conceive a more grotesque lesson to human pride than the skull of Edward the Confessor thus irreverently pulled about in its coffin by a prying chorister, and brought to grin face to face with him through a hole in the lid!

Having satisfied his curiosity, the chorister put the crucifix and chain back again into the coffin, and sought the dean, to apprise him of his discovery. The dean not being accessible at the time, and fearing that the "holy treasure" might be taken away by other hands, he got a brother chorister to accompany him to the shrine about two or three hours afterward, and in his presence again drew forth the relics. These he afterward delivered on his knees to King James. The king subsequently had the old coffin enclosed in a new one of great strength: "each plank being two inches thick and cramped together with large iron wedges, where it now remains (1688) as a testimony of his pious care, that no abuse might be offered to the sacred ashes therein deposited."

As the history of this shrine is full of moral, I subjoin a description of it in modern times. "The solitary and forlorn shrine," says a British writer, "now stands a mere skeleton of what it was. A few faint traces of its sparkling decorations inlaid on solid mortar catch the rays of the sun, forever set on its splendor * * * * Only two of the spiral pillars remain. The wooden Ionic top is much broken, and covered with dust. The mosaic is picked away in every part within reach; only the lozenges of about a foot square and five circular pieces of the rich marble remain."—*Malcolm, Lond. rediv.*

INSCRIPTION ON A MONUMENT ALLUDED TO IN THE SKETCH.

Here lyes the Loyal Duke of Newcastle, and his Duchess his second wife, by whom he had no issue. Her name was Margaret Lucas, youngest sister to the Lord Lucas of Colchester, a noble family; for all the brothers were valiant, and all the sisters virtuous. This Duchess was a wise, witty, and learned lady, which her many Bookes do well testify: she was a most virtuous, and loving and careful wife, and was with her lord all the time of his banishment and miseries, and when he came home, never parted from him in his solitary retirement.

In the wintertime, when the days are short, the service in the afternoon is performed by the light of tapers. The effect is fine of the choir partially lighted up, while the main body of the cathedral and the transepts are in profound and cavernous darkness. The white dresses of the choristers gleam amidst the deep brown of the open slats and canopies; the partial illumination makes enormous shadows from columns and screens, and darting into the surrounding gloom, catches here and there upon a sepulchral decoration, or monumental effigy. The swelling notes of the organ accord well with the scene.

When the service is over, the dean is lighted to his dwelling, in the old conventual part of the pile, by the boys of the choir, in their white dresses, bearing tapers, and the procession passes through the abbey and along the shadowy cloisters, lighting up angles and arches and grim sepulchral monuments, and leaving all behind in darkness.

On entering the cloisters at night from what is called the Dean's Yard, the eye ranging through a dark vaulted passage catches a distant view of a white marble figure reclining on a tomb, on which a strong glare thrown by a gas light has quite a spectral effect. It is a mural monument of one of the Pultneys.

AFTERWORD

In 1820 an irascible English aphorist, Sydney Smith, having suffered, as had many Europeans, just about all the American boasting he could stand, delivered a blast at the upstart's pretensions. Though the Republic had rejected England almost fifty years before, Smith said, it had nothing in the way of arts, manners, or intellect to show for itself. In the midst of his tirade the caustic divine (he was a minister in the Established Church) demanded, "And who, the wide world over, reads an American book?"

His jibe could hardly have been more ill timed, for even as he uttered it, a book was taking shape which everybody in America, just about everybody in Great Britain, and then thousands upon the Continent fell to reading with avidity. In his preface of 1848, Washington Irving tells the bare story of the publication of *The Sketch Book,* though from a combination of modesty and a deliberate intent to mislead he does not give the complete drama of its astounding success. Chiefly what he does not mention is that this book, which was universally hailed in 1820 for its "geniality," its sunny disposition, its cheerfulness, came out of a bitter immersion in failure, loneliness, and dark depression.

Born in 1783, the son of a hardware merchant and deacon in the Episcopal Church, Washington was petted and indulged by his parents, his four older and adoring brothers, and two older and adoring sisters. He later said that they all took pride in his "sensibility." They delighted to play upon it, thus engendering in him "a morbid feeling." That there was such a vein in him is certainly true, and *The Sketch Book* owed much of its appeal for his own generation to this element in his being. But as he came of age the figure he presented to the city was anything but morbid: He displayed a constantly augmenting charm, a taste for fine clothes, a lively humor and an irresistible sociability, an eye for handsome women, and a disinclination to soil his graceful hands in any of the grubby work his family, and his sort of families everywhere in America, were stoutly performing from dawn to dusk, six days of the week. The brothers—perhaps vicariously relishing the freedom they could bestow upon the one butterfly in Deacon Irving's household—gave him two glorious years of a grand tour through Italy, France, England, and Switzerland. Therein he paid little heed to the Napoleonic Wars but considerable to monuments and galleries, and even more to the theater and to the beauty of the women.

Back in New York in 1806, Irving was about the most elegant apparition the plebeian town had ever seen. In accordance with the prevailing injunction of the society, he gave at least the appearance of being engaged in a gainful occupation by going through a few motions of practicing law. But he expended his abounding energy by joining with three or four wits to publish a series of mild skits upon the manners of the citizens, called *Salmagundi,* which makes very pallid reading today. He learned contempt for Thomas Jefferson and democracy, and love for Matilda Hoffman. She died at the age of nineteen, in 1809, and Irving was indeed bereaved. Mawkish legend has sentimentalized Irving's love into a grand passion and Matilda's death into a tear-jerking tragedy. The event was not so spectacular as that, but it did accentuate the "morbid" strain in him and reinforced his tendency to luxuriate in the blissful sorrows of premature death. Yet by exercising a self-discipline he never was again to achieve, he manufactured a surcease from anguish by completing his *Diedrich Knickerbocker's A History of New York.* It was a huge success in America (the subject was too remote from Europe to attract attention there, though fortunately it did not escape the omnivorous curiosity of Sir Walter Scott), and yielded

Irving a profit of $3,000—utterly unprecedented for any writer in the United States of that time.

Knickerbocker is rollicking hyperbole, playing fast and loose with factual history, punctuated with sly off-color jokes that express what had already become for fashionable young men in New York a self-consciously "Rabelaisian" pose, insisted upon the more resolutely as a repudiation of New England. The book piles satire upon that region; in the grotesque figure of William the Testy it viciously caricatures Thomas Jefferson, and in the heroic Peter Stuyvesant allows Irving's petulant scorn for the vulgar masses to break through the comic mask. In sum, it dramatizes the image of Irving as the gayest blade that America had yet produced, the nearest we could boast to match the young dandies of London coffee houses.

Knickerbocker entirely lacks that "kind of melancholy fancying which has in it something sweeter even than pleasure," as he says of "The Pride of the Village," in which melancholy he extravagantly indulges through such *Sketch Book* pieces as "The Broken Heart," "The Widow and Her Son," and "Rural Funerals." Over these even the cynical Lord Byron unashamedly wept. The aspiration for worldy sophistication and an appreciation of polite bawdiness never deserted Irving (though the provincial son of a Manhattan hardware dealer had to work hard to manage them), and these constitute a still-appealing value in his best writing. But between 1809 and 1819 he discovered, and for the rest of his life was to remain happy with the finding, that a lush yet refined cultivation of the gentle tear, interspersed with bonhomie and a pleasant affectation of useless erudition, was readily marketable in the early nineteenth century. For the two years in which *The Sketch Book* was bit by bit appearing, Irving made a profit of $9,000, which no other writer in England except Scott could come near, and none at all in America.

Yet it is not enough to say of Irving that he composed his book only out of a calculation of what the public would buy. After he set the vogue, a myriad of imitators followed it; several of them were successful but are deservedly forgotten today, whereas *The Sketch*

Book, despite its maudlin passages, can be and is read with interest, even with pleasure, by many who long since have consigned "sensibility" to the garbage heap. There was a time, up until very recently, when reprints of *The Sketch Book* left out the graveyard numbers and concentrated on the jovial Christmas passages and on those which were assumed to be approvable by modern standards—"Rip," "Sleepy Hollow," "Mutability of Literature." Yet so to excise is to spoil the unity of the work, a coherence which it does possess despite the piecemeal way in which Irving wrote and published the parts, despite the fact that "Rip" and "Sleepy Hollow" can stand by themselves and customarily are anthologized as "short stories." We must peruse the whole as a unit, observing the conscious alternation of moods— for example, the jolt intended by the shift from "The Wife" to "Rip"—in order to comprehend that Irving had every right to call the result a *book* and not a collection of random "sketches." Though in the expanse of nineteenth-century literature it is not what we denominate a major work—not even so basic to our appreciation of the epoch as are, say, Hawthorne's *Mosses from an Old Manse* or Melville's *Piazza Tales*—still it sustains an intrinsic merit all its own, quite apart from its role as pioneer for both these latter works, or even for the tales of Edgar Allan Poe.

The reasons for the unique excellence of *The Sketch Book* can be precisely recounted in relation to the tastes of 1820, but viewed from the side of Irving's own development they are, briefly, two. The first is the long apprenticeship he had actually served in the art of writing, beginning with a pathetic volume of "dramatic criticisms" he printed back in 1802, professing the author to be (significantly) "Jonathan Oldstyle." The theater in New York at that date presented no challenge to a critic's powers, but even then Irving exhibited a precocious ability to make something out of nothing, just as in *Salmagundi* he almost promoted middle-class New York into a subject worthy of social satire, and as in *Knickerbocker* he wrought a comic masterpiece out of the meager and dull records of New Amsterdam. He had learned lucidity (for decades selections from him have been used in secondary schools on the Continent for teaching beginning students of the language easy and flawless English), the art of handling anecdote, and, above all, the trick of appearing under an alias, as Jonathan Oldstyle or Diedrich Knickerbocker. This device served him well as he assumed the masquerade of Geoffrey Crayon, and doubled the ingenuity by deriving some of the tales from masquerades within the masquerade, such as the "corpulent old Swiss" who tells "The Specter Bridegroom." Wherefore Washington Irving, from 128 William Street in commercial New York, could emblazon his nom de plume on the title page as "Gent." and so himself write like a gentleman.

The second factor in Irving's biography to which we must attribute the quality of *The Sketch Book* is his career between 1815 and 1819. After serving as an officer in the New York militia at the end of the War of 1812 (he saw no action), he was restless and increasingly subject to moods of depression. His brothers again came to his aid and sent him to England, intending that for a while he represent the firm in Liverpool and eventually escape again to Italy. Thus in 1815 he commenced what became seventeen years of "exile." The brothers failed; Irving was left alone, poor, and in an industrialized North of England which was grimier than New York. Except for a few respites, such as his visit to Scott, he sank into a gloom which for him was profound. "It has pleased heaven," he wrote in 1817, "that I should be driven on upon my inner strength." Memories of Matilda pressed him anew—"the agony of her death, the seraphic years of her blessedness." The world had become for him a jarring collision, a heartless pleasure. "I feel like one withered up & blighted—broken heart is like a desert wherein can flourish no green thing—The romance of life is past." For a Washington Irving even to contemplate such desolation was virtually a premonition of death. If he was to survive he would have to write —and write, not like Poe, fantastic projections of his despair, but consoling visions of benevolent humanity, tinged with reflections on death and the decomposition of corpses which would turn them into triumphs for that sensibility which alone could preserve him.

In New York, where for a brief interlude he had tried unsuccessfully to edit a magazine, he had written the two threnodies on the Indians which he now placed judiciously in *The Sketch Book*. These presaged his technique: He strove to invest the Indians, still regarded by most Americans as vermin, with such virtues as might excite tears of compassion. Extending this pattern to the mortuary scenes of jolly old England, and then to the jolliness and the antiquity of the land, and skillfully placing amid this medley of sensibility the two tales designed, as he advertised, to shed "a color of romance and tradition" over America as well, he commenced securing the publication of partial collections in New York. Eventually, with the help of Scott, as he tells us, he got the majestic John Murray to bring out the complete array in a two-volume edition in the summer of 1820. Irving for the time being let drop his cloak of melancholy, gave no more thought to Matilda, and became in London, according to a reliable reporter, "the most fashionable fellow of the day."

Thus we confront the incongruity that the first American literary creation to achieve international recognition centers upon a semi-fictional creation, Geoffrey Crayon, who is a saunterer, a daydreamer, a connoisseur of impressions and exquisite sensations, whose aim in life is to escape "from the commonplace realities of the present," and to lose himself "among the shadowy grandeurs of the past." This is indeed incongruous, because the America of 1820 was well entered upon that gigantic exertion which commenced with the end of the war, which was erecting an industrial, urban, hard-working civilization that in its own eyes and in the eyes of foreign observers was already the defiant vindication of the commonplace. There was virtually no time or place in the United States for anyone to play at what Irving says he did in "Stratford on Avon," to be a lonely wanderer through historic scenes, drinking deep but quiet drafts of inspiration and allowing his mind to be "intensely sensible of the beauty and majesty of nature." Or at least, if any in America had attempted such a career of indolence, he would have had to retreat to Walden Pond, there to forego not only the fashionable but the profitable.

Hence it does seem revealing that the two stories in which Irving strove to weave slight webs of enchantment within the American scene are actually plagiarisms from German folklore. His note at the end of "Rip Van Winkle," saying that the story might have been suggested to Mr. Knickerbocker by the German superstition about the Emperor Frederick, was a calculated design to prevent his readers from noticing that it was in fact an adaptation to the Hudson River landscape of an old German tale, "Peter Klaus." None of Irving's admirers realized this, any more than they understood that "The Legend of Sleepy Hollow" was virtually a translation of Bürger's *Der wilde Jäger*. Only several decades later, after Irving had died with his secret, did nosy scholarship disclose the derivation; but Irving's public, especially in America, would not have cared a hoot had they known it in 1820. Even in New England the discomfiture of Ichabod Crane provided a moment of respite from the domination of the Puritan ethic of ascetic labor. A whole people committed to unremitting industriousness embraced the shiftless Rip, just as they would later let their thwarted longings for vagabondage take them down the Mississippi with Huckleberry Finn.

By the same token we are bound to surmise that a classless society in a raw country, where everything was new, gained a release from the pressures of business or farming when, of an evening, after a day of toil, it could participate in "that foolish fondness for old and obsolete things to which I am a little given." In an economy which took its toll of men at what seems to us a terribly youthful age and of young women at an appalling rate, there were profound consolations in his picture of the dying girl: "The feeble, fluttering, thrilling, oh! how thrilling—pressure of the hand," especially as he could assure this commonplace population that the natural effect of sorrow over the dead "is to refine and elevate the mind." And even those who were complacent about there being no social hierarchy in the new Republic would find a delightful fascination in the class structure of Bracebridge Hall.

In 1825 William Hazlitt, in a great book entitled *The Spirit of the Age,* dismissed Irving as not belonging to the age at all. Both Irving's language and his sentiments, said the Rhadamanthine Hazlitt, are taken from Addison and Goldsmith; he shows no awareness of what the Industrial Revolution is working in Great Britain, and so his writings are "literary *anachronisms.*" But the multitude of Irving's readers in England and on the Continent were untroubled: they wanted the England of Irving, not of Manchester. The hordes of his readers in America were even less perturbed. For Irving himself *The Sketch Book* was a victory of sensibility over a dire threat of disintegration. For his American public it was a welcome interlude from the strenuousness of prosperity, after the reading of which they could return, with refreshed enthusiasm, to the making of more money.

Perry Miller
Harvard University

SELECTED BIBLIOGRAPHY

WORKS BY WASHINGTON IRVING

"Letters of Jonathan Oldstyle, Gent." (with others), 1802-3 Essays

Salmagundi (with others), 1807-8 Essays

[Diedrich Knickerbocker's] *A History of New York,* 1809 Satirical History

The Sketch Book of Geoffrey Crayon, Gent., 1820 Tales and Sketches (Signet Classic CE1614)

Bracebridge Hall, 1822 Tales and Sketches

Tales of a Traveller, 1824 Tales

The Life and Voyages of Christopher Columbus, 1828 History

A Chronicle of the Conquest of Granada, 1829 History

Voyages and Discoveries of the Companions of Columbus, 1831 History

The Alhambra, 1832 Tales and Sketches

The Crayon Miscellany, 1835 Travel Books and Tales
   A Tour on the Prairies (Vol. 1)
   Abbotsford and *Newstead Abbey* (Vol. 2)
   Legends of the Conquest of Spain (Vol. 3)

Astoria; or, Anecdotes of an Enterprise Beyond the Rocky Mountains, 1836 History

The Adventures of Captain Bonneville, 1837 History

Oliver Goldsmith: A Biography, 1840; rev. 1849 Biography

Biography and Poetical Remains of the Late Margaret M. Davidson, 1841 Biography

A Book of the Hudson: Collected from the Various Works of Diedrich Knickerbocker, 1849 Tales and Sketches

Mahomet and His Successors, 1850 Biography

Wolfert's Roost, 1855 Tales and Sketches

Life of George Washington (5 vols.), 1855-9 Biography

Spanish Papers and Other Miscellanies, 1866 Posthumously Selected Tales and Sketches

Abu Hassan, 1924 Posthumously Published Drama

The Wild Huntsman, 1924 Posthumously Published Drama

The Works of Washington Irving (Author's Uniform Revised Edition) New York: G. P. Putnam's Sons, 1860-1, 21 vols.

Complete Works of Washington Irving (includes journals, notebooks, and letters) Madison: Univ. of Wisconsin Press; Boston: Twayne, 1969—

BIOGRAPHY AND CRITICISM

Aderman, Ralph M., ed. *American Transcendental Quarterly*, No. 5 (First Quarter, 1970).

Callow, James T. *Kindred Spirits: Knickerbocker Writers and American Artists, 1807-1855*. Chapel Hill, N. C.: Univ. of North Carolina Press, 1967.

Charvat, William L. "The Conditions of Authorship in 1820." In his *The Profession of Authorship in America, 1800-1870*. Ed. Matthew J. Bruccoli. Columbus, Ohio: Ohio State Univ. Press, 1968, pp. 29-48.

Hedges, William L. *Washington Irving: An American Study, 1802-1832*. Baltimore: Johns Hopkins Press, 1965.

Hoffman, Daniel. "Prefigurations: The Legend of Sleepy Hollow." In his *Form and Fable in American Fiction*. New York: Oxford Univ. Press, 1961, pp. 83-96.

Leary, Lewis. *Washington Irving*. University of Minnesota Pamphlets on American Writers, 25. Minneapolis: Univ. of Minnesota Press, 1963.

McClary, Ben H., ed. *Washington Irving and the House of Murray: Geoffrey Crayon Charms the British, 1817-1856*. Knoxville: Univ. of Tennessee Press, 1969.

Myers, Andrew B., ed. *A Century of Commentary on the Works of Washington Irving, 1860-1974*. Tarrytown, N.Y.: Sleepy Hollow Restorations, 1976.

———, ed. *Washington Irving: A Tribute*. Tarrytown, N.Y.: Sleepy Hollow Restorations, 1972.

Pochmann, Henry A. "Introduction." In *Washington Irving: Representative Selections*. Ed. Henry A. Pochmann. New York: American Book Company, 1934, pp. xi-xcii.

Reichart, Walter A. *Washington Irving and Germany*. Ann Arbor: Univ. of Michigan Press, 1957.

Springer, Haskell. *Washington Irving: A Reference Guide*. Reference Guides in Literature, 6. Boston: G. K. Hall, 1976.

Williams, Stanley T. *The Life of Washington Irving*. 2 vols. New York: Oxford Univ. Press, 1935.

A Note on the Text

This edition of *The Sketch Book* is based on the Hudson Edition, published by G. P. Putnam's Sons, New York, in 1880. The spelling and punctuation have been brought into conformity with modern American usage.